VOWS
OF
VENGEANCE

The Legends of Eldhaven #1

Nathalie Edward

For my little sun summoner Alina,
who made my dreams come true,
and gave me the courage to bring this story to life.

ARENTHIA

The Raven's Cabin

The Librarium

IRONHOLD

PORT ORYNTH

The Buxom Lady

SILVER BAY

BREYVIA

SOLHAVEN

PORT VEYNE

GREYHAVEN

MORDESSA

ZARENTH

MORROW BAY

THAELON

DRIFTWOOD

MOSSGROVE

THORNMERE

N

W   E

S

ELDHAVEN

Contents

1.
Niev

Blood clung stubbornly to the leather of her boots, refusing to wash away even in the downpour, a stark reminder of the night's messy work.

Niev Helvast's boots squelched on the cobblestones, rainwater pooling around her feet in crimson-streaked puddles. She moved through the alleyways of Solhaven with practiced ease, her cloak pulled tight against the storm. The rain drummed against the city, a steady rhythm that drowned out the echoes of her footsteps.

Baron Ogier wouldn't be waking up to see another sunrise. Niev made sure of that. The grim poetry of her work lay in the silence she left behind, the kind that only the Grand Duke Haywood was willing to pay for.

For Haywood, the affair his daughter had with the Baron was more than just a blot on his name, it was an offense that clawed at the very fabric of his carefully curated reputation. In a world where whispers could carve empires and rumors felled kings, his retribution had to be decisive and without echo. That's why he sought Niev's particular set of skills—swift, precise, and quietly lethal. She was the razor-edge his vendettas required, and the Baron had unknowingly signed his demise the moment he decided to bed the Duke's daughter.

The initial assignment had been simple: slip into the mansion, slit his throat, and disappear. But the Baron's paranoia had rewritten the script.

Extra guards, last-minute shifts. She'd spent weeks studying the mansion, memorizing every creak in the floorboards and the hum of the staff's nightly routines. Yet the Baron's fear had turned a clean job into a small-scale bloodbath. Three extra bodies now weighed on her conscience, their lives snuffed out because they'd been in the wrong place at the wrong time.

She didn't stop to dwell on it. Regret was a luxury the Tigress of Solhaven couldn't afford.

As she walked through Solhaven's pristine streets, rain washing the blood off her boots, she couldn't help but think about the city's hypocrisy. The opulence and quiet here were just a mask for the corruption simmering beneath. Solhaven's elite played their games of betrayal and deceit, leaving people like Niev to clean up the mess. And yet, even here, amidst the gilded mansions and iron gates, danger lurked. For Niev, it was always a matter of staying one step ahead—silent, sharp, and always prepared to disappear into the shadows.

By the time she crossed into Greyhaven, most of the blood had vanished from her boots. She left behind the mansion's pretentious calm, allowing herself to embrace the lively chaos as if it were an old friend. The vibrant underbelly of Greyhaven, with its taverns brimming with raucous laughter and conspiracies whispered in shadowed corners, offered a sanctuary from the infernal quiet of streets she'd just come out of.

When the Great War of Eldhaven ended, a luminous statue was erected in Santa Alba's honor, casting radiant light across Solhaven at dawn. The city was meant to be a beacon of hope, a place of renewal and peace. Curtains were kept open so the morning rays that passed through the statue could wake residents gently.

But the city had become divided. The affluent cemented their control by forcing Solhaven's original residents into a shadowed district they dubbed Greyhaven.

It was here that the poor and the criminals found refuge, nestled under the looming shadows of grand mansions that never let light touch the statue of Santa Alba.

Niev smirked to herself, a bitter kind of amusement tugging at the corner of her lips.

Greyhaven, a place she would've once been warned to stay away from, had somehow become her refuge.

She wondered, fleetingly, what her father would think if he could see her now. Almost as if the thought of him was enough to summon his ghost, a memory surfaced, unbidden and unwelcome.

For a moment, she wasn't in Greyhaven's dimly lit alleys, dodging drunks and insistent vendors. Instead, she was walking through polished marble halls, the warm glow of candlelight flickering against gilded walls.

The scent of damp stone and burning tallow in Greyhaven was replaced by the delicate fragrance of fresh parchment and jasmine oil. There had been laughter once. A table set with silver, the quiet hum of conversation over a feast laid out beneath a chandelier that glowed like captured starlight.

Her fingers twitched at the ghost of a memory, a long-forgotten sensation of silk gloves against her skin. She had been someone else back then, someone who knew the warmth of a home, the gentle brush of a mother's hand against her hair, the steady presence of a father who had commanded rooms without needing to raise his voice.

Now, she knew taverns where blood was cleaned off wooden floors with cheap whiskey, where deals were made with a handshake and broken just as easily with a blade.

She exhaled sharply, pushing the thought away before it could drag her deeper. The past was a ghost with nothing left to offer her.

She pulled her cloak tighter and stepped further into the familiar chaos of Greyhaven.

Niev had only known the city as it was now—overtaken by sprawling estates that towered over the square, forever blocking the sunrise. The nobility had turned the northern part of Solhaven into the dimly lit Greyhaven she traversed now, a place where the sun never reached and shadows reigned supreme. Here, among the crowded streets and layered secrets, was the raw pulse of the city, the true face of Solhaven.

The air was thick with the scent of ale and sweat as vendors peddled tarnished trinkets, their voices rising above the din to compete with the laughter and curses of pickpockets weaving deftly through the crowd.

"Get back here, thief!" yelled a stall owner, shaking his fist at a lanky figure who melted into the shadows, nimble as a wraith.

Nearby, women leaned provocatively against doorframes, offering honeyed smiles to potential patrons, their voices promising warmth and escape from the cold reality outside. Drunk men staggered by, their laughter booming like cannon fire in the narrow alleyways, remnants of some forgotten joke echoing off the ancient stone.

The streets seemed to pulse with life, their slick cobblestones reflecting the gaudy glow of street lamps. Every corner buzzed with activity, promises, and peril that defined Greyhaven, a chaotic orchestra of life where survival was an art, not a certainty, a stark contrast to the rigid, closed-off world Niev had left behind mere streets ago.

Ahead, the flickering glow of a crimson lantern beckoned her like a siren's call to shore. The Red Dragon's Lair awaited—a place as much a part of Niev as the dagger sheathed at her side. She rapped on the weathered door in a practiced rhythm, one that spoke of many past visits. A narrow slit snapped open, revealing a pair of disinterested eyes set into a face nearly swallowed by shadows.

"Password?" The voice came gruff and low, more of a grumble than a question.

Niev leaned in, rolling her eyes, "Open the damn door, Goram."

The hinges squeaked in protest as the door edged open. For a heartbeat, Niev lingered on the threshold, letting the warm glow spill over her damp boots. In this place, danger felt like a steady pulse beneath the floorboards, and she thrived on it.

To his credit, the doorman didn't flinch, but the slit clapped shut. She heard the heavy lock click back, and the heavy door creaked open.

The doorman looked up, recognition flickering in his tired gaze.

"Ah, Tigress, didn't think it was you. Just keeping the place secure." he muttered, not meeting her gaze as she stepped past.

"If you think standing idly by a strip of wood is what's gonna keep intruders out, then you've highly overestimated your role, love." she replied coolly, brushing past him into the warmth of the lair.

Inside, The Red Dragon's Lair was a cacophony of subdued voices and urgent planning. The air hung heavy with the scents of candle wax and leather, comfortingly familiar to Niev. Assassins and mercenaries moved with purpose, their conversations a tapestry of ambition and edged intent. Here, she was among kin, bound not by blood but by the shared hunger for survival.

Yet as she neared the far end of the lair, her pulse ticked up a notch. Tensions ran high whenever Saeris demanded an audience, and tonight's fiasco would only sharpen her mentor's scrutiny. Niev pressed on, determined to hold her own.

As she made her way through the crowded room, nodding to familiar faces, she caught snippets of plans, deals going down. A young thief was huddled over maps, plotting his next robbery, while a seasoned assassin discussed poisons with a renowned chemist.

Seated at the corner of the room with a flickering candle casting shadows that danced along the walls, Teagan Blackwood sharpened his blades with the focus of a master craftsman. Known for his expert tracking skills and innate ability to slip into places trouble called home, Teagan was a lithe figure, with dark bronze skin and black curls, who was as comfortable in the underbelly of Breyvia as a fox in its den. He was also Niev's closest friend.

Teagan paused his blade sharpening as she approached, glancing up through dark lashes.

"Saeris is looking for you," he warned her, his voice smooth and unhurried. He returned to his work without missing a beat, the rhythm of the whetstone against steel, a steady reminder of the deadly precision expected within the walls of The Red Dragon's Lair. .

"Thanks for the heads-up, Teag," Niev responded, her tone light and edged with camaraderie. "Try not to wander off if I end up needing someone to find my corpse later."

He chuckled quietly, an amused glint in his eyes. "Oh, please. I'd find you before you had the decency to stay dead."

"Funny," she scoffed. In a world where trust could be a rare currency, Teagan was one of the few she considered reliable, if not predictably rogue. His unique set of skills made him indispensable in their line of work—a master tracker and scout, capable of following trails others would overlook and finding paths through the most treacherous terrain with unerring precision.

Niev turned toward the darkened stairwell leading to Saeris Morraine's office, her thoughts churning over the mess she'd made tonight. Saeris trusted her, mess and all. That much had always been clear. But still, she paused at the oaken door, steeling herself at the mouthful she was about to hear, and pushed open the oak door to the Red Dragon's office, the hinges creaking softly as she entered. The air inside was thick with the scent of parchment and smoke, a familiar scent that spoke of late nights spent planning and plotting within these walls.

Saeris looked up from the spread of documents on her desk, her expression a mix of irritation and curiosity. "Niev," she began, a single eyebrow arching in displeasure. "You want to tell me what in the Nine Hells happened tonight?!"

Settling herself into a chair opposite Saeris, Niev took her time, brushing a loose strand of hair behind her ear. "You know," she replied, a smirk playing at her lips despite the gravity of the situation, "our dear Baron apparently felt his life might be at risk. Imagine that."

"The agreement was simple," Saeris reminded her, eyes narrowing. "Slip in, *slit his throat*," she emphasized, "and leave quietly. A mansion's worth of blood was *not* part of the deal."

Niev leaned back, unfazed by her mentor's criticism. "Yeah, about that. Seems word got around faster than we planned. He hired a few extra hands to hang around his bedroom mere hours before I showed up. Would've been nice if they'd handed me a schedule update. I spent two weeks studying that place. Those extra bodies weren't part of my plan either." she quipped lightly, her voice dipped in annoyance.

Saeris sighed, rubbing her temples. Niev had been thorough: she'd studied the mansion for weeks, mapping out every entrance and exit, memorizing the guard shifts, even listening to the staff's nightly hum as they slipped into sleep. But the Baron's last-minute paranoia had rewritten their script entirely.

"So you thought painting the carpet with their insides was the right call?" Saeris asked, her tone exasperated yet lacking in true malice.

"Well, I *was* going to leave a note," Niev shot back, lips pulling into a grin. "But wouldn't you know, they were fresh out of quills."

Saeris narrowed her eyes, "You're insufferable."

Niev smirked, "Look, the Baron was getting more and more paranoid by the minute. And given the added muscle, it was now-or-never, really. If I hadn't taken my chance tonight, he'd probably barricade himself in a fortress by tomorrow. It was the best possible outcome given the circumstances."

Saeris raised an eyebrow in challenge.

"Okay fine, not *the best* outcome," Niev responded, her grin widening. "I could've shifted and made a meal of them, that would've been less messy, but you know that's not my thing." Her tone was playful, yet the underlying assurance was as clear as her intentions.

Despite herself, Saeris allowed a small chuckle to escape. "Try to keep it cleaner next time. Baron carpets are a nightmare to clean, even with all the rain."

Niev shrugged, rising to her feet. "I'll bring my own broom if it ever happens again," she winked.

"Wait," Saeris called slowly after her. She shuffled a pile of documents, her brow creased. Niev could tell something new was coming, the air was charged with an unexpected anticipation.

Saeris looked up, locking eyes with Niev, her expression smoothing into one of calculated calm. "I've got a new assignment for you," she began, her voice steadier than it had been earlier.

The silence stretched for a moment, Niev frowned, "What is it?" she asked, her voice full of suspicion.

"This task deviates from your usual assignments," Saeris began, her voice steady. ""There's a shipment bound for the Grand Librarium in Arenthia. Inside it, hidden among merchant wares, are documents that have piqued certain interests. I want them."

Niev's brow furrowed, her arms folding tight across her chest. "You're sending me to intercept a merchant's shipment?"

"Correct."

"And that shipment's headed to Arenthia's Librarium," she repeated, slowly. "Inside the most heavily watched archive in the damn country?"

"Not inside," Saeris corrected. "At the doors. You'll arrive ahead of the wagons, wearing the blue robes of a junior archivist. When the delivery clerk signs the ledger, you sign beside him, take custody of the crates, and vanish before they're carried past the marble threshold."

Niev's brows shot up. "So I'm to pose as library staff, walk up to the front gate, and stroll off with state-sealed cargo while half the city's scholars look on?"

"Exactly," Saeris said without a flicker of humor.

"No," Niev said, shaking her head, "Absolutely not."

Saeris ignored her and firmly continued, "We've been led to believe these documents contain information critical to several ruling houses, and it's causing quite a stir. Your skills are perfect for slipping in and out unnoticed."

Niev took a step back. Her voice was flat, absolute. "I said no."

Saeris leaned forward, pinning her with a steely gaze before she could argue further. "I wasn't asking, Niev."

Niev barked a laugh, bitter and incredulous. "You don't need an assassin for this, you need a diplomat with a death wish."

"I need you," Saeris said, unblinking. "You're the only one I trust to get in, read the room, and disappear with the prize."

Niev's expression darkened. "I haven't stepped foot in Arenthia in ten years. And I have no intention of doing so now."

Saeris's stare didn't waver. "Trust me when I say I'm not asking lightly."

"You're not asking at all," Niev snapped. "And I'm not one of your pawns anymore. Find someone else."

"No," Saeris said matter-of-factly. "You're the only one I trust with this—"

"What's in them?"

Saeris hesitated, and that pause told Niev more than she wanted to know.

"We don't know. Only that they hold secrets tied to several ruling houses. Old bloodlines. Power shifts. Hidden allegiances. Whatever's in those records... it's enough to spark a war if it falls into the wrong hands."

Niev scoffed, shaking her head. "And whose hands would that be?"

Saeris ignored her, and Niev noticed the barest lift at the corner of the Red Dragon's mouth, an almost-smile of certainty, not concession.

She counted on me to refuse, Niev realized, pulse ticking faster. Eyes narrowing, she let her gaze rake over Saeris from silver-threaded cloak to measured stance, searching for even a flicker of doubt. There was none. Saeris held herself like a chess master who'd just nudged a pawn, already seeing three checkmates ahead.

"You knew I'd say no," Niev said at length, her voice low and deliberate, "Yet here you are, standing your ground. What are you hiding that makes you think I'll agree to this folly?"

For a heartbeat, silence reigned, then Saeris inclined her head, a predator's courtesy. "Your family's name has come up."

The words struck like a blade between her ribs.

Niev's pulse quickened. "What?"

The room seemed to tilt. Saeris stepped closer, lowering her voice until it thrummed in Niev's bones. "We believe these documents contain information about the ruling witch clan of Arenthia. If I had to guess, Your parents' deaths weren't just a casualty of political maneuvering. Someone wanted them gone for a reason. You retrieve these papers, and they might be the first step to find out why."

Niev's pulse spiked; her jaw tightened against the rush of memory. Saeris continued, each word precise as a scalpel. "You steal those pages, you might finally trace the coin trail that paid for your parents' coffins, and the contract that sold you into a cage ten years ago."

Silence vibrated between them. Outside, a gull screamed over the harbor, distant and raw.

Niev stared at Saeris, disbelief morphing into anger as the full weight of her assignment settled in.

Arenthia... An insidious echo from her past, a place she had no desire to revisit after her parents' brutal murder. And yet, here she was, ordered to infiltrate one of its most guarded sanctuaries.

Saeris tilted her head. "Refuse if you like. But those crates will cross the threshold in seven days. Once the Librarium seals them, not even I can pry them loose."

Niev's fists clenched instinctively, the frustration visibly coursing through her. "I don't—" she sputtered. "You know what that place is to me," she whispered in defeat.

The words tasted like rust on her tongue, bitter and unwelcome. She bit the inside of her cheek, willing the sharp sting to keep her expression neutral, to smother the emotion threatening to crack through the careful mask she had spent years perfecting. Her shoulders stiffened, her jaw locking tight as if sheer force alone could keep the weight of the past from pressing down on her chest.

Her fingers curled deeper into her palms, nails biting into skin, but she refused to unclench them, refused to let Saeris see even a flicker of weakness. A muscle twitched in her jaw, and she forced her gaze to remain steady, trained on a fixed point beyond Saeris' shoulder rather than risk meeting her eyes. The room felt too small, the air too still, and she hated how, for a fleeting second, something raw had slipped through her armor.

Saeris didn't hesitate. "And I know what this mission means to all of us," she countered. "It's not about your past. It's about our future. The future of everyone in Breyvia. You retrieve these documents, and we gain the upper hand in a war that hasn't even begun yet. You refuse, and we're flying blind when our enemies aren't."

They locked eyes, the room electrically charged with tension. Saeris was the closest thing Niev had to family, after she'd saved her from her fate a decade earlier, but she was also the ruthless leader of the Assassin's Guild—unyielding when it came to anything that could bolster her power or bring in substantial rewards.

Niev's anger simmered at the edge, a burning frustration that had nowhere to lash out. Yet, underlying her anger was the deep-seated knowledge that this was the reality they lived in. She pushed back her chair abruptly, the legs screeching against the wooden floor.

"I'll need resources, people, whatever you can give me to make this clean. Don't expect me to do this half-cocked," Niev seethed, her words firm with the determination to control the mission's pace if not its necessity.

Saeris nodded curtly, her expression finally softening at the edges. "Make a list, and it'll be done. But know this: the stakes here are higher than your grudges, and there is no room for messy outcomes."

Without another word, she turned on her heel, slamming the door behind her, the sound echoing like a gunshot through the silent corridors.

As she stormed through the lair, the den of criminals looked on in disbelief, a tumult of whispers and glances following her in the wide eyes of those who knew what outbursts like hers would cost the lesser of their ranks. Niev was the only one who could afford such insolence, one of the few Saeris shared enough history with and trusted to challenge the tenuous chain of command without consequence. Though it seemed now that history was demanding its pound of flesh.

2.
Niev

Rain hammered Niev the moment she stormed out of the Red Dragon's Lair, drenching her before she reached the first alley. Water streamed down her face—cold, unrelenting—but it was nothing compared to the fire burning beneath her skin.

She walked fast, cutting through the maze of Greyhaven's streets, letting the downpour drown out the simmering anger curling in her chest. Every step splashed through puddles, mud clinging to the edges of her boots, but she barely noticed.

Ten years. Ten years of loyalty, of carving out a life from the bones of her past, of doing Saeris's bidding, and this was how she repaid her? Sending her back to that place?

A place she had sworn never to set foot in again.

She scarcely noticed the city around her, the shouts of merchants haggling over rain-dampened wares, the distant clash of steel in a back alley fight, the flickering glow of tavern lanterns reflecting in waterlogged streets. None of it mattered. Not when her past had been dragged from its grave and thrown at her feet.

She exhaled sharply, shaking the thought away.

You know what that place is to me.

She hated that she had said it. Hated even more that it had cracked through her composure.

Her fingers curled into fists, the bite of her nails grounding her. She had spent years hardening herself against the weight of her past, against ghosts that lurked in the edges of her mind. But the moment Saeris mentioned Arenthia, those ghosts had stirred—restless, reaching.

A sudden burst of laughter made her tense. She turned just in time to see a boy dart past her, small and quick, a stolen apple clutched in his fist. A vendor shouted after him, curses lost to the rain.

The boy vanished into a crooked side lane, leaving only the echo of hurried footfalls. The vendor's voice faded, and Greyhaven's rain-born hush rushed back in. In that hollow quiet, memories pounced.

Niev had been that child once, not a thief, but a girl with too much hunger in her belly and too much light in her eyes. A girl who had known warmth and silk and candlelit halls. A girl who had been taught right from wrong by a father who spoke of justice as though it was something that could be carved into the bones of the world, something unshakable and true.

And she had not been alone.

Elias had been there too.

Her twin brother, her other half, before the world had torn them apart.

She could still hear his laughter sometimes, bright, careless, the kind of joy that had no place in the world she had been forced to survive. They had been inseparable, two sides of the same coin, until the night everything burned. Until the night she lost him and her parents forever.

Her throat tightened, and she forced herself forward.

She would have laughed at the irony if it didn't make her sick. What would they think of her now?

She knew the answer, even without asking the question.

Her father had taught her that justice was something to be upheld, something to be fought for. He had spent his life believing in that. She had spent hers proving him wrong.

A gust of wind cut through the streets, whipping her damp cloak around her legs. The chill did nothing to ease the weight pressing against her ribs.

Images flashed, unbidden, through her mind, her mother's soft smile, her father's fierce lessons. She'd spent ten years pushing thoughts of her dead family away, the grief too insurmountable to face. Each memory was a blade, reopening old wounds. She couldn't afford to linger on these thoughts, especially if she was to go back and not get caught. The notion of returning made her feel sick.

Saeris, despite their closeness, had turned ruthless when it came to the mission. Niev had seen the flicker of iron resolve in her eyes. Saeris wouldn't let sentiment jeopardize anything that might augment her power. Loyalty and affection were luxuries, not necessities, in their world. And despite Niev's defiance, she knew, Saeris had ordered; she would obey. There was no other option, not when stakes like these were involved.

She slammed her foot into a puddle, splashing mud up against the stone walls. Her thoughts drifted, unbidden, back to the memory of her father. Feodor Helvast had been a beacon of integrity, a man of God, a warrior who had taught her strength and compassion, embodying the virtues of gentleness in a world often devoid of it.

If only he knew how she used the shapeshifting powers she inherited from him not for good, but to lie, steal, and *murder*.

Each life she had taken felt like a tally against the teachings he'd instilled. Her heart twisted with shame, and she shook her head, trying to dispel the thought before it rooted itself too deeply.

Returning to Arenthia would not only mean confronting the land of her childhood but also facing the demons that her past harbored. The cruelties inflicted there had driven her down a path he would have deemed unredeemable. The red stain of a dozen missions marked her soul, challenging the image of the girl he had once lifted onto his shoulders, the child who had dreamed of a life guided by the light of his wisdom.

Teeth clenched against the chill of the rain, Niev resented her orders, resented Saeris for digging up these forgotten ghosts. The mission ahead represented more than danger, it threatened to stir memories she had buried long ago, and forces she would rather not unleash. Yet within her turmoil, she felt the embers of defiance burning hotter.

Your family's name has come up. Your parents' deaths weren't just a casualty of political maneuvering. Someone wanted them gone for a reason.

She slowed her steps slightly, allowing the rain's fall to drown out the cacophony of thoughts. Her father might have been ashamed, might have pitied the path she'd chosen, but it didn't matter. He was dead. And no amount of shame or wallowing would bring him back.

But if Saeris was right, and there was more to her family's death, she needed to find out everything.

Who gave the order? Why? Had it been calculated years in advance, or was it a decision made in a single moment? And if someone had taken everything from her—her parents, her brother, her home—then what did they have now? Power? Security? A throne built atop the blood they spilled?

Her fingers curled into fists, a slow, burning heat coiling in her gut.

If the ghosts of Arenthia thought they could stay buried, they were wrong.

She had spent a decade surviving, clawing her way through the filth of the world, becoming a blade honed by hardship. And she would carve the truth from the bones of the people who stole everything from her.

For now, she pushed her father's image into the depths of her mind, needing to stay focused. Despite everything, she carried his teachings in the quiet recesses of her heart, hoping they might one day guide her shadowed steps through the storm.

She forced herself to count intersections—one, two, three—until the steady rhythm steadied her breathing. By the fourth turn her rage had cooled to a simmer.

When she finally reached her building, an unassuming structure nestled quietly in a dim alley, Niev was drenched to the bone, and feeling slightly calmer.

The apartment had been the fruit of her work with Saeris, a place solely hers in a city where she belonged to no one but herself.

Ascending the narrow stairway to her apartment, she welcomed the familiarity of the squeaky steps and the faint aroma of old wood. At the top floor, she turned the key, the lock clicking open with a satisfying click.

Her home was compact, but each element was thoughtfully curated to form a sanctuary. Upon entering, she shed her sodden cloak, allowing it to crumple in a heap by the door. The dim light from the rain-dappled windows cast a gentle glow over the room, where her modest fireplace stood ready to warm the chill from her bones.

Niev moved about her space with a reverence born from years of solitude. She absently ran her fingers along the spines of books that filled her shelves, from tales of ancient legends to romance tomes filled with hope and happy endings. There was little luxury to be had in the life she lived, but her books were her most prized possessions. Each one was a companion for the nights she spent anchored by the soft crackle of the hearth.

She crossed the room, pulling back the curtain to reveal the city's expanse. Solhaven sprawled beneath her, a mosaic of lights glittering through the storm. The view was both calming and exhilarating, a reminder of the world that lay beyond her walls.

As the warmth of her apartment enveloped her, Niev tossed her bloodied, rain-soaked clothes into a basin by the door, a ritual to be addressed later. Striking a match, she coaxed a fire to life, watching as tongues of flame hungrily licked at the dry wood, and began to ease the chill from her bones.

Once the fire crackled in the hearth, she left the room behind, seeking solace in the hot shower that awaited. Steam curled around her, obscuring the small bathroom mirror. She stood under the scalding water, letting it wash away the residue of blood and the grime of the city's streets until she felt herself slowly start to calm down.

She wrapped herself in a towel and returned to the main room, her fingers deftly setting water to boil on the small stove. The familiar motions grounded her, but they did little to quiet the storm still raging in her mind. The rain outside blurred the cityscape beyond her window, distorting Solhaven's skyline into something almost dreamlike. If only she had the luxury of slipping into that illusion.

Then came a knock.

Niev stiffened instinctively before crossing the room, pressing her palm against the doorframe. She cracked it open, cautious, but the moment she saw the familiar silhouette leaning lazily against the doorframe, her shoulders eased.

"You looked like you were ready to tear the city apart earlier," Teagan said, tilting his head slightly as if assessing her mood. "Figured you could use a friend."

He lifted a bag, flashing his usual easy grin. For a fraction of a second she pictured a dagger, not a dinner bag, and her shoulders tightened, then the familiar scent of cumin and roasted chicken drifted out, disarming her.

"I brought food," Teagan shrugged, his eyes narrowing. "Are you gonna let me in?"

Niev narrowed her eyes playfully. "Depends. What's in the bag?"

"Spiced chicken and rice, with a side of yogurt garlic sauce." He smirked at the dreamy look that crossed over her face. "I know, I'm a saint."

She chuckled despite herself, stepping back to let him in. "You're a pain in the ass, but that chicken smells too divine not to let you in. Want some tea?"

"Absolutely." He shook the water from his cloak, tossing it over the back of a chair before making himself comfortable like he'd done a hundred times before.

As Niev poured the tea, she glanced down at herself, suddenly aware of the towel wrapped snugly around her. "I should probably put on something more decent."

Teagan stretched out in his chair, all too at home. "Don't rush on my account, darling. I've seen women in far less."

"Yeah, well, you haven't seen *this* woman," she quipped, shaking her head as she disappeared behind her bedroom door.

"We could always change that!" he called after her, the grin evident in his voice.

"You'd love that, wouldn't you?" she tossed back, emerging moments later in a cream sweater and black leggings, her damp hair pulled back, stray tendrils clinging to her skin.

Settling into her chair, she watched as Teagan began dishing out the food. His presence was an easy comfort, a much-needed distraction. But the weight of the conversation with Saeris still sat heavy on her chest.

"So," Teagan said, handing her a plate. "Spill it. What did Saeris say to rile you up this much?"

Niev exhaled softly, her fingers tightening around her cup. "She wants me to go to Arenthia."

The name barely left her lips before Teagan's playful expression faltered, his brows lifting in genuine surprise. "Arenthia?" he repeated. "You're serious?"

"Dead serious," she muttered. "She needs me to retrieve something from the Grand Librarium."

Teagan let out a low whistle. "That place is locked up tighter than a miser's purse. And she wants *you* to slip in and out unnoticed?"

"Apparently, yes." She leaned back, exhaustion creeping into her voice. "Feels more like a fool's errand than a mission. She expects me to gather a list of assets and form a team. A proper one, if I have any hope of pulling this off."

Teagan's fingers drummed against the table, his easy demeanor replaced by something more calculating. "You know I've got your back, Niev. If you need someone, I'm in."

She studied him for a moment, searching his face for any trace of hesitation. There was none.

"I might take you up on that," she admitted, stirring her tea absently.

For a while they ate in silence, the hearth's warmth battling the storm still raging outside. But then, Teagan set his cup down with a quiet *clink* and leaned forward.

"Listen," he said, voice lower now. "I wasn't going to bring this up unless I had to, but... I've heard things about that place. About the Librarium. Lately, it's been attracting the wrong kind of attention."

Niev's brow furrowed. "What kind of attention?"

He hesitated before answering. "Word is, someone's going to extreme lengths to protect those documents."

Something cold twisted in her stomach. "Who?"

Teagan shook his head. "No names. But whoever it is, they're willing to kill for it."

Niev exhaled through her nose, tapping a finger against the rim of her cup. "Well, isn't that just perfect."

Teagan studied her carefully before adding, "Look, you know I'm all for a good heist, but if Saeris thinks you'll be the only one after those documents, she's either lying or underestimating the stakes. And we both know she doesn't make mistakes like that."

Niev sat back, the weight of the revelation settling over her. As if this mission wasn't complicated enough already.

Teagan took another sip of his tea, watching her over the rim of his cup. "So, what's the plan?"

She exhaled, shaking her head. "I don't know yet. But I'll figure it out."

Teagan grinned "You always do."

For now, the conversation shifted back to lighter things, the storm, old jobs, Teagan's latest misadventures. But Niev couldn't shake the feeling that, by the time the night ended, she had more to worry about than just the mission.

Someone wanted to protect what she was after.

And if Teagan was right, they were willing to kill for it.

❋   ❋   ❋

The next morning, Niev rose with a renewed sense of purpose. The storm had passed, leaving Greyhaven slick with last night's rain, the scent of damp earth mingling with the salty tang of the harbor. As she stepped into the streets, the city had already begun its restless routine—merchants setting up stalls, the clang of hammers on steel ringing from nearby forges, and the distant laughter of street children weaving through the crowd.

She tugged her hood lower and threaded through the alleys with the ease of someone who knew every turn. Her destination lay tucked between bustling storefronts—a modest seamstress shop with a faded sign and lace-curtained windows. It blended seamlessly into its surroundings, an unassuming place to the untrained eye. But Niev knew better.

Pushing the door open, she entered to the chime of the overhead bell. The interior was busy, bolts of fabric lined the walls, spilling in soft cascades of jewel-toned silks and humble linen, as the sun filtered softly through lace curtains.

"Myria," Niev called as she stepped inside, her eyes catching the seamstress engaged in a fitting with a customer, her onyx braid swaying slightly as she adjusted the hem of the wealthy merchant's wife's gown.

Myria barely glanced up as Niev entered, but a knowing smirk tugged at the corner of her lips. "My lady," she greeted, her tone warm but edged with amusement. "What can I do for you?" she asked, seamlessly continuing her work with practiced ease.

"I'm in need of some new gowns," Niev replied casually, her eyes innocently roaming over Myria's current customer.

"The usual?" Myria called back over her shoulder, hands expertly pinning fabric into place.

"Something fresh, actually," Niev replied, the words carrying weight beneath their casual exchange.

Myria nodded slightly, a subtle understanding passing between them. "Of course. Give me a moment."

Niev wandered the shop, fingers skimming over the embroidered silks as she listened to the seamstress make her final adjustments.

As far as she could tell, their coded exchange went unnoticed by the customer, who, now satisfied, turned to Myria with thanks. "I appreciate your attention to detail, Myria. Always a pleasure."

"Thank you, Mrs. Alder. I'll have your dress ready in a fortnight," Myria assured. A few more pleasantries, a brief exchange of coin, and with a grateful nod, the merchant's wife swept out the door.

The moment they were alone, Myria turned the lock with a soft *click* and fixed Niev with a sharp look.

"Alright," she said, arms crossing. "What do you really need?"

Niev leaned against the counter, feigning nonchalance. "How much time do you have?"

Myria gave a knowing sigh, already moving to reorganize scattered fabrics. "Enough to tell you that whatever you're about to ask for is going to be a headache."

"I need the robes of an archivist from the Grand Librarium," Niev said, her voice even.

Myria froze mid-motion, then slowly turned to face her.

"You're joking."

Niev lifted a brow. "Do I look like I'm joking?"

Myria exhaled sharply, shaking her head. "Niev, do you have any idea how difficult that is? Even if I could get my hands on the right fabric, the embroidery alone would take weeks. And that's assuming you don't want one imbued with security threads, because if you do, you'll need the real thing, and that's an entirely different beast."

"I know," Niev said simply, offering nothing more.

Myria studied her for a long moment, suspicion narrowing her gaze. "This isn't a normal job, is it?"

Niev hesitated. "No."

Myria let out a humorless chuckle. "Wonderful. Just wonderful. You know, there was a time you used to bring me requests that weren't borderline suicidal."

"We were younger then."

"We were smarter then," Myria corrected dryly.

Niev smirked, but it faded as Myria's expression turned more serious. "I trust you, Niev, but you need to tell me what you're walking into. The Grand Librarium isn't some noble's estate. It's one of the most secure places in Arenthia. You don't just stroll in wearing a fancy robe and expect that to be enough."

Niev met her gaze. "I don't expect it to be enough."

Myria's lips pressed into a thin line. "What aren't you telling me?"

Niev hesitated before finally saying, "Saeris wants me to intercept documents from the Librarium. She says they could alter the balance of power in Breyvia."

Myria scoffed. "Saeris would say the same thing about a particularly well-written tavern menu if she thought it could be leveraged."

Niev sighed. "She says my family's name is in them, Myria."

That made Myria pause.

For all their banter, Myria and Teagan were the only people in Breyvia Niev truly let inside the walls she kept around her history. They didn't know every detail, Niev had never described the screams or the fire or even who her family truly were, but they knew the broad strokes: the massacre that had taken her parents and brother, the night she herself was dragged away in chains. It was an unspoken bond among the three of them; Teagan and Myria never pressed, and Niev never had to wonder where their loyalties lay.

The irritation on Myria's face faded, replaced by a sober, calculating concern. "Your family?"

"Yes."

Silence stretched between them.

Myria glanced away, chewing the inside of her cheek before muttering, "Shit."

Niev crossed her arms. "So, can you help me or not?"

Myria sighed deeply, rubbing her temples. "It's not a matter of can. It's a matter of should. You're playing a dangerous game, and I don't like that you're doing it blind."

"It's not negotiable, Myria."

Myria looked at her sharply. "That's the part that worries me."

Still, despite the hesitance in her voice, Niev could already see it—the gears turning, the reluctant acceptance settling in. Myria didn't like it, but she wasn't about to walk away.

"I'll see what I can do," she finally said, but the look she gave Niev was edged with frustration. "But this will take time. And if I do this, you owe me, Helvast."

"I always pay my debts, Holloway." Niev replied, her eyes narrowing.

Myria snorted. "Good. Because this one's going to be expensive."

Niev smirked. "Wouldn't expect anything less."

Myria shook her head, already moving toward a shelf of fabric. "I'll need to call in some favors. But while I do that, I suggest you start figuring out the second part of this ridiculous plan."

Niev tensed. "Actually... I was hoping you could help with that too."

Myria stilled. "Niev," she warned.

"I want a real archivist's identity. Someone cleared for the Librarium's inner sanctum. If anything goes sideways at the gates, I'll have to walk those crates straight into whatever private vault is expecting them."

Myria swung around, incredulous. "Are you out of your god-damned mind?"

Niev didn't flinch.

"You're talking about scholars who spend half a lifetime earning those sigils," Myria pressed, voice sharp with disbelief. "People vetted, ward-scanned, and followed by stewards who can recite their shoe sizes."

"I know exactly what I'm asking," Niev said, eyes steady. "If the hand-off fails, I need a second door, or the whole play is dead before it starts—"

Myria pinched the bridge of her nose, exhaling hard. Then she met Niev's gaze again, frustration and loyalty warring in her eyes.

"You always drag me into the worst situations, you know that?"

Niev smiled slightly. "But you always come through for me."

Myria groaned. "That's the problem."

The seamstress's silence seemed to stretch on forever. Then, finally—

"Fine," Myria muttered. "Give me a few days. I'll see what I can dig up."

Niev exhaled, tension leaving her shoulders. "Thank you, Myria."

Myria waved her off. "Don't thank me yet. If we get caught...I'll kill you myself before they can."

"Noted."

Outside, the rain had finally ceased. Somewhere in the distance a harbor bell tolled twice—dawn's promise or a warning, she couldn't tell. Either way, the clock was already ticking.

3.
Niev

The Wild Boar reeked of ale, sweat, and secrets. A battered sign depicting a snarling boar, swung above the entrance, its tusks chipped like a drunkard's grin. Inside, voices clashed like swords; the air was thick with the smell of roasting meat and old wood.

Niev slipped through the doorway, the tavern's warmth slamming into her like a punch. The din swallowed her whole—mercenaries bellowing over their drinks, traders bartering like their lives depended on it, and gamblers cursing their misfortunes. A massive wooden boar's head glowered down from above the bar, its glassy eyes gleaming in the flickering candlelight.

Heat from the hearth rolled over her, laced with the metallic tang of old coin and sweat. The noise and scent thick enough to hide a conversation.

She weaved through the throng, ignoring the leers and sidelong glances, and claimed a booth tucked in the shadow of the hearth. A barmaid threaded past with brimming tankards, and Niev caught her eye with a small gesture.

"A plate of whatever's fresh, and a mug of your strongest," Niev said, offering a fleeting but warm smile. It was a practiced gesture, the kind that made her seem harmless, until it didn't.

The barmaid, a sturdy woman with fiery hair and an apron stained with beer, shot her a quick nod and disappeared toward the kitchen. Niev leaned back, the din of the tavern providing a perfect backdrop for her thoughts. She was here for more than food and drink. Somewhere in this den of chaos lay the thread that would lead her to her next target.

When the barmaid returned with a steaming plate and frothy mug, Niev thanked her and ate slowly, her sharp gaze roamed the room, cataloging every detail—the flash of a dagger at a sailor's hip, the coded exchange between two merchants, the wary glance of a man nursing his third pint despite the early hour.

She chewed methodically, her thoughts weaving plans and contingencies, until the barmaid returned, her smile generous but her sharp eyes betraying a keen intelligence.

"How's your breakfast?" the barmaid asked, leaning against the booth with practiced casualness.

Niev raised her mug in acknowledgment, letting the foam kiss her lips before responding. "Not bad. That new cook knows what he's doing."

The barmaid gave her a quick once-over. "Haven't seen you here before."

Niev offered a small smile, lifting her mug. "The food's worth the trip apparently."

The barmaid snorted, unimpressed but intrigued. "That so?"

Niev shrugged noncommittally.

The barmaid chuckled but didn't move away. "Maybe. Or maybe you're after more than a meal."

Setting her mug down, Niev leaned forward slightly, her voice lowering just enough to be heard over the clamor. "Let's say I'm looking for someone," she said, her tone casual. "Who would I ask for information in this *fine* establishment?"

The barmaid's fingers tightened on her tray—a flicker Niev didn't miss.

"Depends who you're looking for," she said carefully.

Niev narrowed her eyes and took a measured sip, letting the moment hang before adding, "The Harbormaster."

The barmaid's smile froze, the light in her eyes hardening into something cautious. Her head tilted slightly, her hand gripping the tray just a touch tighter. "Who's asking?" she said smoothly.

Niev let the silence hang, let the tension simmer just long enough before she leaned back, draping an arm over the booth like she had all the time in the world. "Let's just say Saeris Morraine's Tigress is on the hunt," she replied, her tone laced with dangerous charm. "And the Harbormaster has information she needs."

The barmaid's composure faltered for a heartbeat, her eyes widening in recognition at the mention of the head of the Assassin's Guild and her right hand. Fear flickered across her features before she forced her expression into a careful mask.

Niev followed the woman's gaze. The barkeep, a hulking man with a grizzled beard, had stopped wiping down the counter. His sharp eyes locked onto her, then slid down to the gold coin she was now spinning between her fingers.

Slowly, he nodded. Acknowledgment. Invitation. Warning.

A man near the bar abruptly stood and slipped out the door. Niev tracked him from the corner of her eye, noting the subtle way he kept his head down. Either word was already spreading, or she'd just set something in motion.

Good.

She took a slow sip of her drink and waited.

She traced a circle on the mug's handle, one loop for every second the barkeep stayed gone. By the tenth, impatience sharpened into readiness.

Niev didn't have to wait long. The barkeep disappeared into the back room, leaving the bar momentarily unattended. If the regulars noticed, they gave no sign, too absorbed in dice games and drunken camaraderie, but Niev's focus sharpened. Her hand rested lightly on the hilt of the dagger concealed at her side, fingers brushing the familiar leather grip.

The barmaid returned, setting down another mug on Niev's table without a word. Her earlier smile was gone, replaced by a neutral mask. "Give it a moment," she murmured, her voice barely audible over the tavern's din. Then, with a quick glance toward the back, she added, "When you're called, move fast. Don't make them wait."

Niev inclined her head in acknowledgment and sipped from her mug, letting the warm, bitter ale calm the growing tension in her chest. She knew the risks. An invitation like this often came with more strings than a merchant's ledger. Still, she couldn't afford to hesitate. The Harbormaster held information she needed, and if there was one thing Niev excelled at, it was navigating dangerous currents.

Minutes later the barkeep re-emerged, massive arms crossed over his chest. "Come," he said, voice low and gruff. No room for debate.

Niev stood smoothly, following him through the tavern, past the roaring crowd and into a corridor dimly lit by flickering lanterns. The air shifted, less smoke, more damp wood and cold stone.

At the end of the hall, a wiry guard with a scar across his nose assessed her with a quick, practiced glance. Satisfied, he stepped aside and pushed open a reinforced oak door.

The room beyond was a stark contrast to the rowdy tavern above. Thick rugs muffled sound, and shelves lined with ledgers, maps, and curiosities spoke of quiet power. A single table sat in the center, a lantern casting shifting shadows across the walls.

And behind the table sat the Harbormaster.

He was older than she'd expected, his silver hair cropped short and his weathered face a map of experience. His eyes, sharp as a hawk's, fixed on her the moment she entered. He gestured to the chair opposite him, his fingers adorned with rings that glinted faintly in the lamplight.

"I hear you've been looking for me," he said, his voice calm and measured, almost amused. "I trust you have a good reason."

Niev approached but didn't sit. Instead, she placed both hands on the back of the chair opposite him, leaning forward slightly. "I need information," she said. "And I was told you're the man to get it from."

The Harbormaster chuckled, leaning back in his chair. "Flattery will get you nowhere, Tigress," he said.

Niev raised an eyebrow. He knew who she was. Most people didn't know the face behind the name.

She slid a gold coin across the table. "Let's start with this, then."

He picked up the coin, turning it between his fingers before pocketing it. "A fine opening bid. But before we discuss business, tell me... What is it Saeris Morraine's Tigress is hunting?"

Her smirk died, replaced by hard intent. "I'm looking for some sensitive documents."

The Harbormaster leaned back in his chair, his sharp gaze dissecting Niev's words. For a moment, the room seemed to contract, the weight of his silence pressing against the walls. Then he exhaled a slow breath, steepling his fingers before him.

"You've heard about the sealed consignment headed to the Librarium, then?" he said, his tone measured.

Niev nodded, her expression unflinching. "Word travels fast when certain interests start poking around. Sealed documents, ones that seem to have everyone whispering, enough to make them worth the risk. I need to retrieve them before anyone else gets their hands on them."

The Harbormaster's lips curved into a faint, knowing smile, though it held no warmth. "You're not the only one curious about those documents, Tigress. Arenthia has been stirring with whispers, rumors of secrets worth fortunes, of power better left untouched."

"Then you understand why I need to move quickly," she pressed, leaning forward. "I'm not here to negotiate with you, Harbormaster. I'm here to make sure those documents disappear before anyone can use them. I want the route, the timing, and the size of the escort."

He studied her for a long moment, then let out a quiet chuckle, shaking his head. "Bold, as always." He gestured lazily toward a nearby map spread across the wall, marked with faint lines and symbols. "The Librarium has yet to receive those documents. They're still en route, traveling under a quiet but heavily guarded escort. A precaution, no doubt, given the value of what's inside."

She clenched her jaw, her mind racing. *Good*, she thought. Fewer walls, fewer wards. "How far out are we talking?"

The Harbormaster tilted his head, his eyes glinting like a predator who had just cornered his prey. "That depends on what you're willing to offer in exchange for that information."

Niev slid a second coin across the table, her voice low and resolute. "You'll get more if the information proves accurate. Where are they?"

He pocketed the coin with a smirk, leaning forward conspiratorially. "The documents are being transported by a merchant caravan out of Darsyn, heading to Arenthia. They'll be passing through the Northroad's mountain pass in five days' time."

"The Northroad?" Niev frowned. "Nobody uses it anymore. It's too dangerous."

"Precisely," the Harbormaster said, his voice almost amused. "The perfect route for something you don't want to draw attention to. Of course, dangerous routes have their... hazards."

Niev's mind was already mapping out the possibilities. The Northroad was treacherous terrain, notorious for its winding paths and the brigands who used its natural cover to ambush travelers. If she moved quickly, she could intercept the caravan before it reached the pass, and before Arenthia's interests could close their grip on the documents.

She stood abruptly, her chair scraping against the floor. "You've been helpful, Harbormaster. I'll see to it you're compensated properly when I return."

"Don't flatter me with promises, Tigress," he said with a lazy wave of his hand. "But if you survive this little venture, I'll expect my cut when you're done."

Niev glanced back over her shoulder, her expression hesitant, her voice barely higher than a whisper. "What do those Arenthian documents actually contain, Harbormaster? Why would Saeris want them?"

The Harbormaster's smirk deepened as Niev reached for the door. "So, she *hasn't* told you."

Niev locked her jaw, brow furrowing.

"There's no such thing as *Arenthian* documents, my dear. Breyvia, Arenthia, Thaelon...All of Eldhaven is tied together," he said, his tone dropping into something darker.

Niev's expression hardened, her fingers curling into fists. "What's Breyvia got to do with sealed documents bound for the Librarium?"

The Harbormaster leaned forward, his elbows resting on the table. "Everything. Word is, the documents detail the ledger of a key syndicate—names, locations, transactions. It's all there, black and white, enough to unravel the entire network between our three nations. But here's the catch, those who want it sealed aren't the ones trying to stop the slave trade. They're the ones profiting from it."

What did an entire criminal network have to do with her family's death?

Niev felt the air leave her lungs. The implications struck deep. "And the Librarium is willing to hold onto something like that?"

"The Librarium doesn't pick sides," he replied with a shrug. "It collects, it preserves, and it safeguards knowledge. What happens to that knowledge, how it's used or who accesses it, depends on whose hands get to it first. My guess is that the Breyvian syndicate isn't interested in letting those documents reach the shelves, and neither are the ones trying to protect them from public view."

Her mind raced. The caravan carrying the documents wasn't just a simple transport, this was a powder keg. If the documents fell into the wrong hands, any chance of dismantling the Breyvian network could vanish, along with untold lives.

"Why hasn't someone stopped the caravan already?" Niev asked, her voice tight with urgency.

"Because not everyone knows what's inside those sealed papers," the Harbormaster said, his eyes narrowing. "And those who do are either too scared or too bought off to act. Except you, it seems."

"I'm not scared," she replied quickly as grim determination settled over her. "And no one owns me."

The Harbormaster chuckled softly. "Saeris Morraine might beg to differ."

Niev's shoulders stiffened, but she didn't rise to the bait. "Where exactly is this caravan?" she shot back.

He gestured toward the map on the wall, his finger landing on a crooked trail that snaked through the Northroad's treacherous mountain pass. "Like I said, they'll be here in five days, maybe less if the winds stay in their favor. They're keeping the pace steady but discreet. You'll have to be fast to catch them before they reach Arenthia."

Niev stared at the map, memorizing the terrain. "Anything else I should know?"

The Harbormaster hesitated, then leaned closer, his voice dropping to a whisper. "Only this... If you do get those documents, don't trust anyone. Not even the ones who say they want to stop Breyvia. You don't know how deep this rot goes."

Niev straightened, her gaze unwavering. "I'll handle it."

The Harbormaster watched her go, his expression a mix of admiration and unease. As the door swung shut behind her, the weight of her mission pressed down with renewed intensity.

This wasn't just about secrets or power anymore, it was about lives. Innocent lives, stolen and sold in the darkest corners of Breyvia. If she could intercept those documents, she could expose the rot festering in the kingdom's underbelly.

But first, she had to catch the caravan.

With every step through Greyhaven's bustling streets, her resolve hardened. Thunder grumbled over distant hills. The Northroad awaited, and with it, the chance to bring down one of the most insidious networks Arenthia, and the world, had ever known.

4.
Niev

By the time Niev had finished her errands, the streets of Greyhaven were cloaked in darkness, the moon casting fractured light through the twisting alleys. The air was thick with the scent of damp stone and lingering smoke, the hum of the city still teetering between sleep and sin. She moved with purpose, her footsteps light against the cobblestones, muffled by the night's hush.

The plan was clear: intercept the caravan before it reached the mountains, end the mission early, and avoid setting foot in Arenthia altogether. Every step closer to her old home felt like a step toward a past she'd spent years outrunning. The thought gnawed at her, but she shoved it aside. There was no time for ghosts.

A chill breeze curled down the alley, lifting the edge of her cloak and carrying distant tavern laughter. She rolled her shoulders, ready for the night's work.

A flicker of movement up ahead snapped her from her thoughts.

Niev stilled, instincts flaring, fingers tightening around the hilt of her dagger. A figure stepped from the shadows, slow and deliberate. She reacted without hesitation—closing the distance in a fluid motion, blade pressed against the intruder's throat before he could breathe a word.

"Do you have a death wish?" she hissed, her voice a low, venomous hiss. Her piercing gaze met the man's, searching for any sign of threat.

The man didn't flinch. His breath was shallow, his body rigid with something that wasn't fear. His gray eyes, old but unwavering, held a desperation that didn't belong to someone trying to save his own skin.

"Tigress," he rasped, his voice rough, weathered. "I need your help."

Niev didn't ease her grip. "Who are you? You've got three seconds to convince me not to spill your blood right here."

The man raised a trembling hand, not in defense, but in supplication. "I mean no harm. Please, just listen. I've been looking for you."

Niev's grip on the dagger didn't loosen, her jaw tightened. "People who look for me don't usually live long enough to regret it. What makes you think you're an exception?"

"I know who you are. What you've done," he said, his voice strained but steady. "*You hunt monsters.*"

She tilted her head slightly, the corner of her mouth twitching in a humorless smirk. "And what makes you think you're not looking at one right now?"

The old man's gaze didn't waver. "Because monsters don't protect the innocent. They don't bring justice where no one else will."

Niev froze, his words hitting deeper than she'd expected.

Over the past decade, she'd carved a reputation as Saeris Morraine's Tigress, a blade for hire, Eldhaven's most ruthless assassin. She followed Saeris's orders to the letter, delivering swift, quiet executions that filled the guild's coffers.

But deep down, no matter how much she tried to bury it, she knew the old man was right, there was more to her than that.

Saeris knew it too. Though the Red Dragon never spoke of it, she was aware of the other side of Niev's nocturnal escapades. On nights when Saeris's coffers weren't calling, Niev hunted for herself, seeking out those who preyed on the powerless. Women bound to servitude, children stolen off the streets, and the desperate clawing at survival had all found salvation in her silent blade.

She never stayed long enough to see their gratitude. She wasn't doing it for that.

She did it because no one else would.

Saeris had to know, Niev had never been subtle, but the Red Dragon had her reasons for tolerating it. Tigress had never failed her, not once, and Saeris was too pragmatic to risk losing her deadliest weapon by questioning what she did in her spare time.

The weight of his words pressed on her, heavy and unshakable. Slowly she eased the blade from his throat, but did not sheath it. "Talk fast," she said.

The man exhaled shakily, relief flickering across his face. "My name is Ewan Beylore," he said. "I'm a blacksmith. I've lived in Greyhaven my whole life. But two months ago... two months ago, they took my *son*," his voice cracked.

Niev's grip on her dagger tightened.

She knew what was coming before he even said it.

"'Who took him?'" *She already knew the likely answer.*

"The slave traders," Ewan spat, his voice thick with bitterness. "Those bastards who steal children off the streets and sell them to the highest bidder. I tried to stop them, but they beat me bloody, and stabbed my boy, Finnian, as punishment. They didn't even let me have his body so I could *bury him*," he choked.

That stopped her.

Her stomach coiled, rage creeping under her skin like a slow-burning fire.

The shadows of her past stirred, ugly and relentless. She knew what it meant to be stolen. She knew what it meant to be owned. The chains of memory rattled, but she forced herself to focus.

"The city guard won't lift a finger," Ewan continued, voice shaking with exhaustion. "They say there's nothing they can do. But you... you can do something."

Niev said nothing, her silence pressing him to keep talking.

"I've heard the stories," he went on, desperate now. "How you go after the ones no one else will touch. How you make them pay." His hands trembled, whether from anger or grief, she couldn't tell. "That's why I've been looking for you. You're my last hope."

"I don't know what you've heard, old man, but I can't bring people back from the dead," she said, her face set in a frown.

Ewan reached into his coat, and her dagger was back at his throat before he could move an inch.

"Wait," Ewan said, his movements slow as he pulled out a small leather pouch. He held it out to her, his hand shaking. "This is everything I've got. It's not much, but it's yours if you'll help me. Just... please. Avenge my boy."

Niev stared at the pouch, but didn't take it.

Coin would never be the reason she said yes.

She could walk away. Ignore this. Keep her hands clean of it.

But she already knew she wouldn't.

"You think I do this for charity?" she said, her voice cold. "I have rules. I don't take jobs that don't come through Saeris."

Ewan's shoulders sagged, the pouch trembling in his hand. "Then take it to her," he pleaded, his voice splintering with desperation. "Tell her whatever you need to. But don't let them get away with this. And when you succeed, I'll rest easier, knowing that my son didn't die in vain."

The raw pain in his voice cut through the armor Niev kept around her heart. She looked at him for a long moment, her expression inscrutable.

This wasn't just a job. This was a hunt.

And she never left a hunt unfinished.

She exhaled sharply, snatching the pouch from his hand and tucking it into her coat. It was heavier than she expected. Not just coin, but trust. Hope. Desperation.

"I'll do it," she said quietly.

Ewan sagged with relief, his lips parting as if to thank her, but she cut him off before he could speak.

"On one condition." Her voice was steel. "You forget this ever happened. You never saw me. If anyone asks, the Tigress wasn't involved."

Ewan nodded frantically. "Of course. I—"

Niev turned before he could say anything else, already walking away.

"Save your thanks," she said over her shoulder. "I'm not doing this for free."

But as the city swallowed her back into its shadows, the truth gnawed at her.

This wasn't about gold.

It never had been.

❋ ❋ ❋

Greyhaven's lamps guttered overhead as she crossed the quarter. By the time the dragon-etched door loomed ahead, her decision was set in steel.

The scent of smoke, leather, and spice wrapped around Niev as she pushed open the heavy wooden door of *The Red Dragon's Lair*. The underground sanctuary was alive with movement—shadows slipping between tables, murmured conversations blending with the crackle of the hearth. Assassins, spies, and informants gathered in small clusters, trading secrets like currency. This was the nerve center of Solhaven's underworld, and at its core sat Saeris Morraine.

Perched at her usual seat at the massive oak table, the Red Dragon barely glanced up as Niev entered, idly twirling a dagger between her fingers.

"Back already?" Saeris mused, her voice smooth as silk but edged with steel.

Niev moved through the lair with the quiet confidence of someone who belonged, her strides purposeful. "We need to talk." Her tone was low but urgent.

Saeris tilted her head, curiosity flickering across her sharp features. She gestured to the empty chair across from her. "Sit."

Niev's gaze swept the room. Too many ears. This conversation wasn't for public consumption. Saeris, ever perceptive, caught the hesitation and smirked knowingly.

"Out," she ordered, her voice cutting through the lair like a blade.

The reaction was immediate. The men and women lingering nearby drained from the space without a word. The soft shuffle of boots faded, leaving only the low crackle of the fire.

Satisfied, Niev took a seat.

Saeris waited until the last person was out of earshot before leaning forward, resting her elbows on the table. "Talk," she said with a predatory grin.

Niev exhaled, steeling herself. "Your intel was only half right," she said, keeping her voice even. "The documents exist, but they haven't made it to the Librarium yet. They're in transit, being transported by a secret caravan through the Stoneridge Mountains."

Saeris's expression remained unreadable, but her fingers stopped twirling the dagger. "The mountains are impassable this time of year."

"Not if they take the Northroad."

Saeris tapped a single nail against the wood, her mind already working. "Interesting. And where did you come across this little gem of information?"

Niev allowed herself a smirk. "I had a chat with the Harbormaster."

Saeris chuckled. "That conniving bastard. I assume you applied... *persuasive measures*?"

Firelight flickered across Saeris's face, deepening the shadows under the knife-sharp lines of her cheekbones. For a heartbeat, neither woman spoke.

Beneath the silence lay Breyvia's uglier truths. King Oros—greedy, restless, and obsessed with controlling every vital sea route from Thornmere to the high northern straits—had let corruption bloom so long as coin and influence flowed back to his throne.

The Breyvian syndicate was the crown's unspoken engine: smugglers, slavers, and black-ledger merchants who greased the ports and, so rumor claimed, answered directly to Oros's favorite weapon, Commander Ruarc McCullen. McCullen's reputation was legendary, a naval tactician who could blockade three harbors with two ships, a man so fiercely loyal to Oros that every timbershore captain feared his crimson-sailed flagship more than a storm at sea.

"This is no small claim, Niev," Saeris's eyes narrowed. "The syndicate isn't just some band of cutthroats. Their coin buys lords, guildmasters, constables. And with a king who counts every clinking piece of silver, I'd wager Oros knows exactly what they're doing, maybe even signed off on it."

Niev had witnessed the syndicate's rot on more than one dock: children herded like livestock, hollow-eyed men slumped in chains, cargo holds heavy with bodies instead of grain. She clenched her fists beneath the table, nails biting into her bandaged palm.

"I know," she said quietly. "That's why we move before those documents vanish into some gilded vault, and before McCullen tightens the noose."

Saeris leaned back, her fingers steepled as she regarded Niev. The crackling firelight danced across her calculating expression. "So you're proposing a raid."

"Yes," Niev replied, her voice firm. "We stop that caravan in the mountains before it reaches Arenthia. It's the best chance we've got. Once it's in the Librarium, the documents will be buried under layers of security, and we'll lose our shot."

Saeris tapped her fingers against her chin, a contemplative silence stretching between them. Finally, she spoke. "And you're certain the Harbormaster was truthful?"

Niev nodded. "He's a sneaky bastard, but he's no liar. He wouldn't risk your wrath."

A smirk tugged at Saeris's lips. "Alright," She rose from her seat and began pacing, her mind visibly working through the possibilities. "If this is as big as you say, we'll need to hit them hard and fast. The Northroad isn't easy terrain, and the caravan will be heavily guarded. It'll take precision and the right team. Have you made a list of everything you'll need?"

Niev nodded. "I'll need a tracker, a navigator, maps of the Stoneridge region, and a weapons expert. Someone who can handle explosives."

Saeris arched a brow. "Explosives?"

"If things go south, I want a contingency."

Saeris stopped pacing, turning to face her. "And I suppose you have someone in mind for the last role?"

"Not yet," Niev admitted. "But I figured you might."

Saeris's grin widened. "As it happens, I suspected you'd want extra firepower, so I sent word ahead. There's a man eager to test his toys. A highly skilled *materia*."

The word drew Niev's full attention. Materia were a rare cadre of specialists who could manipulate matter at its most fundamental level, reshaping it as easily as potters shape clay. Some bent metal to their will, fusing blades from scraps on the battlefield; others coaxed threads into living armor or brewed volatile chemicals in thin air. The most gifted could mend flesh—walking triage tents whose hands rewove torn muscle and bone. Versatile in both crafting and combat, a materia was equal parts artisan, alchemist, and walking arsenal.

Niev's mind flicked to Myria, quiet, sharp-tongued Myria, who used her own fabric manipulation to disguise her gifts behind a seamstress's needle and thread. Most assumed she was merely talented with textiles; only few people knew she could stitch silk into an unbreakable garrote or weave shadow-black cloaks that swallowed sound.

Saeris's eyes gleamed as she went on. "He's quick-witted and entirely too clever for his own good, but if anyone can tip the scales in your favor, it's him."

Before Niev could question her further, the heavy door at the far end of the lair creaked open. A shadowed figure stepped inside, backlit by the torchlight from the hallway. The air in the room shifted subtly, charged with something new, something *volatile*.

As the man strode forward, his presence filled the space like he owned it. Tall and lean, he moved with an effortless confidence, his tailored vest snug over his athletic frame. Caramel-brown hair, almost long enough to be loosely tied at the nape, caught the firelight as keen brown eyes swept the room, curious, mischievous, and unabashedly amused.

The satchel slung over his shoulder jingled softly, the unmistakable sound of metal and glass shifting within.

"So *this* is the infamous Red Dragon's Lair." His voice was smooth, carrying the weight of someone who found amusement in everything. He made a show of glancing around before flashing an easy grin. "I was expecting more *fire and brimstone*, but I suppose this will do."

Saeris leaned against the table, her smirk growing wider. "Tigress, meet Caelan Galbraith. Caelan, this is Niev—your new partner."

Caelan's gaze shifted to Niev, his piercing brown eyes narrowing slightly as he studied her with an intensity that was both disarming and magnetic. "*Aah...* The legendary Tigress," he said, his gaze full of mischief. "I was wondering when we'd cross paths."

Niev's expression remained unreadable, but her eyes sharpened. "And you must be the boy with the toys Saeris was telling me about."

Caelan's grin didn't falter. He leaned against the table with an easy swagger. "I didn't realize my *toys* were such a topic of discussion. But, since you seem so interested, I'd be happy to give you a private demonstration." He winked.

Niev's dagger was out before he could blink. The polished steel gleamed under the firelight as she pressed the tip just below his belt.

"Just to make things *abundantly* clear. We're not partners, Galbraith," she said, voice soft as a drawn wire. "I give the orders, you keep the smirk and the wandering eyes to yourself, and maybe, *just maybe*, you'll live long enough to show me those skills you keep bragging about."

Caelan merely chuckled, glancing down at the blade. "A dagger? Really? That's almost *charming*." He tilted his head, feigning disappointment. "I expected something more creative."

"Careful *materia*," Niev leaned in, voice dropping to a whisper. "You're one word away from experiencing how *creative* I can be."

Saeris let out an exaggerated sigh, and slammed her palm on the table. "If you're both done with your pissing contest, we do have a mission to plan."

Niev withdrew her blade with a flick of her wrist but didn't break eye contact.

Caelan chuckled, dropping his satchel onto the table with a *thud*. "Relax, Tigress. I'm not here to waste your time. I'm here to make sure you don't get yourself killed."

Niev arched a brow. "I've been doing just fine without you, thanks."

The tension between them crackled like lightning. They both turned their attention to Saeris, but the unspoken challenge between them remained.

It was clear this partnership would be anything but *simple*, or dull.

Soon enough the Northroad would test them both. For tonight, strategies, and tempers, would have to forge an uneasy alloy.

5.
Caelan

Caelan prided himself on his iron focus and usually quiet demeanor, yet the instant his eyes landed on the Tigress, every disciplined thought in his head scattered like iron filings to a lodestone.

The candlelight flickered, casting long, restless shadows across the map laid out on the oak table. Saeris's fingertip traced the Northroad where it knifed through the Stoneridge range, and across from her the Tigress leaned in—sharp-eyed, all coiled muscle and murderous focus. Niev Helvast didn't just study terrain; she devoured it, the way predators memorize the softest part of a throat.

"The caravan is scheduled to pass through here," the Red Dragon said, tapping a section of the map where the road narrowed between steep cliffs. "If you strike there, they'd have nowhere to run, but taking it won't be easy."

Niev studied the map, memorizing the terrain. "How many men do you think we should expect?"

"Hard to say," Saeris exhaled, considering. "But if this is as important as we think, they won't be traveling light. Expect at least two dozen guards, maybe more."

Caelan let out a low whistle. "Two dozen? And here I thought you were inviting me to something fun."

Niev's glare was sharp enough to gut a man. *God, those eyes.* Dark, focused, unwavering. Like she saw right through him and had already decided she didn't like what she found.

"Feel free to sit this one out, *boy*."

The word landed like a gauntlet. Why did he *like* that? He should have ignored the jab, but some unruly part of him craved the spark in her eyes, and wanted to see it flare hotter. She dragged barbed wire across his composure, and instead of bleeding, he found himself smiling.

Focus, Galbraith, he told himself, but the order went unanswered. Every disciplined instinct urged silence; every reckless impulse wanted to keep prodding until he uncovered whatever made the Tigress bare her teeth.

He lounged back, offering the crooked grin that always aggravated the disciplined. "Now, now, Tigress. No need to wound my pride. Just tell me where to plant the fireworks and when to light the fuse."

She tried to ignore him but Caelan saw her mouth twitch with what looked like both irritation, and reluctant intrigue, and he wondered, with a ripple of dark amusement, why this woman made him want to rile her until sparks flew, even if it burned them both.

Instead, she turned back to Saeris. "I highly doubt the number will be that big. The Northroad is already steep and dangerous. If two dozen men are spotted trying to cross it, it'll be too obvious something's afoot. The numbers won't be large, but they'll be highly trained."

Caelan's smirk faded slightly, his mind shifting gears. "Then why the big caravan? If they're just transporting documents, wouldn't it make more sense to be... less conspicuous?"

"They're using trade as cover," Niev huffed. The sound was almost a scoff, and Caelan found himself watching the way her mouth moved as she spoke, how her lips barely parted when she was irritated. *God, what was wrong with him? He'd just met this woman!*

Saeris cleared her throat, and tapped the map again. "We strike at dusk three days from now. Fog rolls off the Stoneridge cliffs at first light; by sunset it sinks into that pass thick as wool. Perfect cover."

Niev straightened, the candlelight limning her profile in gold. "We'll need rope ladders and anchors on the western ridge. I want eyes on both ends of the bottleneck before the caravan even sniffs trouble." She pointed to Caelan without looking at him. "That fuse you're so eager to light goes here, under the lead wagon. One spark and the road's gone. But wait until we've got our hands on the goods."

"Pulverize the whole ledge?" Caelan arched a brow. "Lovely. I'll whip up something scenic."

Niev finally met his gaze again. *Oh she was definitely annoyed, but was this a flicker of begrudging respect he spotted?*

"Just make sure *scenic* doesn't kill us," she smirked mockingly.

He saluted her with two lazy fingers. "Beautiful destruction, minimal casualties. My specialty."

"Larger goods in plain sight, with the real cargo hidden," Niev continued. "We'll need someone stealthy enough to find where the documents are stashed while the rest of us create a distraction."

Saeris's expression sharpened with something like approval. "This is bigger than your usual jobs, Tigress. You'll need a solid team to pull it off."

"That's what I'm working on," Niev replied. "Also, I'm going to need Teagan."

Saeris raised an eyebrow. "Your little scout?"

"He's the best one we've got," she shot back without hesitation. That sharp edge again, the way her voice didn't allow room for argument. Stubborn, relentless. He should find it annoying. Instead, he was almost impressed.

Saeris considered it for a beat, then nodded. "Fine. But he's not enough. You'll also need a navigator, someone who knows the terrain better than the damn caravan itself."

"Doran," Niev said with a wince. "He used to run smuggling routes through the Stoneridge passes. If anyone knows the land, it's him."

Caelan snorted before he could stop himself.

Niev's eyes snapped to him. "Something funny?"

Her head tilted slightly, dark strands of hair slipping loose from where they had been pinned back, framing her face in an almost careless way. She was a thief, a liar, and a cold blooded *killer*. She had no business looking this good.

Caelan leaned forward, resting an elbow on the table. "Doran? You mean the washed-up smuggler who's more familiar with the inside of a rum bottle than the actual routes?"

Niev narrowed her eyes. "He knows the terrain."

"He *knew* the terrain. Twenty years ago." Caelan shook his head, clearly amused. "You really want to bet your life that he hasn't forgotten half of it between drinks?"

Saeris remained silent, watching the exchange with mild amusement, clearly waiting to see who would win.

Niev exhaled sharply, patience thinning. "If you have a better idea, say it."

Caelan's grin stretched wide. *Oh, this was too easy.*

"Ayda Ravenscroft. The Raven."

Her frown deepened. "Who?"

Leaning forward, Caelan gestured vaguely. "She's a herbalist and navigator. A real one. Travels constantly, has an absurd memory for landscapes, and won't steer us into a canyon because she forgot which way the sun rises." He shot her a pointed look. "Unlike Doran."

"Doran's reliable," Niev argued, arms folded.

"No, Doran's available. There's a difference."

Caelan saw the flicker of hesitation in her eyes. He could see how much she didn't like that he had a point. But that was fine. He wasn't done yet.

"Ayda actually knows the Stoneridge region," he continued. "Not from stories, not from smuggling runs a decade ago. She's mapped half of it herself. If we want to move fast, unseen, and have the best chance of cutting off that caravan before we're outnumbered, we need her."

Niev's jaw tensed, like she was *really* hating that she was considering it.

Saeris, however, was already convinced.

"I like it," she mused. "A fresh perspective. And I've heard of The Raven, she has a reputation for knowing the land better than the locals."

Niev's lips pressed into a thin line. There it was again. That tension in her mouth, like she was biting back a retort.

"She's not a fighter," Niev stubbornly pressed on.

"Not particularly," Caelan agreed easily. "But she doesn't need to be. That's *your* job. Hers is to make sure we don't die from poor planning."

Saeris smirked, clearly enjoying watching Niev wrestle with her pride. "Tigress, if you're really so concerned, take both. Doran and Ayda. Let them prove themselves, and use whoever you trust when the time comes."

Niev exhaled sharply, like she knew she was outmaneuvered. "Fine. But if she slows us down—"

"She won't," Caelan cut in smoothly.

Niev shot him a look. He was going to be in trouble if he started enjoying it too much.

He just grinned.

Saeris seemed deeply entertained. "Alright then. It's settled. Gather your team. Be back here at dawn."

Niev didn't wait for further discussion. She pushed away from the table, already moving towards the door.

Caelan lingered, rolling a stub of chalk he'd idly transmuted from a splinter of stray limestone between his fingers. He caught himself glancing at Niev's retreating back and almost scowled. *Focus, Galbraith. Plans, powder, profit... nothing else matters.*

Yet the steel-line of her shoulders and the precision in her stride tugged at him like a current. Something about her scraped away his surface calm, exposing edges he thought long filed down. She made him reckless, made him *want* to be reckless.

Behind him, Saeris murmured, "Careful, Galbraith. She's not a flame you can toy with and walk away unburned."

He offered a half-smile. "I have no idea what you're talking about."

And as he pocketed the chalk, already imagining the chemical cocktail that would turn rock to shrapnel, he couldn't shake the feeling that this job was about to be a hell of a lot more interesting than he'd planned.

❋ ❋ ❋

The streets were dark, their usual chaos subdued beneath a heavy silence that pressed against the damp walls. Pools of lantern light flickered weakly, struggling against the encroaching shadows that stretched between crumbling buildings. The rain from earlier had left the ground slick, the scent of wet stone lingering in the air. Somewhere in the distance, the faint sound of laughter echoed—muffled, distant, as if swallowed by the night itself.

Caelan moved easily through the dimly lit passages, his hands tucked in his pockets, his gait unhurried. He could feel the weight of eyes tracking their steps, measuring them, deciding whether they were worth the trouble. He didn't glance over his shoulder, didn't tense when a figure melted back into the alleyway just ahead.

But he felt *her* tension.

Niev walked just behind him, her steps as controlled as ever, but there was something in her posture, always rigid and resistant. He didn't need to see her face to know that she was biting back irritation. It simmered between them like a fuse waiting to be lit.

Caelan smirked to himself.

"You always this pleasant on a walk?" he murmured, keeping his voice low and easy.

Silence.

He could practically hear her grinding her teeth.

Oh, this was too good.

She didn't like being led, by anyone, but especially not by him it seemed. He could feel it in the way she walked, just a step slower, her presence taut as a drawn bowstring. He cast a sideways glance, catching the way she kept pace just enough to show she wasn't following, but refused to step fully beside him.

God, she was stubborn.

"Go on then," she muttered finally, quickening her step to match his. Her arms crossed, her irritation practically radiating off her. "Get it out of your system."

Caelan arched a brow, feigning innocence. "Get what out of my system?"

She shot him a look that promised murder.

"You've been waiting to gloat since we left," she said dryly. "Might as well get it over with."

He chuckled, slow and warm. She made this too easy.

"I wasn't going to gloat."

Niev kept staring.

"Alright, maybe just a little," he admitted, shrugging.

She rolled her eyes.

"But listen," he continued, the teasing edge in his voice dulling just slightly. "I didn't suggest the Raven just to get under your skin."

Niev scoffed. "Oh, please."

"I mean it." He ran a hand through his tousled caramel-brown hair, glancing at her. The candlelight from a nearby lantern caught the sharp line of her jaw, the flicker of frustration in her dark eyes.

Caelan had seen plenty of fighters, plenty of people who carried their steel in their posture, in the way they watched the world like they were always calculating how to kill it.

But the Tigress?

She was something else entirely.

He exhaled, shaking his head. "Doran is good, but he's reckless. And that's exactly why we can't use him. You don't need someone who's just 'reliable' or 'familiar.' You need someone adaptable, someone who thinks on their feet and gets shit done."

Niev shot him a look, her skepticism clear. "This isn't some gambling job, Galbraith. It's a raid. And Saeris put me in charge. I've known you for less than a few hours and you've already tried to undermine my authority—"

Caelan stopped walking.

Niev took another step before she realized he wasn't beside her. Her head snapped back toward him, her brows furrowing in irritation at being forced to pause.

"I know how it looks," he said seriously, his usual easy grin absent. "But I wouldn't have suggested her if I didn't think she was the best choice." He held her gaze, letting her see that he meant it. "Ayda doesn't just read maps; she understands terrain in a way I've never seen before. And more importantly, she won't hesitate if things go south."

For a moment, Niev just looked at him.

Her weight shifted slightly, her fingers flexing at her sides. He could see the way her jaw tensed, the way her lips pressed together, the way she searched his face for any flicker of amusement, any sign that he was just saying this to get a rise out of her.

He let her look.

And when she didn't find what she was expecting, that seemed to irritate her more than anything.

She exhaled sharply through her nose, as if the very act of considering his words physically pained her.

Her gaze flickered down, away from his, like she suddenly found the damp stones beneath them more interesting. Then, with a slow roll of her shoulders, she met his eyes again.

She still wasn't convinced. But she was listening.

His mouth twitched. A small victory.

"You'll like her, I promise," Caelan added, smirking now. "If for no other reason than the fact that she'll give me just as much hell as you do."

That got her.

Just the smallest twitch at the corner of her lips, there and gone in an instant. But he caught it.

He could tell she hated that he had a point. It was written all over her features.

But she was thinking about it now.

He could see the wheels turning behind those dark eyes, weighing it, trying to find a reason to shove the idea aside.

Instead, she asked, "You're sure about her?"

There was more challenge than curiosity in her tone.

He grinned.

"Absolutely."

※　※　※

The further they walked, the more the city peeled away behind them. The tight, tangled streets of Greyhaven stretched like veins through the body of civilization, but here, those veins thinned, leading them toward something quieter, something untouched by the filth and fire of the city.

Caelan had spent years navigating the underbelly of Greyhaven, slipping between its gutters and grandeur alike, but even he had rarely ventured this far. The air was different here, fresher, laced with brine and damp earth. The usual scents of crowded alleys—stale beer, rotting wood, the acrid sting of tallow candles burning low—faded beneath the sharper notes of salt and something else. Something green and herbal, crisp and slightly sweet.

Caelan inhaled deeply. *Bergamot and jasmine.*

His gaze flickered sideways toward Niev.

She walked with the same purpose, shoulders squared, cloak drawn tight, her entire presence wired with alertness. But there was something else beneath it, something rigid in the way her fingers twitched near her belt, how her dark eyes flicked to every ridge and hollow around them, scanning, calculating.

He smirked.

"This isn't some trap, you know," he said, watching her out of the corner of his eye. His tone was lighter than usual, but the teasing edge was absent. For once. "You look like you're about to bolt."

She scoffed, but her fingers flexed slightly, betraying her unease.

Caelan liked that she wasn't comfortable out here. He didn't know why, maybe because it was the first time in the past few hours he'd seen her out of her element. Maybe because she carried herself like she had the city in her palm, but here? Here, she was forced to play by someone else's rules.

He wondered if she hated that as much as he enjoyed witnessing it.

Their path wound past a stretch of weathered stone houses, half-swallowed by tall reeds and creeping ivy. The homes here weren't stacked and crowded like in Greyhaven; they were quiet, tucked into the land rather than built to claim it. It was a stark contrast to the Red Dragon's Lair, where everything reeked of leather, ink, and smoke.

But this place?

This place breathed.

His gaze traced the outlines of gnarled trees curling over one of the cottages, their twisted limbs almost protective of the small structure nestled beneath them. A faint trail of smoke curled from the chimney, and warm candlelight flickered through the thick curtains.

"This is it?" Niev asked, arching a brow as she took in the modest, vine-wrapped cottage. "Is she a witch or something?"

Caelan grinned. *Oh, if only she knew.*

"Something like that."

Before she could press further, he knocked, three sharp raps, and stepped back.

A pause.

Then, the door swung open.

A petite woman, barely reaching Niev's shoulder, stood on the threshold. Her strawberry-blond hair was tied in a messy knot, stray strands escaping over her forehead. Sharp hazel eyes flicked between the two of them, catching on Caelan with immediate suspicion.

"Oh, it's *you*," Ayda drawled. "What do you want, Galbraith? Another smoke bomb gone wrong? A potion to fix your bruised ego?"

Caelan grinned. "Missed you too, Raven."

Ayda exhaled, rolling her eyes before her sharp gaze flicked to Niev, assessing rather than judging. Whatever she saw made her expression soften slightly. "And who's this?"

Before Caelan could introduce her, Niev crossed her arms. "I'm Niev," she said curtly.

She was so damn *prickly*.

Ayda raised an unimpressed brow.

Caelan snorted. "This is Saeris's right hand. The infamous Tigress of Solhaven."

Niev's lips pressed into a thin line. He could tell she hated that he'd answered for her.

"I don't exactly introduce myself that way, but yes."

Ayda hummed, tapping a finger against the satchel at her hip. She smiled, but there was something sharp in it. "Good for you, love."

Caelan watched, amused, as Niev's scowl twitched, just a little. A flicker of something that wasn't quite irritation.

He leaned in slightly, lowering his voice. "Told you you'd like her."

She shot him a withering look.

Worth it.

Ayda exhaled through her nose and studied them both for a long moment before stepping back. "Fine. Come in. If I'm going to listen to whatever foolishness you two are about to propose, I might as well be comfortable."

The interior was exactly the same as the last time Caelan was here.

Shelves crammed with glass vials, parchment maps, and stones arranged in odd, intricate patterns. Dried herbs hung from the ceiling, their scent thick in the warm air, and a wooden table dominated the center of the room, cluttered with open books, half-mixed tonics, and what looked suspiciously like an unfinished trap mechanism.

He loved that Ayda still made those.

"Don't touch anything," Ayda warned, her sharp gaze cutting toward him.

Caelan placed a hand over his heart in mock offense. "You wound me, truly."

Niev pulled out a chair and sat, her dark eyes still scanning the space. Cautious. Always cautious. But she didn't look as tense as she had outside.

He leaned against the nearest wall, arms crossed, watching as Ayda moved toward the hearth, tossing herbs into a steaming pot.

"Tea," she explained. "Something tells me I'm going to need to be well-hydrated for this."

"Fair enough," Niev said, leaning forward. "I'm not one to beat around the bush. So here's the deal, I need a strong navigator who can make sure my team and I don't get killed. And according to him, that's you."

Ayda shot Caelan a look. "And you're just going to take his word for it?"

"Absolutely not," Niev said flatly.

Caelan let out a long-suffering groan, tipping his head back against the wall. "Unbelievable."

Ayda shot him a sideways glance. "Don't lump me into whatever fragile ego crisis you're having. I don't need your vouching. Besides," she turned back to Niev, eyes sharp with interest now. "What exactly are we navigating?"

"The Stoneridge Mountains," Niev answered. "We're intercepting a caravan before it reaches Arenthia."

Ayda's brows lifted. "In winter? That's bold."

She stirred the tea, her eyes flicking to Niev with quiet scrutiny. Caelan knew that look. Ayda wasn't just considering the terrain, she was considering Niev. Weighing her. Testing her.

Niev, stoic as ever, held her ground.

Ayda finally exhaled, tapping a finger against the rim of her cup. "And what exactly is this caravan carrying that makes it worth risking your necks?"

Niev hesitated. Not long, but long enough.

"That's on a need-to-know basis," she finally said.

Ayda's fingers tightened around the spoon, her sharp gaze snapping back to the Tigress. She smirked. "Fair enough."

"So, you're in or what?" Caelan asked, feigning nonchalance, but he was watching her carefully.

Ayda was quiet for a long moment before she exhaled through her nose.

"Alright."

Caelan blinked. "That's it? No arguments? No long speeches about how we're reckless?"

"Oh, you're definitely reckless," Ayda said, pouring the tea into small ceramic cups. "But if you're really planning to take down a slave trading network, then I'm in."

Calean instantly felt the tension in the room thicken.

Niev went completely still.

He noticed the way her fingers curled slightly around the cup Ayda had just slid toward her, though she didn't pick it up.

"I never said anything about a slave trading network," Niev said evenly.

Ayda met her gaze, unbothered. "You didn't."

The silence stretched.

He could practically taste the threat in the room. It was thick, like the slow curl of smoke from the hearth, coiling between Niev and Ayda in a silent standoff.

And he was enjoying every second of it.

Niev ignored him. "Then how do you know?"

Ayda tapped a finger against the rim of her cup, unfazed. "Because, love, I make it my business to know what I'm getting into before I agree to anything." Her lips quirked, slow and knowing. "And because someone got to me first."

Caelan's brows lifted. Now *this* was interesting.

Before Niev could ask who, the sound of a door creaking open from the back of the house cut through the room.

Caelan instinctively shifted, hand twitching toward his belt, but Ayda barely reacted, which meant she'd been expecting this.

A shadow moved behind the cluttered shelves, footsteps light and practiced, like a ghost slipping through familiar walls. Then, out of the dim candlelight, a figure emerged, and the second Caelan saw who it was, everything made sense.

Teagan Blackwood.

Caelan bit back a laugh. *Oh, this was about to be good.*

He'd never personally met the man, but he'd heard and seen enough of him around town to recognize him instantly.

The firelight threw jagged shadows across Teagan's face, accentuating his ever-present smirk, the same damn smirk that made it impossible to tell whether he was genuinely amused or just liked to watch people suffer.

He stopped mid-stride, eyes locking onto Niev. Something unreadable flickered across his face before he schooled it back into that same easy arrogance. He exhaled a low chuckle.

"Well, this is unexpected," he mused. "Didn't think I'd be seeing you here, Tigress."

Caelan felt the moment Niev's entire body went rigid.

Her expression didn't change much, her jaw clenched, her shoulders squared, but he noticed. He noticed the sharpness in her breath, the tension coiling beneath the surface of her calm.

And Caelan, ever the opportunist, pounced.

"Oh, this is fantastic." He grinned, stretching back in his chair like all of his nameday wishes had come true at once. "Tigress, you mean to tell me your tracker, your dear old right-hand man, as it were, also thinks Ayda is a better choice than Doran? God above, this is beautiful."

Niev's glare could have melted steel. "Shut your mouth."

Caelan's grin only grew. "I love this for you."

She turned back to Teagan, her temper burning hotter than the tea steaming between them. "Explain," she demanded.

Teagan held up his hands, but the smirk never left his face. "Alright, alright. Before you get that vein in your forehead all worked up, let me be clear, I wasn't going behind your back."

Niev arched a brow.

"Okay, well, technically I was," he admitted. "But only because I was helping."

"Helping," Niev repeated flatly.

Teagan crossed the room, leaning against the table like he owned the damn place. "When you told me about the mission, I figured you'd need a strong team. And when I heard Saeris was pushing Doran for the job, I... Well, let's just say I had some doubts."

Caelan snorted. "Even your best friend doesn't trust your choice. That says so much."

Teagan ignored him, his focus still on Niev. "I've known Ayda for years. I knew she'd be a better choice. So I came here and pitched the job to her myself."

Caelan wasn't laughing anymore.

Not because of the mission. Not because of the behind-the-scenes scheming.

No.

It was the way Niev's expression barely shifted, but her eyes did. Just slightly. Just enough for Caelan to catch the brief flicker of something before she smothered it under her usual sharp edges.

Teagan said he had known Ayda for *years*.

And Niev hadn't known that.

Interesting.

Niev inhaled sharply through her nose. "Without telling me."

"Would you have listened?" Teagan countered.

Niev didn't answer.

Ayda, ever the troublemaker, hummed in amusement, sipping her tea. "You know, this is almost sweet. A bunch of men running around, trying to get me a job." She set her cup down and smirked at Niev. "I'd say I'm flattered."

Niev pinched the bridge of her nose, visibly willing herself not to strangle someone. Instead, she turned to Teagan, eyes narrowed. "How do you know each other anyway?"

Teagan's smirk faltered—just a little.

Caelan caught it.

Teagan glanced at Ayda, who simply shrugged as if to say, *Might as well tell her.*

"I met her years ago," Teagan said, settling onto a stool by the table. "Back when I was still doing more scouting than fighting. Got lost in the middle of nowhere, chasing a bounty, ended up half-dead in the forest from a bad fall and a worse wound."

Ayda snorted. "Idiot fell into a ravine trying to track a man twice his size."

"It was a strategic maneuver," Teagan argued, holding up a finger.

Ayda rolled her eyes. "It was not. Anyway, I found him bleeding out in the woods and, being the charitable soul I am, decided to save his sorry ass. Stitched him up, got him on his feet. Been stuck with him ever since."

Teagan smirked. "And you're so lucky for it."

Ayda leaned her chin on her hand, unimpressed. "Yeah. Lucky."

Caelan watched Niev absorb the story.

She didn't react outwardly, no sharp words, no immediate arguments, but he saw the way her fingers curled slightly against her knee, the way her jaw tightened.

Not anger.

Not exactly.

Something almost like hurt flashed behind her eyes.

He filed that away.

"So let me get this straight," Niev said finally, lowering her hand. "You—" she jabbed a finger at Teagan "—pitched my own mission to a recruit before I had a chance to? Without telling me?"

Teagan nodded, not even a little remorseful. "Correct."

"You went behind my back, again, even after I specifically—"

"Correct," Teagan repeated, wincing.

Niev exhaled through her teeth.

Caelan, smirking, nudged her shoulder. "I am *never* letting you live this down."

She shoved him off his chair.

He hit the floor with a grunt, still laughing.

Niev exhaled sharply through her nose, fixing Teagan with a withering glare. "I swear to all that is holy, if you ever go behind my back again—"

"You'll kill me," Teagan finished for her, smirking. "Yeah, yeah. You say that every week."

Niev clenched her fists, then unclenched them with visible effort. She turned to Ayda. "And you're still in?"

Ayda smirked, enjoying herself far too much. "Absolutely."

Niev studied her, searching for any sign of hesitation. But Ayda's eyes were steady. She had made that decision knowing exactly what they were up against.

Niev seemed to respect that.

She nodded once, decisive. "Alright. Welcome to the team."

Teagan shot a fist in the air. "I'll drink to that!"

Caelan, from the floor where he was still recovering from being shoved, groaned. "Can someone help me up before the toasts start?"

Teagan extended a hand, hauling Caelan to his feet with an exaggerated flourish. "Teagan Blackwood," he said smoothly, placing a hand over his chest in mock seriousness. "Master tracker, occasional troublemaker, and longtime acquaintance of every single woman in this room."

Caelan, ever the performer, dusted himself off and gave an overly dramatic bow. "Caelan Galbraith, explosives expert, master of charm, and fastest contender for the top spot on the Tigress's murder list."

The two men exchanged a glance before bursting into laughter.

Niev exhaled sharply, pinching the bridge of her nose. "Great. They're going to be insufferable."

Ayda smirked. "Of *that*...I have no doubt."

Niev shot her a sideways glance, catching the gleam of dry amusement in her hazel eyes. And after what felt like an eternity, she smirked back.

6.
Caelan

The last few days leading up to the ambush blurred into a restless haze. Maps became their entire world—ink bleeding into parchment as they traced routes over and over, searching for weaknesses, hidden paths, the perfect strike point. The cramped walls of Ayda's cottage bore witness to hours of tension, the sharp scent of burning candle wax and drying herbs thick in the air, doing little to soothe frayed tempers.

Caelan sat at the wooden table, absently spinning a small vial of black powder between his fingers while Niev and Teagan argued over infiltration tactics. Again.

"You're not listening," Niev snapped, hands braced against the table, her glare sharp enough to cut steel. "We can't just storm in with blades drawn. We need to control the fight before it even starts."

Teagan crossed his arms, expression unimpressed. "And I'm saying the second we engage, we lose that control. We should take out the perimeter guards first, pick them off before they even realize they're under attack."

"Which is exactly what I said ten minutes ago," Niev shot back.

"Yeah, but you said it like an ass," Teagan muttered.

Caelan huffed a quiet laugh, earning a sharp look from Niev. He was really starting to get used to her scowl.

"Careful, Blackwood," he mused, still twirling the vial. "That vein in her forehead's about to pop again."

Teagan smirked, and Niev looked two seconds away from hurling another dagger at one of them.

Caelan pushed off the doorframe, leaving them to their latest round of bickering. He had no interest in watching them circle each other with sharp words and stubborn glares all day—not when there was actual work to be done.

He strode down the dim hallway, boots whispering against the wooden floor, and slipped into the small side room he had claimed for himself. It was quiet here, tucked away from the main space where the others had spread their maps and plans. The only sound was the faint crackle of a single candle burning low on the desk, its golden light casting jagged shadows against the cluttered walls.

Caelan exhaled slowly, rolling his shoulders before setting down his satchel. *Finally, some peace.*

He unbuckled the straps and began unpacking his tools with practiced efficiency. Small brass casings, vials of fine black powder, carefully coiled fuse wire, every piece meticulously arranged in front of him. He worked by feel, fingers moving with an artisan's precision as he measured, filled, sealed.

He pressed two fingers to a lump of raw slag and coaxed it apart, the metal softening under his will, stretching into a thin sheet that curled obediently into a perfect cylinder. A pulse of intent, and the seam fused without heat marks. Next, he scraped a calloused thumb across a handful of sand, whisper-light transmutation rippling outward until the grains melted and reformed into flawless vials that cooled in his palm. Chemicals followed—nitre crystals condensed from the damp in the walls, sulfur teased from a half-empty lantern wick, charcoal sifted from the hearth. He measured by instinct, mixing volatile powder that shimmered silver in the lantern glow before tamping it into each shell.

Hours bled away like this: hunched over the table, metal reshaping at a thought, glass blooming into ampoules, explosive slurry swirling with a flick of his wrist.

Controlled devastation. That's what this was.

Most people assumed explosives were blunt instruments—messy, unpredictable, designed only for chaos. *Idiots.* The real art was in precision. Knowing exactly how much force was needed to collapse a wall without bringing the whole building down. Blowing the wheel off a wagon without igniting the cargo inside.

This mission demanded finesse. Niev had been painfully clear about that.

No unnecessary casualties.

Caelan scowled at the memory, his grip tightening on the small metal casing he was working on. As if he was some reckless fool playing with fire for fun.

He might have made a career out of destruction, but he wasn't careless. Everything he built had a purpose. A calculated effect.

He sealed the device in his hand, giving it a small, experimental toss before catching it again. A compact charge, small enough to fit in a palm, just enough to cripple a wagon's axle. Quick, clean, effective.

It would do.

He set it aside and reached for another casing. On and on he worked, assembling a neat line of palm-sized miracles, until the candles burned low and the room filled with the faint tang of ozone.

Eventually, the door creaked open behind him.

He didn't need to look up to know it was *her*.

He could tell from the controlled rhythm of her steps, from the way she hovered just inside the doorway as if already regretting the impulse.

Caelan didn't look up immediately, instead finishing the careful placement of a fuse before speaking. "Something I can help you with, Tigress?"

A pause. Then—

"You've been in here for hours," she muttered, arms crossing over her chest like she'd only just realized she needed an excuse. "The rest of us are about to eat. If you want to, you know... join."

Now *that*, he did not expect.

Niev rarely hesitated. She was a woman of purpose, sharp angles and certainty, not one to stumble over a simple invitation. And yet, she was standing there, trying to sound casual while very obviously failing.

Caelan smirked but didn't turn just yet. Instead, he flicked his gaze toward the candlelight, watching the flame dance across the gleaming metal of the devices in front of him. "Didn't realize I was being timed."

"You weren't," she shot back quickly, then frowned, as if irritated at herself for the unnecessary defense.

Caelan finally glanced at her, the corner of his mouth twitching as he took in the way she lingered in the doorway, arms crossed in that tight, controlled way she did when she was thinking too much.

Niev's gaze flickered over the table, taking in the mess of tools and half-assembled weapons. He didn't miss the way her eyes lingered, not just in assessment, but with something quieter, more thoughtful.

It occurred to him that she had never seen him like this before.

Focused. Meticulous. *Quiet.*

Caelan was many things—reckless, cocky, an insufferable pain in her ass, if her glares were anything to go by.

But for once, there were no smart remarks, no unnecessary flourishes of dramatics. Just his hands moving with careful precision, assembling something that could level a room in seconds.

And she was watching.

Lingering.

She'd gone eerily still, and he couldn't tell whether she liked seeing him like this or not.

"You're good at this," Niev said after a long beat, her voice low, almost reluctant.

Caelan arched a brow. "What, blowing things up?"

She gave him a look. "No. The way you work. It's... precise."

That caught him off guard more than it should have.

He knew how people saw him—loud, unpredictable, the wildcard in a room full of professionals. People assumed he just threw fire and hoped for the best. They didn't see this part. The patience. The calculation. The discipline beneath the chaos.

But at this moment, she *saw* him.

And for some damned reason, that made his pulse kick just a little harder.

"Controlled chaos," he murmured, twirling a small, finished charge between his fingers before setting it down. "That's the trick. Make it look unpredictable when, in reality, you know exactly how it'll end."

Niev hummed, watching him for a moment longer before exhaling. "Well... Just don't forget to eat while you're busy orchestrating destruction."

Caelan leaned back in his chair, tilting his head at her. "Are you... worried about me, Tigress?"

Her eyes narrowed instantly. "No."

He grinned. "You sure? Because it sounds like—"

"Forget it," she snapped, turning on her heel. "You can go ahead and starve for all I care."

She stalked out before he could push further, but not before he caught the way her shoulders tensed—just slightly—at his chuckle.

Caelan smirked to himself, giving the charge one last spin between his fingers before standing.

Well... Dinner did sound good.

And riling her up even more?

That was just an added bonus.

❋ ❋ ❋

By the time they were ready to move, exhaustion gnawed at the edges of their resolve, but there was no turning back.

And after two full days of riding into the mountains, the cold bit deep, cutting through layers of fabric and flesh alike, but Caelan barely felt it. He had grown up in worse places, learned to endure.

The Northroad stretched before them like a silvered scar, winding through jagged cliffs and rolling snowdrifts. A place made for ambushes and death.

Niev led the way, her movements precise, predatory. He watched the way she moved—silent, calculating, dangerous.

It was almost hypnotic. *Almost.*

Ayda's voice was barely a whisper over the wind, guiding them through the treacherous terrain.

"Step left. Ice."

"Watch the ledge here."

"That patch will sink if you're not careful."

She was unnervingly good at reading the land, moving like she belonged to it. Caelan wasn't easily impressed, but he could admit that much.

Ahead, Teagan flickered in and out of sight like a shadow, scouting the path, scanning for signs of movement—tracks that were too fresh, disturbances in the natural rhythm of the night. Every so often, he'd give a silent signal—a raised fist, a shift of his stance—wordlessly communicating what he saw.

Caelan, for once, kept quiet.

His fingers hovered near the vials strapped to his belt, ghosting over the edges of a flask filled with black powder. It was a habit, an unconscious tic. A reminder that when the time came, he'd be ready.

He caught Niev watching him.

"What?" he murmured, voice barely carrying over the wind.

She didn't answer immediately, just studied him for a beat longer than necessary before shaking her head. "Nothing."

Liar.

But he let it go.

The trees began to thin, the forest retreating into open stretches of snow-laden hills. Beyond them, the Northroad unraveled like a pale ribbon in the darkness.

And there—a caravan.

Half-obscured by the falling snow, three wagons crawled forward, their lanterns casting a feeble glow against the storm.

Niev lifted her fist. *Stop.*

The group froze instantly, blending into the landscape like specters.

Teagan reappeared beside them, breath misting in the cold air. "Three wagons. Six guards on foot, armed."

Niev's eyes flicked over the scene, mind working fast. Caelan could see it, the way she mapped it out in her head, sorting possibilities, deciding their next move before anyone else had even drawn breath.

Ayda frowned, peering at the caravan. "They'll see us coming if we move in too soon. Open road gives them too much visibility."

The wind howled through the narrow pass, kicking up flurries of snow. The cliffs loomed over them, jagged and merciless—a perfect place for an ambush.

Niev crouched low behind a boulder, eyes narrowing. The wagons were slow, burdened by their cargo, but the guards were sharp, scanning their surroundings with practiced wariness.

Six on foot, more likely inside. All armed.

Teagan crouched beside her, hands resting on the hilts of his daggers. "We wait until they reach the choke point," he murmured. "Once they're between the cliffs, they're boxed in. No room to maneuver."

Niev smirked. "Good thinking."

Caelan shifted slightly behind her, rolling one of his vials between his fingers. "I can take out the lead wagon," he offered. "Scatter the horses, slow them down."

Ayda exhaled, watching the approaching caravan with an unreadable expression. "That road's icy. If the horses spook and the wagons slide, we might not even have to fight half of them. They'll be too busy trying not to tumble off the edge."

Clever.

Caelan glanced at Niev, waiting. He wasn't the type to take orders, not really, but she was sharp. He wanted to see what she'd do next. And now was not the time to test her patience.

She turned to Teagan first. "You're with me. We take out the ones on foot before they can react." Then her gaze flicked to Caelan. "Wait for my signal. Hit the lead wagon, but don't blow it to the goddamned sky just yet."

Caelan grinned. "Wouldn't dream of it."

Ayda pulled her bow from her back, checking the fletching on her arrows. "And me?"

Niev met her gaze, her expression cold, fierce. "Cover us. Drop anyone who gets too close."

The plan locked into place like the final piece of a well-crafted mechanism.

Caelan exhaled slowly, watching as the sound of hooves and creaking wood filled the air, growing louder. The caravan was nearly at the choke point.

This was it.

His fingers curled around the vial of black powder.

Niev was crouched ahead of him, silent, poised, her twin daggers already unsheathed. The firelight from the caravan flickered against her face, casting half of it in gold, the other in shadow. She looked like a predator waiting for the perfect moment to strike.

God help the poor bastards below.

Ayda nodded once, then slipped into the darkness. The woman was damn near supernatural in the way she vanished, her small frame blending into the terrain as if the earth itself had given her permission to pass.

The moment stretched thin. The calm before the storm.

Then Niev glanced at the tracker.

Teagan smirked. "Try to keep up, Tigress."

And just like that, the first body hit the ground.

Caelan wasn't sure if he blinked or if she just moved that fast. One second the guard was breathing, the next there was a dagger buried in his throat, Niev easing him down like a lover whispering him into death.

Teagan was just as fast, slipping through the shadows like a whisper, his blade already lodged deep in another guard's ribs before the poor bastard could make a sound.

Two down.

Ayda signaled. Seconds before the next rotation.

They slipped into position—

And then came the first mistake.

The blood from that first body had seeped into the snow too fast.

A guard stepped closer to the fallen shadows. His boot nudged something too soft. His brows furrowed—then he saw the dark stain in the snow.

His eyes widened.

"Ambush!"

The word barely had time to echo before Niev silenced him, her blade ramming upward beneath his jaw. His scream turned to a wet gurgle—too late.

The damage was done.

The caravan roared to life.

Swords were drawn, shouts filled the frozen air, and the fight exploded into motion.

Caelan twisted the vial in his fingers before tucking it away. Time to have some fun.

Niev moved like a specter of death, slipping between bodies, stepping into the kill before her enemies even knew they were dead. She was fast—so goddamn fast—a blur of silver steel cutting through the firelight.

Caelan had seen skilled fighters. Hell, he'd fought alongside some of the best. But this?

This was something else entirely.

His breath hitched as he watched her.

She didn't fight like a soldier. She didn't fight like a common killer.

She fought like death itself.

A force of nature honed into a weapon so lethal, so terrifyingly beautiful, that he forgot himself for a second.

Her body twisted, dodging an incoming strike like she had seen it before it even happened. A man lunged for her—she caught his wrist, twisted, snapped the bone in a single motion.

The scream barely left his lips before her dagger found his stomach, pulling free, striking again. Blood splattered, black in the firelight.

Caelan's heart pounded. He couldn't look away.

"Galbraith!"

Teagan's voice snapped him back to reality, and Caelan barely ducked in time to avoid a blade aimed straight for his throat.

He spun, twin daggers flashing, and drove one into the attacker's thigh, twisting the blade before yanking it free. The man screamed, dropping his weapon as blood spurted into the snow.

Caelan wasted no time.

His second dagger slit across his throat, cutting the scream short.

The body hit the ground, steam curling from the fresh blood in the snow.

"Focus, Galbraith," he muttered to himself, shaking off the lingering daze. Now was *not* the time.

Teagan was holding his own, three men circling him at once. Ayda wasn't far, her small frame weaving through the chaos, her arrows barely even cutting skin before her enemies collapsed, poison locking their limbs, their throats tightening as death took hold, and she made her way to the wagons.

Caelan caught a flicker of movement near the second wagon, just beyond the fire. Ayda was crouched near the underside of the carriage, her hands moving fast, prying open a hidden compartment.

The ledgers.

She yanked them free, stuffing them into a satchel.

They had what they came for.

But the moment she turned to run, a guard spotted her.

He was on her in seconds, his fist grabbing the back of her cloak, yanking her to the ground.

Ayda twisted, her dagger slashing, but he was faster.

He knocked the blade from her grip, his knee slamming into her ribs. She gritted her teeth, curling away, reaching for another weapon—

But the man wasn't drawing his sword. *No.*

He wouldn't just kill her. He had other intentions.

Caelan saw it before he heard it.

The way the bastard's grip tightened on her shoulder, the way his other hand—free of a weapon—moved toward her hip instead.

Rage ignited in his blood.

But Niev moved first.

One second she was flesh.

The next, she wasn't.

Her body twisted, bones snapping and reshaping, muscles elongating, tearing apart and reforming, her hands becoming paws, claws extending, her breath deepening into a growl.

Where Niev had stood, a massive tiger landed soundlessly in the snow.

Caelan had never seen anything like it.

A beast of rippling muscle and sunset-colored fur, eyes burning gold in the firelight.

The fight stopped.

For just a second, everyone froze.

Then the real screaming started.

The man who had grabbed Ayda barely had time to react before the Tigress sank her fangs into his shoulder, bone shattering.

His scream died in his throat as he was thrown, like a ragdoll, crashing into the snow with a wet, sickening crunch.

Another man tried to flee but she tore through him, claws raking deep, throat ripping open with one swipe.

Teagan barely had time to dodge as blood splattered onto his boots.

"Stars almighty, remind me never to piss her off," he muttered.

Caelan barely breathed.

The chaos was still raging, the fight still burning, but all he could see was her.

This—this thing of terror and beauty.

Something dark and primal curled in his chest, something unfamiliar, something he didn't have a name for.

All he knew was that he had never seen anything so deadly in his life.

And God help him, he'd never wanted to touch death more.

He turned, just as more guards spilled from the remaining wagons. Saeris was right. There were over two dozen men, but they'd hidden in the caravans, that's why they'd moved so slowly at first.

Shit.

Caelan's breath came hard, misting the cold air, his knuckles tight around his bloodied daggers as he assessed the chaos.

They were outnumbered. Outarmed..

Time was up.

They needed an exit.

Caelan moved without thinking, grabbing a vial from his belt. He twisted the cap, felt the familiar weight of powder shift in the glass.

One throw. One shot.

His aim was perfect.

The vial shattered against the lead wagon.

A beat—Then the world exploded.

A sharp pop split the air as the vial shattered against the front wheel of the lead wagon. The caravan exploded in a column of flame, a shockwave blasting through the battlefield.

The guards screamed as fire engulfed the wagons, horses rearing, wood cracking and splintering under the force of the explosion.

So much for keeping it clean, with no unnecessary casualties.

Smoke billowed into the sky.

Caelan allowed himself the briefest flicker of satisfaction until he saw her.

She had just turned, only just, when the blade found her.

It sank deep into her side.

Caelan's stomach plummeted.

The Tigress roared, the sound rattling through his chest, primal and raw, but she didn't collapse.

Instead, she turned on the man who had struck her, a savage force of fury and instinct. Her claws tore through him like paper, ripping his throat open before he could scream. Blood splattered across the snow, black in the firelight.

And then she staggered.

For the first time since this fight began, Caelan saw her hesitate.

Her massive frame swayed, her body fighting against itself as she tried to stay standing. Tried to force her way through sheer will.

Too much blood.

Caelan felt his stomach twist.

Her body shuddered violently, muscles spasming, the shift ripping through her.

Bones cracked. Fur retracted. Her limbs shortened, twisted, reshaped, her human body fighting its way back, despite the damage, despite the obvious pain.

She hit her knees, bare skin slick with sweat and blood, her hands clutching at the wound.

"Shit."

Caelan was already moving before the thought fully formed, feet pounding across the battlefield. He didn't think, didn't hesitate. He *ran*.

But Teagan reached her side first, daggers spinning as he carved through the last few men standing in their way.

"Can't leave you alone for two seconds, can I?" Teagan muttered, catching her arm.

Niev barely acknowledged him. Her eyes were darting, scanning through the smoke and the wreckage.

Looking for something.

No, someone.

Caelan followed her line of sight, his pulse hammering.

Where the hell was Ayda?

The fire raged behind them, consuming what was left of the wagons.

Then...a shadow.

Ayda emerged from the far side of the wreckage, her small frame weaving between bodies, a satchel slung over her shoulder.

Caelan exhaled, tension draining from his limbs.

They had the ledgers.

For the first time, Niev's posture slumped slightly, the relief breaking through her sharp focus.

Then her knees buckled.

"Whoa—no, no, no—" Teagan swore, reaching for her.

But Caelan was faster.

He caught her before she hit the ground, arms wrapping around her before she could argue, before she could fight him off.

Because he knew she would.

"I'm fine," she rasped, breath shaky. "Put me down—"

"For once in your life," Caelan gritted out, adjusting his hold, "just shut your goddamn mouth."

Her fingers weakly gripped his coat, like she was going to shove him away but her strength was failing.

"I'm going to—"

"—murder me later," he finished for her, voice low, steady. "I know."

She grunted impatiently but it was weak.

That scared him more than anything.

"Just hold still," he muttered, shifting her weight against him. She was cold as ice.

Too much blood. Too much damage.

If they didn't move now—

"We need to go," Ayda's voice snapped through the moment, firm and urgent. "The fire will draw attention. If anyone else is coming—"

"We're not sticking around to find out," Teagan finished, already scanning their surroundings.

"Where?" Caelan demanded, his grip on Niev tightening as she stirred against him.

Ayda's jaw tensed. "There's a cabin hidden deep in the woods, it should be safe. No one will find us," she said, shooting Niev a worried look. "We can tend to her wounds there."

Teagan shot her a look, but nodded. "Lead the way."

And so they moved.

Ayda led them off the road, into the treeline where their escape route had already been mapped out. The terrain was rough, thick with snow and uneven ground as Caelan carried Niev. He didn't ask, didn't check if she was okay with it. Because she wasn't.

Because she would never be okay with being carried, not even when her own body betrayed her.

"Don't you dare pass out on me," he murmured.

And still, he didn't put her down.

Not even when she weakly muttered, "Not giving you—" she swallowed thickly, barely conscious, "—the satisfaction."

Caelan huffed a breath, something almost like a laugh.

"Sure, Tigress." His voice was quieter now. Rough. "Whatever you say."

But she didn't hear him.

Because by then, darkness had already taken her.

7.
Caelan

The wind howled through the mountains, its icy fingers cutting through the trees as Ayda led them through the snow-covered forest. Their breaths curled into the night air, bodies hunched against the cold, boots crunching through the frostbitten underbrush.

The abandoned cabin emerged from the darkness like a specter, tucked into the trees, its weathered frame half-swallowed by nature. The roof sagged slightly under years of snowfall, but the walls still stood strong. Smoke stains marred the stone chimney, and the wooden shutters creaked faintly in the wind.

Ayda reached the door first, pressing a hand to the frame, as if listening to the bones of the place. Satisfied, she pushed it open, revealing a dark, dust-ridden space, the air thick with the scent of old wood and time.

"Let's get her inside," Her voice was firm, as she ushered them in.

Cold air wheezed past their boots as they crossed the threshold, carrying the musty tang of rodent-nests and long-dead fires.

Caelan carried Niev, her body heavy with exhaustion, her breath shallow. Blood had soaked through her clothes, seeping through his arms as he held her upright.

The moment they crossed the threshold, he cursed. "She's getting colder. We need heat, fast."

Teagan was already moving. He strode to the hearth, tossing aside the remains of a collapsed chair, pulling dry logs from the corner of the room. His hands worked quickly, flint sparking against steel.

A small ember caught. Then flame. Then a fire roared to life, chasing the shadows away, casting everything in a flickering golden glow.

Caelan lowered Niev onto a fur-lined rug near the hearth, easing her carefully to the floor. Her breathing was uneven, and her fingers curled instinctively around the wound at her side, pressing against the pain even in unconsciousness.

Ayda knelt beside her, pulling off her satchel. Her fingers trembled as she sliced through Niev's blood-soaked tunic, peeling the fabric away from torn flesh. The gash was ugly—deep, ragged, clogged with dirt from the skirmish. "Teagan, spirits," she barked.

He yanked a flask from his coat and splashed the clear liquor over the wound. Niev hissed through her teeth even while half-conscious; fresh blood welled scarlet against pale skin.

Ayda snapped back into motion. She pressed a warm cloth to Niev's wound, wiping away the excess blood, exposing the deep gash across her side. It was ugly and jagged from the way the blade had torn through muscle.

Caelan clenched his jaw. If the blade had gone even an inch further...

No.

She was alive.

But not for long if they didn't work fast.

Niev groaned, her body twitching slightly as the pain surged through her unconscious form.

Teagan was at her head, brushing damp strands of hair from her forehead, his voice softer than Caelan had ever heard it.

"Easy, Tigress. You're not dying on my watch."

Ayda set the cloth aside and reached for her satchel. From within, she withdrew small glass vials, her hands steady as she measured out herbs, powders, oils—her movements practiced, almost rhythmic. The scent of crushed sage and bitter root filled the room as she mixed, grinding the ingredients together with precise, forceful strokes.

A whisper of something otherworldly hummed through the air as she added a final drop of something viscous and dark.

"This will help with the pain," she murmured as she pressed a small vial to Niev's lips, tilting her head just enough to let the liquid trickle into her mouth.

Ayda wiped the edges of the wound clean with a scrap of linen, clearing the grit, but the flow kept pulsing, too strong for pressure alone. "She's lost too much blood. We need to stitch the wound and stop the bleeding—"

"I'll do it."

Caelan's voice cut through the tense silence, sharp and certain.

Ayda hesitated, her hazel eyes flicking up at him in surprise.

Teagan scoffed. "Where the hell did you learn how to stitch up stab wounds?"

Caelan rolled up his sleeves, not bothering with a response. He knelt opposite Ayda, palm hovering over the torn flesh that ran from Niev's ribs toward her hip—raw, slick, pumping crimson with every heartbeat. With a flex of will he drew three slender shards from the buckles on his belt. They softened and thinned mid-air, twisting into silvery needles finer than a hair. A second gesture teased a ribbon of titanium from one of the shards, spinning it into supple suture wire that coiled around his fingers like living silk.

Ayda's mouth parted in quiet astonishment; Teagan's usual smirk collapsed into uneasy awe.

"Hold her steady," Caelan murmured.

He positioned himself at her side, pressing a firm hand against her hip to keep her from shifting.

"This is going to hurt," he warned.

Then he pressed two fingers to the torn flesh, and the world seemed to hush. Muscle obeyed his intent, knitting fiber by fiber, vein ends kissing and sealing.

Niev flinched violently, a strangled hiss escaping her lips.

The bleeding slowed to a trickle. Ayda sucked in a breath as she watched tissue crawl together under Caelan's touch. He knew that no *materia* could command more than one discipline; yet here he was, metal dancing in one hand, living flesh in the other.

When the deeper layers had closed, he threaded the titanium-silk through his makeshift needle and stitched the outer wound with rapid, perfect loops—each knot melting seamlessly into skin the instant he tied it. Minutes later the gash was little more than a thin crimson seam, already paling at the edges.

Caelan sat back on his heels, the needles dissolving to dust between his fingers. "She'll scar," he said quietly, "but she'll live."

Ayda let out a long, shaky whistle. Teagan stared at him in awe or horror, he couldn't tell. "What the bloody hell are you, Caelan Galbraith?"

Caelan wiped a smear of blood from his knuckles and shrugged, as though he'd merely mended a torn bootlace. "Precisely six foot two of bad decisions," he said, reaching for the cloth Ayda offered to blot the last drops from Niev's skin. "Let's leave it at that."

Teagan barked a brittle laugh, half nerves, half relief.

Ayda tucked a strand of hair behind her ear, still staring. "You didn't just close a wound," she said softly. "You shaped the flesh, guided it. I've seen metal-workers bend iron like clay, but never this."

Caelan looked away. "Metal's easy. Flesh listens if you know how to ask."

Teagan chuckled, tension easing. "Heals metal, stitches meat. Next you'll tell me he brews his own whiskey."

"Only on feast days," Caelan dead-panned.

Ayda finished wrapping a clean bandage around Niev's waist. "Whatever you are, Caelan Galbraith," she said, fastening the last knot, "remind me to keep you very close, and never on the other side of a battlefield."

Caelan met her eyes, the hint of something unreadable flickering there. Then he glanced back at Niev—at the slow, steady rise and fall of her chest. Alive.

For reasons he didn't want to examine too closely, that mattered more than it should.

8.
Niev

She wasn't dead.

That was Niev's first realization.

The second was that she was warm. Too warm. Heat wrapped around her like a heavy second skin, pressing against her back, her legs, her side where—

She hissed softly, fingers twitching as fresh pain jolted through her wound.

The cabin. The fire. The battle.

It all came back in pieces. The snow. The blood. The explosion.

The burn of steel sinking into her side.

She forced her eyes open.

Shadows danced against the wooden ceiling, twisting with the low flicker of the dying fire. The scent of smoke and herbs lingered in the air, sharp but familiar, threaded with something metallic—blood.

Her blood.

Instinctively, she tried to sit up, but her body refused. A heavy ache settled deep in her muscles, her limbs sluggish with exhaustion.

A weight pressed against her ribs—a thick bandage, firm and secure.

Someone had stitched her up.

Memories stirred, flashing quick and fragmented.

Hands. Steady hands. Holding her together, pressing against the wound, keeping her conscious.

Niev blinked hard, clearing the haze from her vision.

It took her a moment to realize she wasn't alone.

Caelan was on the floor.

Soundly asleep.

Niev stilled.

He lay on his back, one arm draped lazily over his stomach, the other bent behind his head. His usual carelessness was there, but in sleep, it looked... different. Less performed. Less like a man who played with death for the thrill of it, and more like someone who, perhaps, had played too long and finally let himself rest.

A few feet away, Ayda and Teagan had claimed the chairs, both wrapped in blankets, breathing deeply in sleep.

But Niev's gaze kept drifting back to Caelan.

To the sharp lines of his face softened by exhaustion. To the way the firelight cast golden shadows along his cheekbones, flickering against the edges of his tousled hair.

She swallowed.

It had been his arms that carried her.

His hands that stitched her up, steady and precise, like he had done it a hundred times before.

He was reckless, cocky, insufferable.

And yet—

He'd saved her.

Niev frowned, shifting slightly on the couch. It shouldn't have mattered.

But she was struggling to reconcile the image of him in the Red Dragon's Lair—smirking, spinning words like daggers, riling her up just because he could—with the man who had pressed his hands against her wound to stop the bleeding, who had carried her through the snow without a word of complaint, who had sat on this floor long enough to fall asleep next to her.

A traitorous warmth curled low in her stomach.

Before she could push the thought away, his breathing changed.

His eyelids flickered. A slow inhale. A shift of muscle.

Then—Caelan's eyes opened.

Niev froze.

For a long moment, neither of them moved.

The golden firelight flickered between them, casting shadows that danced along his face.

His gaze found hers, still heavy with sleep, but sharp enough to pin her in place. And for the first time since meeting him, there was no teasing in his expression. No smug arrogance.

Just something quiet. Something serious.

His lips parted slightly, like he wanted to say something—but for once, he hesitated.

Niev's breath hitched.

He hadn't hesitated before. Not in battle. Not when throwing himself into chaos, playing with fire just to see how far he could get before burning. But now, here, in the dim hush of the cabin, with only the fire and the sound of their breathing between them—

He hesitated.

Finally, in a voice lower than usual, almost reluctant, he spoke.

"You fight well."

Niev let out a weak snort, the corner of her lips curling despite the pain.

"You're not so terrible either."

Caelan's smirk was slow, something almost amused flickering in his gaze.

But he didn't say anything else.

And for some reason, neither did she.

❋ ❋ ❋

Days passed in an unsteady blur.

The storm raged outside, howling through the mountain pass, wind hammering against the wooden walls of the cabin like a beast seeking entry. Snow piled against the windowsills, creeping up the stone foundation like slow-growing ivy, threatening to swallow the structure whole. Inside, however, the fire burned bright, keeping the bitter cold at bay.

Niev hated being confined. She'd never been one to lie still, but her wound forced her into stillness. Caelan had stitched her up better than she could fathom, but the poison in that blade still made every shift send sharp, agonizing pain lancing through her side, a brutal reminder of her own mortality. And she despised it.

Teagan and Ayda took turns checking her wound, but it was Ayda who hovered the most, reapplying salves, steeping herbal teas, making sure the stitches held.

"You move, you tear them open again," she reminded Niev every time she tried to sit up too quickly. "And we will not be stitching you back together a second time."

Teagan did his best to keep her distracted, recounting ridiculous tales—some real, some exaggerated to the point of absurdity. He stretched across the floor, idly flipping a knife in his hand, laughing at his own jokes as he regaled them with stories of cons gone right, cons gone terribly wrong, and the occasional escape from angry lovers. But there was an edge to his humor, a weight in his glances at Niev that he tried to mask.

Caelan, for once, wasn't his usual insufferable self. He didn't try to provoke her, didn't make light of the situation. Instead, he busied himself with the ledgers, poring over the records they had stolen, making notes, cross-referencing names.

Occasionally, he'd disappear outside, checking the surrounding area for signs of unwanted company. When he was inside, he was quiet. Watchful. Bringing Niev food without being asked, setting a cup of warm tea near her hands before walking away.

Niev noticed.

And that unsettled her just as much as the wound in her side.

※　※　※

Niev sat propped against a pile of furs near the hearth, exhaustion tugging at her limbs but her mind unwilling to rest. The ache in her side was duller now, the healing salves working their magic, but the inactivity gnawed at her. She hated being still. Hated feeling weak.

Ayda sat across from her, meticulously grinding dried leaves into a fine powder using a stone mortar. The rhythmic motion was methodical, practiced, her focus sharp as she prepared whatever concoction she had in mind.

Niev studied her, frowning slightly before finally voicing what had been nagging at her.

"Why do you even have a cabin hidden out here?"

Ayda didn't look up, merely scooped some of the powder into a small vial before corking it. "Figured you'd ask eventually."

She placed the vial carefully beside her before reaching for another bundle of herbs, plucking the leaves off the stems with nimble fingers. "My mother was from the Elarian witch clan of Arenthia."

That made Teagan and Caelan pause in their quiet conversation near the table. Teagan shot Ayda a sharp look. "You never told me that."

Ayda smirked. "Didn't really seem relevant."

Niev arched a brow. "An Elarian?"

Ayda nodded. "That's right."

Niev stiffened, exhaling through her nose. The Elarian witches were a minor clan, but still powerful in their own way. Unlike the Nivola coven who ruled Arenthia, the Elarian witches worked in the shadows— diviners, healers, herbalists, and occasionally assassins if the price was right. But they were not known for being forgiving.

"That explains the potions," Caelan mused, leaning against the wall, arms crossed. "But not the location."

Ayda's expression darkened slightly. "Elarians don't take kindly to outsiders."

"Sounds like most people," Teagan muttered.

Ayda gave a humorless chuckle. "Not quite. They don't just dislike outsiders—they ostracize them."

She set down the herbs, rubbing her hands together to rid them of dust. "My father was Breyvian, a trader who got caught up in my mother's orbit. He wasn't from a noble house, wasn't particularly powerful, but she fell in love with him anyway. Her family never approved, they shunned and disrespected him at every turn. Until my mother couldn't take it anymore."

Teagan frowned, his usually playful demeanor shifting to something more thoughtful. "So, what? They ran?"

Ayda nodded. "Built this place together. Lived here for years." She glanced around the cabin, a soft expression flickering across her features. "It was our home."

Caelan tilted his head. "What happened to them?"

"We didn't remain hidden for long," Ayda's fingers curled into her palm, but her voice remained steady. "Her clan found us eventually. Killed my parents for daring to leave. I was ten."

The fire crackled between them, the warmth at odds with the weight of her words.

Ayda exhaled, shaking her head slightly as if dispelling the memory. "They would've taken me back, forced me into the coven. But I ran. Navigated my way through the mountains until I found my way to Breyvia. Figured if I could survive that, I could survive anything."

Niev stared at her, something shifting in her chest. Ayda had been a child when she lost everything. Alone, hunted, and forced to navigate a world that wanted nothing to do with her.

That was something Niev understood all too well.

Teagan sighed, rubbing his hands together before leaning forward on the table. "Well... that was depressingly informative."

Ayda smirked, wiping a tear from the corner of her eye, "Sorry to ruin the mood."

Without warning, a pillow sailed across the room and smacked Teagan square in the face.

"What the hell is wrong with you?" Niev groaned, glaring at him from her spot near the hearth.

Teagan made a muffled noise of protest, peeling the pillow off his face before tossing it lazily onto his lap. "I was trying to lighten the mood."

"By being an insensitive ass?" she shot back.

He gestured vaguely. "It's one of my more charming qualities."

"You have zero charming qualities," Niev muttered, shaking her head.

Caelan tilted his head, studying Ayda with newfound interest. "So that's why you're so damn good with terrain."

"And poisons," Teagan added dryly.

Ayda gave a casual shrug. "I learned how to survive."

Niev let out a slow breath. "I'm sorry."

Ayda's gaze flicked to hers, a hint of surprise in her expression before she smirked. "Don't be. I lived. And now I get to poison the occasional bastard who deserves it."

That earned an amused exhale from Caelan. "You're alright, Ravenscroft."

Ayda smirked. "Don't get sentimental on me, Galbraith. I might poison your next meal just to keep you on your toes."

Teagan groaned. "We are never having a meal I don't personally prepare ever again."

Niev, for the first time in what felt like forever, smiled.

These three were... different. But she was beginning to think she didn't mind that at all.

9.
Niev

That evening, Niev lay stretched near the hearth, exhaustion sinking into her limbs, her body still stiff with the lingering ache of injury. Sleep beckoned, lulling her in the slow drag of firelight and whispered embers, but her mind refused to quiet. Too many thoughts. Too many ghosts.

A floorboard creaked.

Her senses, dulled by fatigue, sharpened instantly. Fingers twitching toward a non-existent dagger at her hip, she cracked open one eye—only to see Caelan standing in the doorway.

Something about his posture—still, tense, caught somewhere between hesitation and resolve—sent a ripple of unease through her. His usual energy was absent. No careless smirk, no irreverent humor.

He stepped forward, a heavy leather-bound ledger clutched in his hands. The firelight caught the taut lines of his jaw, the faint furrow of his brow.

He didn't speak at first, just watched her, then finally moved closer and held out the book.

Niev straightened slightly, ignoring the way her body protested. "What?" she asked, her voice rough from disuse.

Caelan said nothing at first. He simply extended the book toward her, his grip lingering a second too long before he let it go.

"You should see this." His voice was quiet. The lack of bravado or snide comment set her on edge.

Niev accepted the ledger, running her fingers over the worn leather cover before flipping it open. Her eyes flicked over the first few lines, absorbing the neat, deliberate script. Names. Ages. Buyers. Destinations.

The air in the room seemed to thin.

The first page listed children—some as young as three years old. Sold. Bought. Shipped to slave pits, forced into servitude, sent to brothels.

She turned the page. Another list. More names. More horrors.

Another.

And another.

It didn't stop. The list stretched on and on, pages upon pages detailing the systematic selling of human lives, reducing them to numbers in a grotesque ledger of transactions.

Niev's grip on the brittle paper tightened, her nails pressing into the edges. Her stomach twisted, bile rising in her throat. She had killed men in cold blood, slit throats without blinking, watched life drain from the eyes of her enemies without remorse. But this—this was a different kind of monstrosity.

It was deliberate. Organized. And so, so much worse.

A quiet breath behind her made her aware of Ayda's presence. She had moved closer, reading over her shoulder. For a moment, she said nothing, her sharp hazel eyes scanning the entries, absorbing their meaning. Then, without warning, her hand curled into a fist against the table, knuckles turning white.

"This... this isn't just a trade." Ayda's voice was tight, brittle with contained fury. "This is an empire."

A heavy silence fell over the room.

The fire popped, spitting sparks that died on the stone—too small to matter beside the inferno now burning behind Niev's ribs.

Teagan, sitting across from them, exhaled a low curse. He dragged a hand through his hair, gripping the back of his neck as if the weight of the words physically pained him. His usual light-hearted demeanor had vanished, replaced with something hollow and dark.

"I've been going through those ledgers for the past three days, the entries are endless," Caelan's voice was quiet, almost numb. "This trade has been going on for decades."

Niev turned another page, scanning the script with renewed sharpness. There were locations—hidden auctions scheduled in various cities across the continent. Sealed agreements between buyers and sellers. Names of powerful nobles and officials, all with a vested interest in keeping this trade alive.

Her jaw locked.

This wasn't just a handful of criminals exploiting the desperate. This was systemic. Protected. It had infiltrated the highest levels of power, thriving in the shadows of the very nations that claimed to uphold order.

Caelan leaned against the opposite wall, arms crossed over his chest. The firelight cast sharp shadows across his face, accentuating the tension in his jaw, the tightness in his shoulders.

"I knew it was bad," he said finally, voice quiet but edged with something raw. "But this is so much worse than what I imagined."

As Niev flipped through the brittle pages, her sharp eyes scanning the names, a familiar one stopped her cold.

Her breath caught in her throat.

Niev stared at the name as if she could will it to change. As if, by some cruel twist of fate, she had misread it. But the letters remained the same.

Finnian Beylore.

Her grip on the ledger tightened, the edges of the paper crinkling under her fingers. She read the name again, forcing herself to focus past the roaring in her ears.

Age: Eight. Destination: Arenthia. Status: To be auctioned.

His father thought he was dead. Niev had sworn vengeance in the name of a lie.

Her pulse pounded in her ears, a slow, seething fury rising like a tide.

Teagan, who had been watching her closely, frowned. "What is it?"

She released the breath she was holding slowly, steadying herself, then turned the ledger toward him, tapping her finger against the name. His eyes flicked down, and the moment he saw it, his entire body stiffened.

"Shit," he breathed.

Ayda and Caelan exchanged glances. "Alright," Ayda said carefully, "someone explain before I start assuming the worst."

Niev took a slow breath, forcing the words out past the knot in her throat. "A few days before we left Greyhaven, I was stopped in the street by a blacksmith. His name was Ewan Beylore. He was grieving—said slave traders took his son, and when he tried to fight back, they killed the boy and took his corpse as punishment. He begged me to avenge him."

Ayda snapped the ledger from Teagan, her expression instantly hardening. "So, what? The boy is alive?"

Niev nodded. "He's on this list. If I had to guess, they're selling him to the highest bidder in the next auction." Her voice turned rough. "The bastards made a father mourn for a son who was still breathing."

Caelan let out a sharp, disbelieving laugh. Not one of amusement—one of pure disgust. "So they don't just steal lives, they destroy what's left behind too." He rubbed a hand over his face. "Fuck."

Ayda swallowed, staring at the ledger as if it were something rotten. "How old?"

"Eight."

Ayda's knuckles whitened against the edge of the table. She met Niev's gaze, something raw and dangerous flashing in her hazel eyes. "We need to get him out."

Niev nodded once, her grip still tight on the ledger, jaw set, "We're getting all of them out."

The room was silent for a beat.

Then—Teagan exhaled hard, shoving his chair back, raking a hand through his hair in frustration. "Niev, that's a suicide mission."

She had expected the protest. Not because Teagan didn't care—but because he cared too much. Because they'd spent years in this world, wading through blood and shadows, doing what they had to in order to survive. They were criminals, killers when necessary, but there were some lines that weren't meant to be crossed.

And children?

Children were definitely on the other side of that line.

She could see it in the way his fingers curled into his hair, in the sharp pull of his jaw, in the way his breath came just a little too hard.

Teagan wasn't arguing because he thought they shouldn't do it.

He was arguing because he knew they had to.

And because he knew they might not survive it.

"What would you have me do, Teeg?" Niev's voice was quiet, but the weight behind it cut deep. "These are *children*."

Teagan looked at her, something flickering behind his eyes—something heavy, something pained.

She knew him too well. Knew every shift of his stance, every twitch of his brow, every tell in his body language.

He wouldn't argue.

Because no matter how reckless, how impossible, how insanely dangerous it was—he already knew they were going to do it.

Caelan looked at Niev for a long time. When he finally spoke, his voice was light, but the weight behind it was anything but.

"I know when the next auction is."

The room stilled.

Ayda's fingers curled around the edge of the table. Teagan's jaw tightened, and Niev felt something cold settle in her stomach.

Caelan exhaled slowly, then tapped the open ledger. "That's what I've been deciphering the past few days." His fingers traced the ink-stained pages, his movements deliberate, precise. "It's happening in Port Orynth."

Niev's frown deepened. "Port Orynth?"

The name alone sent a ripple of unease through her. Port Orynth wasn't just any city in Arenthia—it was a stronghold of decadence, built into the cliffs that overlooked the Silver Bay. An oasis of wealth and indulgence for the noble elite, hidden beneath the illusion of pristine marble halls and sprawling estates. But beneath that glittering surface, its underground network was *legendary*.

A place where the worst of the worst indulged their vices behind locked doors.

And now, apparently, it was where dozens of children were about to be sold.

Caelan nodded, his expression grim. "Makes sense, doesn't it? The noble houses of Arenthia don't like getting their hands dirty in their own capitals. They move things offshore, use a city that already thrives on underground dealings. Port Orynth's entire foundation is built on bribery and secrecy. No one talks unless they want their tongue nailed to the docks."

Ayda inhaled sharply, shaking her head. "How the hell do you keep something that big hidden?"

Teagan's jaw tightened. "You don't. You just pay the right people to look the other way."

Ayda swore under her breath.

"No, this doesn't make sense," Niev's brow furrowed. "There's no way you can pay enough people to keep this hidden. It's simply too big. We're talking about dozens upon dozens of children, someone would have had to spot them sooner or later."

"Not if they never see the light of day," Caelan said, voice quiet but sharp.

The room stilled.

Niev's stomach twisted. Slowly, she turned toward him, taking in the way he stared down at the open ledger, his fingers ghosting over the ink-stained pages like he was reading something far worse than what was written.

Ayda's brows pulled together. "What do you mean?"

Caelan exhaled, tapping the parchment before finally looking up. "They're kept underground."

A heavy silence followed.

"The Hollow Quarter," he clarified. "It's beneath Port Orynth. A network of tunnels and chambers, carved out of the bedrock. Some say it was built during the Great War—old bunkers, forgotten catacombs, maybe even a failed attempt at expanding the city underground. Doesn't really matter. What does matter is that it's been used for smuggling and illegal trade for decades."

Teagan swore under his breath.

Ayda sat back, crossing her arms. "So you're telling me the children are hidden in an underground maze beneath the most corrupt city in Arenthia?"

Caelan's jaw tensed. "More than that. They're transported through it." He flipped a few pages in the ledger, pointing at a coded line of script. "See this? This isn't just a list of buyers. This is a map of movement. They're taken from the port through the drowned tunnels, moved deeper underground, and then smuggled out through a passage hidden in the Stoneridge Mountains. That's how they've been operating under everyone's noses."

Niev swallowed hard, gripping the table.

"They're never above ground," she murmured.

Caelan nodded. "Not unless they're being shipped out."

The weight of his words settled over the room, thick and suffocating.

Niev's hands clenched into fists. It made sense now. The secrecy, the sheer scale of it all. It wasn't just bribery—it was a carefully designed system. A machine built to swallow children whole, one that had been running for years.

But still, something didn't sit right.

Her gaze flicked to Caelan, watching him carefully as he flipped another page, his eyes scanning the coded entries like he had spent years deciphering them. His movements were too sure, his understanding too precise.

"How do you know all this?" she asked, the question slipping out before she could stop it.

Caelan didn't look up. "Because I pay attention."

Niev narrowed her eyes. "To a city you've never lived in?"

That made him pause. Just for a second. But she caught it.

"You don't know where I've lived," Caelan met her gaze, something flickering in those sharp, golden-brown eyes—something careful. "Besides, you don't have to live somewhere to know how it works."

That wasn't an answer.

Niev frowned. "You're talking about places most people in Arenthia don't even know exist. Even I—" she cut herself off, jaw tightening.

Even she hadn't known. And she'd spent more than half of her life there.

She saw it then, the flicker of curiosity that crossed Teagan's face. He knew her better than anyone, and he'd definitely caught the slip. But thankfully, he said nothing.

Caelan, however, was watching her a little too closely now.

"Maybe I just know the right people." His voice was light, but the weight behind it was anything but.

Bullshit.

But before she could press him, Ayda exhaled sharply, dragging the conversation back into focus.

"This doesn't add up," she muttered. "We're talking about a massive operation—one that's been running for years. There's no way they've kept it hidden without inside help."

Niev's jaw tightened, shaking her head. "We're talking about dozens of children at a time, smuggled through tunnels beneath one of the busiest ports in Arenthia. A single loose thread and the whole thing unravels. Someone, somewhere, would have spoken by now."

Her own words unsettled her.

Because it wasn't just about bribing a handful of guards or corrupt merchants. Port Orynth was the beating heart of trade in Arenthia. Everything and everyone was watched.

And there was one woman who always knew what moved through her city.

In Arenthia, power flowed from the Nivola Witch Clan like blood from a blade. Their matron Adrianna Nivola bound every merchant and dockmaster to fate-spun pacts, her seers reading shipping manifests as easily as runes. Lesser houses like the Elarian survived on healing and prophecy, and the Cheyan witch clan on clandestine wards, but both danced at the edges of Nivola courts, quietly stoking rebellion. If Matron Nivola truly didn't know of children slipping through Port Orynth's undercity, then something darker than corruption was staring them all in the face.

The thought lodged itself in her mind, unshakable.

"How would the ruler of Arenthia not know about this?" Niev said carefully, her gaze flicking over the others. "Matron Nivola has spies in every major trade house. She keeps records of every merchant guild, every dockmaster, every captain who sails in and out of the country. If she doesn't want something in her city, it doesn't stay there. Period."

Silence settled over the table.

Caelan watched her, his fingers idly tapping against the wooden surface, but he didn't interrupt. There was something too sharp in the way he listened.

Ayda frowned. "So either she's turning a blind eye—"

"Or she just doesn't know," Teagan finished.

Niev scoffed before she could stop herself. "Adrianna knows everything."

It came out too fast. Too certain.

She felt Caelan's gaze flick to her, lingering just a second too long.

Niev forced herself to remain still, to school her features into something neutral, but inside, her mind was turning over the facts, trying to piece together a puzzle that refused to make sense.

Could Adrianna really be unaware?

Was it possible that an entire smuggling network had grown under her rule, right beneath her feet, without her seeing it?

She didn't know what unsettled her more—the idea that the Matron of Arenthia's ruling witch clan was completely unaware...

Or the idea that she was involved..

❋ ❋ ❋

Hours later, ledger pages littered the table like shed skin, and the fire crackled, casting flickering shadows against the wooden walls of the cabin. The warmth did little to thaw the cold that had settled into Niev's chest.

For a long moment, they sat in silence, the weight of the ledger pressing down on all of them. The air was thick with something unspoken—rage, resolve, grief in a form none of them had the luxury of expressing fully.

"The event isn't public," Caelan said, breaking the silence. "It's a closed affair, only for high-tier buyers. If we're going to get inside, we need forged documents, sealed invitations, and identities solid enough to pass scrutiny."

Niev exhaled sharply, rubbing a hand over her jaw. "I know someone who can do it."

Teagan groaned, already guessing. "She's going to be pissed as hell, Niev."

"She'll get over it."

"Will she?"

Niev clenched her jaw. "She doesn't have to like it. She just has to do it."

Myria was the only one skilled enough to mimic any handwriting, any crest, any official document with a level of detail that made her the most valuable, and most temperamental—ally they had.

But she was also Niev's friend. And right now, she was going to be *livid*.

Because the last time Niev had asked for her help, she'd vanished before even picking up the damn Librarium robes.

Teagan sighed, rubbing his hands over his face. "She's going to murder you."

"She can get in line."

"You had her running around Solhaven for *days* trying to source that fabric for your Librarium identity, and then you just *never showed up*," Teagan reminded her.

Niev huffed, pushing back against the sharp stab of guilt. "Yes, well it's not like I did it on purpose. We had to retrieve those ledgers, I wasn't strolling around the city ignoring her."

"Sure, let's go with that," Teagan muttered.

"She'll still help," Niev said, resolute. "She's too damn good at what she does not to."

Caelan smirked, resting his chin in his palm. "So you need a woman you've personally pissed off to handcraft our entire cover story? Brilliant."

"Are you done?" Niev snapped.

Caelan chuckled. "Not even close."

Ayda smirked, tilting her head as her expression grew serious. "Assuming we get the invitations, what about our identities? They're not going to let just anyone walk in."

Niev's gaze flicked to Caelan. "That's where he comes in."

Caelan's smirk widened. "Oh? I might like where this is going."

"You shouldn't."

Teagan's ears piqued as he looked at Niev curiously.

"The auction is full of the wealthy, the corrupt, and the worst people Eldhaven has to offer," Niev said, flipping the ledger open to one of the earlier pages, scanning names. "We can't sneak in as guards or staff—too risky. Too many restrictions. But buyers?" She tapped the page, eyes sharp. "Buyers have power. They have access. They move freely."

Caelan arched a brow. "You want me to pretend I'm a buyer?"

"You already act like an arrogant bastard. Shouldn't be too difficult."

He snorted. "Flattered."

Niev ignored him. "You'll pose as a high-profile bidder. Someone rich. Entitled. The type of man who throws coin at anything he finds remotely entertaining."

"I can do that."

"Good. And I'll be your *mistress*," she added.

Caelan blinked. "Come again?"

Teagan choked on his drink. He sputtered, slamming his cup down with a sharp *clack* against the wooden table. "What?"

Ayda, to her credit, didn't even try to hide her amusement. A slow, knowing smile curved her lips as she leaned back in her chair, watching the chaos unfold like it was the most entertaining thing she'd seen in years.

Niev kept her expression carefully neutral, arms crossed over her chest as she leveled him with a look. "You heard me."

Caelan seemed—*stumped.*

His usual sharp retorts, his relentless cocky remarks, *gone.*

His lips parted slightly, his brows knitting together as if he were trying to *process* what she'd just said. Which was a rare sight in itself—Caelan Galbraith, at a loss for words.

Niev would have taken more satisfaction in that if she weren't already bracing for the inevitable.

Then, as if to compensate for his momentary lapse, his expression shifted. That smirk—the insufferable, aggravating, *too damn smug* smirk—crept back onto his face.

"Well," he finally said, sitting back in his chair, "As much as I'd love to be seen parading you around, mind explaining why?"

Niev resisted the urge to throw something at him. "Buyers with mistresses are common. Expected. The women they bring aren't questioned. They're ignored. A rich man parading his latest trophy doesn't raise suspicion—but a man of power walking in alone? That's noticed."

"So what, you're going to bat your lashes and let me buy you drinks all night?" Caelan teased.

"No," she said flatly. "I'll be listening. Watching. The buyers will talk more freely around someone they see as insignificant. And the traders won't look twice at me."

Ayda rested her chin in her hand, eyes glittering with mischief. "I think it's a great idea."

Teagan muttered a curse. "And what am I doing while you two are cozying up to each other?"

"You're getting into the holding cells," Niev said.

Teagan's expression turned serious.

"They'll be kept underground," she continued. "I need you to find them. Unlock what you can. Get them ready to move."

Ayda shifted. "And me?"

Niev's gaze met hers. "You're going after the traders."

Ayda raised a brow.

"We need to get as much information as we can," Niev explained. "Find the paper trail. The ledgers. Records of transactions. Proof of every child they've sold, every buyer, every shipment."

Ayda inhaled slowly, considering it. Then she nodded. "I'll get it."

"Remember, there's no room for mistakes this time," she shot them a warning look. "We don't get the kids out if we leave a massacre in our wake. If we make too much noise, the rest of their network will scatter like rats, and we'll lose our chance to track them."

Teagan rolled his dagger between his fingers. "So, we slip in, steal their prize, and slip out before they know what hit them?"

Ayda, still focused on the map, frowned. "That's easier said than done. These auctions aren't backroom deals in some noble's estate. They take security seriously. Buyers are vetted, identities checked. We won't slip out easily. ."

She sighed, tracing a finger over the map. "There's also the matter of getting Myria on board. And going back to Greyhaven."

"Which is crawling with people looking for us," Teagan pointed out, "Because lady kitty cat *here* decided to shift mid-fight and show her hand."

Caelan exhaled, shaking his head. "If the Tigress of Solhaven can't slip back into her own city, maybe her reputation's been grossly overestimated." His voice was smooth, but there was an edge to it— serious, assessing.

Niev's eyes flicked to him, sharp as a blade, but she didn't take the bait. "We go in quiet. Ayda and I will get to Myria. Teagan, you and Caelan get us an escape route. We're going to need a clean way out after this."

Teagan exhaled, rubbing his jaw as he exchanged a glance with Caelan. "Right. About that."

Niev narrowed her eyes instantly. "Why do I feel like I'm not going to like what you're about to say?"

Caelan, for once, wasn't the one pushing her buttons. Instead, he leaned back against the wall, arms crossed, watching Teagan with amusement—like he knew something she didn't.

Teagan, the bastard, at least had the decency to look mildly uncomfortable.

"Well," he started, dragging out the word. "We're smuggling out a dozen kids, if not more. That's not something we can just walk through the city gates with."

Niev folded her arms. "Obviously."

Teagan shifted in his seat, as if bracing himself. "Which means we need a ship. Preferably with a captain we can trust—"

Something cold settled in her gut. "No."

Teagan kept going, undeterred. "A ship, a crew, and someone who can navigate hostile waters without getting caught. Someone who can make sure we get those kids to safety."

"No."

"Niev," Teagan said, his voice turning serious. "We don't have many options."

Caelan, who had been watching the exchange with open interest, glanced at Ayda. "I take it she's already figured out who we're talking about."

Ayda, sharp as ever, tilted her head slightly. "Who *are* we talking about?"

Teagan sighed, rubbing his temples. "Captain Laughlan Thorne."

Niev's fingers curled into fists before she forced them to relax. Her pulse hammered in her ears, but she kept her face impassive. "You're out of your damn mind."

Caelan let out a low whistle, intrigued. "The pirate?"

Niev turned a sharp glare on him. "He's not an option."

Teagan ignored her. "He's our best option. Laughlan has a ship, a crew, and the kind of reputation that keeps people from asking too many questions. We need someone who can get us and those kids out of here without drawing attention."

"No."

Ayda studied Niev carefully, her gaze flicking between her clenched jaw and the storm brewing in her eyes. "You know him," she murmured, realization dawning. "Not just in passing I gather."

Caelan's grin widened as if he'd just been gifted the most entertaining news of his life. "Ohhh. This is *personal*."

Niev shot him a glare that promised violence.

Teagan sighed again, but this time, there was a touch of exasperation. "You hate him, I get it. But tell me—who else can pull this off?"

Niev's teeth clenched, her fingers twitching at her sides. The last time she'd seen Laughlan Thorne, he'd been drunk off his ass, standing on a tavern table, grinning like he owned the goddamned world. His coat hung loose around his shoulders, his shirt was half-open, and his belt was missing—probably lost in some bet he had no intention of paying.

And then, in front of half the damned tavern, he had tossed a coin in the air, caught it between his fingers, and—with all the smug confidence of a man who had never once been denied anything in his life—looked her straight in the eye and said *"Be a darling and carry my heirs, Tigress."*

The room had gone silent.

She had stared at him, her pulse a slow, burning drum.

Then he had grinned wider, like a man dancing on the edge of a knife, and continued—far too loudly.

"I am now but a slave to the taste of your lips. And I must have more."

She had slapped him so hard his head snapped to the side, the crack of it ringing through the tavern.

Laughter had erupted around them, mugs slamming against tables, men doubling over with amusement.

Laughlan had staggered, blinking as if trying to catch up with reality, then touched his lip, checking for blood.

And then—he had laughed.

"Ah, love," he had mused, voice rough with drink. *"I'll make you my wife eventually."*

She swore then and there never to cross paths with him again.

And now—Teagan wanted to hand him control of their escape?

To put the lives of those children in his hands?

Her stomach churned.

She wanted to strangle Teagan Blackwood.

Not only for suggesting they bring on Laughlan, but for being right about it.

The Sersha Mara was fast, its crew efficient, and Laughlan... Laughlan was too damn good at what he did. He knew the waters like he was born of them. If anyone could get them out unseen, it was him.

And Teagan knew it.

So did she.

She exhaled sharply, her hands pressing flat against the table as if grounding herself. "We don't tell him everything. He gets us in and out, and that's it."

Teagan smirked. "That's the spirit."

Caelan leaned forward, chin resting in his hand, grinning like a man enjoying every second of this. "You wanna tell us what happened between you two, or should we guess?"

Niev threw her dagger so fast, it buried itself in the wood right next to Caelan's hand.

"Fine," he chuckled, raising his hands in mock surrender. "No guessing."

Ayda finally shook her head, exhaling. "You're all unbelievable."

Teagan leaned back, satisfied. "Then it's settled. We get Myria to forge our papers, and we get Niev's former paramour to sail us out."

Caelan, who had been leaning back casually against the table, suddenly went very still.

"...Her what?"

"I am going to *murder* you," Niev said, her eyes shooting daggers at Teagan.

Caelan's grin spread slowly, but there was something sharp beneath it.

"Ah," he drawled, tilting his head at Niev with entirely too much amusement. "So, the Tigress of Solhaven fancies *pirates*."

Niev shot him a deadly look. "Don't."

Niev pushed off the table, rolling her shoulders like she was about to break someone's ribs.

Caelan laughed, but his smile didn't reach his eyes.

"God help you, Teagan, if this goes to hell."

Teagan only grinned. "Wouldn't be the first time, Tigress."

Niev exhaled slowly, dragging a hand through her hair.

Great... Now, not only did they have to infiltrate a heavily guarded auction, but they also had to deal with bloody Laughlan Thorne.

10.
Caelan

The first light of dawn barely kissed the horizon when Caelan and Teagan slipped out of the cabin, boots crunching softly against the snow-packed ground. The storm had died sometime in the night, leaving behind a crystalline stillness—the kind that made the world feel too quiet.

Caelan wasn't sure why the silence unsettled him.

Or maybe, he did.

His fingers curled inside his gloves, flexing idly as they made their way toward the tree line where they'd left the horses days ago. His mind, despite his best efforts, kept circling back to the night before.

To her.

To the way she had burned.

Not with fire, but with a kind of anger that was just as consuming. A storm in the shape of a woman. A force of nature wrapped in blood and steel.

He had known, logically, that Niev was dangerous. That she had been Saeris's right hand for a reason. But seeing her fight—seeing the lethal, razor-sharp precision of her movements, the way she became something more, something terrifying and magnificent in the same breath—had stirred something in him he wasn't ready to acknowledge.

And then, of course, there was the matter of her *former lover*.

Caelan's jaw ticked, a muscle feathering in his cheek.

He wasn't a fool. He had seen how she reacted at the mere mention of Laughlan Thorne. The way her expression had iced over, the barely contained fury that had coiled through her shoulders, the tight press of her lips like she was remembering something she wished she could forget.

And it had bothered him.

More than it should have.

Which was *ridiculous*.

Caelan had been attracted to plenty of women before. He knew the signs, the tells—the slow creep of awareness whenever he was near someone he wanted, the way his mind cataloged every detail with little effort. The shape of a mouth. The way someone moved. A particular quirk of expression.

But this was different.

This wasn't about a pretty woman he wanted to touch—though stars knew that if Niev wasn't so damn insufferable, he'd be thinking about that too.

This was about the fact that for the first time in a long time, someone had unsettled him.

And he didn't like it.

Not one bit.

"You're awfully quiet," Teagan said, his voice dragging Caelan back to the present.

Caelan blinked, shoving the thoughts away with practiced ease.

He pulled his cloak tighter around himself, huffing out a breath that misted in the cold air. "Remind me why we're the ones out here tracking horses at the ass-crack of dawn?"

Teagan, ahead of him, glanced back with a smirk. "Because you're my favorite idiot, and you didn't argue hard enough when Ayda told us to."

Caelan rolled his eyes, shoving his hands into his pockets. "Next time, *you* should argue harder."

Teagan chuckled but said nothing, his focus shifting back to the tracks half-buried beneath a fresh layer of snow. The prints were faint, but they were there—their horses had bolted during the ambush, scattering into the mountains like they had better places to be.

Caelan sighed. "We should've tied them up better."

"Should've," Teagan agreed. "But then again, I wasn't expecting you to blow up a caravan either."

Caelan grinned. "Are you joking? That was the highlight of the night."

"Besides," he added, "She was hurt, and we needed a way out. What else should I have done?"

Teagan didn't argue, but looked at Caelan with a knowing smile on his face. The two fell into a quiet rhythm, following the trail. The mountains were treacherous—rocky cliffs that sloped into thick patches of pines, winding paths carved by rivers long since frozen.

The silence stretched, broken only by the occasional call of a distant crow.

The cold chewed at them as they trudged across the drifted yard in search of the horses. Powdered snow swirled up around their boots; Caelan's breath fogged white, frosting his lashes. He flexed his still-aching fingers which were now stiff as iron.

He stamped once, teeth chattering. "Stars, I'd kill for the cabin's hearth right now," he muttered. The wind nipped harder, and he tucked his collar up to his ears. "Think the girls are still sleeping?"

Teagan huffed out a laugh that became a cloud of steam. "Ayda? Probably. Niev? Not a chance. By now she's probably awake, glaring holes through the rafters and counting seconds until she can tear out of that cabin."

Caelan pictured it—Niev pacing, coiled, hating the enforced rest while he froze his backside off in the snow—and a wry grin tugged at his mouth. "Figures," he said, tightening his cloak as they pressed on toward the stables.

Teagan frowned slightly, adjusting the strap of his satchel. "How bad was her wound, really?"

Caelan was quiet for a moment before sighing. "Bad enough that she needs the rest. Not bad enough to kill her. I'm pretty sure she's too stubborn for that."

Teagan loosed a breath, kicking at a patch of frost-covered grass. "You stitched her up fast. Didn't hesitate. Even the most skilled healer would've flinched seeing a wound like that.." He paused, his gaze flicking sideways.

Caelan tensed.

Teagan wasn't a fool. He picked up on details others ignored, fit pieces together that most people never realized were missing. Caelan had been careful about what he let slip, about how much he let them see.

But that night... that night, he hadn't been careful at all.

The firelight. The blood. The steady press of needle through torn flesh. His hands had moved on their own, precise, practiced—too practiced.

Teagan cleared his throat, his voice dropping. "Look, I've worked with other *materia* before. They bend steel, reshape stone—one element, that's the rule. But last night you had metal floating in one hand and skin weaving under the other like you'd done it a hundred times." He met Caelan's eyes. "How is that possible?"

Snow crunched beneath their boots as Caelan rolled his shoulders, but the tension in them didn't ease.

For a long moment, he didn't answer.

The wind howled softly through the trees, stirring the silence between them.

Teagan let it stretch, not pressing, not pushing—just waiting.

Finally, Caelan exhaled a slow breath, misting in the cold air. His gloved fingers flexed at his sides, like he could still feel the pull of thread between them.

"I was born in Thaelon," he said, voice quieter than usual. "In the slave camps of Zarenth."

Teagan went still.

Caelan didn't look at him. He kept walking, stepping over a fallen branch, his tone measured, detached—like the words weren't his own, like they were someone else's story that he was simply retelling.

"My parents were slaves," he continued. "That was all I'd known them to be. And all I was supposed to be, too." A faint, humorless smirk flickered across his lips. "My powers didn't start showing until I was well past my sixth nameday."

Teagan remained silent, his expression unreadable.

Caelan exhaled, shaking his head. "But a materia manifests where need is sharpest. People got hurt all the time, and I had a gift that could put them back together. Didn't take long for them to realize I was more useful with steady hands than breaking my back in the mines. So the slaves started hiding me, protecting me."

He paused, letting the weight of those words settle between them.

Caelan clenched his jaw, staring at the path ahead. "It kept me alive. For a while." Nights spent hunched in shadows, cupping another slave's torn flesh, whisper-shaping tissue until screams faded to sleep—that part he left unsaid. "Metal, flesh—doesn't matter. Need teaches you what practice never will."

Teagan's voice was quieter now. "And then?"

Caelan smirked, but there was no amusement in it. "And then I left."

Just like that. Simple. Clean. A blade through a vein.

But Teagan wasn't fooled. No one *left* a slave camp. But he wasn't about to push further.

"That's why you were so careful with her," Teagan murmured, eyes sharp. "That's why you didn't hesitate."

Caelan didn't respond.

Because what was there to say?

He wasn't the only one with blood in his past. He wasn't the only one with scars stitched into his skin. Caelan pushed the memories back—like he always did.

They walked in silence for another mile before Teagan abruptly held up a hand. Caelan stopped beside him, following his gaze toward a small grove nestled between jagged ridges.

"There," Teagan murmured.

Caelan squinted. A dark shape moved among the trees. Then another. The horses.

"Well, that was easier than expected," Caelan mused.

Teagan shot him a dry look. "You just jinxed it."

He wasn't wrong. Tracking them was one thing. Catching them was another.

The first two horses, still saddled and tired from their unexpected adventure, were easy enough to approach. Teagan murmured something low, soothing as he grabbed the reins of the first. The second barely resisted, ears flicking as it huffed out a breath.

The other two, however, were nowhere in sight.

Caelan sighed dramatically, resting his hands on his hips. "Well. Guess we're walking the rest of the way."

Teagan frowned, scanning the ridge. "They could still be close. Give me a second."

Caelan leaned against a tree, watching with vague amusement as Teagan searched the area. Tracking was Teagan's thing—not Caelan's.

A few minutes passed before Teagan exhaled sharply, shaking his head. "They're gone. Either ran too far or got spooked into the deeper ridges."

"Great," Caelan muttered, running a hand through his already messy hair. "Two horses. Four people."

Teagan gave him a flat look. "Yeah, that's typically how math works."

Caelan huffed out a breath, adjusting the saddle on one of the horses. "You think Niev is gonna throw another dagger at me when she realizes she has to share?"

Teagan smirked. "Oh, absolutely."

Caelan chuckled under his breath, though something about the thought made his pulse tick faster.

❀ ❀ ❀

By the time they returned to the cabin, Niev and Ayda were already outside.

Ayda stood with her arms crossed, watching them approach. "You're late."

Teagan sighed dramatically, swinging off his horse. "We had to track them through the damn mountain. Not exactly easy."

Ayda walked past him, barely glancing at the two horses before making her decision. Without a word, she climbed onto Teagan's horse, settling behind him as if it had never been a question.

Caelan grinned. "Damn, she didn't even hesitate."

Niev frowned, then slowly turned to look at the remaining horse. Then at Caelan.

Then back at the horse.

Caelan's grin only widened. "Is there a problem, Tigress?"

"I'd rather walk," Niev muttered, arms crossing over her chest.

"Oh, come on," Teagan called from where he sat in the saddle. "We don't have time to be choosy."

Niev shot him a glare before exhaling sharply.

Caelan leaned against the saddle, watching her with far too much amusement. "I'd offer you a choice, but unfortunately, we only have the one horse."

"Tragic," she deadpanned.

"I'm sure it is," Caelan agreed, not even trying to hide his smirk. "Now, come on, up you go."

He watched as Niev approached the horse, her movements sharp, controlled—too controlled.

She was tense. Not from the wound. He'd seen enough injuries to know when someone was favoring a weakness. This wasn't that.

No, this was something else entirely.

Her fingers curled and uncurled at her sides, her shoulders tight beneath her coat. She was stalling, though she'd never admit it.

Caelan bit back a smirk.

This woman had faced down killers, fought through an ambush, taken a sword to the side—but sitting in front of him on a horse was what finally had her hesitating.

Oh, this was going to be fun.

Still, she stepped forward, ready to mount on her own, because of course she was.

But Caelan moved first.

His hands found her waist— firm, unyielding— and he lifted her effortlessly, ignoring the sharp inhale she made as she landed lightly in the saddle.

For the briefest moment, her hands latched onto his shoulders, fingers digging in as she steadied herself.

Caelan felt that grip everywhere.

Niev snapped back fast, shoving his hands away as if burned. Her glare could've melted steel.

"You absolute—"

"Careful now." He kept his voice even, lower than usual, something teasing but unreadable beneath it. "Wouldn't want to tear those stitches."

She looked like she was weighing whether or not to stab him.

"I'm fine," she snapped, adjusting herself stiffly in the saddle.

Caelan climbed up behind her, settling into place. The moment he did, his smirk faded just a fraction.

Shit.

He hadn't accounted for this.

For the way her back pressed against his chest, how he could feel the warmth of her even through the layers of fabric.

Or for her scent—bergamot and jasmine, fresh from her morning shower—filling the space between them.

They were in the middle of nowhere! How the hell did she manage to smell like that?!

It was distracting. Far too distracting.

For the way his own pulse kicked slightly harder than it should.

Caelan shifted slightly, clearing his throat. "Comfortable?"

"Shut up."

His grin snapped right back into place.

Oh, this was going to be the most torturous and entertaining ride of his life.

11.
Niev

The rhythmic crunch of hooves against the frozen earth filled the silence as the four of them made their way back toward Greyhaven. The air was crisp, the morning sun barely warming the frost-covered landscape, but Niev barely felt the cold.

She was too aware of the man sitting behind her.

Too aware of the steady rise and fall of his breath against her shoulder, of the way his arms caged her in, fingers occasionally adjusting the reins near her waist.

Too aware of the heat of him, pressed against her back.

She kept her eyes locked on the road ahead, determined to focus on anything that wasn't Caelan Galbraith and the infuriating way he *existed*.

A raven flapped from a birch branch, scattering frost in a glittering cascade.

It wasn't working.

Especially not when the man in question shifted slightly in the saddle, his thigh brushing against hers, his fingers adjusting their grip on the reins—*completely unnecessary*, she was sure of it.

Niev scowled. "Are you doing that on *purpose*?"

"Doing what?"

She could hear the smirk in his voice.

Her fingers twitched where they rested against the front of the saddle. She was going to *strangle* him.

Ahead of them, Teagan turned slightly in his seat, shooting her an insufferable grin. "You two sound awfully quiet."

Ayda, comfortably seated behind him, didn't even hesitate. "Oh, suspiciously so."

Niev gritted her teeth.

Caelan just chuckled behind her, low and smug, his breath grazing her ear.

She resisted the urge to shove him off the damn horse.

The road stretched on, winding through the snow-laden trees. The crisp scent of winter mixed with the distant salt of the sea, the landscape shifting as they left the harsher mountain trails behind.

A band of mist unfurled across the hollows, carrying the wet-loam smell of thawing fields. Pines gave way to skeletal orchards, their black branches clacking overhead like wooden wind-chimes. Somewhere ahead, unseen streamlets chuckled beneath ice. Each mile felt warmer, softer—and far too exposed.

Despite the tension knotting in her spine, Niev had to admit—this was the easiest ride she'd had since leaving the cabin. Her wound ached, but it was tolerable.

Not that she'd ever admit it, but Caelan's nearness steadied her as much as it irritated. His body moved easily with the rhythm of the horse, his hands firm on the reins, his core balanced enough that she didn't have to fight against him. It should have been unbearable.

It wasn't.

Which only made it worse.

"Relax, Tigress," Caelan murmured, his voice a lazy drawl at her ear. "I don't bite."

"Well, I do," she turned to him menacingly, her eyes suddenly shifting amber. "So, shut your mouth."

Teagan barked out a laugh ahead of them, throwing a glance over his shoulder.

Ayda chuckled, adjusting her hold on Teagan's waist as the horse trotted down a steeper path. "He probably deserved it," she heard the witch mutter to the tracker.

Niev smirked. At least someone had sense.

Caelan sighed dramatically. "Feeling awfully unappreciated back here."

"Good," Niev muttered.

His arms flexed slightly as he adjusted the reins, his hold subtly tightening, drawing her an inch closer against him.

She stiffened.

Caelan, *bastard* that he is, pretended not to notice.

"Wouldn't kill you to be a little grateful, you know," he mused, as though they were discussing the weather.

Niev scoffed, lifting a brow. "For what exactly?"

"For the company," he mused lazily, voice dripping with amusement. "The smooth ride. Or maybe for saving your life and fetching you a horse at the crack of dawn because I'm an impeccable gentleman."

She scoffed. "That last one is a blatant lie."

"Ouch."

Ayda snorted. "You'll live."

The group fell into a companionable silence, the wind whistling through the trees as their horses carried them steadily forward.

But still, something nagged at her.

She didn't owe Caelan anything, not really. But the truth sat heavy on her chest, stubborn and insistent.

She *had* almost died.

And he *had* carried her all the way to the cabin. *And* stitched her wound.

Niev exhaled slowly, the words crawling up her throat like splinters. "Thank you."

Caelan stilled behind her.

"For saving my life," she added quietly.

His hands remained steady on the reins, his posture unchanged, but she felt his focus shift.

After a beat, he leaned in, his breath warm against the shell of her ear. Too close. Too smug.

"You're welcome," he murmured.

She jammed her elbow into his ribs.

Caelan let out a sharp grunt, jerking back. "Bloody hell, woman."

Teagan burst out laughing. Ayda just shook her head.

Niev smirked, finally comfortable again. "Impeccable gentleman, my ass."

The road stretched on, and Niev tried to focus on their destination.

Not on the warmth of the body behind her.

Not on the way his presence made her feel oddly steady.

Just on the mission ahead.

Because once they reached Greyhaven, there would be no distractions.

No lingering warmth.

Just the plan. The forged papers. The upcoming auction.

And dozens of children who needed saving. *No pressure.*

✴ ✴ ✴

Dusk bled gold into indigo as the weary road delivered them to a dusty crossroads town—a cluster of timber buildings pressed against rolling farmland, well north of Solhaven's coastal sprawl. Traders from every direction paused here before tackling the high grasslands beyond; the only gate was a split-log arch, but iron lanterns swung from it and a slow stream of wagons and pack mules shuffled through.

Niev tugged her hood low, eyes sweeping the rutted street.

She didn't trust crowded places. Too many eyes. Too many whispers.

Teagan was already dismounting. "I'll scout ahead," he muttered, already angling toward the shadows. "Make sure we're not walking into a trap. There's a tavern two doors up. Wait for me there."

"Be quick," Niev called after him.

He tossed her a lazy salute before disappearing into the crowd, melting into the evening bustle like a ghost.

Ayda dismounted with practiced grace, securing her mare to a hitching post outside the tavern's sagging porch. The sign—an outrageously curvy barmaid hoisting a tankard—creaked above them in the prairie wind—*The Buxom Lady*.

Niev eyed the establishment with a mix of wariness and resignation.

It was exactly the kind of place she would expect Teagan to suggest—rowdy, warm with the scent of roasted meat and spiced ale, filled with too many people packed too close together.

"Charming," Caelan murmured sarcastically beside her.

Niev rolled her eyes and swung off the horse before Caelan had the chance to help her down, landing with only a mild protest from her healing wound. She was fine. She would keep being fine.

They stepped inside, warmth immediately wrapping around them.

The tavern was loud, filled with the clatter of mugs slamming against wooden tables, laughter spilling over from drunken conversations, and the thick, greasy scent of fried food clinging to the air.

A barmaid passed them, expertly balancing a tray of drinks while batting off a man's wandering hands with a well-placed slap.

Niev exhaled sharply. At least the staff was competent.

She strode toward the bar, resting a hand on the rough wooden counter. "We need two rooms," she said. "And warm basins of water sent up, along with meals."

The bartender, a thick-armed man with a permanent scowl, eyed her with disinterest. "Silver upfront."

Niev slid the coins across the bar, watching as he bit one before pocketing them.

"Upstairs, last two on the left," he grunted before signaling one of the serving girls. "Basins and meals will be up soon."

She grabbed one of the keys, tossing the other to Ayda as they stepped away from the bar. Only once they were out of the bartender's earshot did she explain, keeping her voice low.

"We're not splitting up more than necessary. Two rooms. One for us, one for them."

Teagan, who had reappeared at her side, frowned slightly. "Could've gone for four. We have the coin."

"And have one of us alone if something goes wrong?" Niev shook her head. "Not happening."

The wooden stairs creaked under their weight as Niev and Ayda ascended, their boots leaving faint traces of melted snow behind them. The warmth of the tavern dulled the lingering cold, but the exhaustion from the past few days still clung to Niev like an unwanted shroud.

She tightened her grip on the key, leading the way down the dimly lit corridor. The lanterns cast flickering golden light against the cracked walls, their soft glow making the space feel smaller, more intimate.

Once inside, she closed the door with a quiet click and let go of a breath she hadn't realized she was holding.

The room was simple—a sturdy bed against the far wall, a wooden washbasin already set near the hearth, and a narrow table with a single rickety chair. It was hardly luxurious, but it was private, and for tonight, that was enough.

Ayda set her satchel down by the bed, rolling her shoulders before stretching her arms above her head. "Well, as much as I enjoy the feeling of dried blood and road dust on my skin, I'd rather not smell like a stable for dinner. I'll go first."

Niev nodded, sinking onto the edge of the bed with a quiet sigh as Ayda disappeared into the washroom.

For the first time in what felt like days, she let her body relax. The tension in her shoulders uncoiled, her hands unclenched, and the ever-present alertness that sat like a blade in her spine dulled—if only just a little.

Outside, the tavern's lively noise filtered through the walls, laughter and music a distant hum beneath the sound of water pouring from the basin in the adjoining room.

She reached for her satchel, unbuckling the worn leather flap and pulling out a clean tunic. As she did, her fingers brushed against something small and smooth—a glass vial.

By the time Ayda emerged, her damp strawberry-blond hair clinging to her neck, Niev had taken her place in the washroom. She let the warm water soothe the lingering ache in her muscles, scrubbing away the grime of the road.

When she stepped back into the room, toweling off her hair, Ayda was perched cross-legged on the bed, braiding a section of her drying hair with idle focus.

Niev set the towel aside, reaching into her satchel again. She retrieved the small vial, uncorking it with a practiced motion, and patted a few drops of the oil onto her neck and wrists before rubbing them together.

Ayda's nose wrinkled slightly before she smirked. "Have you been carrying those scented oils the entire time?"

Niev chuckled, capping the vial and slipping it back into her bag. "My life has little luxuries, Ravenscroft. You take them when you find them."

Ayda smirked, shifting slightly as she adjusted the blanket over her lap. "Listen, I'm not judging. It's the little things, yeah? A warm bath, a decent meal, and soft silk sheets."

Niev huffed a small laugh. "Exactly."

Ayda leaned back against the headboard, crossing her arms. "So that's your thing then? Carrying expensive oils around while the rest of us stink like wet leather?"

Niev snorted, stretching her legs out in front of her. "I'd hardly call it my *thing*."

Ayda smiled teasingly. "So what else does the Tigress do in her free time? Other than making impossible plans to save the unfortunate."

"I—" Niev started with a hesitant smile, "read mostly."

Ayda blinked. "You...read? What, like books?"

The sheer disbelief in her voice made Niev laugh.

"Yes, books. You sound like I just told you I knit in my free time."

Ayda raised both hands. "Forgive me for being shocked that *you* spend your free time reading grand tales by candlelight."

Niev gave her an unimpressed look. "What exactly did you think? That I spent my time sharpening knives and brooding in dark alleyways?"

Ayda made a thoughtful hum. "A little, yeah."

Niev shook her head, but amusement glimmered in her eyes. "I actually have an entire wall of books back in my apartment."

"Now *that* I have to see," Ayda tilted her head, studying her as if seeing her in a new light. "What kind?"

Niev shrugged. "Stories of far-off places, impossible odds, people who carve their names in history. That sort of thing," She hesitated, then added with a small smirk, "And romance."

Ayda's brows shot up. "You? The woman who's stabbed, or threatened to stab, every man we've met so far?"

Niev shot her a knowing look. "Liking a good romance and stabbing men are two very different things."

Ayda snorted, tucking a strand of hair behind her ear. "So what, you sit by the fire reading about swooning maidens and gallant heroes sweeping them off their feet?"

"Maybe?" Niev said teasingly, "Or ones where the heroines stab their enemies and save the prince."

Ayda laughed. "Now *that* I would read."

The conversation drifted into a comfortable lull, the fire crackling softly between them.

The golden glow of the hearth painted flickering patterns across the wooden walls, the warmth stretching lazily through the small space. Outside, the muffled sounds of the tavern below filtered up through the floor—muted laughter, the occasional scrape of a chair, the clinking of mugs—but in their room, everything felt quieter.

Niev leaned back slightly, running her fingers through her damp hair, the scent of bergamot and jasmine curling faintly in the air. Ayda stretched out her legs, absently tracing the hem of her sleeve with her fingers, her gaze distant as if still half-lost in the conversation they had just shared.

There was something different about the air now.

For the first time since this journey had begun, there was no challenge in Ayda's expression, no guarded appraisal, no unspoken weighing of threats and intentions. And Niev felt it too, in the way her shoulders had gradually relaxed, in the way she wasn't sitting on the edge of the mattress as if prepared to launch into action at any second.

It was rare to sit like this.

To not be sharpening a blade, strategizing an attack, or keeping her senses stretched taut.

To simply exist in the quiet company of someone else.

Ayda shifted slightly, adjusting her position against the headboard, the subtle creak of the mattress filling the room. A stray lock of hair had fallen loose from her braid, brushing against her cheek, but she made no move to fix it. Niev's gaze flickered toward the window, where frost clung to the glass, glad they had the luxury of a warm bed.

A draft slipped through a crooked shutter, carrying the faint clang of a distant forge and the earthy smell of turnip fields beyond the palisade—small reminders that this town was only a night's rest, not a refuge.

The fire crackled again, a log shifting, sending a burst of embers flickering up the chimney. The light danced across Ayda's face, catching the sharp angles softened by exhaustion.

Niev exhaled slowly. She wasn't one to easily make friends. But for some reason, she was glad for the witch's company.

Ayda hummed, breaking Niev from her train of thought. She shifted slightly as if considering something before speaking. "You sounded... *familiar* with Arenthia earlier. When we were discussing Port Orynth."

Niev's hands stilled over her satchel's buckles.

For a long moment, she said nothing.

She could lie.

It would be easy.

But something about the way Ayda had softened, the way she wasn't prying so much as offering a quiet space to speak—it made the truth feel less dangerous.

Finally, Niev exhaled, her fingers tightening around the strap of her bag. "My mother was Arenthian."

She didn't look up as she said it.

There was a pause.

Then, quietly, Ayda asked, "a witch?"

Niev nodded, her throat tightening slightly. "Yes. But she died years ago, and I haven't stepped foot in Arenthia since."

The words felt heavier than she expected them to.

She saw the flicker of something in Ayda's expression—understanding, curiosity, but also restraint.

Ayda could have asked for more. She could have pried, pushed, demanded details Niev wasn't ready to share.

But she didn't.

Instead, she leaned back against the headboard, exhaling through her nose. "Hell of a thing, isn't it? The probability of two Arenthian witches finding each other like this?"

Niev smirked, grateful for the shift in conversation. "You'd think the universe had a sense of humor."

Ayda let out a low chuckle. "Or terrible foresight."

Silence settled between them, not uncomfortable, but reflective.

Then Ayda sighed, tilting her head against the wall. "I miss it sometimes."

Niev glanced at her. "Arenthia?"

Ayda nodded. "The land, at least. The forests stretched endlessly, the rivers clear enough to see the fish swimming beneath them. And the air—God, the air there is nothing like here."

Niev's lips pressed together, something raw twisting in her chest. "It was beautiful."

Ayda studied her. "But?"

Niev hesitated. Then, with a slow breath, she said, "But I would kill to not have to step foot in it again."

Ayda's gaze darkened slightly. "Yeah."

Another stretch of silence.

A knock at the door cut off whatever Ayda was about to say.

Niev sat up slightly, glancing toward the door just as Teagan's voice rang through the wood.

"Ladies, we come bearing gifts," he announced proudly. "And by gifts, I mean lukewarm food and subpar company."

Ayda sighed dramatically. "Oh, joy."

Niev smirked as she pushed off the windowsill and crossed the room, opening the door to find Teagan grinning like he had just pulled off the heist of the century. He held a tray stacked with bowls, steam curling faintly from them. Behind him, Caelan leaned against the hallway wall, balancing a second tray on one hand while holding a pitcher of ale in the other.

"We figured we'd eat together," Teagan said, breezing past her into the room without waiting for an invitation. He placed the tray on the small wooden table near the fire. "You know, in case the two of you started getting ideas about conspiring against us."

"Too late," Ayda deadpanned. "One of you will be dead by morning."

Niev snorted, as both men entered, balancing trays of food between them, the scent of roasted meat and spiced ale filled the small room.

But it wasn't the meal that caught her attention.

It was the two thick slices of chocolate cake Caelan casually placed onto the table with a smirk.

Niev froze. Her gaze locked onto the dark, glossy layers, the dusting of powdered sugar on top, and the way the soft cake looked impossibly rich with what looked like candied cherries in the middle.

"You got chocolate cake?" The words left her before she could stop them, her voice almost reverent.

Caelan shrugged, looking far too pleased with himself. "What can I say? I may or may not have bribed one of the barmaids and sneaked into the kitchen."

Niev barely heard him. She was already reaching for the plate, her usual guarded expression slipping entirely as she lifted a forkful, eyes practically gleaming with anticipation.

"You absolute godsend," she murmured as she took a bite, groaning softly as the taste melted on her tongue. For a brief, blissful moment, she forgot entirely who she was sitting with. "I could almost *kiss* you."

The words hung in the air—sweet, reckless, impossible to snatch back.

Heat scalded the back of her neck. *Saints, Niev, what is wrong with you?*

She stared down at the fork as though it had betrayed her, willing the moment to rewind, to swallow the slip before anyone else could react.

The room went completely still.

Caelan's head snapped up so fast it was a wonder he didn't give himself whiplash. Ayda blinked. Even Teagan looked momentarily thrown, the smirk on his lips faltering as he stared at her.

Niev paused mid-bite, trying very hard to ignore the words she'd just said.

Slowly, she lowered her fork, clearing her throat.

Ayda was the first to break. She let out a loud, delighted laugh, her shoulders shaking as she nearly spilled her ale. "Oh, that's it," she gasped, wiping at her eyes. "We've found it. The Tigress does have a weakness, and it's sugar."

Teagan let out a low whistle. "Didn't think I'd see the day."

Niev, too pleased with her cake to be properly annoyed, shot Ayda a look of mock offense. "I'll have you know," she said, stabbing her fork dramatically into the slice. "I would go to extreme lengths for a good slice of cake."

Teagan smirked, leaning forward on his elbows. "Well, if you're to be taken to your word. Then, you owe our boy here a kiss."

Niev scoffed, rolling her eyes, but the corners of her lips twitched upward. "I said *almost*. Don't get carried away now."

Ayda snickered, and Niev huffed, trying to look indignant, but the effort was half-hearted at best. The rich chocolate melted on her tongue, warm and indulgent, and if they wanted to tease her for enjoying it, so be it.

She pointed her fork at Teagan instead. "If you *really* wanted to make yourself useful, you'd have stolen me a third slice."

Ayda snorted. "She's insatiable."

"That's one word for it," Teagan muttered, shaking his head.

Across from her, Caelan had gone oddly still. His usual wolfish grin had eased into something softer—corners of his mouth tilted, eyes crinkling at the edges the way they had when he'd stitched her side. No quip followed. Just that quiet, baffling smile aimed straight at her.

He looked like he had uncovered some grand secret that no one else had been privy to. And the worst part? He wasn't even gloating about it.

He just kept *smiling at her.*

Niev narrowed her eyes, suspicion flickering through her pleasure. "What?"

Caelan's grin widened. "Nothing. I just—" He shook his head, smirking, but there was something almost *fond* in the way he studied her. "I'll keep that in mind for next time."

She rolled her eyes but took another bite, hiding her smile behind her fork.

Below, a door slammed and a burst of laughter spilled onto the street, then faded. Upstairs the four of them sat in the hush that follows shared food, firelight licking the walls while outside the crossroads town exhaled into night.

12.
Caelan

The air in the room was different tonight. The fire's pop sounded louder, and even the ale smelled sweeter—lavender-honey instead of bitter grain. The tension that had weighed on them for days had loosened. Conversation flowed more naturally; the silences, less sharp.

For the first time, they weren't just reluctant allies plotting their next move. They almost felt like... something else. Not quite friends. But close.

Caelan leaned back, letting the hum of conversation settle over him like a blanket. He wasn't used to this—ease. The quiet between people that didn't require suspicion. It unsettled him more than the tension ever had.

Teagan rocked back on two legs of his chair, grinning. "Alright, let's make this interesting with a game."

Niev raised a brow. "A game."

"Yeah. It's a thing people do, Niev. To *bond*."

Ayda snorted.

Teagan ignored her, grinning like a man about to stir trouble. "The rules are simple. You either answer a question honestly, or you take a drink." He gestured toward the pitcher of ale Caelan had smuggled from the kitchen earlier, figuring they'd need something to dull the edges of whatever came next.

"Nothing too scandalous. I promise," he added with a wink.

Niev's expression flattened. "I'm sure that's a lie. But fine," she muttered, grabbing the pitcher and pouring herself a drink. "As long as drinking is involved."

Caelan smirked. Of course she'd play along—never one to back down from a challenge, even a stupid one like this. There was a steadiness to her, something unshakable. He hadn't decided yet if that made her the most dependable person in the room... or the most dangerous. Probably both.

He picked up his own cup, taking a slow sip, more to watch her than anything else.

Teagan beamed. "That's the spirit."

He tipped his chair back onto two legs, stretching his arms behind his head. "Alright," he said, a slow grin creeping onto his face. "I'll start easy."

He turned to Ayda. "Favorite place you've ever been."

Ayda hummed, swirling the last of her drink. "The Elarian Highlands." She went on, "You'd have to see it to understand but, it's not just fields. It's endless. Rolling green hills that stretch so far you swear the land itself breathes. In the summer, the air is thick with lavender and wild thyme, and when the wind rolls in from the cliffs, you can see storms crawling across the sky for miles before they ever touch the ground. There's a quietness to it—like the world hasn't quite figured out how to be cruel there yet."

The room was silent for a moment, the fire crackling softly behind them.

Caelan stared into the flames, picturing it. Not because he longed to go—he didn't. But because he wanted to understand the kind of person who would. Ayda spoke like someone who'd seen too much, and still hoped the world might surprise her. He didn't know whether to envy that or fear it.

Teagan let out a low whistle. "Alright. That was... poetic."

Ayda lifted her cup, shrugging "You asked."

Teagan turned to Niev next. "What about you?"

She hesitated, then finally said, "Mossgrove."

Niev's gaze softened, her fingers tracing absent patterns against the rim of her cup. "It's a small village on the Island of Thornmere."

Teagan's frown deepened. "I didn't know you went to Thornmere."

Her lips pressed together briefly, as if she'd already said too much. But then, after a long pause, she exhaled slowly.

"My father used to take me there," she admitted, her voice quieter than before.

Caelan stilled. Her voice had shifted—barely—but enough to make him pay closer attention.

There was something buried in the way she said it, something deeply intimate for some reason, but he couldn't pinpoint what.

"I was young," she continued. "We'd stay for a few weeks at a time. There was this waterfall tucked away in the cliffs just outside the village. We'd bring food and sit by the water for hours." A ghost of a smile tugged at her lips. "He tried to teach me how to fish once."

Teagan snorted. "Oh yeah? How did that go?"

Niev huffed a soft laugh, shaking her head. "I *hated* it. I didn't have the patience for it. He'd sit there, still as stone, waiting—*actually waiting*—and I'd just throw pebbles into the water, bored out of my mind."

The firelight flickered across her face, casting deep shadows along the sharp lines of her features. She looked softer in that moment. Not weak—never weak—but human, vulnerable in a way Caelan rarely saw from her.

And for the first time, he saw it.

The grief.

The kind that settled deep in the bones because you didn't know how to set it down. The kind you didn't talk about unless it slipped out by accident. It was the same kind of weight he carried.

But then, just as quickly as it had surfaced, she schooled back her features. Tucked away the frayed edges of whatever had cracked open inside her and turned her attention onto him, her voice a little too even.

"Anyway," she said, tone deliberately casual. "What about you?"

"Mordessa," he said after a beat.

Teagan raised a brow. "Mordessa? That wasteland?"

Caelan smirked faintly. "You see wasteland. I see freedom."

Ayda tilted her head, studying him. "Go on."

Caelan leaned back against the wall, spinning his empty cup between his fingers. "Mordessa is the last place in Thaelon where the empire doesn't have its claws buried deep. It's wild. Lawless, sure, but... no kings, no lords, no masters. Just people surviving. No one gives a damn where you're from or who you used to be. Out there, you get to be *anybody*."

When he was done, Calean looked up to see Niev staring at him with newfound curiosity and a knowing look. She quickly averted her gaze.

Teagan rubbed his hands together with a grin that spelled trouble. "Alright, round two. Ayda—Who was your first kiss?"

Ayda rolled her eyes so hard it was a miracle they didn't fall out of her skull. "Seriously? That's your big question?"

He spread his hands innocently. "It's a classic!"

She muttered something into her cup that sounded like a curse and took a drink instead.

Teagan groaned. ""Coward."

"I'm doing the world a favor."

"Fine. Niev. Same question." Teagan gave her a pointed look.

Caelan glanced sideways at her, expecting silence or sarcasm—maybe a glare sharp enough to cut Teag clean in half. He knew by now that she wasn't the type to share easily, and definitely not the type to entertain teenage nostalgia. He'd seen her deflect with wit, with ice, with a blade, if necessary. There was no way she'd actually answer.

But Niev didn't hesitate. "His name was Beckett. I was fifteen. It was... underwhelming."

Teagan looked delighted. "Underwhelming how?"

"Let's just say his breath and technique were bad enough, they put me off kissing boys for the next three years."

Ayda snorted mid-sip. "Oh gods."

Teagan burst out laughing, slapping the table. "That poor bastard."

Caelan didn't laugh—at least not loudly—but the corner of his mouth lifted in a smirk. He glanced at Niev, catching the faint smile playing on her lips as she looked down into her cup. When she noticed him watching, she arched a brow, as if daring him to comment. He didn't. But the smirk lingered.

Teagan leaned forward, resting his elbows on the table with exaggerated curiosity. "Alright then. Now I *have* to ask—who's the lucky bastard who broke your so-called *vow of celibacy*?"

Niev's gaze snapped to him. Slowly. Her eyes narrowed into the kind of look that usually preceded violence.

Teagan grinned wider. "Oh no," he said, dragging out the words like a man cracking open a secret. "It was Thorne, wasn't it?"

She didn't answer. Didn't blink. That was answer enough.

Teagan cackled, shoving back from the table in victory. "It *was*! Laughlan Thorne! I knew it! I *knew* there was something too smug about that bastard."

Niev sipped her drink with slow, lethal calm.

Ayda, on the other hand, looked far too entertained. She leaned an elbow on the table and tilted her head toward Niev. "Alright, but seriously. How handsome is this man exactly?"

Niev exhaled through her nose, as if regretting every life choice that had brought her to this moment. "Unreasonably."

Ayda raised her eyebrows. "Ah. Dangerous category."

Teagan nodded solemnly. "That's the worst kind. Right up there with 'smells like pine, smoke, and sin.'"

Niev narrowed her eyes at him. "Are you describing him or yourself?"

"I contain multitudes."

Caelan hadn't said a word. But his cup sat untouched in his hands, and his jaw had tightened slightly—not enough for anyone to comment, but enough for Niev to notice.

Of course it was Thorne. That name kept crawling back into the room like a curse.

He'd never even met the man for God's sake. It shouldn't matter. He knew that.

But for some reason, it *did*.

Niev returned her attention to her drink. Her expression was unreadable now—controlled, composed, carefully neutral. But her fingers tapped absently against the rim of her cup.

Teagan, oblivious or just bold, opened his mouth again.

"God, now I'm picturing it—sweaty sparring, lingering glances, forbidden late-night confessions—"

"Teagan," Niev said, without looking up. "I swear to God—"

"All right, all right!" He raised his hands, laughing. "I'm done. No more digging up your tragic romantic history."

Ayda grinned. "You say that, but you're still thinking about it."

Teagan gave her a wink. "It's called imagination, Ayda. You should try it sometime."

The room hummed with warmth, the fire crackled, and the ale flowed as the Tigress cleared her throat and looked up with a mischievous grin. "Alright, my turn to ask. Ayda. Worst decision you ever made in bed."

Ayda's jaw dropped. "Oh, come *on*."

"You brought this upon yourself," Niev shrugged, all innocence. "Answer or drink."

Ayda grumbled and threw back a gulp of ale. "Soldier. Bad lighting. Wrong tent."

There was a beat of stunned silence and then the room *exploded*.

Teagan doubled over, nearly falling out of his chair, gasping for air. "Wrong *tent*?!"

"I don't want to talk about it!" Ayda shouted over the laughter, red-faced but grinning.

"Was he at least—" Teagan started, wheezing.

"No! And shut up!"

Even Caelan barked a laugh at that, and Ayda pointed a warning finger at him.

"Don't you dare."

"I didn't say anything," he said mildly, but his expression betrayed him.

Teagan wiped tears from his eyes. "Alright, alright. Who's next?"

But before anyone could answer, Niev straightened, her cup forgotten on the table. The glow from the fire cast shadows along her cheekbones, flickering with the movement of the flames.

She looked across the table—past Teagan, past Ayda—and locked eyes with Caelan.

Her voice, when she spoke, was calm—quiet. But it shifted the air between them like a sudden change in wind direction.

"What's the thing you're most afraid of?"

The room stilled.

Even the fire seemed to hush, its crackling softened under the weight of her question.

Caelan didn't answer. Not immediately. His grip on his cup tightened just slightly—small enough that most wouldn't notice, but Niev did. She didn't look away.

The question hadn't been said with cruelty. There was no heat in it. No challenge. Just... weight.

Caelan could've made a joke. Dodged it. Taken a drink.

Hell, if it was anyone else asking, he would have.

But he didn't.

The heat in her molten brown and amber eyes compelled him to answer truthfully.

"I'm afraid," he said slowly, voice lower than before, "that everything I've done was for nothing. That I clawed my way this far, survived things I shouldn't have, and in the end... none of it will matter."

Ayda's gaze dropped to the table, her fingers tracing a slow line through the condensation on her glass. Teagan leaned back, staring into the fire like it might give him something else to say.

But Niev didn't flinch. Didn't look away. She nodded—just once.

"I get that," she said.

There was no pity in her voice. No softness, either. Just truth.

Recognition.

It was worse than pity, somehow.

It meant she saw him.

Caelan's throat tightened and he tore his gaze away from her.

Teagan cleared his throat. "Well. That got heavy."

Ayda snorted quietly. "You started it."

"Did not."

"You literally brought the ale and said, 'Let's make this interesting.'"

"Okay, maybe I started it a little," he admitted. "Still. I thought we'd land somewhere closer to 'embarrassing hookups,' not 'soul-crushing existential dread.'"

Niev leaned back in her chair, crossing her arms. "You didn't specify the rules."

Ayda raised her cup in a lazy salute. "That's on you."

The tension eased again—not entirely, but enough for the warmth to creep back in around the edges. But beneath the lingering jokes, something had changed.

There was a crack in the walls they'd all built around themselves.

But none of them seemed to be in a hurry to patch it.

Ayda took another sip of her drink, then gave Teagan a sideways glance. A slow smile tugged at her lips.

"You know," she said casually, "you've been awfully good at getting everyone else to spill their secrets tonight."

Teagan blinked. "What? I'm just the host. The facilitator."

Ayda tilted her head. "Uh-huh. And how many questions have *you* actually answered, oh great facilitator?"

Teagan opened his mouth, then promptly closed it again.

Caelan couldn't help the flicker of amusement that touched his face. He sat back in his chair, watching as Ayda leaned in like a cat who'd just cornered something small and squirmy.

Teagan huffed. "Fine. You want something embarrassing? Hit me. I can take it."

Ayda's grin widened. "Alright then. Most humiliating time a woman rejected you. And I want details."

Teagan groaned, flopping dramatically back in his chair. "Why do I feel like I walked into a trap?"

"Because you did," Caelan muttered.

Ayda leaned on her elbow. "C'mon, Teeg. Let's hear it."

He let out a long-suffering sigh. "Okay. Fine. I was seventeen. There was this girl, Marys, and I was *convinced* she fancied me. I mean, she laughed at my jokes, she touched my arm when she talked—classic signs, right?"

Ayda looked delighted already. "Go on."

"So I sneak into the stables one night—she worked there, right? I leave this whole dramatic note in her saddlebag. Flowers, a poem, the whole thing. Pure romantic genius."

Caelan raised a brow. "You wrote her a poem?"

"I was *young and in love*," Teagan shot back. "Well, not *in love* per se, but *in-fatuation* at least. Anyway, the next morning, I'm waiting to see her reaction. She walks out, reads the note... and bursts out laughing. Not in a *good* way. In a full-body, can't-breathe, wiping-tears-from-her-eyes kind of way."

Ayda winced. "Ouch."

"She *read it out loud* to her friends. Called me 'Teagan the Tragically Tender.'"

Niev burst out laughing—actual, full-bodied laughter that shook her shoulders and made her clutch her side. Her head tipped back, eyes crinkled at the corners, and Caelan could swear he saw tears forming in the corners of her eyes.

She was light and fire, and for a second, he wanted to bask in it. But he knew better. He'd spent too long surviving to let his guard down now. That kind of brightness had a cost. It lured you in, made you hope, and then it burned you alive.

"God," she gasped, trying to catch her breath. "The *tender*? What exactly was she referring to that was *tender*?"

Ayda nearly spit out her drink. Teagan threw his hands in the air. "That was *not* what she meant!"

Niev wiped under her eyes, still grinning. "You sound like a tragic bard who cries the morning after."

"I *do not cry after*," Teagan snapped, pointing a finger at her while everyone else laughed harder.

But try as he might, Caelan couldn't look away from Niev.

There was something about her laugh—real, unguarded, warm in a way she rarely let herself be. It lit her from the inside out, softening the angles of her face and turning her usually sharp eyes into something brighter. Lighter. Alive.

He'd seen her fight.

He'd seen her furious.

He'd even seen her grieve.

But the way she laughed—truly laughed—caught him off guard.

Her face, usually carved in stone, was soft now. Her eyes weren't sharp or calculating—they were alive, lit with something unburdened. And for a second, just a second, she didn't look like the weapon the world had forced her to become.

She looked... free.

And Caelan didn't know what to do with that.

It wasn't attraction. Or maybe it was. But it was more than that, too. It was the recognition of something he didn't yet have the courage to name. Something that made his chest feel too tight and his thoughts too loud.

She was dangerous—not because of her power, not because of what she could do with a blade or a glance—but because *this* was the part of her no one expected. The part no one saw coming. The part that could slip past his defenses without ever drawing a sword.

And she didn't even know she was doing it.

He looked away, back toward the fire, jaw flexing.

Whatever this was—this thing coiling up inside him, slow and certain—it was not part of the plan.

It couldn't be.

But it was there now.

And he wasn't sure he knew how to stop it.

"I almost left the country," Teagan added dramatically. "I spent a full week hiding in the forest out of pure shame."

Niev snorted again, "Yeah, I bet you did."

Caelan chuckled, shaking his head. "Now *that's* soul-crushing."

"Right??" Teagan pointed at him. "Women are cruel creatures."

"That we are," Niev raised her glass proudly, taking it as a compliment.

Ayda laughed. "That Marys was a fool. This kind of earnest tragedy? Some girls would kill for that."

Teagan sniffed. "That's what I've been saying for years."

The warmth returned—real, this time. It buzzed through the room like the afterglow of a storm, crackling but calm. Caelan let himself lean into it, just for a moment. The comfort of the fire. The weight of tired limbs. The strange, fragile thing they'd all been building—whatever it was.

But even then, he couldn't take his eyes off Niev. Not when she was still smiling like that.

She was going to be the end of him, he thought again hopelessly.

13.
Niev

I'm afraid that everything I've done was for nothing. That I clawed my way this far, survived things I shouldn't have, and in the end... none of it will matter.

Caelan's voice still echoed in her head.

Hours had passed. Maybe more. The fire had burned down to glowing embers, and the men had slipped off to their respective room, ale-drunk and laughter-dulled. But Niev hadn't moved.

She sat near the window now, elbows resting on the sill, watching the wind ripple through the grass just beyond the edge of the inn. The moon was thin and high, and the sky above it cloudless, distant, unbothered. A few stars blinked down at her like they knew better. Like they'd seen a thousand people like her and Caelan come and go—battered, burned out, thinking they were unique in their brokenness.

But what he said—*what he meant*—stuck.

Because God help her, she understood it. More than she wanted to.

It wasn't the words that hit her, not really. Plenty of people feared insignificance. Plenty feared regret. But *his* fear wasn't rooted in insecurity—it was rooted in exhaustion. He'd *done* things. Survived things. And not just for himself, that was the part that haunted her.

He'd fought and scraped and bled for something. And now he was afraid it would all amount to dust.

She lived that feeling.

It was the same one that crept into her gut in the dead hours of the night, the one that asked if all her sacrifices—her loyalties, her silence, her obedience—had ever actually *meant* anything. If she'd truly protected what mattered... or if she'd just been surviving out of habit.

Niev exhaled slowly, pressing her forehead against the cool glass. It was ridiculous how clearly she could still hear his voice. Low. Rough-edged. Like he hadn't meant to say it but couldn't stop himself.

And the way he'd looked at her after—like he regretted letting her see it.

But still, he'd been truthful, and that was the dangerous part. Because Caelan wasn't just angry or brooding or damaged. He was *honest*— sometimes despite himself. Honest in the ways that mattered.

And people like that were rare. *Too rare.*

Which meant she couldn't afford to trust him. Not fully. Not yet.

She straightened from the window and folded her arms, trying to shove his voice into the quieter parts of her mind. The ones she didn't look at unless she had to.

Outside, the wind shifted again, brushing past the stone walls like a whisper of something still waiting.

Behind her, the inn creaked gently as someone moved. Probably other patrons walking through the hallway.

Niev turned quietly from the window, the room dim with moonlight. Ayda lay sprawled across her half of the bed, one arm dangling off the edge, breathing slow and even. A deep sleeper, thank God. She'd never have let Niev leave without a comment or questions.

The air in the room felt too close, too full of the things she wasn't ready to name. She slipped on her boots, wrapped her cloak around her shoulders, and eased the door open with careful fingers. The wood creaked softly—nothing more than a breath—but she paused anyway, waiting for any sign that Ayda had stirred.

Nothing.

Niev stepped out into the narrow hallway, the air cooler and still. She pulled the door shut behind her, turning—

—and stopped dead.

Caelan stood just a few feet away, halfway out of the room he shared with Teagan. His hair was slightly mussed, dark strands falling loose around his face. He wore a black tunic and a cloak not yet fastened, his hand still at the clasp. His hood was down, but his posture was already coiled like someone prepared for silence and shadows.

He looked up. Their eyes met.

Neither of them moved.

The inn was too quiet. The space between them too loud.

So much for avoiding him.

She cleared her throat, arching a brow. "Couldn't sleep?"

He nodded once. "Something like that."

His voice was low, husky with fatigue—or maybe something else.

Niev hesitated for half a breath, then tilted her head toward the stairs. "I'm going for a walk. If you'd rather not stare at the ceiling for the next hour, you can come."

She turned and began down the steps, not waiting for his answer.

But she heard him follow.

Outside, the night was crisp. Cool enough to make her glad for her cloak, though not unpleasant. The streets of the village were mostly deserted, save for the occasional torch bracketed to a stone wall, sputtering in the breeze. Above them, the sky stretched wide and quiet, moonlight spilling across the rooftops like spilled silver.

They kept their hoods drawn low, boots quiet against the cobblestones.

Neither spoke at first.

But she could feel him beside her.

Too close. *Not close enough.*

She was hyperaware of everything—the sound of his footsteps matching hers, the quiet shift of his cloak, the line of his jaw beneath the shadow of his hood as the fabric grazed his stubble. He walked like someone who'd spent too long in dangerous places. Every motion economical. Controlled. Silent.

She didn't know when she'd started paying attention to the way he moved. The shape of him. The quiet strength in his frame. But now that she had, it was hard to stop.

"Didn't take you for the sleepless type," she said finally, her voice low enough to be swallowed by the wind.

He glanced sideways at her. "Didn't take you for the 'I like to take walks under the stars' type. Yet, here we are."

She smirked. "It's not for the stars. It's to try and shut my thoughts off."

"Ah," he said. "So a peaceful stroll, then."

"Clearly."

They rounded a bend, the path widening near a small grove just beyond the edge of the town. The trees there leaned in close to one another, their branches tangled like they were sharing secrets.

Niev stepped off the cobbled road and onto the dirt path that led between the trees. He followed without question.

"Most people lie," she said, her voice barely above a murmur. "When you ask them what they're afraid of. They throw something pretty at you. Or vague. Something they've practiced."

"I've never been good at practiced answers... Not with you," he added tentatively, his jaw clenching.

"No," she murmured. "You haven't."

They reached a low rise where the trees thinned and the sky opened again above them. She stopped at the crest of the hill and looked out across the fields. The tall grass swayed under the moonlight, silver-tipped and restless.

She folded her arms across her chest and glanced at him. "You're not what I expected."

He turned to her, brow raised. "What did you expect?"

She considered him for a moment. "Arrogant bastard. Probably with a drinking problem."

He huffed a quiet laugh. "That's not *entirely* wrong."

"But not right, either."

He looked at her for a long moment, then stepped closer. Not enough to crowd her, but enough that she could feel his presence more sharply now. The heat of him. The quiet steadiness.

"And you?" he asked. "What did you expect me to think of you?"

She looked back out at the field, the night wind lifting strands of hair from beneath her hood. "Does it matter?"

"Yes," he said simply.

She looked at him then, eyes searching his face, his posture, his stillness. "I expected you to see the Tigress. Saeris's mean, ruthless, and bloodthirsty mercenary."

He tilted his head. "And what do you want me to see?" he whispered.

She didn't answer right away. Because she didn't know. Not really.

But she held his gaze. And for once, she didn't hide.

The silence stretched between them again—tense, charged, full of all the things they weren't saying.

When she finally looked away, it wasn't out of discomfort.

It was because her heart had started to beat faster.

The wind stirred the grass below them, brushing across the field in rippling waves. Neither of them spoke. The silence felt thick with everything that hadn't been said. The night held its breath around them, quiet and still.

Niev's eyes drifted back to the horizon, to the far-off mountain range beyond. Somewhere past that lay Port Orynth. The secret underground tunnels. The guards. And the children.

Her arms folded tightly over her chest again, but this time it wasn't from the cold.

"Do you really think we'll succeed?" she asked, voice low, barely above the rustle of the wind. "That we'll actually be able to save them?"

She didn't look at him when she said it. Couldn't.

There was too much weight behind the question.

He was quiet for a few seconds. Then—

"I don't know," he said honestly. "We've planned as best as we can. Timed every step. Mapped every weak point. We've accounted for everything we *can* account for."

She turned to him then, the moonlight catching the side of his face, tracing the edge of his jaw.

His eyes softened. "But that's not what you asked."

"No," she said softly.

He looked down into her eyes then—his gaze steady, unwavering. "I'm going to get those children out, Niev... or I'll die trying."

She stared at him, her breath caught somewhere between her lungs and her throat.

He meant it. There wasn't a hint of bravado in his tone. No arrogance. No blind optimism.

Just plain and devastating truth.

And the way he said *her name.*

She hadn't expected this. Not from *him.* Not from the man she'd once pegged as another outlaw with a grudge and a sharp tongue.

But this man—the one standing in front of her, cloaked in shadow and moonlight, speaking of life and death like they were promises—was something else entirely.

In that moment, she felt like they were two sides of the same coin.

Because she would've said the same thing. Because she had.

And now, somehow, he had the gall to stand there and *mean it* the way she did.

She turned to look at Caelan—studying every inch of his face. Looking for whatever strange, quiet fire lived inside that made him so willing to sacrifice himself for this cause.

Her chest tightened, emotion swelling in a place she'd long thought was dormant. It clawed its way up, pressing behind her ribs until she had to shove it down again, fast, before it could make a mess of her voice.

Her throat was tight, but she managed to breathe through it. "You make it sound so noble."

"It's not noble," He huffed, glancing at her. "It's just the right thing to do."

She swallowed hard, then looked away, trying to steady herself.

When she spoke again, her tone was lighter. Just enough to cut through the heaviness between them. "Well, I suppose I'll have to make sure you don't get killed. Wouldn't want to lose my cover."

His brow arched, amused. "Your cover?"

"Well, I *will* be posing as your *mistress*," she said, folding her arms and giving him a sideways look. "In the midst of dozens of leering, disgusting men. I expect protection, praise, and the occasional expensive gift."

He actually laughed at that. "Still can't believe that was your idea."

"I told you. No one expects the Tigress to be *anyone's* mistress. That's why it works. Besides, men will see whatever they want to see—a pretty woman hardly seems like a threat."

He shook his head, grinning faintly. "It's reckless."

"It's brilliant."

"It's *dangerous*."

She gave him a sly look. "So am I."

He didn't respond right away, but his smile deepened. "We'll make a convincing pair, you know," he said, "if you can manage not to murder me halfway through."

"That depends," she said, eyes narrowing. "Are you going to be insufferable?"

"Probably."

"Then it's a toss-up."

He stepped closer, just enough that she had to tilt her chin slightly to meet his gaze.

Their breath mingled in the cool night air, warm against the wind.

And then, without warning, he leaned in—just beside her ear, his voice low and intimate.

"You don't need to worry about anything, *darling*," he murmured. "I'll take good care of you."

Her breath caught in her throat.

She hated how it made her heart stutter. Hated how her skin reacted, how her stomach flipped, how a thousand thoughts scattered behind her eyes like startled birds.

Her fist itched to strike him—but she stayed rooted, chest caged in panic and something like want.

She should knee him in the groin for getting this close.

He didn't move either—just lingered there a moment longer, like he was waiting for her to push him back. When she didn't, he slowly pulled away, his eyes never leaving hers.

There was tension between them now—thick and tangible, strung tight between every inch of space they *weren't* touching.

She forced a smirk, though her voice came a touch lower than usual. "You'd better. I'm quite the high-maintenance lover."

She felt rather than saw his reaction; a long, slow inhale, the brush of warmth as he drew nearer. His eyes darkened, amused, and something far more urgent, flickering in their depths.

Caelan's voice dropped an octave, low and teasing. "*Oh darling...* pampering you would be my greatest pleasure."

He offered her a crooked smile, heat rolling off him in waves.

Niev's blood thundered in her veins the moment his words brushed past her ear.

Her pulse spiked so violently she nearly leaned into him—then jerked upright, fury and desire tangling in her gut. Her fists clenched at her sides, nails biting into her palms. She could feel the rush in her cheeks, hot and insistent.

The promise in his words hung between them, raw and electric, and Caelan's grin told her he wanted nothing more.

And just like that, he drew back, the heat of him lingering in her veins as the world settled into silent vertigo. Another gust of wind rolled past them, carrying the scent of ash and pine. The moon dipped behind a passing cloud, and for a brief moment the world went dark.

But Niev wasn't thinking about the moon.

She was thinking about how close he still was.

How she was physically restraining herself from getting even closer.

And how she wasn't ready for what that meant.

14.
Caelan

He couldn't remember the last time silence had felt this loud.

They stood at the edge of the grove, not touching, not speaking. But everything in him was still tuned to her—every breath, every flicker of movement, every damn heartbeat. The wind moved her cloak gently around her legs. Her hair stirred where it escaped her hood, dark strands catching silver in the moonlight.

She hadn't stepped away.

That was the part he couldn't stop replaying.

When he'd leaned in—close enough to feel the warmth of her skin, close enough to whisper what he meant—she hadn't pulled back. She hadn't laughed it off. She hadn't cut him with a look.

She'd just... stood there.

Let him in.

Just for a second.

And now he couldn't seem to put his feelings back in the box he'd kept them in since they met.

It had been easier when she was just the Tigress. The blade in the dark. The one you didn't cross, didn't question, didn't look at too long unless you wanted to get burned.

But tonight—God, *tonight*—he'd seen everything she tried not to show. Her laugh. Her grief. Her fear, when she thought no one was watching.

And now, she wasn't just the Tigress anymore.

She was *Niev*.

And that was far more dangerous.

She turned away first, her boots crunching lightly on the dirt path as she made her way back toward the road. He followed without a word, falling into step beside her like it was second nature now.

The walk back to the inn was quiet, but not strained. The air between them still buzzed, the unspoken things hanging like smoke. But neither of them reached for it. Not yet.

By the time they reached the door, her expression had settled back into something neutral. Controlled. But not cold.

She glanced up at him, one hand on the handle.

"We should leave early," she said. "Before sunrise."

He nodded. "I'll make sure the horses are ready."

She hesitated, like she wanted to say something else. But then she nodded once, almost to herself, and slipped back inside.

Caelan waited until the door shut behind her before he let out the breath he'd been holding.

He stood there for a long moment, the cold brushing against his skin through the fabric of his tunic, grounding him. Reminding him what this was.

A mission. A risk. A line they couldn't afford to blur.

He had a role to play. She did too.

But none of that changed what had just happened.

And none of it changed the fact that she was under his skin now.

He could feel her there. Lodged like a thorn he couldn't pull out.

And he wasn't sure he wanted to.

He lingered in the silence, fingertips grazing the doorframe as if to catch a trace of her scent. Moonlight pooled at his feet, and for a moment his pulse thundered so loudly he thought she might hear it on the other side. He pressed his hand to his chest, willing his heart back into a steady rhythm, but the tremor in his fingers betrayed him. His breath caught— half in the chill, half in the memory of her nearness—before he shoved it down and turned away.

Caelan slipped back into the room quietly, shutting the door behind him. Teagan was sprawled across his bed, one leg hanging off the edge, snoring like a dying bear. Caelan moved past him without comment, dropping into the chair near the hearth.

The fire was out. Just a few embers remained. He closed his eyes and let the heat of those few dying embers wash over him. Fingertips brushing the cold iron of the poker, he nudged a spark into life—tiny orange fingers clawing at the dark—before dropping back into the chair.

He watched the fire catch and falter, mirroring the war raging behind his eyes. A soft exhale escaped him as he leaned forward, elbows on his knees, the echo of her breath still warm against his ear. In the silence, her presence settled beside him like a living thing—sharp, insistent, and utterly inescapable.

He stared at the embers until they faded into darkness, his own words echoing back through his mind.

You don't need to worry about anything, darling. I'll take good care of you.

It had been a joke.

Except it hadn't.

And that, more than anything, was the problem.

He closed his eyes, just for a moment.

And the past came for him like it always did—quiet at first, then all-consuming.

❋ ❋ ❋

The air in the camps was always thick. With smoke, with sweat, with the kind of silence that meant survival. Even when people cried, they did it soundlessly.

He was just a boy then—barely ten. Old enough to know better, too young to do anything about it.

His mother's hands were always cracked and red from the soap vats. The lye ate through skin like it was nothing. She used to hum under her breath while she worked. A soft, tuneless sound. It didn't carry hope. It didn't carry comfort.

He knew she did it just to remind herself she was still alive.

His father worked the quarry wall, breaking stone from dawn until nightfall. He came home with blood in his teeth more days than not.

They never complained. Not once.

But it was the way they watched the guards with their heads slightly lowered. The way they flinched at shouting, even when it wasn't meant for them. The way they didn't speak unless they had to.

That was what taught Caelan what fear really looked like. Not panic. Not screaming.

Just... silence.

One night, when he was twelve, he saw a girl taken from the line outside the food station. She couldn't have been older than seven. A guard pulled her by the arm, said she was "defiant." She hadn't said a word. Just looked him in the eye when she handed back the empty tin.

That was all it took.

Caelan never saw her again.

He hadn't spoken for three days after that.

He remembered sitting in the dark beside his mother while she wrapped a clean strip of linen around his father's hand. He'd crushed three fingers that day under a falling stone, and the bone had pushed through the skin. No one treated it. No one would.

His mother didn't cry. Didn't speak. Just worked, careful and fast.

When she was done, Caelan remembered the way she'd looked at him— tired, worn, her eyes hollow, and said, softly:

"You survive, Caelan. You survive, and when you can fight, you fight for your life, my son."

That was the first time he'd ever heard her speak like that.

Not like a mother, but someone older. Angrier.

Someone who remembered freedom.

He never forgot that night. Not the look in her eyes. Not the quiet promise that lived behind her voice.

He wished she was still alive. So he could've gotten her out. Or died trying.

But that didn't matter now.

His parents were dead, but the camps still existed. The Empire still took children. Still broke people down until they forgot their names.

And as long as that was true, he wouldn't stop.

✳ ✳ ✳

Caelan jerked awake sometime before dawn, breath sharp in his chest. Teagan still snored in the corner, curled into the rough wool blankets like a wounded animal. The fire was long dead, its hearth cold and caked with gray ash.

Frost glimmered on the low wooden windowpane, spiderweb cracks glittering in the pale light. His boots whispered against the splintered boards as he stood, every joint protesting the chill that seemed to seep through the cracked plaster walls.

He slipped aside the heavy linen curtain and pressed his forehead against the glass, peering out at the narrow cobblestone road winding eastward through the silent village. Lanterns swung in their iron brackets, guttering weakly in the predawn breeze.

A thin line of light cracked over the distant ridgeline, painting the sky in bruised pinks and golds. And as the world slowly brightened, Caelan made himself a silent vow.

He would not let them disappear.

Not like the girl in the line. Not like his parents. Not like too many others before. Not this time.

The world was still wrapped in darkness when Caelan slipped from the inn's back door, cloak drawn tight against the lingering chill. Lantern light pooled softly in the low hallway, but beyond that, all was quiet—save for the faint clink of distant pans in a kitchen long since shuttered. He paused for a moment on the threshold, listening to the hush of sleeping rooms, and let the cold air clear the last traces of sleep from his mind.

Dew clung to the cobblestones in jewel-bright beads as he made his way to the stable, each step deliberate so as not to wake the world around him. The horses nickered softly at his approach, damp flanks shifting in the half-light. He knocked twice on the post before lifting the latch, then moved through the stalls with an almost ceremonial calm—brushing coats, checking hooves, easing each creature into stirrups and saddles. Dawn might still be hours off, but in the pale promise of this morning, Caelan felt everything align around the simple certainty of a journey beginning.

By the time the others began to stir, Caelan had already saddled the horses. The inn's courtyard was still half-shrouded in mist, dew glistening along the fence rails and the leather straps of the tack. He moved with practiced efficiency, each motion quiet and deliberate. He liked mornings like this. No chatter. Just clear focus on the task at hand.

He was checking the cinch on his stallion when he heard footsteps behind him—soft, measured.

He didn't need to turn to know it was her.

"I thought I was early," Niev said.

"You are."

She stood beside him now, hood down, cloak already fastened. Her hair was braided tight against her scalp in a way that gave her an even sharper edge. She looked composed. Focused. But her eyes flicked toward him—just once—before sweeping past to the saddled horses lined along the fence.

She didn't speak again.

Just walked to his stallion, grabbed the pommel, and mounted behind the saddle in one fluid motion.

Caelan froze.

He turned slowly, staring at her, brows lifting before he could stop himself.

She didn't even look at him—just adjusted her cloak and settled herself like it was the most natural thing in the world.

And yet, just yesterday, she'd rolled her eyes so hard she nearly lost them when they told her she'd have to ride with *him* instead of Teagan.

She could've taken Teagan's horse—he hadn't even shown up yet. She'd gotten here early, and had every chance to spite him. But she didn't.

She just got on. No complaint. No smirk. No bite.

And that alone put him on edge.

She was always sharp, always posturing—*what was this?*

He didn't trust it.

He passed her the reins without a word. Their fingers brushed—brief, unintentional—but it was enough to stir something low and restless in his chest.

She didn't comment. Neither did he.

Ayda and Teagan joined them shortly after. Ayda with a sleep-mussed scowl, Teagan with a grin that said he'd slept better than anyone had a right to.

"Everyone ready to play traitor, mistress, and noble scum?" Teagan asked, swinging easily into his saddle.

"Hardly a stretch for you," Niev muttered.

Ayda smirked as she mounted. "Try to behave. We'll be in Greyhaven by midday if we don't get waylaid."

Caelan swung up behind her, settling into the saddle.

And immediately regretted every decision that had led to this moment.

His thigh pressed flush against hers, the hard curve of her back molding to his chest as the stallion shifted beneath them. He could feel the heat of her body seeping through heavy leather, each hitch of the saddle jarring his spine. Her hood brushed his cheek when the horse took a step, and his fingers locked around the reins she'd draped over his wrist—slick with dew and her damp cloak. Every inch of him tensed, the grip in his calves, the ache in his shoulders, the sudden ache in his guts.

They rode in formation—Niev and Caelan leading, Ayda and Teagan a short distance behind. The first hour passed in silence, save for the occasional clatter of hooves and the caw of distant crows. The trees grew thinner as they traveled south, the land flattening into long, low fields veiled in fog.

Caelan kept his eyes on the road but his mind wasn't still. He replayed their plan, their backup plan, and the fallback for the backup. But between every calculation was the echo of her voice—of *last night*. Her breath catching when he leaned close. The look in her eyes when he told her she didn't need to worry.

He shouldn't have said that.

He meant it.

But he shouldn't have said it.

She had enough to carry without him complicating things.

But the truth was, he *would* take care of her.

Because somewhere along the way, it stopped being about the mission. Stopped being about—

He hissed as her shoulder brushed against his chest. Just a light graze. But it yanked him out of his thoughts nonetheless.

Caelan blinked, refocusing on the road ahead. The trail narrowed slightly as the terrain sloped downward, and Niev adjusted her posture to keep balance.

That's all it was, he told himself.

An unintentional shift. But then she did it again.

Leaning ever so slightly back into him—not enough to be obvious. Just enough to make him feel it.

He stiffened, breath caught halfway in his chest.

Another curve in the path, and this time her hand moved, sliding a fraction farther along the saddle horn. Her knuckles brushed his fingers.

She didn't pull away. Didn't apologize. Didn't even acknowledge it.

Caelan's eyes narrowed slightly, not at the road—but at *her*.

She wasn't shifting for balance. She was doing this on *purpose*.

The realization sank in slow and hot—just like the flush creeping up the back of his neck.

Yesterday, she'd threatened to strangle him for shifting in the saddle too much. Today, she'd mounted his horse before the others even showed up, and now she was making the ride a lesson in restraint.

This was payback.

Every slight movement brought her closer. Every tiny lean into him blurred the lines between accident and intention until he didn't know where one ended and the next began.

And God help him, she was enjoying it.

He could feel it in the tension of her back—the subtle looseness of her shoulders. Not relaxed, not really. But *amused*.

She was doing this to unsettle him, and it was *working*.

Caelan clenched his jaw and refocused on the path, posture rigid. He wasn't going to give her the reaction she wanted. Not yet.

He could feel the smile she was holding in. It made something tight and slow burn in his chest.

She was infuriating.

She was brilliant.

And right now, she was absolutely in control.

As the road straightened and the trees thinned, her movements grew even less subtle. More deliberate. She leaned forward slightly under the guise of adjusting her reins, which shifted her hips back against him. Then, as if she hadn't just knocked the air out of his lungs, she casually tilted her head, letting a few strands of hair slip free and brush against his jaw.

He didn't breathe for a full second.

The air between them was too warm, despite the wind.

She shifted again—this time a small roll of her shoulders that pressed her spine flush against his chest. Not for balance but just to *rattle* him.

God, she was *insufferable*.

Caelan's hands tightened on the reins. He'd held the line this long. Kept still. Focused. Disciplined. But if she thought she could keep doing this without consequence—

She leaned again. Slower this time. Lazier. Like she was getting comfortable.

He moved. Splaying his palm on her stomach and pushing her back against him. Just enough to close the space between them. His chest pressed against her back, his breath warm against the side of her neck as he dipped his head.

She froze. *Finally.*

He leaned in—close, too close—his mouth just beside the curve of her jaw, and let his voice slip into something low and quiet and dangerous.

"Are you sure you want to play this game, Tigress?"

He felt her breath hitch—but just slightly. Barely enough to notice.

She didn't turn to look at him. Didn't push him away. Didn't say a word.

Which meant he'd gotten to her, too. *Good.*

Because she'd started this. And now?

He was all in.

Niev was still for a long moment.

And then, just when he thought he might have actually broken through that impossible composure of hers, she turned.

Slowly. Deliberately.

She glanced back over her shoulder, meeting his gaze full-on, eyes dark with amusement and something else—something that turned his insides into molten lava.

And then she gave him the most *wicked* smirk.

"I have *no idea* what you're talking about," she said, voice honey-sweet and positively dripping with mock innocence.

Caelan exhaled slowly through his nose, lips curving into a dry, humorless smile.

She turned back around, perfectly composed, sitting tall in the saddle like nothing had happened—like he hadn't just whispered into her skin or felt the catch in her breath.

And he realized then that she wasn't rattled.

She was *thriving*.

She wanted the game.

And God help him, so did he.

15.
Niev

They slipped through the rear postern first, pressing into the flurry of travelers funneling toward the main gates. Niev kept her face buried in the shadow of her hood, one hand lifting the edge of her cloak to mask her profile.

Caelan mirrored her, his dark cloak pulled high. All around them, the patrols of Commander McCullen—crimson-sashed and hawkish-eyed—scanned the crowd for signs of the Tigress. They moved as part of the tide, bodies brushing past, voices rising in the chaos, until at last they neared the open gates without drawing a single glance.

The gates of Greyhaven creaked open, and midday poured in like floodwater. Noise. Motion. Heat radiating off sun-warmed stone. Sprawling gray walls towered on either side, but inside was a crush of color and sound. Market stalls spilled into the streets. Couriers wove between wagons. Somewhere nearby, a vendor shouted about spiced plums while a child tried to barter with a chicken. It was loud. Chaotic. And exactly what they needed.

Niev kept her hood low, her steps steady. Caelan dismounted first and offered her a hand.

She accepted it. Not because she wanted an excuse to touch him—she assured herself. But because they'd reached some kind of truce and she wasn't one to deny chivalry.

When her boots hit the cobblestones, he gave her the smallest smile and looked away without a word.

She let her gaze track him for half a heartbeat too long. That quiet confidence—damn him—it was growing on her.

Ayda sidled up beside her, muttering as they passed a fruit stand whose owner was threatening two young children already running away clutching injured hands. "If that old woman swings her cane one more time, I swear to God—"

"She's blind," Niev said dryly.

"She *aimed*, Niev."

Niev bit back a smirk. "Let's keep moving."

Behind them, Teagan snorted and caught up, pushing his hood back just far enough to give Caelan a look.

They reached the corner of a busy intersection, where carts bottlenecked and voices overlapped in a noisy tangle. Niev slowed just enough to let the others draw in closer, forming a tight cluster beneath the awnings of a spice merchant's stall.

"This is where we split," she said under her breath. "Ayda and I will find Myria. And get her to work on those new identities."

Caelan raised a brow. "You're sure you can trust her?"

"With my life," Niev said. "But she hates me just enough right now to make this difficult."

"She did say she'd melt your daggers if she ever saw your face again," Teagan mused.

"She says that every time."

Teagan leaned against the edge of a stall, arms folded, looking far too pleased with himself.

"And while you two go charm the forger you *abandoned* mid-job," he said, "Caelan and I will go knock on the Vowbreaker's door."

Niev turned her head slowly, a crease forming between her brows. "Vowbreaker?"

Teagan grinned. "You know. Laughlan Thorne. The one who shattered your three-year vow of romantic abstinence with a single kiss? Ring any bells?"

Ayda coughed into her hand, failing miserably to hide her laugh.

"I hate you," Niev muttered.

"I just think it's impressive," Teagan went on. "It's not every man who can claim to be the Tigress's first—"

"I *swear*—"

"I meant kiss," he said innocently. "Caelan, back me up."

"Absolutely not," Caelan scoffed. "You're on your own, mate."

"I will stab you in front of witnesses." Niev said.

"And they'll all say I had it coming," Teagan grinned.

Caelan rolled his eyes, exhaling slowly—something between a sigh and a smirk.

Niev didn't look at him. Not directly. She didn't *have* to.

She could feel his attention like heat. Quiet and steady, as ever.

"We'll meet at the apartment by midnight," she said, stepping back. "Don't be late."

Teagan gave a mock salute. "Don't worry. We'll have Laughlan wrapped in a bow for you."

Caelan finally spoke. "Let's just get it done."

Their eyes met—hers and his.

He didn't have to say *be careful*. It was there, plain as the set of his jaw.

She dipped her chin once in reply.

Then she turned, tugging her hood lower, and melted into the crowd with Ayda at her side.

The moment they were out of sight, Ayda nudged her elbow. "You're staring at him."

"I was watching our flank."

"Mm-hmm."

Niev didn't respond.

Didn't explain how being close to him made her feel like she could breathe and burn at the same time. Didn't admit that she liked the way he moved—quiet, calculated, steady like the edge of a drawn blade.

Instead, she let the crowd swallow them, thickening the deeper they went.

Greyhaven at midday was nothing like the cold, silent fortress it was at night. This part of the city pulsed with life—merchants shouting prices from behind sun-bleached awnings, children darting through puddles, and the occasional clatter of armored boots that made Niev instinctively draw her hood lower, elbowing Ayda to do the same.

The two women moved fast, slipping through the press of bodies like smoke.

They took the side streets when they could—narrow lanes tucked between mismatched buildings, where peeling shutters and hanging laundry painted a different version of the city.

Niev led them with the ease of someone who knew the layout by heart, one hand brushing the hilt at her hip more from habit than need.

Ayda stuck close, her gait casual, her posture relaxed—but her eyes were sharp, always scanning. They passed two patrols without incident, ducking behind a fish cart for the second one, the stink of brine thick in Niev's throat.

"Forgot how much this place reeks," Ayda muttered, barely audible.

Niev didn't respond. She was watching the alley ahead—narrow enough that most wouldn't give it a second glance, choked with crates, broken furniture, and the lingering scent of hot iron.

"This way."

Ayda followed without question as Niev led her down the alley, their boots quiet on the uneven stones. A rusted metal sign swung overhead, barely legible anymore. Just a faded emblem of thread and flame—Myria's mark.

The back entrance was a narrow wooden door wedged between two broken shutters, hidden beneath a collapsing overhang. Most wouldn't know it was there unless they were looking.

Niev knocked twice, waited, then pushed it open.

She crossed the threshold into the hushed workroom, where the rich scent of old velvet mingled with oil and the faint tang of singed linen. Sunlight slanted through a high window, igniting dust motes that floated like flecks of gold in the air. Beyond her, the steady hum of a lone sewing machine was the only sound.

She paused, gesturing for Ayda to wait by the door, then closed and locked it with a soft click. The silence that followed felt charged—until a voice cut through it, sharp as a tailor's shears. "You have some *damn* nerve."

Niev didn't flinch. She stepped forward instead, toward the row of half-finished robes on mannequins and the thick curtain that separated the back from the storefront.

Myria swept the curtain aside with the dramatic fury only she could pull off.

She wore a deep burgundy work apron over a plain dress, streaked with chalk lines and old thread. Her hair was pinned in its usual chaotic knot, silver needles stuck through like weapons, and her eyes—

The fury in those almond-shaped, onyx eyes could skin a person.

"You vanish for *weeks*," Myria shrieked, stalking forward. "Weeks! After dumping an impossible commission on me. You didn't pick up the robe, you didn't *pay*, and you didn't even have the decency to send a single goddamned message. You could've been dead for all I knew!"

Niev didn't answer right away. She waited, watching as Myria circled around a dress form like a predator deciding which part to bite first.

"I'm not dead," Niev offered, shrugging innocently.

"Oh, well that's *reassuring*," Myria snapped. "Should I alert the guilds? Make a commemorative sash?"

Ayda leaned in from behind Niev, murmuring dryly, "She missed you."

Myria ignored her. "Do you know how hard it is to forge a Librarium seal that passes a real scan? *Do you?* I had to bribe *three* different spellweavers just to get the base glyph. One of them wanted my *spleen.*"

"You still have your spleen," Niev said calmly, eyes narrowing.

"Barely."

Myria jabbed a finger toward a pile of neatly folded dark fabric. "And I finished the robe. Against my better judgment. Sewn with glyph-thread, lined with concealment wards, *and* tailored to your measurements from *memory*, which is frankly a miracle considering how much you fluctuate when you're stressed—"

"Thank you," Niev interrupted before it could spiral further.

That stopped Myria short.

Just for a moment.

She blinked, and then narrowed her eyes, growing immediately suspicious, "Why are you here?"

Niev glanced at Ayda, hesitating for just half a breath, before biting her lip and muttering, "I need your help again."

The room fell into a hush so deep it pressed in on them—long enough for Myria's shoulders to slump. She sighed and dragged a hand down her face, smearing a streak of charcoal across her cheek. "Of course you do."

"I'll pay this time," Niev said.

"You'll pay *double*," Myria snapped. "Upfront."

Niev winced but nodded. "Fine."

Myria's eyes cut over to Ayda for the first time, taking her in with a sweep that was far too thorough to be casual.

Niev knew immediately what the seamstress was seeing. Slim frame. Rolled sleeves. Ink-stained fingertips. A faint pulse of warding magic under the collar.

Myria's brow arched.

Ayda arched one right back. "You're not going to ask who I am?"

Myria smiled, a sharp glint in her eyes. "I know who you are."

"Oh," Ayda blinked. "Well... That's ominous."

Myria turned back toward the shelves, already pulling bolts of fabric and loose scrolls from their cubbies.

"I make it a point to know who's wrapped up in Niev's chaos," she said. "Especially when they're dragging spell residue that smells like shadowroot and moon ash."

"Fair," Ayda replied, then added with mock formality, "For the record, I take zero responsibility for this lady's past nonsense. I always pay what I owe. *On time.*"

Niev blinked dumbfounded. "Traitor," she said, hand to her chest in mock offense.

"Not a traitor," Ayda said, wrapping her arm around the Tigress's shoulders. "Just financially responsible."

"She's as insufferable as they come," Niev muttered toward Myria.

"*She*—" Myria said, looking pointedly at Ayda, "is an upgrade from the usual company you keep."

That earned a genuine laugh out of Ayda.

Niev just sighed. "We need forged identities. Four. Fast. You already have the seal. And I need those tracking spells you bought off all of it. I want them to pass clean."

Myria folded her arms. "You're walking into something bad, aren't you?"

"Yes."

"You're dragging Teagan into it too, aren't you?"

"Yes."

Myria squinted. "That's three—You, Teagan, and the witch. Who's the fourth?"

Niev didn't hesitate. "Caelan Galbraith."

She didn't explain. Didn't ask if Myria had heard of him.

She just looked at Ayda, and Ayda, of course, grinned.

Myria stared for a moment, then let out a sigh like the weight of the entire world had just been dumped into her arms. "I swear, you attract chaos like it's a hobby."

Then she turned on her heel and disappeared into the shelves.

"You've got until sundown," she called over her shoulder. "After that, I'm locking the door, and if you try to come back again with a dramatic entrance and no payment, I *will* strangle you with a cheap loincloth."

"I'll take that as a yes," Niev muttered, following her in.

Behind her, Ayda whispered with a grin, "She's definitely fond of you."

16.
Caelan

"Tell me exactly what you promised him," Caelan said, his voice clipped as they weaved through the thinning crowd.

Teagan was grinning.

That was never a good sign.

"It was a necessary compromise," Teagan replied, gesturing with one hand like he was recounting a tavern tale and not, presumably, orchestrating his own death. "A little detail. A sliver, really."

"You promised him a *what*?"

Teagan held up both palms. "I promised him *flexible terms*."

"That's not an answer."

"It's an answer *you're not going to like*," Teagan admitted cheerfully.

Caelan swore under his breath and kept walking. The sun had long since dipped below the upper ring, painting the stone alleys in dusk-colored shadow. Niev's apartment sat tucked in the old quarter near the canal—unassuming, quiet, and precisely positioned for fast exits in three directions. Typical of her.

"She's going to kill you," Caelan said.

"She'll understand."

"She *won't*."

"She *might*."

"You're smiling like you *want* her to stab you."

"I just think," Teagan said, turning sideways to avoid a stray cart, "that she's going to be more impressed than angry. You know how she gets when someone does something reckless but effective."

"You think this counts as effective?"

Teagan shot him a sideways look. "We got the *Sersha Mara*, didn't we?"

Caelan didn't argue. He couldn't. Laughlan Thorne didn't give away favors, and he certainly didn't rent out his infamous ghost-painted ship to just anyone. They needed him.

Still, Caelan had hoped—*really* hoped—that Niev's past flame would turn out to be some half-drunk, sea-stained brute with a voice like gravel and the manners of a rabid dog. Instead, Laughlan Thorne had been everything Caelan *didn't* want him to be.

Composed. Clean-cut in that roguish, *on-purpose* way. Lean and graceful with a swagger that wasn't put on but earned. His clothes were travel-worn but fine. His eyes were too sharp, his smirk too practiced, and his voice carried that effortless confidence that could convince you to sail into a storm and smile while doing it.

He'd greeted Teagan like an old friend and Caelan like a mild inconvenience.

And the worst part?

Caelan had understood it.

The charisma. The way people leaned in when Thorne spoke. The way he seemed to have gravity around him, like everything bent slightly toward his orbit. Niev had avoided all mention of the captain—but Caelan had always assumed the memory of him was mostly irritation and a bit of bad taste.

Now, he wasn't so sure.

He didn't *ask* if there was still something there.

Didn't need to.

Because even if there wasn't, Thorne would try anyway. He wasn't the type to walk away from a challenge. And Niev? God help him, she was definitely *worth* the challenge.

Caelan had barely spoken during the meeting, letting Teagan do most of the fast talking while he watched. But the longer it went on, the more that quiet turned into clenching tension just behind his ribs.

He told himself it was about the terms of the deal.

He knew it wasn't.

And now, as they rounded the final corner, the noise of the market behind them, the canal glinting dark and narrow between the buildings, that unease hadn't faded. It settled under his skin like a bruise, tender and slow to heal.

Niev's apartment sat above a faded bookshop with no name, a rusted lantern swaying lazily above the door.

As they climbed the stairs, laughter floated through the window above.

Teagan slowed.

"Well that's suspicious."

Caelan arched a brow. "What?"

"That," Teagan said, pointing up. "That's *Niev. Laughing.*"

Caelan blinked, just once. Then he heard it again—faint, unmistakable, a warm breath of amusement layered beneath Ayda's sharper laugh.

"Definitely suspicious," Teagan muttered.

They climbed further up the stairs, and Caelan knocked twice against the painted wood. Footsteps followed. Then the door creaked open—

And he forgot whatever he was about to say.

Niev stood framed in the doorway. Her hair was down—unbound and still damp at the ends, the strands dark and clinging in gentle curves along her collarbone. A few pieces stuck to her neck where the water hadn't yet dried, and he hated how his gaze caught there—how the hollow of her throat seemed suddenly more dangerous than any blade she'd ever drawn.

The scent hit him next. Faint, but impossible to ignore—bergamot and jasmine. It wrapped around him, subtle but insistent, and he could already tell it would linger in his head longer than it should.

She wasn't in her sleek traveling cloak or one of her meticulously tailored outfits either.

Just soft black trousers that clung in all the right places and a loose linen shirt, collar slightly open, sleeves pushed to her elbows like she'd just rolled them up a minute ago.

He knew it was unintentional. She hadn't done any of this *for him*. But it still hit like a punch to the ribs.

And the worst part?

She didn't even seem to notice.

Her gaze flicked between the two of them, unreadable as ever.

"You're late," she said.

Teagan stepped forward, completely unfazed. "But successful."

She narrowed her eyes. "Define successful."

Teagan gave a wide grin. "Thorne said yes."

She crossed her arms. "What did it cost?"

Caelan opened his mouth to answer.

Teagan beat him to it. "He just said we'll cross that bridge when we get there."

She blinked once. Slowly.

Then stepped aside and gestured them in. "Fine."

The door shut softly behind them, and the sound of the city outside faded into a low murmur beneath the floorboards.

Niev's apartment was small—but not cramped. It was clean, quiet, and impossibly lived-in. And *not* at all what Caelan expected.

His eyes swept the space slowly, taking it in.

The bookshelf was the first thing he noticed—tall and crowded to the brim, shelves sagging under the weight of thick tomes and battered spines. Some books were carefully stacked, others shoved in sideways, and there were scrolls wedged between the gaps like afterthoughts. A few had scraps of paper tucked between the pages as makeshift bookmarks. Every inch of it spoke to obsession. Study. *Intention.*

To the left, the kitchen was equally telling. Not pristine, not decorative—but *used.* The kettle still steamed faintly on the iron stove, a few mugs sat drying on the rack, and the faint scent of peppermint tea clung to the air. There were herbs strung neatly by the window. A chipped ceramic jar full of dried fruit sat open on the counter.

The warm familiarity of it made his chest tighten, as if he'd uncovered a secret chamber in a house he thought he'd fully explored. He stopped mid–step, missing Teagan's next question and Ayda's approving hum by the bookshelf, until a sharp poke jabbed him below the ribs. He blinked, looked down, and found Niev's dark eyes studying him.

"You okay there?" she asked, one brow arching.

He opened his mouth. "It smells like—"

"Cookies," Ayda said from across the room, already nosing through the jar on the counter. "Divinely gooey chocolate chip cookies."

Caelan turned his head slowly, wide-eyed.

He stared at Niev.

Cookies?

The ruthless assassin of Greyhaven... *baked?*

Her expression didn't shift. She just shrugged, heading past him toward the kettle. "You were late."

As if that explained everything.

Caelan watched her walk away, still trying to reconcile the image of her flipping a dagger into a man's throat with the scent of baked goods and peppermint.

He was failing.

Spectacularly.

Who the hell was this woman?

He paused in the doorway, letting the last wisp of cookie-scent curl through his thoughts like a taunt. He drew a deep breath, smelled the peppermint in the air, and squared his shoulders. With a quiet nod to himself, he crossed the low-lit room, footsteps soft on the wooden floor, and slipped back into the fold of the group waiting by the hearth.

Everyone had gathered. Ayda lounged in the worn chair by the hearth, fingers tapping a rhythm against her thigh. Teagan leaned back on the couch, boots kicked up on the edge of the table with the smug air of a man pretending his part was already done. Niev stood near the kitchen, arms crossed, hip resting against the counter, watching a dark-haired, porcelain skinned woman he assumed was Myria like a hawk.

Myria, of course, held the center.

She was perched on the edge of a stool, sleeves rolled, spectacles slipping down her nose, several wax-sealed folders stacked beside her. Her hair was pinned up in a chaotic knot.

"You're going in as nobility," she said, flipping open the first folder. "Specifically, a mid-tier delegation from the eastern territories of Rotharym. Not important enough to be watched closely, not obscure enough to raise suspicion."

She turned to Caelan first, handing him a folder with precise calligraphy etched into the corner. "Lord William Dhoran. Reclusive. Inherited wealth. The kind of noble whose name gets you in the door but not in the history books."

Caelan flipped the folder open. The details were impeccable. Land holdings, a falsified lineage, even a forged estate crest.

"You'll play it quiet. You're there to indulge yourself, not impress anyone. And you've brought—" she turned to Niev with a smirk, "—your *lady*."

Niev took her folder without comment.

"Lady Keira Wendlyn," Myria continued. "Former court musician's daughter, elevated by your interest. Too pretty to be respectable, too clever to be ignored."

Teagan whistled. "So she's the scandal."

"She *is* the scandal," Myria replied. "And depending on how things go, possibly the distraction."

Teagan cackled. "I *love* that for you."

Niev shot him a look.

Caelan's gaze flicked to Niev. *Oh, she was a distraction alright.*

Myria moved on to Ayda. "You're her handmaid. Eyva. You've served her since childhood, or whatever excuse you feel like giving, as long as you perfect the art of being invisible. You'll carry the documents, intercept the whispers, and slip whatever you can past the servants. Stay close, listen, and don't use magic unless you want to be dragged out by the throat."

Ayda gave a mock salute. "Yes, ma'am."

Teagan leaned forward eagerly. "And me?"

Myria handed him his folder with a long-suffering sigh. "You're Mathis Dhoran. The disgraced cousin. Terrible with money, worse with women. You gamble, you drink, and you attend elite auctions under the protection of your more responsible relative."

Teagan opened the file and laughed. "You wrote a *whole* backstory for that?"

"I didn't have to," she said, deadpan.

Ayda actually *wheezed*.

Teagan gave her an exaggerated bow. "Rude."

Once the folders were distributed, Myria stepped back from the table. "Your papers, seals, and invitations are all inside. You'll find payment records for the auction and enough fabricated transactions to sell the illusion."

She pulled a scroll from her satchel and unrolled it.

The map of Port Orynth sprawled across the table — etched in faded ink and annotations that looked like they were written in at least four different handwritings. Streets, landmarks, estate placements... and beneath it, a second layer. Shadowed lines. Arrows. Passage markers.

The Hollow Quarter.

Myria looked up at Niev, who stepped forward, planting her palms on either side of the map.

And when she spoke, her voice was calm. Measured. *Commanding.*

"This is the estate," she said, tapping a square block etched with heavy ink near the marble district. "It was once owned by Chancellor Esvaren. Now it's a private auction house with a veiled patron and rotating guards. The auction will be held in the lower hall, here."

Caelan didn't need to glance at the others to know they were all watching her the same way he was. She moved with total control. A woman who didn't just expect others to follow—she *calculated* how to make them do it.

She traced a circular chamber marked beneath the estate with her fingertip.

"The children are kept in cells two levels below. They're moved through a ventilation tunnel into the catacombs during shipment. That's where we extract."

Her hand moved again—across the parchment, toward the narrow line leading out of the estate. "A drain tunnel leads to a locked gate here.

The guard rotations are inconsistent, but this passage is unmonitored. From there, it's half a mile through the Hollow Quarter. Tight turns. No light. Two checkpoints. If we get past those, we reach the sea caverns."

Caelan's gaze locked on the point she indicated. He'd seen this on the ledger pages before—the outline, the trail of ink between payments. But now, hearing it from her lips, seeing the way she dissected it like a surgeon, it struck differently.

He watched her eyes as she looked up, catching each of them in turn.

There was no fear there. Just steely determination.

"The *Sersha Mara* will be waiting offshore. If we miss the extraction window, we don't get another one. There won't be time for second tries."

Teagan let out a low whistle. "This is your idea of a good plan?"

"It's the only plan we've got," Niev said. "We don't get to choose the battlefield. Only how we move on it."

Caelan watched the line of her jaw. She didn't blink. Didn't flinch.

He'd fought beside soldiers, rebels, mercenaries—but none of them could hold a room like she did. She didn't just believe the plan would work. She *needed* it to.

He didn't know what terrified him more—the fact that she'd make this plan work, or that she'd get those children out no matter the price she had to pay.

Because he could see it on her face—she didn't fully expect to make it out alive. All that mattered to her now was how many she could save before the walls came down.

And that, more than anything, scared the living shit out of him.

Ayda studied the map, brow furrowed. "What about the wards?"

"They're concentrated around the main estate and auction hall," Niev replied. "We just need to avoid using any magic. If you cast, you alert the whole damn sector, and we're as good as dead. Which means every move from the moment we enter has to be clean."

When she finished, she straightened and looked around the room. "We leave in the morning. So, try to get some sleep. You'll need it."

Ayda stretched her arms over her head. "So... cookies, anyone?"

Caelan didn't answer. He was still watching Niev.

Still thinking about the fact that this woman who just mapped an impossible rescue with a steady hand and a plan for every turn—had baked cookies earlier because they were late.

And somehow, *both versions* of her felt real.

And no matter how much he told himself to keep a line between them—

She made him forget there was supposed to be one at all.

17.
Niev

They rode for nearly two days, threading south through Breyvia's wide wheat fields—golden waves that lapped at their stirrups in the early light, and skirting the brackish lagoons of Port Veyne where fishing skiffs drifted at anchor. At dusk on the third evening they reached the foot of the Stoneridge Mountains, its jagged peaks blotting out the sky.

There, hidden in a thicket of yew, they found the old smugglers' tunnel—an arched passage hewn into the rock long ago, damp and echoing with distant drips. Torches lit, they spurred their horses inside, the cold stone walls closing in until at last they emerged on the far side into Arenthia's rolling coastal hills.

By dawn, Port Orynth unfolded before them like a mirage of marble and smoke.

Set against the jagged cliffs that bled into the Silver Bay, the city shimmered in the dying light—its pristine facades and domed estates catching the sunset like polished bone. Gilded gates and fluted columns gave it the look of something divine, untouched. But Niev knew better.

This was a city built for performance. Draped in wealth. Masked in perfection.

And beneath it—beneath the alabaster courtyards and perfumed terraces—was something ancient and rotting. A hunger. A network of tunnels carved through the earth like veins through flesh, pulsing with secrets the nobility paid handsomely to ignore.

The Hollow Quarter.

It was down there that the true heart of Port Orynth beat.

And it was down there that the children were waiting.

They rode in through the eastern gate under the guise of privilege—noble names stitched into their clothing, forged papers tucked into velvet satchels, and the kind of practiced indifference that passed for wealth.

It worked. *Of course it did.*

This city didn't care who you were—only how much gold you carried and how good you were at pretending.

By the time they reached the inn on the edge of the noble quarter, the sun had sunk beneath the cliffs and the sea winds had turned sharp and briny. The innkeeper barely looked at them, more interested in the seal on Caelan's ring than any conversation.

One night. That was all they needed.

One night to settle in and become someone else.

They climbed the stairs two at a time, the worn stone steps leading them to a suite tucked into the corner of the third floor. High enough to watch the sea, quiet enough to avoid attention. The air inside was thick with incense and polished wood. Velvet drapes muffled the wind. The golden light of dusk spilled across the floor like spilt oil.

Niev closed the door behind them with a quiet click.

Ayda was already shrugging off her cloak, unceremoniously dropping it across the chaise as she kicked off her boots.

"Heavens," she muttered, rubbing at her calves. "Remind me never to agree to travel as a servant again. I think that horse hated me on purpose."

"You *did* tell it it had an unfortunate face," Niev said dryly, crossing to the wardrobe.

"It did," Ayda grumbled.

Niev's fingers floated a hair's breadth from the wardrobe door before she let gravity pull it open and hung the gown Myria had tailored for her.

Later, under the hiss of the shower, she scrubbed the road's dust and sweat from her skin until her muscles protested. When she stepped out, towel-wrapped, the silence of the room felt thick, expectant.

She eased the crimson chiffon from its wrappings and let it unfold across the bed, the fabric catching the dying light and gleaming like captured sunset. Each fold shimmered; the deep V of the neckline whispered of daring, the thigh-high slit a silent challenge. Niev pressed her palm to the embroidered surface—it felt as sharp as diamonds, cold at first, then warm under her skin.

Ayda drifted forward, boots soft on the rug. The flicker of lamplight in her eyes sharpened into a smirk of approval. "You're going to break hearts in that."

Niev's lips quirked as she stepped behind the folding screen, gown in hand. Her voice drifted through. "That's not what I'm here to break."

When she stepped free from behind the folding screen, the dress seemed to come alive around her. The silk pooled at her feet and then clung—magnetic—to every curve, as if it had been spun for her alone. She lifted her arms, letting the long sleeves settle like liquid fire down her wrists, and felt a thrill the delightful weight of luxury, each bead and embroidered vine kissing her skin like a whispered promise.

Niev ran a fingertip along the carved pattern at her hip, marveling at how something so soft could feel like armor. A ruthless assassin, yes—but tonight, she was also a woman draped in molten ruby, equal parts danger and desire, and she savored it.

She had to give it to Myria—that woman could weave magic into fabric and turn her wildest dreams into reality.

There was a moment of quiet as Ayda sank onto the bed, her eyes tracking Niev with a heavy sigh.

"I know why this matters," she said softly. "I do. How could it not? But... Why does it feel so *personal* to you? Why does it feel like it's *eating* you up?"

Niev didn't answer right away, just unwrapped the jewelry quietly. She lifted the delicate golden hoops—each one crowned with a glinting ruby—and with a final steadying breath, let the slender chain of the plunging necklace fall between her breasts, its filigreed pendant nestled at her heart like a whispered promise.

Then, her voice almost a whisper, she said, "Because I was one of them."

Ayda who had slipped into her celadon gown with practiced efficiency and tugged the silk fabric over her head, stood up straighter.

Niev took a deep breath and continued, "My parents were killed when I was fourteen," she said. "My brother too. I don't even remember how many men there were. Just... blood. Everywhere."

Ayda said nothing as she cinched the faded bodice tight at her waist, and smoothed the skirt until it hung evenly.

"I was dragged away before the bodies stopped bleeding. They didn't ask who I was. They didn't *care*. They took me away from my home in Arenthia. Sold me within the week."

She turned then, her gaze steady but unreadable.

"They brought me to Solhaven. To the Silk Lotus."

Ayda's breath caught.

Niev nodded. "Yes. *The* Silk Lotus."

Ayda slowly tied her hair back with a silver pin, then fastened the simple onyx slippers at her heels, her voice barely above a whisper. "But that place is—"

"Famous. Expensive. Untouchable. I know." Niev's lips curved upward without warmth. "They dressed me like a doll. Taught me to pour wine and play the lute. Trained me to smile on command."

As Ayda reached for the chipped pewter mirror on the dresser, she glanced up at Niev.

"And then, they sent in my first client," the Tigress continued. "Some bloated merchant from the coast with too many rings and too little restraint."

Niev's eyes were far away now, but her voice remained steady.

"His hand barely grabbed me. But I guess it was enough for all the grief, fear, and anger I'd bottled up to come pouring out. I shifted. I don't even remember choosing to. I just... reacted. Clawed half his face off before they were able to take me off of him."

Ayda turned around slowly, her expression torn between horror and awe.

"I don't know what Madame Irene would've done to me if it wasn't for Saeris," Niev said, adjusting one of the cuffs at her wrist. Her voice dipped slightly—not hesitant, but softer.

"She was in the room. Watching from the shadowed alcove, like she always did. I hadn't even noticed her. Not until the blood hit the floor and everyone else screamed."

She paused, hands stilling at her waist.

"She didn't scream."

Niev looked over at Ayda, something unreadable flickering behind her eyes.

"She just stepped forward. Looked me straight in the eye. Calm as anything. Like I wasn't a half-starved, feral child covered in someone's blood. And then she told Irene she'd take me. Paid three times my price and walked me out that same night."

Ayda blinked, her voice quiet. "She bought you."

"She *saved* me," Niev said. And her voice didn't waver—but something in it cracked just slightly. "She could've let me rot in that brothel. Let them chain me up as the filthiest of men had their way with me. But she didn't. She pulled me out, trained me, fed me, protected me. When no one else in the world had use for a half-wild girl with too many teeth and too much rage—*she* did."

She picked up her mask, turned it over in her hands.

"I know what she is," she added, after a long moment. "Saeris Morraine is ruthless. Cold. Cunning. She uses people. She's used *me*."

Niev's lips pressed into a thin line.

"But she also taught me to use myself."

She set the mask down and turned.

"And if she hadn't, I'd have killed myself in that brothel."

Ayda stepped closer, her voice low. "You love her."

"She *protected* me. Better than my mother ever could," Niev said, her voice strained. "Saeris is the closest thing to family I've had in years. She turned me into something no one could ever cage again. And I'll never stop being thankful for that. No matter how cruel she can be."

She looked down, smoothing the front of the gown.

Ayda crossed the room in two strides and wrapped her arms around her.

Niev froze.

But after what felt like forever, she let herself be held.

She let her friend, because that's what Ayda had become, her *friend*, hold her like something worthy of protection.

When Ayda pulled back, her voice was low and fierce. "We're going to end this. Every last one of them."

Niev nodded, her throat bobbing, eyes glistening with tears.

Then turned to the mirror.

The woman who looked back at her was sculpted in blood and silk. Her gown draped like molten flame, gold shimmering at her throat. Her hair, half-pinned and curled just so, framed her face like a crown. Her lips were painted a deep, wicked red.

Finally, Niev picked up a thin vial of scented oil—bergamot, jasmine, a hint of pink pepper, and dabbed it along the curve of her throat.

"You look like vengeance," Ayda whispered.

Niev met her gaze in the mirror. "Good."

Let them look. Let them want. Let them underestimate her.

Because by the time they realized what she truly was—it would already be too late.

18.
Caelan

The hallway outside their suite was dim, lit only by the soft amber glow of a single wall sconce. Caelan adjusted the cuffs of his tailored coat, black with gold trim, the fabric so fine it itched. Myria had done a brilliant job, and he *hated* it.

It felt wrong, all of it—clean seams, polished boots, jeweled rings that didn't belong to him. But this was the role. This was the face they needed the world to see.

Lord William Dhoran. Wealthy, aloof, indulgent. A man who moved through the world like nothing could touch him.

He inhaled, letting the mask settle across his features, and stepped toward the suite door—only to freeze the moment it swung open.

Caelan's breath caught the instant she stepped into the sconce's glow. The gown's blood-red fabric clung to every swell of her hips, tracing the gentle curve of her waist before splitting high along her thigh in a daring slash that left her leg exposed in all its bronzed, flawless glory. Its bared décolletage plunged between her breasts in a deadly V. Her lips—painted the same rich red as her dress—parted in a slow, knowing smile, and Caelan felt heat bloom through his chest like wildfire.

At her throat, a slender chain of beaten gold dipped low, the pendant brushing the hollow of her cleavage like a promise of fire.

Every inch of her was designed to lure him in—the way her hair cascaded over one bare shoulder, the arch of her neck tipped back just so, the subtle dip of her gaze that dared him closer.

By the time she closed the distance between doorway and stone floor, Caelan's throat was parched. Each breath she drew filled the corridor with jasmine and bergamot, weaving around him until his world narrowed to the subtle rise and fall of her chest, craving her touch.

But despite all of this, it was her eyes that undid him.

Dark and burning, framed by lashes so long and precise they looked like they'd been sculpted. Lined just enough to make you notice the shape of them—how they tilted up ever so slightly at the corners, how they narrowed like a challenge when they landed on you.

She was devastating.

Caelan's gaze lingered too long.

He knew it. Knew he should look away—say something dry, something cool to reset the air between them. But the words didn't come.

He just stood there, unable to tear his eyes from the curve of her lips, the subtle gleam of her skin in the lantern light, the steady, molten fire in her gaze.

And then, before he could stop himself—

"You're exquisite," he said.

The words landed softer than he meant them to. Too bare. Too *true*.

Niev stilled.

Her eyes searched his face, something sharp flashing beneath the surface—surprise, maybe. Or something that ran deeper. Her lips parted, just slightly, as if she hadn't expected the honesty. Not from him. Not *now*.

And then—her smile changed.

It deepened. *Real*. Slow. Dangerous.

Because she knew exactly what had just happened.

He hadn't said it as part of the game.

He hadn't said it like a man playing pretend.

He'd said it like someone who was already *gone*.

And she *felt it*.

She stepped closer, closing the last inch between them. Her fingers rested against his chest, just lightly, as if to remind him she could feel his heartbeat, and knew exactly what it meant.

"Careful, my lord," she said, voice silk and smoke. "You're starting to sound sincere."

Caelan swallowed hard. "I am."

Her brows lifted behind the mask. And a wild laugh escaped her.

Caelan's throat worked once before his voice caught up.

"You're going to destroy everyone in that room."

"Including you?" Niev's voice dipped into a teasing purr behind the mask, her eyes glittering with mischief.

Caelan felt a rush of heat bloom in his chest, bright and intoxicating. Every nerve tipped toward her, his breath catching as he stared at the curve of her jaw, the glint of ruby at her earlobe. "Especially me," he admitted, voice low.

"Good," she said, smirking beneath the mask. "That's the plan."

The electric spark between them lingered in the air long after her laugh died away. Caelan's pulse thrummed like a war drum, as he fought the instinctive urge to slide his hand around her waist, pull her back into that room and devour every inch of her in the half-light—

What the hell was wrong with him?

He clenched his teeth, furious at himself for almost losing control over the flaring heat in his veins. This was no private tryst but a deadly mission. Now was *not* the time to get distracted. He dropped his hand, which had unconsciously slid to her hip, and took a measured breath, his pulse roaring in his ears until only purpose remained.

With one last glance—ice in his veins, steel in his gaze—he slipped his arm through hers, and together they descended the stairs, Ayda and Teagan already waiting by the carriage outside. Ayda looked elegant in a simple celadon gown, quiet and composed, her expression already locked into her role. Teagan looked wildly pleased with himself, draped in a deep emerald coat that shimmered with every movement.

"You're late," he said, but his grin slipped the moment he saw Niev. "Dragon's teeth. You look like sin."

"Careful, *Mathis*," Niev purred, her voice velvet. "I am your cousin's for the night."

Ayda bit back a laugh. Caelan swore Teagan blushed.

They stepped into the carriage without another word, doors shut, wheels turning. Outside, the city was glowing—lanterns casting golden halos through the fog as they made their way toward the marble district.

Caelan sat across from Niev, and for what felt like the hundredth time in her presence, couldn't bring himself to speak.

She didn't look at him. But she didn't need to.

He felt her like gravity—quiet and inescapable. A pull beneath his skin.

The carriage wheels hummed over cobbled stone, the rhythmic clatter barely audible above the rustle of silks and the occasional creak of leather. Outside, the city passed in soft, flickering glimpses. Gas lamps stretched like constellations across the boulevards, golden halos bleeding into mist. Nobles wandered beneath the archways, laughter and music drifting on the sea breeze.

But even the beauty of it—the marbled walls, the manicured trees, the scent of salt and citrus in the air—felt wrong. Too clean. Too perfect.

This city was a gilded tomb.

And somewhere beneath their feet, behind stone and lock and coin, children were being hidden. Bartered. Caged.

Caelan's jaw tightened.

He shifted his gaze to the others.

Ayda sat near the window, her mask in place, her profile calm—but he could see the tension in her hands, the way her fingers flexed against her skirts. Teagan lounged with theatrical ease beside her, but even he wasn't fidgeting. That told Caelan everything.

He looked back to Niev.

She was still as a statue, back straight, one hand resting on the edge of the window. Her gown shimmered faintly in the lantern light, every inch of her a portrait of indulgence and seduction. But beneath the surface, he could feel it—the tight coil of tension. The sheer control it took for her to sit still like that.

He wasn't sure which part undid him more—the performance, or the fact that she could wear it so convincingly and still remain herself underneath.

Focus, he told himself. *Stay sharp.*

But his thoughts churned, restless.

He kept seeing flashes of what could go wrong—guards blocking their path, Ayda forced to break her silence and triggering a ward, Niev caught in a trap meant for someone else. Or worse—her walking headlong into danger, not because she didn't know better, but because she *knew exactly what she was risking*.

She wasn't just committed. She was ready to die for this.

And he didn't know what scared him more—that she might not survive...

Or that if it came down to it, *he'd choose to save her* over the mission.

His eyes drifted back to her face. Or what little he could see of it.

Her lashes were long, framing eyes like smoke and amber—eyes that assessed you. Stripped you bare. Even behind the mask, they held that same impossible clarity.

Her lips were still painted that wicked, ruined red. The curve of them unreadable. She hadn't spoken since the carriage began moving. Hadn't teased him. Hadn't even glanced his way.

And yet...

She *felt* him watching.

He was sure of it.

Every second, every breath between them hung heavy, charged.

He wanted to speak. To say something—anything—that might sever the thread winding tighter through his chest. But nothing came.

Because this wasn't just lust anymore.

This was more than that.

And it was starting to scare the hell out of him.

The carriage rounded the final bend.

Through the narrow window, the Esvaren Estate began to rise into view.

A towering structure of curved stone and pale marble, bathed in the warm glow of hundreds of suspended lanterns. The gate was wrought iron and gold, curling into delicate shapes that looked like ivy, like smoke, like a trap waiting to snap shut. Masked guests swept through the main entrance in glittering gowns and embroidered cloaks, their laughter too high, too bright.

Music spilled from the open windows—strings and piano and something slower beneath it, darker.

The masquerade was already in full bloom.

The carriage slowed.

Caelan inhaled through his nose, held it. Exhaled.

Niev finally turned her head, just slightly.

Her eyes met his. And for the briefest heartbeat, there was nothing between them but heat and everything unsaid. Then she spoke, soft and poised.

"Well?" she murmured. "Ready to pretend you *own* me?"

Her voice was velvet. But the challenge in it was unmistakable.

Caelan leaned forward, fingers closing around hers with a care that betrayed everything he was trying to hide. His voice came out barely a whisper, only for her to hear.

"I'm not pretending anything."

Something shifted in her expression and her lips curved, slow and wide, into the kind of smile that made it very, very hard to think.

The carriage came to a stop.

The door opened.

And together, hand in hand, they stepped out into the glittering den of vipers.

❋　❋　❋

The gates yawned open on silent hinges, and Caelan stepped into the belly of the beast with Niev on his arm.

The guards at the gate bowed as they approached, eyes scanning the forged seal on his ring, then dipping toward Niev with barely restrained curiosity.

She moved like she belonged here. Like the Esvaren Estate had been built just to frame her silhouette in candlelight. Heads turned before they even reached the steps, gazes lingering, drawn in like moths.

So much for not drawing attention, Caelan thought.

Warm light spilled across the marble threshold, painting gold over their joined hands as they crossed into the Esvaren Estate. The scent of honeyed wine, polished wood, and some kind of rare orchid oil hit him immediately—sweet and cloying, enough to make his stomach knot.

Inside, the ballroom stretched wide and gleaming, a domed cathedral of excess.

Everything glimmered. The floors were veined marble in black and ivory, polished so clean they reflected the masks of the guests above them like ghosts. Crystal chandeliers swayed slightly from the high-arched ceiling, casting fractals of light across satin and silk. Gold leaf lined the edges of the pillars. Strings of soft music drifted from an elevated quartet tucked into an alcove, the notes floating like perfume.

And everywhere, nobles danced and laughed and drank as if the world outside didn't exist.

Caelan's skin crawled.

Because this—this lavish display of curated wealth and manufactured delight—was the reward. This is what you bought when you sold lives. When you traded in flesh and innocence and the silent screams of children in chains.

He kept his expression smooth. Empty. His fingers tightened on Niev's hip as they moved further in, a subtle pressure only she would notice.

But inside, the weight of the mission pressed harder.

A servant passed with a silver tray. Another offered a goblet of sparkling wine. Caelan declined both with the faintest shake of his head.

To his right, Teagan peeled off with a grin and a twirl, already sinking into his role as the indulgent cousin. His emerald coat shimmered as he swept into the crowd, exchanging compliments and empty praise like he'd been raised in this world.

On Caelan's left, Ayda gave him the briefest of nods, then turned and slipped down a side corridor without a word. She moved like smoke— soft, unnoticed.

Now it was just the two of them.

She moved beside him with that same devastating grace—gown shifting like blood with every step, her mask catching the chandelier light in flashes of gold. Her hand still rested on his arm, light but steady.

He kept glancing at her, unable to stop his eyes from roaming all over her.

And she caught him.

Of course she did.

A flick of her eyes. A curve of her lips. A silent reminder to *focus*.

Niev leaned toward Caelan, just enough for him to feel the whisper of her breath against his neck.

"Eyes on the stairs," she said. "Left corner. The host just arrived."

Caelan didn't glance immediately—he followed her cue, turned casually toward the wine table, and caught the man in question from the edge of his vision.

Tall. Masked in white and silver. Robes tailored to within an inch of opulence.

But it wasn't the clothing that made Caelan's spine stiffen—it was the signet ring on the man's finger. A deep obsidian stone carved with an eight-pointed sun.

Caelan had seen that ring before.

Etched in ink on one of the ledgers. Next to codes. Names. *Lot numbers.*

Brennan Darrow, head of the slave traders network.

The man was laughing at something, his voice smooth and slow. He leaned in toward a woman with a sapphire feathered mask, brushing his lips over her knuckles.

Brennan Darrow moved like he owned the air. He stood at the base of the grand staircase, a circle of simpering nobles orbiting him as if his presence granted them relevance. His mask was silver, sharp along the cheekbones, and his black coat shimmered faintly with silver thread. Polished. Imposing. Effortlessly cruel.

Caelan didn't let his eyes linger long. Just enough to note the direction of Darrow's gaze, the subtle flicks of his fingers when guards passed—an unspoken code, perhaps. The way every servant near him moved with stiff, calculated silence. *Too stiff.*

He and Niev circled the edges of the ballroom, always close enough to watch, never enough to draw attention.

To anyone else, they looked exactly as they were meant to—an indulgent noble and his impossibly beautiful consort, gliding through the crowd like they owned it. Their pace was unhurried, their posture loose, easy. Every movement was a performance.

But beneath the surface, tension wound tighter with every step.

Caelan could feel the burn of her arm against his. The heat of her body through the layers of fabric. Every time her gown brushed his leg—chiffon against wool—it sent a flicker of awareness through him, hot and sharp. Deliberate or not, it was maddening.

Each step closer to Darrow's position forced them to lean deeper into the charade. Heads tilted. Fingers grazed. His hand slipped around her waist more than once.

At one point, Caelan dipped his head low, lips near her ear.

"Bergamot," he murmured, the scent curling around her skin. "Jasmine too. But there's something else..."

Niev blinked, caught off guard. Her breath hitched.

He tilted his head, drawing in slowly like he was cataloging it, committing it to memory. "Tell me," he murmured, "What is it?"

She turned her head toward him, the faintest edge of surprise slipping through the mask of her expression.

"Pink pepper," she whispered, her eyes fixed on his lips.

Caelan smiled satisfyingly. "You smell like danger."

Her breath left her in a laugh—soft, unguarded, almost flustered.

It was the most honest thing she'd given him all night.

Her palm slid up his chest, fingers brushing over the buttons of his coat, resting just above his heart.

Like lovers sharing secrets.

The touch was brief. But he felt it long after she let go, a phantom imprint that refused to fade. His chest was still burning where her hand had been, and he swore her perfume was stronger now.

She smiled at a passing guest, bright and warm behind the mask, voice syrup-sweet.

Then, without looking at him, she murmured, "You could at least *pretend* you're enjoying yourself."

Caelan hummed low under his breath. "I thought I was doing quite well."

"No." Her tone was silk with a bite. "You're stiff. Guarded. Not very convincing for a man parading his mistress through a room full of nobles."

He barked a laugh. "*Stiff* is exactly what I'm trying to avoid being."

She froze.

Not visibly—not in a way anyone else would catch—but he felt the subtle shift in her body. The slight hitch in her breath. The pink that bloomed along her throat and rose beneath the edge of her mask.

It was glorious.

He leaned in a fraction, lowering his voice just for her. "What would you suggest I do?"

She tilted her head slightly, eyes still forward, mask gleaming in the candlelight. "Touch me like you mean it. Look at me like I'm yours."

Caelan drew in a sharp breath, his eyes finding hers.

Gently, deliberately, he pressed his hand to the small of her back and guided her a step away from the crowd. Another. Then turned her—slow, smooth—until her back met one of the marble columns lining the edge of the ballroom.

His palm skimmed from the curve of her waist, up her ribs, then slipped down again—fingers trailing along the slit of her gown. Brushing her bare skin.

Niev stilled, but didn't stop him. Her lashes lowered. Her breath hitched—so slight it could have been mistaken for nothing.

Except he was watching too closely to miss it.

Caelan leaned in, voice a whisper against the shell of her ear. "Better?"

Her lips curved. "Getting there."

His hand slid beneath the crimson fabric, the cool silk giving way to warm skin as he traced a slow, deliberate path up the inside of her thigh. Niev's breath hitched; she pressed closer, the hollow of her waist arching into his palm.

"I think you're enjoying this," he murmured, voice husky with something that wasn't entirely pretense.

Niev tilted her chin, her mouth just inches from his now. "I think *you're* forgetting we're supposed to be acting."

He stared at her—the red of her lips. The rise and fall of her chest. The way her fingers had curled into his shirt like she needed something to hold onto.

"I haven't forgotten," he murmured.

His eyes dropped to her mouth—lush and stained ruby—before drifting back to those dark, unreadable eyes. "I'm just... *deeply committed*."

A soft exhale escaped her, a sound so intimate it might have been a secret between them.

Before he could press her further—before he could say or do the next thing that might've pulled them past the point of pretending—they heard it.

Brennan Darrow's voice. Close. Too close.

Caelan didn't turn immediately. Just shifted enough to catch the sound without drawing attention.

"...Go check my office," Darrow was saying to one of his guards. "I can't find the key on me. Must've left it out on the desk. I want it locked up. Immediately."

Caelan froze. His gaze snapping to Niev.

Ayda.

Caelan's heart kicked hard in his chest. She had stolen that key off him, and was supposed to be in that office—*right now*—stealing the prison keys.

If the guard got there first—

"What do we do?" he asked under his breath, voice low, clipped. "If she's caught, everything goes to shit and she's as good as dead! We can't reach her in time."

Niev didn't blink.

She looked past him, toward the center of the ballroom, her expression smooth as ice—calm and calculating even as the fire burned behind her eyes.

And then her jaw set.

"Leave it to me," she said.

He grabbed her wrist lightly. "Niev—"

But she was already gone.

She moved with the kind of poise that belonged to royalty—gown sweeping, mask glowing, her presence cutting through the room like a knife through silk. Every step she took turned heads. Every glance she gave dragged eyes to her.

And then—she stopped. Right beneath the chandelier.

A servant carrying a tray passed between them, and when the crowd cleared—

The Tigress started singing.

The first note unfurled like velvet—low, smooth, arresting.

And the room stilled.

Conversation died mid-laugh. Glasses froze mid-air, and the ballroom stilled around her, heads turning with practiced curiosity... then awe.

The music—previously a pleasant hum beneath conversation— shifted seamlessly to follow her lead. The string quartet adjusted their tempo, their melody bending instinctively around the raw beauty of her voice.

Caelan couldn't move. No one could.

Her voice sounded like a spell. There was something unnatural in it— *not* inhuman, but otherworldly. Like her voice didn't come from her throat, but from somewhere deeper. Somewhere older.

It wrapped around the room. Slipped beneath ribs. Tugged at memory, at ache, at longing.

Somewhere behind him, a noble exhaled audibly. Another clutched the stem of his glass like he'd forgotten how to drink.

Niev sang, and the room *worshipped* her.

Her voice was low at first—quiet, full of ache and emotion—like a wound stitched shut too tightly. Like someone who had learned to carry heartbreak so elegantly, the world mistook it for poise.

She sang of masks.

Of being seen, but never *known*.

Of how easy it was for others to make her into a monster, an object, a weapon—when they hadn't seen the nights she bled, the cost of every sharp edge she wore.

And God, it wasn't just a distraction anymore.

It was a confession wrapped in velvet.

Every noble in the room was watching her.

But *he* was the only one who heard what she *wasn't* saying.

She sang of love too—deep, reckless, bone-deep love she kept hidden beneath silence and silk. Love that wasn't neat or beautiful or easy. Love that burned.

And Caelan suddenly felt as if the ground beneath him had gone soft. Like he was hearing something he wasn't supposed to. Like she'd peeled herself open with a single note and showed him everything she tried to keep buried.

Because it wasn't about them—not the nobles. Not the guards. Not even Brennan Darrow, who now stood slack-jawed, visibly entranced, his wine forgotten in his hand.

It was about her.

She was *everything*. And Caelan was dying to touch her. *Anchor* her. Make her stop singing just long enough to tell her she wasn't what they said. That he *did* see her. That he wasn't looking at a mask anymore.

He was looking at Niev.

And he was already too far gone.

When she hit the high note—clear, aching, impossibly pure—he felt it like a thread pulled tight across his chest.

And when she finally let it go, silence dropped like a curtain. It stretched for what felt like forever.

Then the room exploded into applause. Scattered at first. Then surging. Roaring.

But Caelan still hadn't moved.

The guard had stopped.

Darrow was clapping now too, a tight smile on his face. Entranced. Curious. *Still.*

Caelan's pulse slowly began to ease.

Ayda had time.

Niev had bought it.

And in the middle of the glittering, breathless ballroom, with gold above her and red crystals clinging to her like flame—

She bowed her head just slightly.

Then turned, with the full weight of the crowd's attention trailing behind her, and walked straight back toward him.

Caelan stepped forward without thinking, hand out, ready to catch her.

Her fingers slid into his.

Still warm.

Still steady.

Still hers.

"Next time," she murmured, breath brushing his jaw, "*believe me* when I say I've got it handled."

He stared at her.

And finally—he smiled.

But the moment Niev returned to his side, the wolves came sniffing.

Guests drifted toward them like moths to flame, their masks unable to hide wide eyes and thinly veiled curiosity. Nobles of every stripe—young, old, bored, or drunk—angled for her attention like it was oxygen.

"She sings like an exquisite nightingale," one older lord murmured, clutching his wine as if he'd just seen a miracle.

A woman in silver silk leaned in toward Caelan, laughing behind her fan. "Where on the map do you *find* women like that, Lord Dhoran? Or did you have to build her from magic and sin?"

Caelan gave her a polite smile that didn't quite reach his eyes. "Trade secret, I'm afraid."

Another man—bolder, already two glasses too deep—clapped Caelan on the shoulder. "If you ever tire of her," he slurred, "I'd pay dearly for just a night—"

Caelan's hand slid casually to the small of Niev's back, his tone still easy. "*Unfortunately*, I don't share well."

There was laughter, but something in his eyes must've landed, because the drunk stumbled backward with a muttered apology and a sudden interest in the buffet.

More followed. A small circle formed—ladies with glittering fans, lords with smirking mouths. All with praise on their tongues.

Niev smiled, dipped her head in graceful acknowledgment, all quiet charm and practiced demureness.

But Caelan could feel it—the heat simmering just beneath her skin. Her body still humming from the performance. Her pulse under his fingers.

"Truly," a golden-masked gentleman said, "you must share her. Just one song. Let her come sing at my mansion, just for one night."

"I'm afraid I don't share," Caelan said, tone cool and final. "Not my wine. Not my coin. And definitely not my woman."

That drew a few scandalized gasps and indulgent chuckles. The crowd began to drift away, most of them content with admiration from a distance.

Niev's smirk was wicked as she leaned into him. "You're enjoying this far too much."

"Watching the world fall at your feet?" Caelan said. "I fint it endlessly entertaining."

But his amusement flickered when a young woman in seafoam green approached, eyes locked shamelessly on *him*.

"Well," she purred, tapping his arm with a lace-gloved finger, "I must say, you're the most well-behaved man I've seen tonight. Not even a glance for anyone else."

She looked pointedly at Niev. "What a lucky lady you are."

Before Caelan could respond, Niev shifted in closer, threading her arm more firmly through his, and pushing that simpering woman's hand away.

"Oh, I am," Her smile was honeyed death. "And he glances plenty, to be fair, just in the *right* direction." she said, pulling his chin up so he was looking her square in the eye.

The woman blinked, faltered, and curtsied herself right back into the crowd.

Caelan grinned, teeth flashing as he leaned toward Niev's ear. "Was that jealousy, *Tigress*?"

She tilted her head primly. "You're mine until this assignment ends. And I don't like sharing either. So, you best remember that."

"Mm... Lucky me."

But then—before he could say anything more—the air shifted.

The sound of laughter faded beneath the low murmur of attention refocusing. A ripple passed through the guests like wind through tall grass.

Darrow was approaching with a confidence that made Caelan's fingers tighten against Niev's waist.

The man didn't look at anyone else.

Only *her*.

He stepped into their space with an oil-slick smile and no invitation, one hand already reaching for hers, brushing his lips for a beat too long on the back of her knuckles.

Caelan's blood turned to ice as he felt Niev's whole body stiffen beside him—shoulders drawn tight, spine rigid, her fingers curling reflexively around his arm.

It was the first time he'd seen the Tigress scared.

As Caelan's arm locked across her stomach, a possessive, protective hold that looked casual, Darrow raised a brow. Amused.

"Apologies my lord," Caelan said smoothly, lips near Niev's ear as he spoke, but his eyes locked on Darrow. "But I was just about to take my lady dancing."

He smiled. Sharp. Unblinking.

There was a long pause.

Then Darrow inclined his head, slow and elegant. "Of course. I wouldn't dream of intruding."

And then he turned, vanishing once more into the crowd.

Caelan didn't loosen his grip as he moved her towards the rhythm of the ballroom, gliding into the current of dancers.

She didn't resist. Her hand slid into his without a word.

The music swelled—something slow, something aching, and they moved as if they'd done it a thousand times before.

He held her close. Closer than etiquette allowed. One hand settled at the small of her back, his thumb beginning to trace soft, deliberate circles through her dress.

She was still rigid. Shoulders tight. Mouth silent.

"Talk to me," he murmured, his breath brushing the curve of her ear.

"Later," she said, her voice quiet. But her fingers flexed ever so slightly against his shoulder—like she needed the contact as much as he did.

His jaw tightened. "You know him."

"Yes."

"He's hurt you before."

"Yes."

Caelan was going to kill Brennan Darrow.

He exhaled slowly, circling her through the turn. His fingertips kept moving, soothing along the base of her spine. He wasn't sure if he was trying to calm *her* or himself. Probably both.

But she was softening. Bit by bit. The tension in her frame easing, dissolving under his hand like frost in the sun.

"Just talk to me," he said again, gentler now.

She looked up at him then, just briefly, and something in her expression made his chest ache. *Later.* That was all it said.

And God help him, he'd wait. He wouldn't push her, not until she was ready to be truthful with him.

From the far end of the ballroom, movement caught his eye.

A flicker of celadon velvet near the servants' alcove.

Ayda.

Her mask was back in place, her hair pinned as it had been, and no one noticed her slip along the edge of the crowd. She moved like a shadow, but her eyes found his.

And she nodded once. *She had it.*

The keys. The ledger. The proof.

Caelan felt the shift in Niev's posture too—how her back straightened, her weight subtly shifted toward the door. It was time to move.

He spun her gently into a final turn, their hands parting with practiced grace. When they stepped away, it looked like nothing more than the end of a dance.

No one watched them slip through the back hallway.

No one noticed Ayda and Teagan vanish a beat later.

The air in the servant corridors was colder. Quieter. The music faded behind them as the stone walls swallowed their footsteps.

And still—

Caelan could feel the warmth of her body against his palms.

19.
Niev

The ballroom's echoes faded behind them.

The glittering chandeliers, the delicate string music, the poisoned smiles—it all vanished like a dream as soon as the door closed behind them.

The stone corridor stretched narrow and dark, lantern sconces flickering every few paces. The ground was slick beneath her feet, the damp air wrapping around her like a second skin. Every breath felt weighted.

She crouched near the wall and reached beneath her skirts, fingers finding the delicate heels strapped around her ankles.

Courtesy of Myria's ingenious tailoring, both heels snapped off cleanly in her hands in just two quick cracks.

She straightened, steadier now, and slipped them into a hidden pocket under her dress. One less sound to give her away.

Behind her, the soft shuffle of movement—then warmth.

Caelan shrugged off his dark coat and draped it over her shoulders without a word.

The gesture was maddeningly gentle. Thoughtless in the way that showed he was thinking about her.

She swallowed the lump rising in her throat and kept her eyes forward, but her fingers curled into the lining of the coat like it was armor.

It smelled like him.

Lavender, mint and amber.

Steady, Niev.

But her hands were trembling.

Because Brennan Darrow was walking around above them—alive, wealthy, untouched.

And he didn't even *remember her.*

Not a flicker of recognition.

Not a pause.

He had stared her dead in the face, pressed his mouth to her knuckles like she was nothing but a pretty thing to pass around—

And had no idea she was the girl he sold away ten years ago.

She remembered his voice that night. Polished. Pleasant. The way he chuckled when the gavel dropped. The way his signature glinted beneath the auctioneer's seal.

She'd been fourteen.

Screaming, clawing, dragged in chains through the palace tunnels after her family's blood stained the marble floors.

Her parents. Her brother. Gone.

And that *bastard* had sat in the audience of her ruin and called it business.

She had spent every year since building herself from blood and steel and rage.

And he had no idea who she was.

Like she was just another number on his ledger. Cattle to be sold.

Her vision blurred for a moment, just a flash, and then she felt a grounding hand on her lower back.

Niev looked up into Caelan's eyes only for them to soften at whatever he saw on her face.

She didn't know what to make of this man.

This devastatingly beautiful man who was slowly unraveling all the walls she'd built around her.

Niev shook her head. *Now was not the time to think about this.*

They met Ayda and Teagan at the stairwell.

Ayda had shed the servant's shawl and now carried a leather-bound ledger tucked beneath one arm and a keyring clutched in her hand. She looked flushed but pleased—alive with the kind of adrenaline that came from getting away with something you absolutely shouldn't have.

Teagan arched a brow. "You two put up quite the performance. If I didn't know any better I would've thought it was real."

Niev didn't rise to the bait. Neither did Caelan.

"We have what we came for?" she asked Ayda.

Ayda nodded, handing over the ring of keys. "Ledger's full of coded transactions. Some names I recognized. Others..." She shook her head. "You're going to want to see them."

"We will," Caelan said. "Later."

Because right now, every second mattered. They didn't speak again as they descended.

The entrance to the tunnels was hidden beneath one of the older wine cellars—Myria had given them the map. Three staircases, two locked gates, and a hatch carved into the stone floor beneath stacked barrels of Dornish red.

It took all four of them to shift the barrels quietly.

Niev slipped the key into the rusted lock and turned it once, twice—then again with more force until the mechanism groaned and gave way.

The hatch yawned open.

And stale air rolled up to meet them.

It smelled of old earth. Mold. Oil. Saltwater.

Ayda wrinkled her nose. "What a vile smell."

Niev took the lead, descending the iron rungs one at a time until her shoes hit uneven stone. The others followed silently, shadows falling in behind her.

The Hollow Quarter.

A maze beneath Port Orynth—part bunker, part catacomb, part black market artery no one ever spoke of aloud. The tunnels were carved out of bedrock, narrow in places, wide and arched in others, like the bones of some long-forgotten beast. Water glistened in cracks along the floor. The walls were damp. The air pressed in from every side.

They moved without speaking, their footsteps muffled by centuries of dust and filth.

Niev's senses stretched wide—listening for movement, for voices, for the whisper of steel being drawn too close.

She didn't hear anything yet. But that didn't mean they were alone.

They passed old torches, most burnt to stubs. A few freshly lit. *Foot traffic.* That was both good and bad. It meant they were on the right path. It also meant the guards weren't far ahead.

She glanced back once, her skirts gathered in one hand, the other holding a small dagger at her hip. Teagan moved like a shadow beside her, one hand resting lazily on the hilt of his curved blade. Ayda brought up the rear, eyes glowing faintly in the dark.

"Left fork," Niev said softly. "That's where the cargo holds should be."

She turned left. And the tunnel narrowed. The silence here was thicker. Not dead—*watching*. Like the walls themselves knew what was coming.

"Another guard checkpoint should be just ahead," Ayda whispered. "Two men, based on the map. Maybe three."

Teagan nodded once. "According to the whispers I heard upstairs, they won't move anyone until tomorrow night."

"Remind me again how many?" Caelan asked behind her.

Ayda's voice dropped. "Eighteen."

Niev's stomach turned.

"Mostly girls," Ayda added. "Ages seven to thirteen. All listed by lot number. No names. Just descriptions."

Teagan swore under his breath.

Ayda paused, crouched near a junction where three paths split. She touched the ground briefly, reading the faint footprints in the dust. "Right. That way."

Niev followed without hesitation.

They passed empty storage rooms. Rusted crates. One door with blood dried brown on the hinge. A long-forgotten kitchen, crumbling and still stocked with mold-blackened supplies.

"How secure is the holding cell?" Caelan asked, voice low as they moved.

Teagan answered this time. "Two guards posted at all times. Reinforced steel bars. Same locking system as the others."

"We have the keys," Ayda said.

"Still need to clear the room," Caelan replied.

Niev said nothing.

Her mind was already moving—tracking guard rotations, the most efficient angles of approach, the steps between where they were now and where those children waited.

Then Teagan added, "There's another route out. Narrow, but usable. It comes up near the southern docks. They move shipments that way if things get too hot in the city."

"Escape route?" Caelan asked.

Teagan nodded. "If we don't have time to go back through the estate, it's our best shot."

Niev pressed a hand against the wall as they passed beneath another low arch.

The stone here was colder. Tighter.

She could feel it in her bones—the turn coming. The moment when they'd stop moving through shadows and start pulling steel.

She slowed for just a step, letting her fingers trail across the wall as the shadows seemed to come alive around her.

They were almost there.

The footsteps echoed before the man came into view.

One guard. Alone. Whistling softly down the tunnel with the bored cadence of someone too comfortable in his routine.

Perfect.

Niev raised a hand, signaling the others to stop.

She stepped back into the shadows, back pressed to the damp stone wall, breath stilling. Caelan stood behind her. She felt the heat of him, his blade already half drawn.

The guard rounded the bend—young, square-shouldered, and cocky, with a slack grip on his spear and a faint smirk on his mouth.

He didn't even see it coming.

Teagan moved first, silent as a whisper. One hand clamped over the man's mouth. The other drove a dagger beneath his ribs, swift and clean. The guard convulsed once, then crumpled.

Caelan caught the body before it hit the floor. Together they hauled him into a narrow alcove off the main tunnel. Niev knelt beside him, examining the uniform—heavy gray jacket, steel-toed boots, a brass ring of keys at his belt.

"Strip him," she said.

Teagan arched a brow. "I prefer dinner first, but alright."

"Shut up and help," Ayda muttered.

In a flurry of motion, they peeled the guard's uniform free, tossing the ruined undershirt aside. The body was dragged into the back of the alcove and tucked into a rotted supply cabinet.

Niev crouched down and took a long look at the guard's face and build. She closed her eyes and drew in a slow breath—then paused, standing up abruptly. Caelan's eyes flicked up just as she began unzipping the back of her blood-red gown.

He froze, gaze locked on her exposed shoulder. Niev's hair tickled her neck as she slid the decadent fabric down her arms. When she caught Caelan's stare, she narrowed her eyes and shot over her shoulder, "Do you mind?"

His cheeks flared as he snapped his gaze away, mutely averting his eyes while Niev peeled the gown off and folded it neatly. Teagan chuckled low. "I can't believe you're worried about your wardrobe at a time like this."

Niev tossed him a cool look. "This dress is far too good to ruin."

Ayda stepped forward and gently tucked the gown into her satchel. "Myria's going to love this," she murmured as she zipped it closed.

Niev exhaled and let her arms hang bare as she settled back on her heels. Bones cracked. Her limbs narrowed and reshaped; her hair darkened and grew shorter, coarse and cropped. Shoulders broadened; her face twisted and reformed—down to the faint scar along the guard's jaw—until, at last—

She stood among them, the spitting image of the very guard they'd just killed.

Teagan let out a low whistle. "That's still the creepiest damn thing I've ever seen."

Caelan looked at the dead guard, then at Niev, then back at the guard. "That is eerily uncanny."

She smirked, before donning the uniform, tucking the keys into her belt, and pulling the cap low over her brow. The boots were a tight fit, she'd gotten the feet too big, but they'd hold.

She cleared her throat.

"Let me handle the next one," she said—her voice now a dead ringer for the dead man's. "Wait until I give the signal."

The others melted into the walls like shadows.

Niev—now the guard—strode down the tunnel.

She turned the corner and spotted the second man leaning against the archway that guarded the holding cell. He looked up and grinned.

"Back already?" he called. "Thought you were taking your break."

She shrugged, mimicking the guard's usual slouch. "Figured I'd stretch my legs. You know how it is."

He chuckled, shifting his spear. "Well, at least it's quiet tonight. Barely any screaming."

Niev smiled. Then closed the distance between them in a flash. And drove her dagger through his throat.

He gurgled, shocked eyes wide, fingers scrambling at her uniform as his knees gave out. She eased him to the ground, blade already drawing back.

Teagan was there an instant later, catching the body.

They stuffed it into the same alcove as the first.

Two bodies. No alarms.

Teagan reached for the second guard's uniform, already stripping his outer layer. "Guess it's my turn to play pretend."

❋   ❋   ❋

The cell door creaked open.

Even though the keys made no sound turning in the lock, even though every step had been measured and silent, the moment the iron hinges groaned open into the dark — it felt like a scream.

The smell hit them first.

Sweat, dirt, the sour sting of fear that had nowhere to go. Like it had soaked into the walls, fed by weeks—months—of waiting for a door to open and mean something else.

The room wasn't large. Maybe twenty feet across, low-ceilinged, with damp stone walls and a single guttering lantern that threw trembling shadows over everything.

The children were huddled in the far corner.

Some stood. Most didn't. The youngest ones were curled together like animals—thin arms wrapped around thinner legs, eyes wide and hollow.

Their clothes were little more than rags.

Their faces, bruised and too quiet, turned toward the open door like they didn't dare believe it was real.

No one made a sound. No one moved.

Niev stepped in first. Her boots scuffed the stone, and several of the children flinched. She scanned the group, her gaze moving quickly across each face until she found him.

Second row. A little taller than the others. His cheekbone split and healing badly, but the resemblance was uncanny—the line of his jaw, the squareness of his shoulders.

"Finnian Beylore?" she asked gently.

The boy blinked.

She took a single step closer. "Your father sent me."

Finnian didn't speak. His mouth parted slightly, but no sound came. And in that moment—despite the dirt, the bruises, the weeks of terror—he looked like a boy again. Just a boy.

"I promised him," she said softly, "if I found you, I'd bring you home."

Behind her, Caelan shifted his weight. Teagan stayed quiet. Ayda stood just beyond the door.

Niev crouched. Slowly. Arms resting across her knees. Kept her hands visible. Her voice, when she spoke again, was low. Gentle.

"Don't be scared. I'm not going to hurt you."

A few of the older ones exchanged glances. Most of the younger children scurried back. A girl near the back, maybe twelve, lifted her chin like she didn't believe it.

"Are you here to beat us again?" the girl asked, voice rasped from too much silence.

Niev flinched, and then realized she still looked like the guard.

She unclipped the dagger from her belt and slid it gently across the floor—away from herself. Then she shrugged off the guard's coat, pulled the cap from her head, and let it drop to the floor.

She closed her eyes, exhaled slowly, and shifted back into herself again—tall, dark-haired, jaw sharp, eyes fierce.

A gasp rippled through the children like a wave.

Some scrambled back. Others just stared—open-mouthed, wide-eyed, not with fear but with something like mistrust.

"I'm not here to hurt you, I promise," Niev said quietly. "I'm here to get you all out."

The girl who had spoken earlier stepped forward. Her hair was matted, one eye swollen, but her voice was strong.

"Why?"

Niev hesitated.

She felt Caelan at her back, his presence solid and still. Teagan somewhere behind him, shifting his weight. She didn't need to turn to know Ayda had gone still too.

They were waiting for what she'd say.

"Because," she said slowly, "A few years ago... I was where you are."

The silence was so deafening you could hear a pin drop.

She didn't look back. Didn't waver as she went on. "They didn't call me by my name. I was just a number on their ledger. And they sold me to the highest bidder. I thought that was the end of my life," she said, swallowing the lump in her throat. "But it wasn't."

The girl's eyes narrowed. Her fists clenched at her sides. "What happened?"

"I survived," Niev said. "I found people who helped me fight. I became someone they couldn't touch. And I'm here to make sure no one has to suffer the same fate again."

Another heartbeat passed.

Then another girl, smaller, barely ten, whispered, "What do we do?"

Niev knelt.

"You walk with me," she said. "That's it. You walk. And I'll make sure no one ever puts a hand on you again."

Behind her, Caelan shifted. But she felt it then. The quiet storm of him.

The way his eyes bore into the back of her skull like she'd torn open her chest and handed him something she hadn't meant to give.

Teagan let out a slow breath. Almost a laugh—but without the humor.

"Bloody hell, Niev," he muttered, voice low.

But she didn't flinch. Didn't hide.

Because this wasn't about her anymore.

This was about every child in the room looking at her now like she was *real*.

Like she was *hope*.

And for the first time in years—maybe ever—

She felt like she had a *purpose*.

The rage. The scars. The years she'd spent becoming something terrifying.

It was all for this.

20.
Caelan

"We don't have much time," Caelan said, voice steady but soft. "There's a route through the tunnels. It leads to the southern docks. There's a ship waiting. You'll be safe there."

Still, no one moved. The children just stared at them silently, unable to understand.

Until Ayda stepped forward.

She knelt beside a girl with tangled hair and whispered something too quiet to hear. The girl blinked once. Then nodded. Just barely.

And then she reached out and took Ayda's hand.

That was all it took.

One thread pulled loose from the fear — and the whole knot began to unravel. The children rose slowly, limbs stiff and cautious. Some leaned on each other. Others limped. But they moved.

God, some of them were little over *toddlers*. Their faces were pale in the lantern light. Tired. Hollow. But they moved.

And Caelan kept count as they passed him—Eighteen. Just like Ayda said. *Eighteen lives.*

His hand found the hilt of his blade and stayed there. Just in case.

Ahead, Niev walked alongside the girl who had spoken up first. The sharp one. She didn't hold her hand—Niev wasn't the hand-holding type—but she stayed close. Quietly protective. Her long strides slowed just enough to match the girl's smaller ones.

Caelan couldn't stop replaying her words in his head.

Ten years ago... I was where you are.

He knew she was haunted. Knew she'd been through things most people couldn't name, let alone survive. But hearing it—*feeling it* in her voice as she said it aloud for the first time—it had cracked something open inside him.

She hadn't flinched when she told them.

She'd looked straight at that child, that room, that past—and *owned* it.

He wasn't sure when the line had blurred—between admiration and want, between respect and something deeper, sharper, more consuming. But somewhere between that old cabin in the woods and the tunnels of the Hollow Quarter, it had happened.

He'd fallen in love with her.

The sharp, haunted, stubborn woman who never backed down. The one who carried her scars like armor and still fought for people who had nothing left.

He didn't know what that meant for either of them, not yet.

But he knew one thing:

He would do anything to keep her safe.

"Footsteps," Teagan murmured beside him, breaking his train of thought.

Caelan's head snapped up.

He heard it too—faint, but growing louder.

Shit.

Teagan nodded toward a branching tunnel behind them. "We've got five minutes. Maybe less."

Caelan glanced at the children. They wouldn't run fast. A few could barely walk without help.

"Time to move," he said.

He quickened his pace to catch up with Niev. She didn't look at him, but her body shifted slightly, recognizing the tension in his.

"The dead guards have been spotted," he murmured.

"Shit," She tensed. "How long?"

"Four, maybe five minutes."

"Then we walk faster."

And they did.

The line stretched down the tunnel—Niev and Caelan at the front, Ayda guiding the children through the middle, and Teagan holding the rear. The passage narrowed, the light thinning. The stone turned slick again, and cold air curled up from the deeper shafts below.

Caelan's jaw clenched.

The thought of the guards catching them—of any of those children being dragged back screaming into that cell—

No.

He wouldn't allow it.

Even if he had to block the damn tunnel with his own damn corpse.

"Almost there," Niev whispered.

He glanced ahead.

A flicker of movement—light, low and golden—beckoned from around the final bend.

The hatch.

The escape route.

The dock.

Salvation.

Caelan exhaled—slow, steady, hand still on his blade.

After what felt like forever, the tunnel gave way to air.

Sharp with sea salt and smoke. The wind howled low through the jagged grate that opened out to the hidden docks just below the city's edge.

Caelan stepped through first and there it was.

The *Sersha Mara* anchored low and silent at the hidden pier. Gangplank lowered. No flags. No lights. Only a single lantern swinging at the bow, its flame barely visible through the mist. Laughlan had made good on his promise.

They'd made it.

But the moment snapped in half as soon as Teagan turned his head back toward the tunnel and muttered, "Shit."

The footsteps were louder this time. *Coming fast.* Too close.

If they made it out of the tunnel and the guards caught sight of them loading children onto a *ghost-painted warship* — it was over. The entire mission would collapse. Every name in that ledger would vanish. The auction would relocate. The children would disappear again, this time forever.

And Niev—

No.

Caelan made his decision in a breath.

He turned to the others. "Teagan. Ayda. Get the children on the ship. Now."

"What?" Ayda said sharply. "What are you—"

Caelan grabbed her shoulder. "Just go."

Ayda's eyes narrowed, her breath caught. "Caelan—"

He stepped forward and gripped her shoulder so tightly his knuckles went white. "Get them on that damn ship. Go!"

Her eyes—bright with outrage and fear—flickered to Niev's. "I can't just—"

"Get the hell out of here!" His voice trembled, but he was iron-straight.

Ayda pressed heel to the stone and fled, her cloak billowing like a dark banner. She disappeared in the fog with the first trembling group of children.

Caelan turned to Niev. The air seemed to close in on them. She stood rooted to the spot, chest rising and falling too fast, eyes fierce and glinting with unshed tears.

Her gaze locked on his like she already knew. Like she'd known before he even spoke.

"No," she breathed.

He stepped forward, cupped the side of her face. The moonlight caught the curve of her jaw, the stray curl that clung to her temple. Caelan let himself touch her like it mattered. Like he might never get the chance again.

He pressed his palm flat against her cheek, thumb brushing the scar there. "Trust me," he said, voice raw.

Niev's throat bobbed. She gripped his wrist as if to hold him in place—fingers digging into leather. "*Please—*"

His voice cracked. "I have a plan."

He leaned forward and kissed the corner of her mouth—one fierce, desperate brush—and then pivoted away.

Niev's cry tore from her throat, ragged with betrayal. "Caelan!"

Then he turned and ran.

Niev screamed his name, but Teagan was already behind her, arms wrapping tight around her middle, dragging her back as she thrashed with animal fury, heels scuffing the slick floor.

"*Let me go—!*"

Caelan didn't look back. He sprinted toward the distant light of the carriage, tunnel walls swallowing his silhouette.

His boots thundered over slick stone as he tore down the tunnel he'd mapped a dozen times in his head. He drew the leather pouch from his pocket—its iron striker and tar-soaked fuse a promise burned into his palm.

He hadn't told them. Because he hadn't been sure they could make it this far.

But now—now that the children were safe, now that he'd seen Niev lay her heart down like an open wound, he knew what he had to do.

The estate above them, the ballroom gilded in blood, the cells and cages carved into the Hollow Quarter's ribs—they couldn't stand.

Not after this.

He reached the corridor bend and skidded to a halt as he caught two armed guards mid-sprint.

They saw him and raised their blades—

Caelan didn't hesitate. He lunged. Steel met steel. Sparks rang through the tunnel like a bell struck too hard. He drove one back with a blow to the throat. The other caught him in the ribs, shallow but sharp.

He turned. Countered. And slid his blade across the guard's torso.

Breath ragged, blood wet at his side, he knelt and ripped the pouch open. Pulled the first fuse from where he'd hidden it under the floor grate near the central crosspoint.

He struck the flint once. Twice.

Flame caught the end of the fuse.

It hissed along the tarred cord, splitting off into the web he'd buried through the ballroom's base, the western cellar, the loading tunnel, and beneath Darrow's private quarters.

One flame to purge it all.

One match for every name lost in these walls.

He'd promised them a clean escape.

And he'd be damned if they looked back and saw this place still standing.

The roar began as a low rumble. A heat born somewhere far behind his spine.

Then the world cleaved open.

Fire raced down the tunnel behind him, eating air and silence alike. He sprinted, lungs burning, feet slipping on stone slick with blood and oil.

He didn't look back. Didn't have to, as the heat chased him like a beast set loose from hell.

He reached the far tunnel bend and flung himself around it—just as the first fireline reached the ballroom fuse.

And then—

The world went white.

Flame erupted behind him—*up* through the stone, *out* through the tunnel, *through* the mansion above like a fist through rotted silk.

The explosion ripped the air apart.

The floor bucked beneath his feet.

A blast wave chased him like a tidal surge made of ash and fury.

The sound came a second later—deafening, full-bodied, as if the sky had been torn open and left screaming.

He hit the ground hard, and rolled.

Debris rained down in searing embers. The tunnel behind him howled with fire, and in the distance—far above, far beyond—the estate *collapsed.*

21.
Niev

Children tumbled up the gangplank two at a time, Teagan catching the smallest by the waist while Ayda's calm hands guided the next. The Sersha Mara rocked beneath their feet, deck timbers groaning as each pair of boots found purchase. Down below, the crew moved like shadows—silent, efficient—herding them into the hold without a single question.

But Niev lingered on the pier's edge, wind tearing at the hem of her stolen tunic and whipping strands of hair across her face. Her lungs burned with salt-edged air, but she wouldn't breathe until she knew he was alive. Beyond the dock, the tunnel entrance yawned black, a ribbon of smoke curling into the night sky—no movement, no answer.

Ayda's fingers closed around her wrist, firm and insistent. "We have to go—"

"I'm not leaving without him." Niev's voice was steel.

Ayda's eyes flickered with desperation. "We don't even know if he—"

"Do not finish that sentence."

Teagan's voice cut in, low and furious. "Goddamn it, Niev, we don't have time—"

And then the world shattered.

A keening crack like the sky splitting in two echoed off the cliffs, and the tunnel mouth behind them erupted in fire. First a ribbon of flame, then—Boom—a blast wave surged outward so fierce it slammed Niev back against the pilings. The air trembled with heat and the stench of singed stone.

No sooner had the echo died than a second blast thundered from above: the mansion rent apart by its own foundations. Gold and crimson fire ballooned skyward, a living beacon that painted the bay in hellish light. Rock and ember rained down, and the sea's surface glowed like molten metal.

Niev's knees buckled. Salty spray from the dock splashed her face as she staggered back, heart hammering so loudly she was certain it would burst. Through the haze of smoke and flame, all she could see was that tunnel mouth—now a burning wound in the cliffside, and beyond it, the promise of a man she might never reach again.

From somewhere high on the deck, she heard the voice of the devil himself.

"*Get on board, dammit!*" Laughlan roared from the helm. "We're pulling out with or without you!"

"SHUT THE FUCK UP THORNE!" Niev screamed back, but her words dissolved in the roar of flames.

Teagan cursed at her side—"Niev—"—but she heard nothing but the crackling inferno and the pounding of her own heart. Ayda's frantic tug on her sleeve went unnoticed.

All she saw was the tunnel's black maw, now a furnace of collapsing stone and fire, and no sign of Caelan.

A crewman yanked at the mooring line. The Sersha Mara's hull shuddered, readying to slip free. *Without him.*

Niev's fists clenched at her sides, jaw locked. She would have unleashed hell on this entire city before she let him perish alone.

Then—a flicker of movement caught her vision.

Through the haze of smoke and embers, a figure stumbled from the tunnel's edge like an avenging wraith.

Niev's heart *stopped*.

He emerged, singed and bleeding, coat gone, shirt tattered—one arm pressed to a ragged wound at his side, the other dragging a scorched remnant of his coat across the stones.

Alive.

Niev moved before she could think. Her boots thundered over the damp ground, nostrils flaring against the acrid air. She met him as his knees buckled, catching him under each arm.

"You stupid, reckless, impossible man," she whispered, voice trembling as she pressed him upright.

He leaned into her, forehead resting against her temple. His breath was ragged, but he managed a crooked grin. "I told you," he rasped. "I always have a plan."

She laughed—half tears, half relief—just as Teagan's voice cut through the chaos. "*For the love of all that is mighty, get your asses on this ship before it leaves without you!*"

Ayda was already there, waving frantically from the gangplank.

Niev threw Caelan's arm around her shoulder and helped him forward.

"You are *not* allowed to die on me," she muttered in warning.

He didn't smile. But his fingers curled around hers.

"Not tonight love," he said.

Together, they climbed aboard. The Sersha Mara slid away from the dock, vanishing into the mist of Silver Bay, leaving only smoke, ash, and the fading roar of fire behind.

❋ ❋ ❋

She didn't let go of him until they were on the deck.

Not when the plank trembled beneath their weight, not when the children scrambled to the edges to see what had happened, not even when Ayda reached out to help.

She guided Caelan to the deck and lowered him down gently, her hands shaking as she peeled the remnants of his shirt from his back.

The cloth came away black and half-fused to his skin. Her stomach turned.

Burns laced across his upper back and left shoulder—angry, raw, some already blistering. His arm, too. Red and torn, a sickening gleam of damaged flesh where the fire had caught him hardest.

A metallic tang swam in her mouth.

Caelan's jaw clenched and his breath rattled—like fragile glass threatening to shatter. He said nothing, but the tight twist of his fingers around her arm told her everything.

She reached for the small flask at her belt—pure water, cool and inadequate, and tilted it over his wounds. The hiss of steam rose where droplets hit burnt flesh, and Caelan's shoulders jerked in a stifled shiver.

"I'm fine," he rasped.

"You're *not* fine," she insisted, pressing her palm against his side as though she could hold him together.

"We made it."

"That doesn't mean I want to watch your skin fall off," she replied tersely, not giving him the chance to argue.

Niev felt the ship lurch beneath them—oars slipping free, the rudder cutting through dark water. The Sersha Mara slipped away from Silver Bay, its wake dissolving the flames behind them.

She rose on unsteady legs, her breath coming in ragged gulps. As the wind whipped her hair and salt stung her eyes, she exhaled a shuddering sigh. They were safe. For now, at least.

A cackle of laughter cut through the air as the ship lurched forward. Niev's hair, still streaked with ash, whipped across her face as she looked up, and there, backlit by the dying embers of the quay's blaze, stood Laughlan Thorne.

He lounged against the mainmast with the easy arrogance of a pirate. His coat—midnight blue velvet with gold embroidery—hung as unscathed as if it had never felt a cannon's breath. Beneath the loose tail of his sandy blond hair, the corner of his mouth curved into a crooked scar-tipped grin that held both menace and mischief.

"Well, well, well," he drawled, voice rich and low. "Look who decided to join their own rescue party."

Niev's jaw snapped tight, but Caelan only growled, his eyes never leaving the deck. "Shut up, Thorne."

Laughlan clicked his tongue in mock disappointment, swiveling his gaze to take in Niev's soot-stained tunic and singed skin. "That's no way to thank a man for saving your arse."

"You didn't save anything," Caelan cut in, his voice gravel-rough.

"Did too. Look at you. Charred like a roast. Drenched in smoke. Took your sweet time."

Caelan finally turned his head—just enough to glare at him. "I'll kill you when I can lift my arm."

At that, Laughlan threw back his head and laughed—a sound like a half-remembered storm rolling in off the sea. Then he spotted Ayda, lounging against the railing, cloak slipped just enough to reveal the sapphire of her gown. His grin sharpened as he straightened, smoothed his coat, and turned the full force of his charm on the witch. "You must be the infamous Ayda. My darling, you are far too radiant for this dreary company."

Ayda blinked, caught off guard. "Excuse me?"

Laughlan caught her hand before she could retract it and pressed a kiss to her knuckles. "Captain Laughlan Thorne. At your service—or inconvenience, depending on the mood."

Ayda snorted, "Do you always introduce yourself like the hero of a tavern song?"

Laughlan took an exaggerated bow. "When the audience deserves it."

Ayda didn't pull away immediately. Her lips twitched at the corners. "You're absolutely ridiculous."

"Only on my good days, love."

She cast a glance toward Niev and gave a quiet laugh. "I get it now."

"Get what?" Laughlan said sheepishly, looking between both women.

"Why *she* wants to strangle *you*."

Laughlan winked. "That's how I know she's always thinking of me."

Then he turned, shifting his full focus on Niev. His eyes landed on her shirt, the ash clinging to her skin, the wreckage of smoke and fury behind her. But his grin softened—just slightly.

He uncrossed his arms and leaned closer, all easy confidence. "I've been dying to see you in something other than your leathers. Though I confess... I hoped it would be my shirt you were wearing."

Niev stared at him like she was deciding whether to kick him or throw him overboard.

He winked. "Welcome back, Tigress."

Niev's eyes rolled so far back into her head she almost got dizzy.

Laughlan's voice drifted over the deck. "I must say my dear Blackwood, now that she's here, I find myself immensely pleased with our little bargain."

"Teag, what is this imbecile talking about?" Niev narrowed her eyes at Teagan.

The pirate leaned in, cocky as hell, his grin widening. "One mission. One favor. *One thank you kiss.*"

"What did you say?" she replied, her voice lethally quiet, spine stiffening, .

Ayda let out a strangled snort, her cloak brushing the rail as she fought back laughter.

Caelan's chest rose in a hard cough, yet his eyes never left Teagan—pure, homicidal intent.

Teagan, feigning innocence, leaned against the railing and gave a guilty shrug. "It was the only way he'd say yes."

Caelan's voice dropped to a lethal rasp. "You're so dead."

Teagan winced. "I regret everything."

"Oh, *do you?*" Niev snapped, rising to her feet like a thundercloud wrapped in silk. "Because *I* didn't agree to anything!"

"Technically, it was about the ship," Teagan tried. "Not you."

"You *traded me* for this absolute insufferable—"

"Charming," Laughlan supplied.

"*—braggart—*"

"Rogue."

"*—peacock of a pirate—*"

Laughlan's eyes sparkled. "I like where this is going."

"Shut *up.*"

Niev turned back to Teagan and grabbed a handful of his hair. "If you ever—*ever*—make another decision about *my* personal life without asking me, I will cut out your tongue and shove it so far up your ass, you'll be tasting your own shit for *days.*"

"Ow—" Teagan raised his hands, his eyes widening into saucers "Alright, alright." he said, rubbing at his sore head.

"And you—" she turned on Laughlan, fire rising—"If you so much as lean in for that foolish kiss, I'll rip your face using my bare hands."

Laughlan sighed dreamily. "I find that prospect...quite motivating."

She threw up her hands in exasperation, hair whipping around her shoulders. "Unbelievable!"

She wasn't sure if she wanted to scream, stab someone, or throw herself into the sea just to get a moment of *peace*.

Somewhere behind her, Caelan muttered, "I hope this damn ship sinks."

She was exhausted. She was furious.

And the man she cared about — *cared* about, whether she liked it or not — had nearly died blowing up a fortress of filth while these two bastards were bartering her like a bottle of wine.

And the worst part?

He was *still bleeding*, still leaning back against the mast with smoke in his hair and that maddening calm in his eyes like everything was just *fine*.

Her heart pounded for him. For the explosion. For the kids now tucked away below deck. For the storm still rising inside her.

She took a deep breath. And another.

And then growled through gritted teeth, "You're both lucky I'm too tired to deal with your shit right now."

Laughlan chuckled.

Teagan very wisely, for once, kept his damn mouth shut.

22.
Caelan

The sea was black like ink—heavy and vast beyond the warped glass of the cabin window. Moonlight danced in broken streaks across the waves, and the hull creaked with every shift of the ship beneath him.

Caelan sat on the edge of the narrow cot, jaw tight, trying to breathe through the pain burning down his left side.

The shirt was already ruined—scorched, half-stuck to the torn skin beneath. His ribs ached like they'd been used as battering rams, and his shoulder pulsed in slow, deep waves that reached all the way down his spine.

The door creaked open behind him. And Niev stepped inside, quieter than the sea, carrying a basin of clean water and a small glass bottle of what looked like very cheap, very strong ale.

Her steps were cautious. Measured. He could almost hear the words she didn't know how to say. She set everything down on the table beside him and stood there for a moment, hands at her sides, expression unreadable.

"Teagan's trying to entertain the children," she said finally. "Ayda's helping them get settled. There's a crew member below deck who actually knows first aid, but..." Her gaze dropped to the burns. "I didn't really trust anyone else."

He nodded once. "Thank you."

She didn't reply. Just stepped closer and sank to her knees beside him.

Her fingers moved to the edge of what was left of his shirt. Carefully, she peeled the fabric back, slow and deliberate so it didn't tear what skin hadn't already been ruined.

When she saw the full damage, she hissed.

"God, Caelan..."

He didn't look at her. Just kept his eyes on the sea.

"I've had worse."

"That's not as comforting as you think it is."

She soaked a cloth in the water, wrung it out, and pressed it lightly to the worst of the burns. He sucked in a breath but didn't flinch.

She worked in silence for a few moments, cleaning away soot and ash, the soft scrape of cloth against skin the only sound in the room.

Then, quietly, she asked, "Where did you learn to be so stoic?"

He let out a low breath, not quite a laugh. "The camps."

That made her pause.

And maybe it was the way she stilled.

Maybe it was the fact that she didn't look at him with pity—just waited patiently for him to open up to her. So he did.

He told her everything. Not all at once, not in perfect order, but in that quiet, cracked way things came out when you didn't have the strength to hold them anymore.

He told her about the labor camps in Zarenth.

About how his parents had been taken there before he was even born. How he never saw open sky until he was eight. How he remembered the sound of chains before he knew what his own name meant.

He told her how his father died of starvation, and how his mother followed soon after—starved of love, hope, of anything that could keep a person alive in a place designed to break him.

He told her how silence had been safety. How he'd stopped crying because it drew attention. How the guards didn't care if you were a child when they had orders.

How he eventually escaped. And how the guilt of it—the *fact* that he got out when so many didn't—had never really left him.

And when he was done, he finally looked at her—

Only to find silent tears trailing down her face, clean lines carved through the soot on her cheeks.

The sight broke his heart, because he knew then that the Tigress didn't just cry *for* him.

She cried for the world they lived in. For the children robbed of their names and their parents and their childhoods. For the kingdom that devoured its own.

For the grief she carried, and the grief she could see in him now—open, unhidden, and no longer his alone to bear.

And after what felt like an eternity, Niev wiped her tears with the back of her sleeve and poured a splash of alcohol onto another cloth. "This is going to hurt," she warned, her voice steadier than before.

She pressed the cloth gently to the wound along his shoulder. The sting was immediate and brutal, sending fire racing down his arm, but he didn't move. His body tensed under the pain, but her hand came to rest just above the burn—firm, grounding. Her touch wasn't hesitant. It was careful, precise. Not clinical, but *deliberate*, as though she didn't quite know how else to offer comfort.

"I'm sorry," she said after a moment, her gaze still on his skin.

He exhaled, eyes fixed on the far wall. "It's not your fault."

"Thank you," she continued. "For telling me."

He glanced down at her then, his chest tight as he saw her reach for the bandages next, her fingers brushing his arm as she shifted to sit closer. He didn't miss the way her breath stilled at the contact. Didn't miss his own reaction, either. Her touch left a trail of heat across his skin, and suddenly the burn in his shoulder was nothing compared to the one beneath it.

Neither of them spoke as she began to wrap the gauze around his upper arm. Her movements were careful, deliberate, as if the care she offered could make up for everything he had endured. It couldn't—but it warmed his heart all the same. And maybe that was worse. Because it made him want things he hadn't let himself want in a very long time.

His thoughts drifted to the ballroom. To the scent of her perfume in the dark. The heat of her body against his as they circled the room in a game that had felt like anything but. The way her laughter had slipped through her teeth when he'd whispered against her skin, the way her fingers had pressed just a little too hard against his chest.

It had been pretend. A charade they'd had to do.

But it hadn't felt like it. Not to him.

He wanted to ask her. Wanted to bring it up now, here, in the safety of this quiet space. But the words stuck behind his teeth, too fragile to risk. Because he knew what he felt now, clearly and without question. He loved her.

And he wasn't ready to say it.

Not because it wasn't true—but because he didn't know what she'd do with the truth. She was steel and smoke and sharp edges, and if he gave her something too real too soon, she might slip away before he ever got the chance to see what they could be without all the walls between them. So he said nothing.

Instead, he watched her. The curve of her neck as she leaned over his shoulder. The furrow in her brow as she pulled the bandage tight. The way she bit the inside of her lip when she focused—completely unaware of how much it affected him.

Caelan couldn't help the way his body kept shifting instinctively under her touch. The way his leg brushed against hers as she leaned in. The way his breath caught when her fingers grazed too close to the hollow of his collarbone. His body was traitorous—pain-drenched but greedy for contact. For her.

Her hands hesitated once. Twice. But she kept going.

When she reached the final pass of the wrap and began to knot it off, her voice dropped into something softer. Less composed.

"You're making it very hard to finish this bandage," she whispered.

He let out a breath that sounded like a desperate laugh. His eyes found hers, the corners of his mouth lifting. "You make it very hard, just in general."

The words hung in the air, bold and unrepentant.

Her fingers faltered.

Then she flushed—bright red, a shade he hadn't seen on her before, and barked a laugh so sudden it made him grin.

"I can't believe you just said that," she muttered, half-laughing, half-mortified. "Are you delirious?"

"Maybe," he said, not quite embarrassed. But close. "I nearly got blown up. I think my filter didn't make it out alive."

Her laughter softened, fading into something quieter as her eyes lingered on his mouth for just a second too long. The energy between them shifted again—no longer playful, but charged. Like something raw and dangerous had just been unwrapped, and neither of them was ready to hide it again.

He leaned in, just a little. So did she.

The air grew tight between them, dense with every unsaid thing that had been building since that night they'd met in the Red Dragon's lair. Since the first time she looked at him like she was trying to decide whether to kiss him or kill him.

Her hand still rested against his shoulder, the warmth of her touch bleeding through the bandages, through his skin, straight into his bloodstream. Caelan couldn't look away from her. Not from the curve of her lips, still parted in breathless laughter. Not from the flush still blooming high on her cheekbones. Not from the way her eyes had shifted—no longer guarded, no longer teasing, but lit with something raw and open.

The silence between them pressed in. Like the space between two sparks before the flame.

Her breath skimmed his jaw as she leaned in ever so slightly, her eyes flicking down to his mouth just once before darting back up.

He moved slowly, giving her every chance to pull away—but she didn't. Her gaze held his, dark and steady, as he reached out, slowly and deliberately, placing a hand at her waist and guiding her gently onto his lap, easing her down across his thighs until they were face to face. The motion was tender, careful of his injuries, but intimate in a way that sent his pulse thudding.

She didn't resist. She came willingly, straddling one of his legs with elegant control, the remaining fabric of her trousers drawing tight across her hips, as her knees braced on either side of him. Her hands were on his chest, fingers splayed against his skin just above the bandage. And still, she didn't speak. Her eyes searched his, daring him to move first.

His fingers trembled as they threaded into her hair, then curled behind her neck with a possessive certainty. He paused just long enough for her to catch her breath—lips grazing along her jaw, the rough edge of stubble against her skin—before he closed the distance.

When he kissed her, there was nothing tentative about it. Their lips met like they'd been waiting their whole lives to collide—hot, urgent, and a little unsteady from everything that had happened in the last few hours. She tasted like salt and smoke, like mint on her breath and fire in her blood. Her fingers clenched in the fabric of his shirt, holding on like she needed him to keep her upright.

And then her *scent* hit him again, just as it had in the ballroom. That maddening blend of bergamot and jasmine, wrapped in heat and shadow. Her skin, her hair, her warmth—all of it embedded in that citrus and spice, and it hit him like a punch to the ribs.

He broke from her lips just enough to breathe, his forehead brushing hers as he muttered against her mouth, "Fucking bergamot."

She laughed softly, smiling into the kiss, and then deepened it with a hunger that made his head spin.

The kiss turned hotter, messier. Her hips shifted against him, arms twining around his neck, and he welcomed all of it. Let her take what she wanted. Gave it just as fiercely in return.

He didn't know how long they stayed tangled like that, caught in a haze of kisses and half-broken breaths, but when she finally pulled back, her leg slid across his lap, and stilled.

Her body went quiet.

Then her eyes widened, just slightly, before flicking down and back up to his.

Caelan didn't move. He didn't even blink.

He just kept his gaze locked on her mouth, the ghost of her kiss still burning on his lips, and said—dry, hoarse, and entirely unrepentant—"I told you."

Her cheeks flushed crimson.

And then she laughed—truly laughed—as she dropped her forehead to his uninjured shoulder, burying her face in him like it was the only place in the world she trusted.

He smiled against her temple, drawing his arm around her waist and holding her there.

A sharp knock at the cabin door shattered the moment.

Niev froze against him, lips parted, breath still warm on his skin. Her hand remained on his chest for a single heartbeat longer—then she jerked back like she'd been caught stealing something sacred.

Caelan watched her scramble off his lap, her cheeks flushed, her movements quick but not quite composed. She smoothed her tattered shirt, tucked a curl behind her ear, and took a long, steadying breath—though it did nothing to hide the pink still blooming across her throat. And Caelan realized there was no sight in the world as entertaining as a *flustered* Tigress.

Another knock.

"Niev?" Ayda's voice filtered in, muffled but unmistakable. "You in there?"

Caelan closed his eyes for half a second and exhaled through his nose. Of course it was Ayda.

Niev shot him a warning glance, *don't say a word*, and called out, "Yeah. Just—one second."

She looked down at him then, lips twitching like she couldn't decide whether to laugh or curse the timing of the universe.

"*Just one second?*" Caelan raised a brow, trying very hard not to look too smug. "You gonna tell her we were just reorganizing bandages?"

She narrowed her eyes. "You're *not* helping."

"I'm not trying to."

Niev shook her head, a breathless smile curling at the corners of her mouth despite herself. She leaned in, tugged the blanket back over his lap with careful precision, and gave him one last lingering look. Caelan cracked a smile so wide his cheeks hurt.

Then she stepped away, straightened her spine, and opened the door.

Ayda stood on the other side, arms crossed, eyes narrowing the moment she took in the scene—Niev flushed and breathless, Caelan shirtless and bruised beneath the rumpled blanket, the air thick with something not at all subtle.

Ayda smirked. "Well," she said. "We're healing quite well I see."

Niev didn't even blink. "What do you need?"

"The crew's managed to hang hammocks for the children in the hold. We didn't want them sleeping in the berthing space with the rest of the crew. They're finally settling in. I've healed as many as I could—ship's surgeon helped, but he's overwhelmed. Teagan's been running morale."

She paused.

"And he *may* have let it slip that the pretty lady who saved them also sings like an angel."

Caelan turned his face slightly, biting back a laugh. Niev did not.

"What is wrong with this idiot?" She groaned, dragging a hand down her face. "Does he *actually* have a death wish?"

Ayda's smile widened. "The little ones are asking for you by name. Apparently they want to thank *Lady Niev* for saving them."

"Lady Ni—" Niev repeated, her voice strangled halfway between disbelief and horror. "This is becoming *ridiculous*."

Caelan couldn't help himself. He bit down on a smile, the ache in his shoulder suddenly secondary to the delight curling in his chest. Her mortification was *genuine*, and far too entertaining.

Ayda was already slipping through the door like a shadow.

"You better not leave me with them!" Niev hissed, hot on her heels.

"I wouldn't dream of it," Ayda replied sweetly over her shoulder, with all the innocence of someone walking away from a fight they absolutely started. "But if you don't come soon, Teagan said he'll perform a dramatic retelling of your heroics."

The door swung shut in Niev's face. The silence deafening once more.

Then Caelan laughed. A low, hoarse sound that still made his ribs protest, but it was worth it as Niev rounded on him, eyes sharp.

"Not. A. Word."

He raised his uninjured arm in mock surrender, still grinning. "I wasn't going to say anything."

She arched a brow. "Good."

He tilted his head. "Though now that you mention it... you are *very* maternal."

Her eyes narrowed into slits. "How dare you."

"I just think it's sweet," he went on, voice innocent but his expression anything but. "The way you sing to your children."

"I do not *sing* to my—"

"Soft voice. Gentle hands." He sighed dreamily. "Lady Niev, protector of the small—"

"Shut your *bloody* mouth."

He smiled slowly, that infuriating, roguish smile. His gaze dropped briefly to her lips before returning to her eyes.

"Well," he murmured, voice low and smug, "I think we've established you know exactly how to do that. If you *want* to."

She flushed instantly. And it was glorious.

But instead of storming out, she stepped toward him, leaned in close enough for her breath to graze his cheek, and whispered, "Careful, Galbraith. That blanket won't protect you forever."

Then she straightened, pulled open the door with a flick of her wrist, and vanished into the corridor—leaving him stunned, smiling, and completely ruined.

23.
Niev

Caelan's laughter echoed down the corridor behind her, low and rough, and *infuriatingly pleased* with himself. She could *feel* the smugness radiating off him like a heatwave.

Still, her mouth curved of its own accord.

The air was cool in the passage, laced with salt and tar and old wood, but it did little to ease the warmth she carried with her. It lingered along her collarbone, pooled low in her stomach, and burned at the tips of her ears. She walked slowly, not trusting her knees yet, one hand trailing the wall for balance—part of her still felt like she was floating.

She'd kissed men before. Well, she'd kissed only two men, but it had *never* felt like this. That was dangerous territory. Emotion had always been her sharpest blade, and she'd long since learned to keep it sheathed. But Caelan had a way of slipping past her armor. Of seeing the fracture lines without flinching.

When she was sure the corridor was empty, she lifted her fingertips to her lips. They were still warm.

The memory of his kiss came back in pieces—heat and hunger, the softness of his mouth against hers, the way he'd tasted like smoke and blood. He hadn't hesitated. Hadn't pushed too far, either. He'd just *held onto her*.

God... What had they done?

She exhaled slowly and kept walking.

Eventually, she stopped outside the cabin Laughlan had assigned them for cleaning up when they first boarded the *Sersha*. The door was shut, quiet, unassuming. But the moment her hand touched the latch, she felt everything crowd back in at once—her name on the children's lips, the sting of ash still clinging to her clothes, the weight of Caelan's body burning against hers like a brand.

She slipped inside and closed the door behind her.

The cabin was modest but not unpleasant. The ship's sway beneath her feet was gentle, steady. A basin of fresh water sat on the side table where someone—probably Ayda—had left clean cloth and a bundle of fresh bandages.

Niev leaned back against the door, fingers still tingling.

She'd trained too long and bled too often to be shaken by a single kiss, no matter how good it had been.

But this hadn't been just a kiss. It had been *a break in the dam*. And once it had cracked, everything she'd buried beneath control and caution started leaking through.

She hadn't meant to feel anything. Not for him. Not like this.

But when he ran back into that tunnel—when she saw his silhouette vanish into smoke and stone—something inside her had splintered.

She had felt terror. Real, visceral terror.

The kind that came with the understanding that *if he died, something in her would not come back from it*.

She hadn't let herself feel that way since she was fourteen years old.

Since the night they'd dragged her out of her home and into the hell that was Breyvia.

Since the last time she'd lost someone who mattered.

Her fingers curled against her palm as she leaned her head back against the cabin door, eyes closing against the heat that prickled behind them.

She was in so much *trouble*.

❋ ❋ ❋

The ocean air hit her the moment she stepped back onto the deck.

It was brisk and clean, carrying the scent of salt and sun-warmed wood. The wind tugged gently at the loose waves of her damp hair as she emerged from below, freshly washed and wrapped in a clean tunic that fell mid-thigh over black trousers.

The last, faint memory of sunset had vanished, swallowed by the vast, star-pricked black. Only the celestial scatter of diamonds overhead offered any light, their faint glow barely enough to reveal the ship's dark silhouette against the endless, inky sea. The ship rocked gently beneath her feet, steady and rhythmic, as though the *Sersha* was content with its stolen cargo of survivors.

Everyone was already gathered on deck.

Niev was surprised to see the children were awake and huddled in loose clusters along the far side, their expressions subdued but brighter than they'd been below. Teagan sat among them with the ease of someone born to cause trouble, carving out a space with his voice alone. He gestured wildly with his hands as he told some absurd story about a prince who'd tried to marry a goose and ended up cursed by a swamp witch. The children were hanging on every word—wide-eyed, barely chewing their food as they watched him.

It smelled divine. Rich spices. Caramelized onions. Braised meat. Something garlicky and slow-cooked that made her stomach twist with sudden, almost painful hunger.

She followed the scent toward the galley table where the ship's cook, Thadros—wide-shouldered and perpetually dusted in flour—was handing out tin plates with a practiced rhythm. His skin was weathered bronze, his beard curled like sea foam, and his voice was deep enough to shake the deck when he laughed.

He spotted her instantly and grinned. "Well, well. Look what the sirens dragged in."

Niev smirked as she accepted a plate from his outstretched hand. "Good to see you too, Thad."

"You're lucky you showed up when you did. I was about to feed your portion to that pretty boy of yours."

Niev smiled at the mention of Caelan. "I'll fight him for it," she winked.

Thadros winked. "No need. I always have an extra portion saved just for you."

She thanked him with a nod and drifted away from the bustle, finding a quiet spot near the portside rail. The wood beneath her was warm from the sun, her plate already steaming with food that smelled better than anything she'd eaten in weeks.

She'd just taken her first bite—rich, savory, laced with thyme and butter—when a shadow lingered near the edge of her vision.

She looked up.

The girl stood with arms crossed, dark eyes sharp beneath thick lashes. Her hair was braided tightly down her back, her chin lifted in the way children did when they were trying not to look vulnerable.

It was the one who'd questioned her in the cell.

Niev set down her fork. "Hi," she said softly.

The girl didn't respond at first. Then, with all the bluntness in the world, she said, "Ayda said it was your idea to come and get us out."

Niev raised an eyebrow. "It was."

The girl grunted, seemingly satisfied with her answer. She took a cautious step closer. "My name's Talia."

Niev inclined her head. "I'm Niev."

"I know." Talia looked at her plate. "You gonna eat all that?"

Niev offered the corner of her roll. Talia sat down beside her without waiting for permission.

They didn't speak for a while. Just sat, shoulder to shoulder, chewing in companionable quiet. Niev didn't know what surprised her more— that the girl trusted her enough to sit this close, or that Niev didn't feel the urge to flee.

The little girl broke the silence first.

"Were you really sold under that mountain?"

It wasn't a question. Not really. Niev didn't answer right away. Her gaze drifted to the edge of the horizon, where the stars burned bright against the waves.

"Yes," she said at last.

Talia nodded once, like that made sense. Like it explained *everything*. She picked at the edge of the roll, tearing off a piece with her teeth, chewing slowly.

"Ayda made a list," she said after a long pause. "Of everyone's names. Where we're from. Who to send letters to."

"She did," Niev said softly, setting her plate aside. "She's thorough like that."

"She told us we'd get back to our families."

"You will," Niev said, with more certainty than she felt. "We'll help get you home."

Talia didn't answer right away. She stared out over the rail, eyes squinting against the dying sun, her small fingers going still in her lap.

Then, very quietly, she asked, "What about the ones who don't have families to get back to?"

Niev turned to look at her.

Talia didn't flinch under the gaze. "Some of us were taken from orphanages," she said. "Or workhouses. A few don't remember much at all. What happens to us then?"

There it was. The question with no clean answer.

Niev swallowed against the knot rising in her throat. She had braced herself for the stories. The trauma. The broken bones and empty stares. But not this—this calm, clear voice asking the question she'd asked herself a thousand times growing up: *What happens to the ones no one comes looking for?*

She took a breath, slow and careful.

"We'll find a place for you," she said. "Somewhere better. Somewhere safe."

"Safe how?" Talia asked, still watching her. "Like... will someone take care of us? Or do we just get older somewhere else?"

Niev didn't know how to answer that. She could lie. She'd done it before. Smiled, reassured, fed hope like it was enough to fill a stomach. But not with this girl. Not when she looked at Niev like she already knew the answer.

"We don't have it all figured out yet," Niev said honestly. "But you won't be alone. Not again."

Talia studied her a moment longer, weighing her words like currency. Then she nodded. "Okay."

Just that.

A small word that added an enormous weight on her shoulders.

They sat in silence after that, the waves rolling steady beneath them, the stars blooming one by one across the velvet sky.

Talia had just finished her food when a tiny shadow approached from the edge of Niev's vision.

She turned her head, and her breath caught.

The little boy couldn't have been older than five. Pale hair tangled in soft waves, cheeks smudged with bruises, eyes wide as moons. He held a tin cup in both hands like it was the most important thing in the world, his fingers barely big enough to curl around the rim.

"Is it true you can sing?" he asked.

The question struck Niev like a blade, making her throat tighten. Because it wasn't the question alone—it was the *voice*. So small. So hopeful.

She blinked and looked out across the deck, instinctively searching for an anchor.

Caelan sat not far, half reclined against the rail with his long legs stretched out, a plate forgotten beside him. One arm wrapped in bandages, eyes shadowed by fatigue—but they were locked on her. Focused. Unmoving. The moment their eyes met, something in her steadied.

She turned back to the boy.

"Sometimes," Niev said quietly.

The little boy brightened and sat beside her like they'd always known each other. "Will you sing something now?"

Niev hesitated. All around the deck, movement slowed. The lull in conversation. The soft clink of tin against wood. Teagan's story faded into silence mid-sentence. Even the wind seemed to hush. Dozens of eyes lifted—waiting to see how she would react.

She scanned their faces. And then looked back at Caelan, who gave her the smallest nod of encouragement.

The wood of the ship was warm against her back as she leaned into it, closing her eyes for just a moment longer than necessary. The scent of the sea was sharp in her lungs—brine and woodsmoke and the faint sweetness of Thadros's spices still lingering in the air. But beneath it all was that low hum of expectation, drawn taut across the deck like a bowstring waiting to snap.

The first note left her lips like something half-remembered—gentle, unsure, wrapped in the quiet remnants of a life she'd buried a long time ago. But the wind caught it anyway. Carried it out across the deck like a secret unspooling, like a spell spoken in reverse. The waves calmed beneath it, as if listening. The creak of rope and timber fell silent. Even the sea seemed to still for her as she started singing.

The others, they stand, in perfect array,
I strive to always please them, in their well-worn way,
But my heart rings false, a discordant lay,
'Tis not my fault, if I wander astray.

She could hear her mother's voice in the notes. How she used to hum while brushing Niev's hair, low and rhythmic. How it used to lull her into sleep.

That was before the palace. Before the fire and the blood and the sound of footsteps outside her door that would never be soft again.

Her fingers curled against her thigh as she sang on, pouring memory and grief and something like longing into each verse.

My earth was never round, nor my spirit so meek,
This world is not my home, and so the truth I must speak,
But dreaming's the solace I seek,
When my spirit's weak, and I rise to flee...

Children leaned in closer, shoulders brushing, some wide-eyed, others with lashes lowered, heads resting on knees. A few of them clutched one another's hands—not in fear, but in stillness. Even the youngest, the ones too tired to stay upright, sat quietly in laps or blankets, heads bobbing gently to the rhythm.

Niev barely noticed when their tears came.

A boy near the mast wiped his cheek on his sleeve and didn't pretend it was anything else. A girl with a crooked braid buried her face in another's side. No one told them to stop. No one told them to hush.

And still the wind carried the sound—over the railings, down the ropes, through every open window and hatch. It echoed along the ship's hull and disappeared into the darkening sky like a prayer no one had the right words to make.

> *From solitude's grasp, I yearn to be free,*
> *In doubt's bitter draught, I find my decree,*
> *And lands far and strange, shall set my soul free...*
> *Dreaming is my solace—for eternity.*

When she let the last note fall, it disappeared slowly—drawn out across the water until it faded into nothing. The silence afterward was complete. Whole. Reverent.

Niev didn't open her eyes right away.

When she finally did, it was to the face of the boy who had asked her to sing in the first place. His mouth was slightly open, eyes still wet but shining with something fierce. Gratitude, maybe. Or that simple, soul-wrenching thing only children knew how to give without holding back— *wonder.*

The boy didn't speak.

He just tucked himself against Niev's side, and laid his head on her leg like it was the most natural thing in the world.

And Niev—who had spent a lifetime earning silence, carving out spaces where no one could touch her—let that small child burn a hole through her heart.

24.
Caelan

The children had finally gone to sleep.

Below deck, the creaking hammocks had quieted to gentle, rhythmic sways. A few still whimpered in their sleep, shifting against woven blankets and the makeshift cushions of spare linens, but most had given in to exhaustion. Curled into one another like wildlings in a den, they slept with the stubborn clutch of those who didn't yet believe they were safe.

Above them, the ship drifted through still waters—its hull groaning now and then, as the lanterns swung low, their glow flickering across coiled lines and weather-stained wood. The moon sat swollen and cloud-wrapped over the Sersha, casting a cold halo over the sea.

The crew's laughter had faded to murmurs. Even Thadros in the galley had stopped whistling. All that remained now was the hush—the ship breathing in time with the tide, a fragile moment suspended between danger and what came next.

And Caelan... He didn't know what came next.

He stood at the rail for a long time before moving.

The salt air scraped gently against the burn still healing beneath the bandage on his shoulder, but the ache barely registered. His thoughts were heavier than pain. He leaned against the wood, eyes drifting down the length of the deck.

They'd done it.

Somehow, they'd actually done it.

They had walked into the jaws of Port Orynth's elite, burned a mansion to the ground, and freed nearly eighteen children from a future of chains. It should've felt like victory. He should've felt relief.

Instead, all he could think was—*where the hell do they go now?*

Some had families waiting. That was something. Ayda had been meticulous about gathering names, coaxing stories from fractured memories. But others... too many others... had no names left. No homes. No one who would look for them.

And then there was Niev.

She'd stood before them like some mythical creature as she sang. She'd laid herself bare in front of everyone—children, crew, *him*—and turned her pain into something the whole ship held its breath to hear.

He didn't think she even knew what she'd done.

Didn't think she understood how her voice, trembling and strong, had swept over them like a tide. He had watched it happen—those children, battered and voiceless, looking at her like she was the first real thing they'd ever seen.

And he—

He had looked at her like a man drowning.

Because he couldn't get enough of her. His hands ached to touch her. To steady her. To carry the weight she refused to set down.

So when he saw her, seated at the edge of the forecastle with her back against the mast and her knee pulled close to her chest, he wasn't surprised.

He understood now why the Tigress didn't rest. Why she could never just stay quiet, not when she still had pieces of herself left to give.

The wind lifted the dark strands of her hair and tangled them against her cheek. The sea light gilded her skin in blue and silver, her silhouette carved like sculpture against the night. Her shoulders were bare, the borrowed shirt slipping low, collarbone etched in shadow. And her eyes—half-lidded, distant—were fixed somewhere beyond the black horizon—on lands unseen, or memories he didn't yet know.

Caelan watched her for what felt like the longest time, letting the image of her burn itself into him, the way it always did. She never looked soft, not even in stillness. But there was something quieter in her now. A tired grace. A quiet defiance.

Something that made his chest tighten the longer he stood there.

Eventually, he walked toward her, boots soundless over the worn planks.

She didn't look up as he approached, but he knew she'd heard him.

"Couldn't sleep?" he asked, settling beside her with a wince as his bandaged shoulder adjusted.

Niev shook her head slightly. "Didn't try."

He nodded, leaning back against the warm wood behind them. The silence stretched, but it wasn't uncomfortable. They had become good at that—sitting inside the weight of things unsaid.

She shifted beside him, her shoulder brushing his arm, and he couldn't help it—he looked at her again. The firelight caught the slope of her cheekbone, the faint smear of soot still clinging to her jaw. Her eyes were tired, but there was a softness in them now that hadn't been there days ago. Maybe not ever.

"I used to think," he said after a moment, "that people like us weren't meant to save anyone."

She turned slightly toward him, brows drawn, listening.

He swallowed. "We survive. We fight. We burn bridges and break chains and keep going. But saving people... that always felt like something someone else got to do."

He heard her exhale through her nose, a slow sound.

"Maybe we're not saving them," she said. "Maybe we're just... giving them the chance to save themselves."

He looked down at her, and her eyes lifted to meet his.

God, that *look*.

Everything in him ground to a halt. The wind stilled. The ship faded. The sea could've vanished and he wouldn't have noticed.

She gave him the smallest smile—barely there, almost shy—and in that moment, it would've taken nothing to lean in. To press his forehead to hers. To tell her every word that had been clawing its way up his throat since the first night she threatened to kill him with a hairpin.

He shifted, slow and quiet, and sat beside her.

Their sides touched.

The heat of her soaked into him, steady and immediate. His pulse jumped. She didn't pull away.

She tilted her head toward him slightly, that same smile still ghosting her mouth, and he could see it now—the curve of her lashes, the specks of amber in her eyes, the way her breath hitched almost imperceptibly as he turned to face her fully.

He opened his mouth—

And the moment shattered.

"Are we interrupting something?" Ayda's voice cut across the deck, not unkind, but laced with just enough mischief to make Niev instantly straighten.

Caelan exhaled sharply, blinking back the haze. He glanced up to find Ayda already climbing the last few steps of the deck, Teagan just behind her with his arms crossed and that maddeningly smug tilt to his mouth.

"No," Niev said, far too quickly.

Ayda arched a brow.

Teagan didn't say a word—just raised both hands in mock surrender, though he didn't look the least bit sorry.

Caelan leaned back against the mast, willing his heartbeat to return to normal.

Ayda lowered herself to the deck with a tired sigh, tugging her cloak tighter around her shoulders as she sat cross-legged in front of them. Teagan followed, less graceful—half-drop, half-flop—and stretched his long legs out with a groan like he'd aged a decade since sundown.

"Couldn't sleep either?" Caelan asked dryly.

Teagan smirked. "Sleep's for people who don't have orphans to house and criminals threatening to stab them in their sleep."

"Only if you keep talking," Niev said, not missing a beat.

Ayda snorted.

But it faded quickly, as the silence that followed pressed in—not heavy, but expectant. They all knew why they were here, and it wasn't just to bask in the starlight or pass time with banter.

Ayda pulled a folded piece of parchment from inside her coat, smoothing it across her knee. Caelan recognized the list—names, ages, scraps of remembered homes, places, fragments of lives the children had managed to clutch onto in the dark.

"Some of them remember towns," Ayda said, her voice quieter now. "Penthos. Driftwood. A handful from Greyhaven and its outskirts. We'll need to go through each one and see who we can reunite."

Teagan glanced over her shoulder, brow furrowed. "That's assuming any of those places are still safe."

"It's a start," Ayda said. "We know Finnian's father is a blacksmith in Greyhaven, but he said his uncle is also a merchant in Port Veyne. Claims he has a ship of his own. That's one we can verify quickly. We might even ask him for help to transport the other children."

"And the rest?" Caelan asked.

Ayda hesitated.

Then, softly, "Some of them came from orphanages. Half-forgotten institutions on the edge of Breyvia's coast or the wrong side of Solhaven. A few were pulled straight from the streets."

Teagan's jaw worked, but he didn't speak.

Niev's voice came, quiet but firm. "They can't go back to that."

Ayda nodded. "I know."

The wind brushed Caelan's face, cool against the heat building beneath his skin. He looked at Niev then, really looked, and saw something in her posture that hadn't been there before. Not the tight coil of readiness or that elegant, lethal stillness she wore like armor.

This was different.

Almost... uncertain.

"I might know a place," she said at last.

All eyes turned to her.

Niev exhaled slowly, fingers toying with the edge of her sleeve. "There's a town called Mossgrove in southern Thornmere. Remote. Quiet. My father's mother lives there... or did. I haven't seen her in over a decade. But if she's still alive, and still the woman I remember..."

She trailed off, but Caelan knew what she wasn't saying.

If anyone could make a home for the forgotten, it would be her.

Teagan gave a low whistle. "Thornmere, huh. That's a long journey."

"I never said it would be easy," Niev added defensively.

Caelan studied her in the silence that followed. Her jaw was tight, her eyes shadowed—but there was a kind of fragile conviction in her voice. Like the idea had just taken root inside her and she was trying to let it grow before it collapsed beneath the weight of everything else she carried.

He reached across the space between them, let his hand brush against hers—just once. Grounding. Real.

"We'll go," he said. "All of us."

Teagan ran a hand through his hair, dragging it back from his face. "We could dock in Breyvia first. Port Veyne is the closest stop. Less open sea, faster return for the ones with families."

"But also," Ayda added, "the most likely place they'll be watching."

That pulled a grimace from him.

Caelan leaned forward, elbows on his knees. "We lit up a noble estate like a pyre. We slaughtered a small army of private guards and hijacked a trafficking ring in one of Arenthia's most corrupt cities. Do you really think they won't be watching *all* the coastal gates?"

Teagan didn't argue.

Because they all knew he was right.

"Port Veyne's a good place for hiding," Teagan said eventually, tone slower now. "But not with eighteen kids who've never stepped on a ship before and still flinch every time a boot hits the deck. We're dragging a storm behind us."

Caelan nodded. "Then we outrun it."

Ayda glanced at Niev. "You really think this grandmother of yours would take them in? All of them?"

"I don't know," Niev admitted. "I haven't seen her in over a decade. But if anyone can turn a fractured house into something solid again, it's her. And Mossgrove is not on anyone's patrol map. Not the Empire's. Not the guilds. Not even the bounty circuits."

"Too far out. Too wild," Caelan murmured.

"Exactly," Niev said. "We go there first. Get the orphans safe. Then circle back through the south to Port Veyne. Only six of the children have confirmed relatives. We can take them ourselves. Quietly."

Teagan let out a long breath and finally nodded. "It's not the worst plan we've ever had."

Ayda gave him a dry look. "That's not saying much."

But she reached for the parchment anyway, running her finger down the list again. "I'll reorganize the names. Mark the ones we'll take to Thornmere. We'll need to keep records of everything—what they remember, who they mentioned. It'll help when we double back."

Niev rubbed a hand over her face. "We're going to have to keep moving until we're sure no one's coming after them."

"They will come," Caelan said. "Eventually."

"I know." She looked at him. "That's why we can't let the trail lead to them."

And there it was again—*that look*. That threadbare, terrifying resolve that lived beneath her skin. That willingness to carry every weight herself if she had to. Even now, when the mission should have been over, when they'd burned the past behind them, she was already bracing for what came next.

"Then we stay ahead of the fire," he said quietly.

Ayda gathered the parchment, rising slowly. "I'll start sorting. Maybe tomorrow, we can talk to the kids about it. Gently."

Teagan pushed to his feet with a grunt. "And I'll convince Laughlan to steer around storm belts without charging us extra for it."

Niev gave him a flat look. "Good luck."

Caelan pushed off the mast with a quiet grunt, rolling his shoulder as stiff muscle protested. The sea breeze had turned cool now, brushing over the deck in languid currents, and for the first time since they'd set sail, the air didn't taste like ash.

"We should all try to sleep," he said, looking pointedly at Niev. "Even you."

Ayda nodded, rubbing the side of her temple. "God knows we've earned it."

They began to rise, slow and heavy, the weight of the past days settling now that the worst was—if not behind them—at least paused. But just before they could break apart fully, Ayda stepped forward, fingers digging into her satchel.

"Niev," she said, haltingly.

The Tigress turned, brow furrowing. Ayda hesitated, then pulled a folded stack of old, yellowed parchment from the inside pocket. "When I was in Darrow's office... when I found the keys, I—" She paused. "There were files. Records. Names. Older ones. Don't ask me why, but something made me grab them."

Niev's eyes fixed on the pages.

"I didn't have time to look," Ayda said, voice quieter now. "But... I thought maybe you might want to. I don't know why. Just... felt like I was supposed to take them."

For a long moment, Niev didn't move.

Then, slowly, she stepped closer and took the stack from Ayda's hands. Her fingers lingered, just briefly, over the edge of the parchment. When she finally looked up, her eyes were different—softer. The sharpness was still there, but something else threaded through it now. Gratitude.

"Thank you," she said, her voice barely audible.

Ayda gave a small nod and stepped back, letting the silence hold the weight between them.

And then, of course, Teagan ruined it.

"Well, I suppose the rest of us should go crawl into our measly hammocks below decks," he drawled, stretching his arms overhead with a groan. "While our brave, wounded hero here gets a whole cabin to himself. Must be nice."

Caelan didn't miss a beat. He turned, eyes locking with Niev's.

"I'd gladly switch," he said. "Or make room for one more."

The words hung there, suspended in the thick night air.

Niev's gaze held his. She didn't blush. Didn't look away. But the corner of her mouth lifted, slow and deliberate.

"You got hurt blowing up an entire estate," she said softly. The words hung between them, heavy with more than just gratitude. She didn't say *for me*—but it was there, unspoken, threaded through the way she looked at him. "You've earned that room."

A beat passed. Then another.

"Well, my offer still stands," he murmured, his eyes locked onto her lips.

She gave him a heated look. "I'll keep it in mind."

And with that, she turned, vanishing into the shadows of the stairwell with Ayda beside her.

Caelan stood there a moment longer, watching the space where she'd been. The warmth of her shoulder still lingered at his side.

Only when she was out of sight did he finally turn toward his cabin.

And God help him—he hoped to dream of her, even if he didn't sleep.

25.
Niev

Belowdecks was a patchwork of soft snores, creaking wood, and the occasional rustle of blankets. Lanterns had been dimmed to their lowest setting, casting the hammocks and makeshift bedding in flickers of warm amber and long curling shadows. Niev moved quietly through the narrow corridor between sleeping children, her steps practiced and silent, her heart still riding the aftershocks of the conversation on the forecastle deck.

She passed Ayda curled like a comma in one of the wider hammocks, one arm dangling down, fingers twitching faintly with dreams. Teagan was sprawled out nearby, already snoring softly with a blanket kicked halfway down his chest.

Niev pulled herself into her hammock with a slow exhale, body folding into the sway of it. The canvas gave beneath her weight, cradling her in a strange, familiar rhythm. She laid her arm across her chest, staring up at the timber slats of the ceiling just inches above.

For a while, she listened to the sound of breathing. A chorus of lives she hadn't known existed days ago. Dozens of hearts still learning what safety felt like. Her own heart was a quieter thing, stitched together with too many memories and not enough time to sort through them.

Eventually, sleep pulled her under.

❋ ❋ ❋

She was small again.

Knees tucked beneath her, back pressed to the cold stone wall of the corridor just outside her mother's chamber. The flickering of a candelabra down the hall did nothing to soften the sharpness of the shadows and voices on the other side of the door.

"I warned you, Elowyn" her grandmother's voice cut like a blade— measured, furious, controlled. "I warned you what mixing our line with Thornmere blood would cost."

Inside, her mother didn't answer at first. Only the quiet rustle of fabric. The heavy hush of someone bracing for impact.

"My children are strong," her mother said eventually. "Both of them. In their own way."

"Strong?" The Matron's voice rose. "You've wasted centuries of power on a boy. Elias will never rule the clan. He was born to waste his gift. And she—" A pause. A sneer thick in the silence. "She's nothing but a wild beast—with her father's cursed bones and feral blood."

Niev flinched.

She was too young to understand all of it. But she understood the bitterness. The disgust.

"She's powerful," her mother whispered. "You've seen what she can do."

"I've seen enough," the Matron spat. "Her shapeshifting is not a gift— it is a mutation. Filthy. Untamed. No witch will ever follow her."

"She's still your heir."

"She is not," her grandmother hissed. "She will never be my heir. No child of mine who shifts like a beast and cannot wield true witch power will ever sit on the throne."

Another pause. Longer. Colder.

"You had one duty," the Matron said. "To give me a daughter strong enough to carry on the line. An heir worthy of our name. And even that you failed."

Niev didn't remember how long she sat there after the silence fell. But when the door finally opened and her mother emerged, eyes red and shoulders slumped, Niev turned her face to the wall and pretended not to cry.

❀ ❀ ❀

She woke with a jolt, heart pounding.

For a few disoriented seconds, she didn't know where she was.

Darkness pressed in from all sides—low wood overhead, thick wool beneath her hands. Then the soft creak of the ship reminded her. The pitch of the ocean. The quiet sigh of wind passing through the rigging. She wasn't in a cell. Or the Silk Lotus. Or the palace.

She was on the *Sersha Mara*.

And she was safe.

She dragged in a breath and let it out slowly. The panic didn't disappear, but it loosened its grip—slightly. Enough that her thoughts began to unfurl, sticky and restless.

Her mouth was dry.

Her skin felt damp with sweat.

She reached up, pressing her palm to her chest where her heartbeat still thudded with a rapid, uneven rhythm. It had been *years* since she'd dreamed of her grandmother's voice. Of that narrow hallway behind the throne wing. Of the quiet way her mother cried when she thought no one was listening.

Niev squeezed her eyes shut, trying to force the memory away.

But it clung like oil.

The disappointment in her grandmother's voice, venomous and cold. *"You disgraced this family when you married that man. A savage from the woods. You could've had power. A legacy. Instead, you chose weakness. And now you come crawling back?"*

The venom in those words still bled through time.

Niev had only been ten. Too young to fully understand why her mother had been cast aside. Too old to believe it wasn't already too late to save her. She remembered hiding in the corridor, back pressed to the stone, knees drawn up to her chest. She remembered biting her sleeve to stop herself from crying.

She remembered the look on her mother's face when she finally emerged—like something had shattered inside and would never be repaired.

Niev blinked herself back to the present.

The ship was quiet, the hush of sleep settling like a blanket across the hammocks. The youngest children curled like pups in corners and crates. Ayda murmured once in her sleep across the way, and Teagan had somehow lost his entire blanket to the floor. Only the occasional creak of timber broke the stillness, and somewhere above, she could hear faint footfalls of the night watch pacing overhead.

She wouldn't sleep again.

Not tonight.

Carefully, she shifted her legs over the side of the hammock. A child's small foot was nestled inches from her own, twitching in a dream. Niev smiled faintly and adjusted the child's blanket before rising.

She found her coat. Pulled it on.

The air belowdecks was cold now, the kind of chill that came with the last breath of night before sunrise. Lanternlight glowed faintly against the hull walls, and she made her way toward one of the small benches beside a riveted porthole. It wasn't much, but it was hers for now.

The satchel sat where she'd tucked it the night before, heavy with its burden.

She pulled it into her lap and unfastened the knot.

The ledger rustled open.

The pages inside were fragile, the parchment browned at the edges, the ink faded but legible. Neat, bureaucratic handwriting lined every row—precise, uncaring, the kind of penmanship that made it easy to forget each line represented a stolen life.

She skimmed the first few entries.

Children's names. Approximate ages. Acquisition location. Holding time. Destination. Final buyer code. Price.

It was like reading a butcher's log.

A flicker of nausea coiled in her gut.

She flipped the page. And the next. Her fingers hesitated at some names—too young, too familiar—but she kept going. Her body still ached from the mission, from sleeplessness, from the memory of the tunnels. But something in her refused to stop. Something urged her forward.

Each name felt like a stone dropped in water. Small waves, until the ripple became a roar.

She paused now and then. Let her eyes close. Let her fingers rest.

But she *couldn't* stop.

There were too many names.

Too many children.

And then—

She saw it.

And everything inside her *stilled*.

There it was. Her name. Her real name. Before the world had taken it and twisted it into something else.

She stared at it like it might vanish.

And then, just beneath it—indented with the same scratchy pen, barely visible—

Was another name.

Elias Nivola.

She blinked.

Once.

Twice.

The page didn't change.

Elias Nivola.

And for a long moment, everything inside her just *stopped*.

Her hands trembled violently. The air left her lungs in one sharp, broken sound.

"No," she whispered. "No, no, no—"

Because he had *died*. She had *seen* the blood. She had felt his fingers slip from hers. She had lived every *day* with the silence where his voice used to be. Elias, who had been born beside her, lived beside her. Elias, who used to steal her bread when they were children and then split it in half and give it back. Elias, who could recite lines from books he wasn't supposed to be reading, and who used to fall asleep with his head on her shoulder during carriage rides. Elias, who had tried to fight off the men who came for them.

She could still feel the ghost of his grip on her wrist.

The way he had yelled her name when they tore them apart.

She hadn't just lost her brother.

She'd lost half her soul.

She stared at the names—*their* names—like they were carved into her skin.

For ten years, she had carried their deaths. Like lead in her lungs. Like thorns beneath her ribs. She had built her rage, her sharpness, her purpose on the ashes of a family stolen too soon.

And yet—

Elias Nivola. Marked alive. Processed. Sold. Redirected.

The note beneath it said only: *Lot #47 rerouted. Sold to unregistered buyer. Escort redirected to Zarenth.*

There was no final sale line. No confirmation of death. Just a blank, empty space.

And Niev broke.

Her body folded forward over the page, fingers clenched tight as the sob burst from her chest like a wound reopening. Her breath came in ragged gasps, the kind that left her shaking with the force of it. Tears blurred the ink until his name bled into hers.

She wanted to scream.

To vomit.

To tear the ship apart plank by plank until someone told her *what was happening*.

Her twin. Her other half. *Alive.*

A keening sound broke from her throat. Too soft to wake anyone. But it hurt. It *hurt*.

She clutched the folder to her chest, rocking forward, breath catching again and again like her lungs didn't know what to do anymore. She didn't feel the tears until they hit her knees.

Niev couldn't stop shaking.

Everything she had been—all the steel and silence and fury—cracked. And beneath it was the girl who had waited too long for someone to come for her. The girl who had been left behind and made herself a weapon because it was easier than being vulnerable.

And after what felt like forever, the rage returned. Not the cold, calculated sort she wore on her belt like a blade—but the wild, furious grief of a girl who had begged for someone to save her family and gotten silence in return.

She didn't even know what she would do now.

Where she would go.

Who she would have to kill to find him.

But she would.

God help whoever stood in her way.

Because this wasn't just a mission anymore.

This was blood.

This was her brother.

And she would burn the whole of Eldhaven to the ground if it meant hearing his voice again.

※　※　※

The sky had begun to pale.

The softest shade of blue-grey spilled across the horizon, bleeding into the dark as the stars receded, one by one. The sea rocked gently beneath the *Sersha Mara*, each wave like a quiet exhale. Dawn hadn't broken yet, but it hovered—waiting.

And Niev was still on her knees.

The ledger lay in her lap, pages bent and crinkled where her fingers had gripped too tightly. Her face was dry now—hollow. As though the storm had passed through her and left nothing in its wake but scorched earth and silence.

She couldn't remember how long she'd been sitting there. Time had dissolved after she saw the name.

Elias.

Elias was alive.

Or had been.

And the grief of *not knowing* was almost worse than the grief of loss.

Her mouth was still open, slightly parted as if her lips hadn't figured out how to close again. Her arms ached from holding the book. Her bones felt distant. Detached.

When the hatch creaked open behind her, Niev didn't move.

The cold wind off the sea curled around her shoulders like a second skin, but she stayed exactly where she was—knees pressed to the deck, the ledger clutched like a wound in her lap.

She heard the footsteps first—rushed, heavy, familiar.

"Niev?" Ayda's voice. Closer now. Sharper with worry. "Niev, what—?"

Then Teagan. "God—what happened?"

Still, she didn't look up. Didn't speak.

The silence stretched, thick and heavy, until it began to take shape in their throats—frantic and clawing. She felt Ayda drop to her knees beside her, a hand brushing her shoulder, hesitant and gentle, as if Niev might crumble to dust at the slightest touch.

But it was Caelan's voice that anchored her.

Low. Steady. Desperate in a way he rarely allowed himself to be.

"Talk to me, love."

She lifted her head slowly. Her eyes were unfocused, lashes damp, and her breath came too shallow. She moved as if underwater, arms trembling as she offered the ledger to Ayda, fingers barely holding on.

When she spoke, her voice rasped out of her throat like it had been torn loose.

"My brother," she whispered. "Elias. He's alive."

Ayda froze. Her fingers curled around the ledger, cautious and reverent, like it might bite or break if she held it too tight. Her eyes scanned the pages—brows drawing together, breath coming faster.

And then she saw it.

Elias Nivola.

Sera Nieva Nivola.

The breath left her in a sharp, audible gasp.

"Holy God Almighty," Ayda whispered. "Niev—Niev, this is—"

She stopped. Her hand flew to her mouth.

But it wasn't horror on her face. Not pity. It was something else. Something deeper.

Recognition.

"Niev," she breathed, like she was saying her name for the first time. "Oh dear God."

Teagan stepped forward, confusion tightening his features, voice rising. "Someone tell me what the *hell* is going on!"

Ayda turned the ledger, her hands shaking. "Look."

Teagan leaned in. His eyes moved across the page, reading the names aloud like they might rearrange into something that made more sense.

"Sera Nieva Nivola... Elias Nivola..."

His voice faltered. He looked at Niev. Then back at the page.

Then something shifted in his expression. Slowly, very slowly, he straightened, like the truth was catching up to him in real time.

"Who's Sera Nieva?" he asked, though he already knew.

The silence that followed was cavernous.

Ayda stared at Niev, wide-eyed.

"You're the lost heir of Arenthia," she said, barely a breath. "Adrianna Nivola's granddaughter."

Niev didn't confirm it. Didn't deny it either.

There was no more room for secrets. Not after this.

She closed her eyes and exhaled shakily. The wind bit at her cheeks. Her fingers ached.

But all she could think was how tired she was. So, so tired.

26.
Caelan

Niev didn't speak at first.

She just sat there, curled in on herself, her fingers clenched so tightly that Caelan was half convinced they might crumble. Her shoulders had rounded forward, her head bowed low. Her body was there—kneeling, breathing—but her mind had gone somewhere else entirely.

It was the silence that shook him the most.

The Tigress who never let herself crack. Who had walked into fire and monsters and ballrooms full of leering nobles without blinking—was shaking.

He stepped forward before he even realized he'd moved, his voice breaking the silence.

"...You're Elias's sister?"

Her head snapped up, eyes wide and wild. All the blood drained from her face as she stared at him. "What?"

Caelan didn't look away. "I knew Elias. He was with me in Zarenth."

Around them, the air shifted like glass cracking under pressure.

Ayda gasped, quiet and sharp. Teagan muttered something under his breath. But Caelan wasn't looking at them.

He was looking at her. Only her.

She stared at him like he'd just split the world in half with a sentence. Like she couldn't decide whether to scream or collapse.

Her voice came out strangled. "You *knew* him?"

He nodded, slow and solemn. "It was years ago. When I was a boy. He was... quiet, but not soft. Kind, in a way most people didn't know how to be in a place like that. He helped keep some of the younger ones alive. Gave up his rations sometimes."

He paused, watching her carefully.

"I didn't know his full name. Just Elias. But he told me once... he had a sister. Said she was his twin."

Niev made a sound—half breath, half whimper. Her body trembled, and her eyes shimmered, but she didn't blink.

Caelan forced himself to keep going, even as something twisted in his own chest.

"He used to talk about her. Said she was fire and teeth and too smart for her own good." A faint, broken smile tugged at the corner of his mouth. "He said he'd find her again someday. Said if she was alive, she'd probably be fighting like hell."

Niev's eyes blurred again. Her lips parted around a gasp, her hands shaking harder now, knuckles white against the edge of the ledger. Then she exhaled, a sound so broken it barely made it past her lips. "He's alive," she rasped.

Caelan's expression sobered. He dropped beside her, kneeling on the opposite side. His eyes searched her face. "But Niev... that was years ago. Before I escaped."

Her eyes snapped to him again, desperate. "But you *saw* him. You knew him."

"Yes. I did. I swear it."

"Then there's a chance he might still be in there," she whispered.

"Maybe," Caelan said gently. But the grief in his voice was quiet and honest. "I don't know what happened to him after. I don't know if he made it out. I wish I could say for certain. But I can't."

She blinked rapidly, fighting back another wave of tears.

"I *have* to find him," Niev said, her voice like steel. "I don't care what it takes. I don't care where he was taken. I'm going to find him."

Her fists clenched against the cold.

"I have to," she said, voice cracking as she looked pleadingly at Caelan.

He reached out. His hand closed gently around her elbow, grounding her as she swayed beneath the weight of it all. He didn't rush her. Didn't try to pull her to her feet. Just waited—his eyes steady on hers, his grip solid.

"We'll find him," he said, voice low but certain. "Together."

And he could see then how hard the word *together* hit her.

Her mouth wobbled as she stared at him, searching for something— maybe disbelief, maybe fear—but there was none. Only quiet conviction. And the tiniest ghost of a smile crept across her lips, fleeting and fragile, but real.

Then the moment shattered.

A frantic shout rang out across the deck.

Boots pounded overhead. A bell clanged once. Twice. Then came the sharp sound of a whistle, followed by the thud of running footsteps on the stairs.

One of the younger crewmen—barely more than a boy—burst into view, panting, wide-eyed. "Captain says to get to your stations. Now! We've been spotted!"

All four of them snapped to attention.

Laughlan's voice boomed above, already halfway up the stairs to the helm. "To your posts, you crusty fools! We've got company!"

Teagan appeared at the foot of the mast, blades half-drawn, scowling. "Company? Who the hell—?"

"Darrow," Laughlan bellowed from the helm, spinning the rudder hard as the *Sersha Mara* banked into a sharp turn. "That bastard's ship just came up on our starboard. Either he survived the fire, or he's got a twin as ugly as him. Either way—we're being hunted."

Teagan swore with enough venom to blister the paint off the hull. "I *saw* that estate go up. No one should've walked out of there."

But Niev was still. Too still.

Her eyes didn't shimmer with tears anymore. The storm that had gutted her minutes ago was gone—drained from her face like ink bled from parchment. In its place, something colder had taken root.

Caelan knew that look.

He'd seen it in the faces of men right before they charged into a line of spears without armor. In the set jaw of a woman who stepped into fire rather than bow. Hell he'd worn it himself only a day before.

It was the look of someone about to do something *very, very stupid.*

"Keep the children below," she said, voice like drawn steel. "And don't let them come up. No matter what you hear."

Ayda froze. "Niev—"

"I'll handle it."

Caelan took a step forward. "Wait, what do you—?"

But she was already moving. Boots silent on the deck. A flash of crimson as her coat fell from her shoulders and hit the wood. She climbed the railing without hesitation, her back straight, her eyes locked on the dark waters ahead where a shadow loomed on the horizon.

"Niev!" Caelan shouted, his heart in his throat. "*Don't—*"

She leapt.

The wind ripped past her as she hit the water with barely a splash.

One blink—she was there.

The next—gone, disappeared beneath the surface.

Caelan lunged to the edge of the deck, eyes scouring the waves. Nothing.

Just the black churn of water, bottomless and cold.

He gripped the railing hard enough to hurt, his breath coming too fast, too loud in his ears. His thoughts crashed through his skull like waves against rock—*what was she doing, why didn't he stop her, what if she didn't come back up—*

No splash. No sign.

Just empty sea.

She'd disappeared like a blade slipping beneath the skin of the world. And his heart was *slamming* against his ribs, trying to climb out of his chest. The only sound in his ears now was blood. Fury. Fear. *Please God—*

And then—

The ocean *shifted.*

Something stirred deep below.

And the waves exploded upward in a burst of white foam and coiling scales.

A monstrous form breached the surface, long and coiled, its glistening body as dark as obsidian and lined with jagged silver ridges. The head alone was the size of a wagon, crowned with fins like blades, eyes glowing deep gold, intelligent and furious beneath the surface.

And Caelan—still clutching the rail, breath caught in his throat—couldn't move.

Because somehow, impossibly, he *knew*.

The serpent was *her*.

Niev had shifted into a bloody sea-bound *leviathan*.

And it turned its head toward Darrow's approaching ship with the unmistakable grace of a creature born for war.

Ayda gripped the railing, jaw slack. "*Mother of stars...*"

Teagan's hand dropped from his sword, eyes wide. "She's not just a shifter," he muttered. "She's a *myth.*"

Caelan didn't move. He couldn't.

All he could do was watch as Niev—the woman he loved, the girl who had been stolen, the warrior who had clawed her way back—rose from the waves like a wrathful beast, fury made flesh and scale.

The serpent coiled once beneath the surface—then vanished.

A single ripple marked its absence, and then, just beyond the bow of the *Sersha Mara*, the water split with a violent crack.

She surged upward.

A massive column of scaled muscle, all speed and precision, cut through the waves like a blade through silk. Her body writhed and snapped through the sea with unnatural velocity—no creature that size should move so fast. The glow of her eyes lit the foam from beneath, golden and vengeful, and with every lunge forward, her wake slammed like thunder against the hull of Darrow's ship.

Then came the first strike.

The serpent rose and *smashed* down onto the deck of the enemy vessel with bone-shattering force.

Wood *splintered*.

Men *screamed*.

The ship groaned beneath the impact, and before any of them could recover, she whipped her body sideways and sent a cluster of soldiers hurling into the air. Some landed hard against the deck. Others didn't land at all.

Limbs flailed—one arm bent clean backward, another figure struck the mast with a sickening crunch.

And then—

From the depths of the dark water, they came.

Sirens.

At first, only shadows—darting shapes just below the surface, swift and shimmering. Then faces emerged—inhuman, beautiful, eyes as pale as moonlight and lips stained red. They circled the serpent like loyal wolves, and every time she flung another man from the deck, they caught him.

No screams.

Only a sudden silence as sailor after sailor vanished beneath the waves, pulled down by pale arms and sharp teeth.

This wasn't a battle. It was a *massacre*.

On the *Sersha Mara*, no one moved.

Ayda stood frozen beside Caelan, lips parted in mute horror. Teagan gripped the railing, knuckles white, no jest on his tongue for once.

The crew stared too, dozens of hardened pirates and smugglers, and not one of them breathed.

Because what they were witnessing wasn't war.

It was *retribution*.

Then the serpent reared back, water sluicing off her silver-scaled body in curtains, and for a breathless moment, she hung in the air—impossible, terrible, divine.

And as she came down—

She *shifted*.

In the *blink* of a heartbeat, the massive coils vanished into a flare of magic and shadow and flame, and from their center fell *Niev*.

Barefoot, bare-armed, soaked in saltwater, landing like judgment itself on the ruined deck of Darrow's ship.

Her dark hair clung to her back and shoulders, dripping. Her chin lifted. Her eyes glowed—still gold, still otherworldly—and her clothes, or what was left of them, clung like seafoam to her skin.

She moved forward. Unarmed. Unhurried.

Like a predator with no doubt left in its bones.

Caelan's heart pounded as he leaned over the rail, watching her walk across the splintered deck, straight toward the man who had ruined her life.

Toward *Brennan Darrow*.

27.
Niev

The wreckage of Darrow's ship groaned beneath her feet.

Salt clung to her skin like armor, her breath still tasting of ocean and blood and the shift. Magic flickered just beneath her flesh—raw, volatile, alive. The siren-song of the sea still thrummed in her blood, the echo of her serpent form winding through her limbs like an aftershock. She could still *feel* the water pressing around her body. Could still smell the copper tang of terror pouring off the men who had survived her descent.

Smoke rose in thin trails from shattered lanterns. Splinters littered the deck like bones. The mast creaked, half-leaning. And somewhere below, water had begun to leak in.

She didn't care.

All she could see was Brennan Darrow.

He staggered at the far rail, those ridiculous self-important robes clinging to him, now soaked, torn, and streaked with grime. He leaned on a ruined barrel, one hand pressed to a bleeding temple. His perfect composure shattered, he still tried to carry himself like some sanctified martyr—though now he limped, lip split, eyes wild.

He had stopped barking orders the moment she struck.

Now, he stared at her with pure, unfiltered fear.

And Niev watched the flicker in his gaze—the almost-recognition, the buried memory itching at his instincts—but it never quite surfaced.

Of course not. He didn't know her. Not as the terrified girl sold to the Silk Lotus ten years ago. Not as the daughter of the woman whose throat he'd coldly ordered slit. Her family. Her life. Everything he'd destroyed.

He didn't remember.

But it didn't matter anymore. She'd *make him* remember.

But she would make him.

She took a deliberate step forward, each footfall ringing across the splintered deck. The few remaining crew backed away, hands twitching toward weapons. A weathered gunner spat curses and raised his flintlock.

"Kill the witch!" Darrow snarled, staggering to his feet. "Seize her, you curs!"

He spat blood onto the deck. His voice wavering on the edge of hysteria.

Niev smirked as his gunner charged.

In one fluid motion she dropped to the balls of her feet, weaving under his swinging arm. Her hand shot out to catch his wrist; bone snapped with a dry crack. She kicked his shin, and he pitched forward, half his body dragging across jagged wood until his skull rattled against the deck in a sickening thud.

As Niev stalked towards Darrow, a low hum thrummed beneath her skin—an ancient pulse she'd never felt before. At first it was almost tender, like water seeping between her bones, but with each heartbeat it flared hotter, angrier. The deckboards at her feet darkened, as if ink had spilled in spreading rivulets around her boots.

She froze, startled by the living darkness, but a slow, fierce delight curled in her chest. The shadows slithered up her calves, pooling at her hips, then shot outward in jagged tendrils that wrapped around Darrow's ankles. His eyes went wide as he felt the chill of darkness binding him in place.

Niev's breath caught in her throat—she'd never meant to command the shadows, only to stand before him and make him pay. Now the gloom thickened, solidifying into shapes that hovered in the corners of her vision. Two blades of night shimmered with oily light in her hands. She didn't know how she'd drawn them forth, only that the power drummed at her temples, wild and uncontained, and she reveled in the dizzying rush of it.

Darrow scrambled back, convulsing with panic as memories he couldn't name flickered in his eyes. The crew froze, a primal terror igniting in their chests—not illusions, but something older, more visceral, as if the darkness itself had come alive. Niev's pulse thundered, a triumphant roar behind her ribs, and the shadows pulsed in answer, squeezing tighter around Darrow until he sagged to his knees, stripped of every scrap of arrogance, leaving only his pale, frantic face visible in the gloom.

Her own eyes burned silver, like distant stars wrenched from the night sky. Niev let one of the onyx blades vanish into a fit of smoke as she reached out, her fingers curling around Darrow's jaw, thumbs brushing the split at his lip.

He spluttered, panic gouging his voice. "Please—have mercy—"

"You slit my parents' throats, watched them *die*," she whispered, each word a blade. "And then sold me, and my brother into chains... Did you ever spare a thought for mercy then, Brennan Darrow?"

His eyes darted to hers, desperately seeking a way out. "Please—I'm begging you—"

Niev gave a mirthless laugh. "It's too late for begging now," her eyes roamed his face like a hungry predator. "But answer my question, and I *might* make your death...less painful."

His eyes bulged, shadows suffocating him. Her hand gripped his jaw so tightly her nails drew blood from the gauges in his cheeks. "Who sent you after the heirs of Arenthia?"

He rasped out a strangled breath, eyes darting as if the answer might melt away before he spoke it. "Don—Don Arin—"

Niev's grip tightened, the eel-black shadows thickening around his wrists like choking snakes. "Speak clearly," she commanded, voice low and cold.

"His name is Don Arin Alvania!" Darrow gasped. "He... he paid me in gold, gave me his signet to seal the contract. I've never met him face to face—But I swear it was his doing!"

A slow smile curved Niev's lips, cruel and beautiful. She released his jaw, letting the darkness draw back inch by hungry inch until Darrow's knees hit the deck with a sickening thud. He wheezed, rubbing the raw cut at his lip, blood smearing his fingers.

"You've done well, Brennan," she whispered, voice deeper than the void, "Now pray that God has more mercy on your soul than I did."

Darrow's eyes bulged as he scraped himself upright, tears and blood mingling on his cheeks.

A cold smile curled on Niev's lips as magic shimmered down her fingers like oil on water—dark, smooth, endless. The wind rose around her, seawater and shadows curling up from the deck as if answering her call.

It erupted from her palm in a column of flame-veined shadow—obsidian light bursting skyward, rippling out in rings that cracked the air.

Darrow looked at her in horror as the deck beneath her *screamed*, splintering in spiderweb fractures. The magic poured from her fingers, *through* her veins, like it had always been there—waiting.

Waiting for her to remember who she was.

Wind howled from nowhere. The rigging snapped taut. Lanterns burst into sparks. A vortex of shadow spiraled up behind her, and Darrow stumbled back like the deck had come alive beneath him.

His lips moved.

But Niev wasn't listening.

She stepped forward, magic flickering across her skin like lightning under flesh. Her voice when it came was low.

"This—" she said, and a bolt of energy cracked from her palm, catching him square in the chest. He flew backward, slammed into the mast, and crumpled to the floor, coughing, gasping. "—is for my father... Feodor Helvast, who you murdered in cold blood like he was *nothing*."

Darrow tried to rise, "Please—"

Another strike—this one seared across his arm, flaying skin, igniting fabric.

"This is for my mother. Elowyn Nivola. Who begged for mercy before you slit her throat."

He screamed now. But she didn't stop.

A jagged arc of magic whipped through the air and snapped his leg out from under him with a sickening *crack*.

"This is for my brother. Elias Nivola. The prince of Arenthia who you sold like cattle."

She stalked forward, slow and terrible.

"And this one—" she whispered, standing over him as he writhed, bloody and broken, eyes wide with something like recognition now. "— is for me."

She raised her arm, her shadows turning into a sharp obsidian blade.

"And for every child whose life you stole."

Before he could beg forgiveness, she swung her blade—an obsidian crescent humming with hunger. In a single, fluid motion, she swept it across his throat. Time fractured in that instant. Darrow's scream split the air, his fingers clawed at empty darkness, and his head slipped free from his shoulders, rolling onto the deck in a shining arc of gore.

The severed head lay upon splintered wood, eyes frozen wide in disbelief, as the shadows Niev commanded drifted back into her form, carrying every drop of spilled blood with them. The world snapped abruptly into harsh morning light, the deck's ruin suddenly stark and silent.

Niev stood above the lifeless corpse, chest heaving, the last echo of his terror still thrumming in her veins. She watched the blood- and shadow-streaked plank for a long moment, feeling the primal power pulse beneath her skin.

The silence afterward was louder than the screams had been.

She turned to see the remaining crew of Darrow's ship—those still standing—stared at her like she was the end of the world.

Maybe she was.

She took one step toward them, blood-soaked and glowing, and they *scattered*.

Some ran.

Some *leapt* overboard.

Right into the waiting arms of the sirens below, whose high, lilting song rose in perfect harmony with the thunder of crashing waves.

It was a massacre.

A reckoning.

And Niev—barefoot, burned, with salt crusted in her lashes—stood at the center of it all like a living storm.

She looked up at the *Sersha Mara*, at the deck where Caelan and her friends stood watching her, hand clenched around the railing, jaw tight with something between awe and horror.

And then Niev felt the storm inside her collapse, her legs buckling as the fierce blaze of vengeance drained from her veins, leaving her hollow, exhausted, and utterly spent.

28.
Caelan

He had seen death before.

He had been the cause of it many times. Clean kills. Dirty ones. Desperate ones.

But nothing—*nothing*—had ever looked like *this*.

The deck of Darrow's ship was slick with blood and firelight, the mast cracked in two, sails burning to ash. Bodies floated facedown in the water. Others never surfaced at all.

And Niev stood at the center of it—drenched, silver-eyed, the sea curling gently behind her like it belonged to her.

Caelan couldn't breathe.

Not because of the carnage, though the stench of it hung thick in the air. Not because of the sirens, still crooning beneath the waves as they fed on the last of the crew. But because of *her*.

Because of this infuriating, and terrifyingly beautiful woman, who was carved of fury and shadows, with magic burning under her skin and vengeance singing in her blood.

He had always known there was something more to her. Had felt it in every glance, every fight, every time she'd looked at him like she wanted to devour the world just to make it right.

But seeing it—*all of it*—laid bare like this?

Ten years of silence.

He pressed his knuckles to his mouth, gripping the railing with the other hand, trying to ground himself in the wood, and wind, and truth of what had just happened. Teagan stood beside him, for once saying nothing. Ayda's face had gone white. Around them, the crew of the *Sersha Mara* stared in stunned, reverent horror.

"She took down an entire ship," one of the crew whispered. "All by herself."

And as Caelan looked back at Niev—barefoot, salt-streaked, her silver eyes burning—she sank to her knees on Darrow's collapsing deck. The water, churned to foam by the sirens below, lapped at her calves, but she didn't rise.

"She's going to sink with that ship," Caelan rasped as realization dawned on him, scrambling for purchase on the slick planks. He bent over the ship's edge, ready to dive into the churning water below, but Ayda's hand closed around his wrist and yanked him back.

"Don't be a fool," she hissed, eyes wide. "Those sirens will drag you under in an instant."

He wrenched his arm free. "I'm not going to stand here and watch her drown!"

"You won't be much help if you get eaten either!" Ayda shouted in exasperation.

But their argument was cut short when the lookout—one of Laughlan's deckhands—cried out from the stern, voice trembling. "Look!"

Both of them snapped toward the water as a sudden swell rolled back from the hull of Darrow's wrecked vessel. In that instant, the surface of the sea rose in a perfect, colossal hand—fingers of water curling beneath Niev's knees, lifting her gently upward.

Ayda staggered back, jaw dropping. "What on God's good earth—"

Caelan's heart pounded so hard he thought the deck would shudder beneath him. Niev, still on her knees, blinked in confusion, arms lifting instinctively as if to steady herself on the intangible palm. Her eyes widened, stunned, looking almost mesmerized by the liquid cradle that bore her.

Caelan's eyebrows scrunched in confusion. He scanned the deck of the Sersha Mara, seeking the source of this impossible tide. But everyone seemed as shocked and transfixed as him, until he locked eyes with Teagan, who stood a few paces away. The tracker's hands hovered at his sides, fingers flexing and twisting in a pattern too precise to come off as natural.

Caelan felt a cold click of dread. The wave that carried Niev across the gap was no gift of the sea alone.

Niev didn't lift a hand. Didn't flinch. She simply let the sea *carry* her.

Lifting her into the air on a wave of water and shadow, gliding her across the distance between ships like a figure from myth. Her feet didn't touch the deck of the *Sersha* until the very last second.

And when they did—

She landed like an angel of death descending to earth.

Soaked in saltwater and blood.

Hair tangled, skin kissed with bruises and shadow magic, the remains of her clothes clinging to her like some rabid beast crawling out of hell. Her eyes still shining bright silver like starlight.

No one moved.

The entire crew—rough, hardened, most of them killers—stood frozen. Some still clutched weapons. Others held their breath like a wrong exhale might draw her wrath.

Even the *children* stared.

Because Ayda hadn't kept them below.

Because *everyone* had seen.

Even Talia. Even little Finnian.

All of them wide-eyed and silent as they watched the girl who had sung to them the night before step onto the deck like a *monster* from their parents' stories.

But when Caelan looked at Niev, it wasn't fear on her face.

Not entirely.

It was something colder.

Expectation.

She looked at them—all of them—and waited.

Waited to see who would run. Who would *recoil*. Who would look at her now with the horror she knew she'd earned. And when her eyes found *him*—

Caelan felt her dare.

Go on, she seemed to be saying. *Look away. Turn from me. Show me I was right to keep you all at a distance.*

But he didn't.

He closed the distance between them in three strides, and then he was there—his hand in her hair, his other arm wrapping around her waist, pulling her flush against him, as he caught her lips with his and kissed her fiercely. In front of *everyone*.

She tasted like blood, and salt, and sweat. But none of it mattered.

Because this—*this*—was the woman he loved.

Not just the assassin. Not just the myth. Not even just the girl who had survived.

But the force of nature who had stared down monsters and taken them down.

She kissed him back with equal fire, her fingers curling into his shirt, clutching like she needed him to anchor her. Like she wasn't sure the storm had passed until he touched her.

When they broke apart, her chest was heaving, her eyes wild. Still waiting. Still wondering. Then, with a slow blink, the silver starlit glow in her eyes faded, settling back into their familiar golden-brown warmth.

Caelan's breath feathered over her lips as he leaned in, the world narrowing to the space between them. His hand rose, trembling with something like awe, as his thumb traced the arc of a bloodstain on her cheek.

He drew a breath so deep his chest ached, then spoke, voice low and intimate. "I love you."

Her breath caught, and her eyes snapped up to his.

"I love you, Niev," he said again, because he needed her to believe him, to hear the raw truth in his words. "God help me, I have for a long time. And I'm done pretending otherwise."

The deck had gone quiet again.

He didn't care.

Let the crew watch. Let the children stare.

He would've said it in front of all of Eldhaven.

Because this woman had just single handedly saved all of their lives, *again*.

And she was still standing there—barefoot, blood-soaked, trembling with something too complicated to name—and Caelan saw only her. Her shadow-dark hair clung to her shoulders, her skin bruised and burning, yet in that moment she was more radiant than any sunrise.

He stepped forward, closing the last inch of space, and gathered her to him. She met him just as fiercely, her fingers clutching his shirt.

When they broke apart, he rested his forehead against hers, voice softer now, a vow on his lips.

"No matter what darkness comes next, you will never face it alone."

The silence stretched—thick and heavy as the blood still drying on the boards.

Caelan kept his hands on her, half-afraid she might vanish if he let go.

"Remind me," Teagan said, his voice cracking into the hush like a whip through glass, "to never, ever get on your bad side."

Caelan turned just in time to see him standing a respectful few feet away, hair windblown, mouth drawn in mock solemnity. His eyes flicked to the wreckage behind them. "God, Niev. I mean... I've seen you slit throats, threaten nobles, knock men twice your size on their asses—but this?"

Caelan saw Niev brace herself for the fear and judgement that would come next.

Then, mercifully—

"I don't know about the rest of you," Laughlan drawled from behind them, "but I think I speak for every warm-blooded man on this deck when I say that display *definitely* awakened something hot in me."

Several sailors barked out surprised laughter. Teagan let out a low whistle.

Ayda made a noise of pure disgust. "What the hell is wrong with you?"

"Too long at sea, love," Laughlan said cheerfully. "Too long and far too sober."

Even Caelan cracked the barest smile.

But it was Niev's reaction that held him.

She didn't roll her eyes. Didn't bristle or snap at the captain.

She just turned her head slightly, met Laughlan's gaze across the deck—

And smiled gratefully.

Caelan had to give it to the bastard.

Laughlan might be cocky, inappropriate, and a walking headache most of the time—but *he understood people*. Understood when to press and when to ease off. When to offer a knife, and when to offer a joke. And right now, when every set of eyes on the ship had been filled with awe or fear, the captain had chosen laughter.

And it had worked.

He'd diffused the moment before it could hurt her.

Niev didn't thank him, but Laughlan tipped an invisible hat, as if he felt her thanks anyway.

And for the first time since she'd returned to the ship, Caelan watched her exhale.

Her shoulders dropped by half an inch. Her spine relaxed just enough to stop trembling.

And though her hand was still stained red, she didn't tuck it away.

She let them see her.

And they didn't run.

Neither did he.

He just stood at her side—quiet, steady, ready.

Because he'd never been more sure:

This woman, storm-forged and shadow-wrapped, was *his*.

And God help anyone who tried to take her from him.

Eventually, Teagan stepped forward and did something that surprised all of them.

He pulled her into a hug. No jokes. No winks. Just quiet, steady arms around her.

"In case there was any doubt about what I was going to say," he said, voice low now, almost reverent. "You did what needed to be done. And I'd follow you to the end of the world."

Caelan's eyes drifted from Teagan to the water now still as glass, and a cold flicker of suspicion sparked in his chest, but he buried it beneath relief.

Niev didn't return the tracker's embrace, not quite, but she let him hold her. When he finally pulled back, Ayda stepped into the space he'd left. One brow lifted, a sly smile tugging at her lips. "So... should I be calling you *Matron* now?"

Caelan saw Niev flinch before the words even finished leaving Ayda's mouth. Her jaw tightened, her eyes darting toward the carnage littering the waves. The wind caught her hair again, tugging loose strands across her face, but she didn't brush them away.

"No," she said, and her voice was iron. "You shouldn't."

Ayda blinked, surprised.

"I was never going to be heir," Niev continued, her gaze still locked on the wreckage. "Adrianna Nivola made her shame of me quite clear from the start. She never would've named me her successor. Not when I couldn't wield magic."

Caelan watched Ayda's face soften.

"After what we just witnessed," she scoffed, "I'd beg to differ."

Niev's brows furrowed. "I don't know what that was," she said after a beat. "I've never been able to wield any magic. I've always just been a shapeshifter... like my father."

"Well," Ayda replied, her tone trying for lightness, "I think Adrianna might be proven wrong yet."

But it didn't comfort her. Caelan could see it.

She'd just unlocked power she knew nothing about after *twenty four years*.

Her eyes drifted again—back to the ruined ship, to the floating bodies, to the water now red and quiet.

And the way her shoulders pulled in, like she was bracing for a weight only she could feel...

Caelan wished he could carry it for her. But for now, he just stood close, their hands brushing, waiting to anchor her again when she needed it.

Because she *would* need it.

And he would be there.

29.
Niev

That night, Niev lay curled in her hammock belowdecks, staring up at the low, wooden beams just inches from her face, and tried not to think about the dozen children sleeping around her. Or the ones who weren't.

She'd never been one to sleep well, but now it was damn near impossible. Not with the weight of the ledger still fresh in her mind, or the salt on her skin from the storm she'd unleashed. She kept replaying the expressions on their faces after it was over—the horror, the awe, the confusion.

What did they see when they looked at her now? A protector? A monster?

The quiet rustle of movement pulled her gaze to the right. Small feet shuffled near the floorboards, hesitant. Then came a whisper-soft voice, barely above the creak of rope.

"You awake?"

Niev turned her head and found Talia standing there, barefoot and clutching a threadbare blanket around her shoulders. Her dark eyes shimmered in the dim lantern light.

"I just wanted to say thank you," Talia said, stepping closer. "For saving us again."

Niev opened her mouth, but nothing came. Not yet.

Talia took it as permission and climbed onto the edge of the hammock, legs dangling off the side. "I know some people were scared. But I wasn't. Not really. I thought... you looked like a story. Like something out of the books my sister used to read to me before—" she stopped, swallowed. "Anyway. I want to be strong like you. Fierce like you."

Niev's throat tightened. Her voice when it came was soft and raw. "You already are."

Talia's smile bloomed—quiet and proud.

"I mean it," Niev added, shifting slightly. "You survived something no one should have to. And you're still standing."

A small noise—like a sniffle or a stifled breath—echoed from nearby. Niev glanced around.

Two more children were awake. Then three. A few had propped themselves on elbows, others were just watching, faces solemn but open. One of the youngest gave a small, sleepy nod.

And something in Niev cracked. The warmth was unfamiliar—but welcome. It spread through her chest like sunlight on water.

"Alright," she whispered, clearing her throat. "Back to sleep, little rebels."

Talia grinned and slid down from the hammock. "Yes, ma'am," she added mockingly.

Niev watched them all settle in again. It took time, but eventually the small breaths evened out, the bodies curled back into safety, and the hush returned. She waited a few more minutes, just to be sure.

Then she slipped off the hammock, gathered her coat, and climbed the stairs to the upper deck.

The night was colder up here. The wind sharp enough to bite through the lingering dampness of her shirt, but she welcomed it. Needed the clarity.

The moon hung low and yellow over the horizon, and stars blanketed the sky in thick constellations. The sea below glimmered in places, and the creak of wood and sail offered the only rhythm.

She found Laughlan at the helm, one hand on the wheel, the other holding a chipped mug. He didn't startle when she approached.

"Don't suppose you're bringing me a drink?" he asked, grinning into the wind.

"Afraid not," she said, stepping beside him. "Just gratitude."

"Well, damn. Guess I'll take that too."

She leaned her arms on the edge of the rail, staring out at the waves. "You got us out. You got those children out. And I just want you to know that I am thankful for everything you've done," She hesitated, then said quietly, "And what you said this morning—"

He looked over at her. "Are you about to get all emotional on me, Tigress? Because I left my handkerchief in my other trousers."

She rolled her eyes. "Forget it."

"Nah, don't walk away now," he said, clearly amused. "You were doing so well. That was almost sincere."

She shook her head but didn't move. They stood in silence for a moment, watching the horizon shift as the ship carved through the waves.

Then, more softly, he added, "I meant what I said earlier. I'm glad you came back."

She glanced at him sidelong. "You were mostly being a flirt."

"I *am* mostly a flirt," he said with a smirk. "But I wasn't lying."

Her gaze dropped back to the sea.

"Still," he added, drawing out the word. "I'll admit I'm a little heartbroken."

"About?"

"You choosing broody and beautiful down there instead of me."

That earned a small smile. "What makes you think I chose?" she said playfully.

"Semantics," he said breezily. Then he sobered just a little. "But he's a good man, that one. Been through more than most. Loves you like it'll tear him in two. I can see it plain as day."

She didn't answer—but she didn't have to. The silence between them turned full.

Laughlan shifted his grip on the wheel, his voice losing some of its usual irreverence. "Listen... once we dock in Driftwood, I've been thinkin'."

Niev looked up at him, curious.

He nodded toward the shadowed horizon, where the hills of Thornmere would rise come morning. "You're takin' the Breyvian lads back to Solhaven next, right? Their families. The ones still waiting for them."

"That's the plan," she said cautiously.

"Then let me take the rest. The ones whose families aren't in Breyvia. I've got a fast ship, a crew that listens, and I know the coast better than anyone. I'll get them home."

She stared at him, not entirely sure she'd heard him right. "You'd... do that?"

Laughlan glanced over, something earnest flickering beneath the lazy grin. "Of course I would. I've got space, rations, and enough coin to grease the right palms. You shouldn't have to carry all of it."

Niev's throat felt thick. She opened her mouth. Closed it again.

He wasn't doing it for show. Wasn't asking for praise or recognition. He was just... offering.

They talked logistics for a few more minutes—how they'd divide the manifests, who would go with which crew, how Ayda could help organize the records while Teagan kept the kids from mutinying with boredom.

But when it was done, and the plans were set, she just stood there staring up at him.

At last he paused and glanced at her, one brow lifted. "What is it?"

Her voice was softer than the breeze through the rigging. "You're a good man, Laughlan Thorne."

He froze, then let out a short, startled laugh that cracked open his composure. "Don't spread rumors like that," he murmured, rubbing the back of his neck. "I'll never get laid again."

She snorted, but didn't let her eyes drift. There was a vulnerability there—a steady, honest pulse—that she seldom allowed him to see. Without another word, she stepped forward, lifted one hand, and pressed her fingers to his cheek. His skin was warm as her lips brushed his cheek.

He stood rooted, his eyes widening into saucers.

She offered him a half-wry smile. "I suppose you've earned *one* thank-you kiss after all."

He cleared his throat, sliding into an awkward bow as if to disarm the moment. "Well then," he drawled. "You should probably get some sleep. You've got a brother to save and a grumpy lover boy to look after."

She rolled her eyes, stepping back into the shadows. "I hate you."

"You love me," he called after her with a softer edge this time.

And maybe, in a way, she did.

❊   ❊   ❊

Niev left the deck and didn't realize how far her feet had carried her until the creak of the stairwell gave way to the dim corridor below. The sounds of the ship—creaking wood, distant gulls, the occasional thud of footsteps—were muffled here, as if the whole world had dipped beneath the surface and held its breath.

She paused outside Caelan's cabin door, but her hand didn't rise to knock. Instead, her fingers curled slightly, and she stared down at them.

They were clean now. She'd washed in the sea twice, scrubbing her skin raw with the water below deck, until she was pink and swollen, with no traces of blood or ash.

But still, her hands didn't feel like her own anymore.

The weight that had been coiled in her chest since the fight—since the moment she raised her hand on Darrow's ship and the shadows bent to her—was still there. Humming. Alive.

The sensation was... strange. Like her body remembered something her mind had long since buried.

She lifted her hand slowly. Watched her fingers spread as shadows tickled at her fingertips. The air around her hand thickened almost imperceptibly, dense with a subtle pressure. A flicker of something moved at her wrist—nothing she could see, not really, but she *felt* it. Like waves rolling in from a distance. Like the hush of a tide coming in behind her ribs.

Magic.

Her magic.

Not shapeshifting. Not a weapon someone else had forged and placed in her hand.

This had come from *within her.*

She had grown up hearing she was empty. Broken. A Nivola child without a shred of witchcraft. Adrianna had called her a curse behind closed doors and a disappointment in front of them. No matter how hard she trained, how many bruises she wore like armor—nothing had ever stirred. Until now.

But why? Why *now*, after all this time? What had changed?

Her body hadn't. Her blood hadn't.

But something else had cracked wide open.

And maybe that was it. Maybe she'd been holding the door shut all these years with grief, and rage, and shame. Maybe it had needed a moment of truth—of purpose—for the storm to finally break loose. Or maybe, Adrianna was right, and she *was* cursed.

She took a breath. Closed her eyes. Let the magic rise.

Just to *feel* the shadows curl warmly around her skin, cool as riverwater, slick as ink. A part of her. The part she'd been told didn't exist.

Her throat tightened, but she swallowed it down. There would be time to unravel it all later. To ask questions, to test limits, to wonder if this power would ever truly be hers to keep.

But not now. Because her heart wasn't pounding from magic right now.

It was pounding for him.

For the man who had kissed her like she was real. Like she hadn't filled the sea with blood. And for a second, doubt creeped into her mind.

What if he didn't mean it? What if it was a mistake?

Niev shook her head, and stepped toward the door. She knocked once, and waited.

A heartbeat passed.

Then another.

Inside, she heard a rustle. A sharp breath.

And then the soft squeak of floorboards as he approached.

The door creaked open.

Caelan stood in the doorframe, his shoulder still wrapped in clean linen, a faint sheen of sweat on his collarbone from the residual heat of sleep. His hair was tousled, his eyes dark and alert, and yet still softened the moment they found her.

Her voice was quieter than she meant it to be. "Still got room for one?"

He didn't speak. He just stepped aside, granting her the space, the choice.

Niev entered. The door shut behind her with a soft *click*, and the air between them thickened with awareness.

He watched her from a short distance as she shed her cloak and placed it carefully on the small hook near the cot. Her fingers hesitated at the edges, like she needed the act of folding and hanging to keep herself from unraveling.

She didn't turn around right away. She wasn't sure what to say. The storm inside her hadn't calmed. If anything, it was louder now—waves of thought crashing hard against the fragile walls of her composure.

"You don't have to say anything," Caelan said gently, his voice low and steady behind her. "Not unless you want to."

She turned then. Met his gaze. The golden light from the lantern caught the edge of his jaw, now thick with stubble, the hollows of his cheeks, the soft curve of a half-smile that was as much invitation as reassurance. And by God, he was beautiful.

Not just in the way his body moved, or the way his eyes seemed to see through everything—but in the quiet strength he offered her without asking for anything in return.

Niev's throat was tight. She crossed the room slowly, and sat beside him on the cot. Their legs brushed. His warmth seeped into her.

"I felt it," she said finally, voice low, almost reluctant. "Before I came here. Down in the corridor. It's still... inside me."

That is *not* what she'd come here to talk about.

But once the words were said, everything else came pouring out of her.

"I don't know why it's happening now," she went on. "I've lived with the silence for so long. With everyone telling me I didn't have it. That I wasn't enough. That I wasn't a true Nivola. I believed them."

Her fingers found the edge of the bandage on his arm, grazing it gently.

"I built everything I am on surviving without it. Without magic. Without any kind of inheritance from my mother. And now..."

She looked at her hand.

"It's like I've been holding my breath my whole life. And tonight, I can finally breathe again."

Caelan reached out, brushing her hair back from her face, tucking a loose curl behind her ear.

"What you did," he said, "wasn't born in this moment. Maybe that power's always been yours. It was just waiting until you stopped needing permission."

Her eyes flicked to his. Soft. Searching.

She wasn't used to being seen like this.

But she wanted him to see her. The real her. Even if it scared her senseless.

"I don't know how to be like this," she whispered, gesturing between them "It feels like I'm splitting in two."

Caelan tilted his head slightly, his fingers still trailing gently through her hair.

"You're not splitting," he murmured. "You're expanding."

She snorted, but let out a breath she didn't know she'd been holding, and leaned forward—just a little. Enough for her forehead to brush his.

"Did you mean it?" Niev asked, barely above a whisper.

The moment it left her lips, she regretted it—not because she didn't want the answer, but because she didn't know if she could bear it. Her gaze dropped to her lap, her fingers curling in the hem of her tunic to keep them steady.

She couldn't look at him. Not yet. Not for this. And that made her feel more ashamed and angry with herself than anything else. She was the Tigress of Solhaven, she knew a thousand ways to kill her enemies. But she sat there squirming like some simpering fool.

Niev riled herself up so much, she almost got up and left.

But then she felt the bed shift beneath her as Caelan leaned forward. His hand came to rest lightly beneath her chin, coaxing her face up gently.

And when she finally lifted her eyes, she found him waiting, raw and unflinching.

"I meant every word," Caelan said softly, his fingers brushing her cheek.

"I love you Niev Helvast," he murmured, his hazel eyes burning into hers. "Or should I call you Sera?"

Niev winced at the mention of her real name. "No," she insisted, voice tight. "Just... Niev."

She couldn't explain the shame she felt at hearing her old name. The contrast between how she was raised and who she grew up to be too big for her to accept.

"You should know," Niev's throat tightened, her voice hoarse. "I'm not exactly easy to love or hold on to."

A slow smile curled at his mouth—dry, crooked, entirely *him*.

"Niev," he said, a low laugh rumbling in his chest. "I was born and raised in a slave camp. I wouldn't know *easy* if it slapped me across the face."

Despite herself, she barked a laugh.

He chuckled with her, and for a moment, it was just the two of them. The darkness. The creak of the ship. The warmth of their shared breath. That rarest kind of comfort—unspoken and unshakeable.

Then he grew quiet. His hand slid from her chin to the side of her neck, his thumb brushing beneath her ear with aching tenderness.

"But holding on to you..." he said, his voice dipping lower, more serious now, "has been the most natural thing in the world. As if my mind, my body, my *soul*—all decided the moment they saw you that you were it for me."

Her breath caught, as Caelan's eyes burned into hers, steady and honest in a way that both thrilled and terrified her.

"The only thing that terrifies me about you," he said, "is how afraid I am of losing you."

The ache inside her chest cracked wide open.

She reached for him. He met her halfway.

Their mouths met in a kiss that was far more than a promise—it was a plea, a tether, a battle cry and a surrender all at once. Her fingers tangled in the back of his shirt as she leaned into him, as he pulled her gently onto his lap with a groan against her lips.

The kiss deepened, searing and breathless, the kind that stole time and thought and air. Caelan's hands gripped her waist as though she were slipping from him, thumbs digging gently into the curve of her spine. Niev pressed closer, straddling his lap, her knees sinking into the mattress on either side of his thighs, her fingers in his hair, tugging with growing desperation.

His mouth trailed from her lips to her jaw, to the slope of her neck, drawing a gasp from her throat as her head tilted back. Every place his mouth touched left her burning. Her body, which had so long been a fortress of control, trembled with want.

Clothes shifted. Fabric slid.

A low sound escaped him as her hands slipped under his shirt to trace the lines of muscle beneath—familiar now, but still intoxicating.

She felt him—his need for her, hot and heavy between them, unspoken but undeniable.

She wanted it. She wanted *him*.

But when his hand slid up her thigh, brushing the hem of her tunic, when the kiss turned hungrier, when they were seconds away from losing themselves—

She stilled.

"Caelan," she breathed, her voice a ragged whisper against his mouth.

He pulled back immediately, concern blooming in his eyes.

She wasn't trembling from desire anymore.

She shifted off his lap, standing just out of reach, her hands shaking slightly as she ran them over her arms.

"I'm sorry," she said quickly, too quickly. "I didn't mean to— I just—"

"Hey," his voice was soft. Steady. "It's okay."

She couldn't look at him. Not at first. So she turned her back, standing in the glow of the low lantern, shadows catching on the soft edges of her shoulders. Niev took a deep breath and closed her eyes, bracing herself for the confession she was about to make.

"My parents," she began, her voice tight, "were God-fearing people. They raised me to honor my soul. My body. And I know that sounds like a joke now... after everything I've done."

She swallowed.

"I've killed. Lied. Stolen. I've betrayed people. I've led men to their deaths. I've done things that—if my parents saw me now—they wouldn't even recognize me."

She paused trying to regain the confidence to go on.

"I've committed every sin under the sun to survive since they died. But the only thing I had left—the *only* thing I could still choose—was this. My body. And I swore I wouldn't give it away. Not unless it *meant* something. And even though I've broken every other promise I've ever made to myself, I haven't broken this one. Because if I ever do find a man insane enough to marry me one day, I want him to at least have that."

Her voice broke.

"So, I've never—beyond kissing, I've never been touched like that. Not by any man."

She turned around slowly.

Her eyes were wide and wet and raw. And terrified.

"I'm not saying no forever. I just... I need you to know that I can't. Not now. Not like this."

Caelan stood—his presence solid as stone, but warm as fire.

And when he reached her, he didn't pull her back into bed. He didn't press for more. He wrapped his arms around her, one at her waist, the other cradling the back of her head, and he *held* her.

"I would've never asked for more than you were willing to give," he said into her hair.

She exhaled, slow and trembling, pressing her forehead into his shoulder.

"I meant what I said," he murmured. "You're it for me. And if this is how you love—fiercely, deliberately, like it's sacred—I'd wait ten years, and then ten more, if that's what you needed."

Her breath hitched. A single tear slipped down her cheek.

"You terrify me," she whispered.

"Yeah," he said with a soft laugh. "You terrify me too."

She laughed with him as he softly wiped her tears with his thumbs.

Then Caelan tilted her face up with a single touch, and kissed her again.

Not with hunger this time, but with reverence.

And in that moment, Niev knew that despite all her mistakes, choosing Caelan was the best decision she'd ever made.

30.
Caelan

Caelan woke slowly, cradled in warmth that felt impossibly steady for a ship still adrift at sea. The familiar creak of timber and the rhythmic sway of the Sersha rocked gently beneath him, but for once, his body wasn't tensed against it. It was still. Unburdened.

Because Niev was curled into him, her breath soft against his neck, one leg tangled lazily with his.

Her dark hair fanned over his chest like ink spilled across parchment, one hand resting just below his ribs, her breathing slow and even. His arm had gone slightly numb beneath her, but he didn't dare move. Not yet.

Not when he could lie there and memorize the way she looked when no one else was watching.

In sleep, her sharpness faded. The wariness that always haunted her eyes was gone, replaced with something unguarded—almost innocent. Like the girl she might've been if the world had been kinder.

He leaned down just slightly, breathing her in.

Bergamot and jasmine.

He didn't know how a single scent could undo him the way it did, but bloody hell, it *did*. Twined with the memory of her mouth on his, her skin against his hands. Her smell had become some kind of addicting opioid to him.

He shifted carefully, pressing one last kiss to the crown of her head before untangling from her body with the sort of reverence usually reserved for holy things.

She stirred just slightly as he left the cot, but didn't wake.

Caelan pulled on a clean shirt, tugged on his boots, and padded to the door as quietly as his frame allowed.

The sunlight hit him hard as he stepped onto the upper deck.

The sky above was painted in gold and blue, the morning light dancing across the waves like spilled fire. Crew members were already at work, moving barrels and crates, laughing slowly among themselves. The scent of salt and woodsmoke lingered in the air, mingling with the faint aroma of cooked oats and honey from below.

He was halfway to the railing when a familiar voice called out.

"Well, well, well." Laughlan's grin was already halfway to feral. "If it isn't the lucky bastard of the hour."

Teagan leaned on a coil of rope beside him, arms crossed, eyes gleaming. "A certain Tigress disappeared from her hammock last night and has yet to be found. You wouldn't know anything about that, would you Galbraith?"

Caelan sighed, dragging a hand down his face. "Please tell me you two have something better to do."

"Better than speculating how long your girl's gonna stay in your bunk?" Laughlan looked mock-horrified. "Perish the thought."

"She's not—" Caelan started, then stopped. Glanced toward the sea. "She's not a topic for your amusement."

That made both men shut up for half a second. Then Teagan smiled, a little softer this time.

"Fair enough."

Laughlan, of course, had no such filter.

"I gotta say, though," he drawled, squinting toward the horizon, "that's a woman who could set a man's bones on fire and then stitch them back together with the same hands. I really thought I'd win her back some day, you know," he said longingly as Teagan snorted and patted him on the back.

Caelan didn't respond. He didn't need to.

Because she *had* chosen him. And that was still sinking in.

Laughlan cleared his throat and nodded toward the distance. Caelan followed his gaze.

A rugged coastline had begun to take shape—low, forested cliffs draped in morning mist. The faint outline of buildings appeared between trees, pale stone and timber, carved into the natural curves of the land rather than forced upon it. The docks extended out into the bay like a curled hand, quiet and tucked into the mouth of a cove.

Driftwood.

The port city of Thornmere. Niev's birthplace.

"She'll recognize it soon," Laughlan murmured. "We'll be there by midday. We'll pull in slow, take the crew to resupply. The kids with families stay onboard."

"I'll stay too," Teagan added. "Ayda and I'll keep them busy."

Laughlan turned to Caelan. "That leaves you and Niev. Based on what she said, her family estate's half a league inland."

Caelan nodded. "We'll take the orphans to her grandmother."

"Aye," Laughlan raised a brow. "Guinevere Helvast."

"You know her?" Caelan asked, frowning.

"Do I know her?" Laughlan said with a smirk. "Let's just say that I would *not* want to be on that woman's bad side. She's the scariest, sharpest, most terrifyingly decent woman in all of Thornmere. If she opens her doors to those kids, they'll be the safest orphans in the whole damn continent."

Caelan tightened his grip on the rail, jaw shifting as a sharp wind whipped across the deck. It was stupid. Petty. He knew that. Laughlan had a way of knowing everyone, everything. It was part of his charm. Part of why people followed him.

But it didn't make the small twist in Caelan's gut feel any less real.

Because the bastard didn't just know *of* Niev — he *knew* her. Well enough to joke. To see past her sharp edges. To recognize the woman behind them without flinching. And now he knew her grandmother too, apparently.

The same woman Niev had only mentioned in a quiet, tentative voice, as if she wasn't sure she'd even be welcomed back.

He exhaled through his nose.

He didn't want to dwell on it. Didn't want to give jealousy room to grow. Not when she'd fallen asleep curled against him like it was the most natural thing in the world.

But then—

He remembered her voice the night before.

"No man has ever touched me like that."

And just like that, his tension shifted.

Jealousy didn't evaporate. But it folded into something else. Not pride, exactly — though some feral part of him *did* feel possessive at the thought of her telling him something so sacred.

But more than that, it was gratitude.

Not because she'd saved herself.

But because *he* didn't have to carry the rage of imagining hands that didn't deserve her. Words whispered in her ear by men who didn't see her. Didn't understand the storms that lived inside her chest.

She'd made her own vow in the face of a world that had taken everything from her — and somehow, that piece of her remained untouched.

And now, she'd let *him* hold onto it.

He let the wind cool the heat behind his eyes.

It didn't matter how many people had known her before. How many stories had been shared. How many truths were buried in the folds of her past.

Because last night, she'd given *him* a truth no one else had ever been given.

And for that, he would spend the rest of his life proving he was worthy of it.

✳ ✳ ✳

True to his word, Laughlan got them to shore by midday.

Driftwood rose out of the morning mist like a secret that didn't want to be kept.

The port town was exactly what its name promised—salt-worn, sea-stained, and weather-beaten to its bones. The buildings leaned into one another like drunkards with stories to tell, roofs bowed under the weight of age and wind. Nets hung drying from posts. Fish guts were swept into gutters that stank even in the cool air. The voices of merchants and sailors wove together in a low, constant hum, like the town itself had never learned to rest.

Caelan disembarked with one hand on his sword hilt, more out of instinct than necessity. The Sersha groaned at the dock behind him, her sails drawn in, her crew already fanning out with practiced ease. But the moment his boots hit the salt-drenched planks, something in his chest coiled tight.

It wasn't the smell. Or the chaos.

It was *her*.

Niev walked just ahead of him, the children trailing behind like shadows too small for their own grief. Her stride was steady, but he could feel the shift in her body. The subtle way her shoulders stiffened. The way her hands balled into fists and then slowly unfurled at her sides, like she was fighting to control something she didn't want to show.

He didn't know if it was the town or the ghosts waiting in it, but she was changing right in front of him.

She wasn't putting on one of her masks. This was her peeling one off.

The streets were narrow and slick from the sea air. Locals leaned out of windows or huddled under awnings, their eyes following Niev like they weren't sure if they were looking at a ghost or a memory. The children were quiet—Talia close on Niev's right—each of them wearing the same wary look.

A market stall opened on their left, heavy with baskets of clams and mussels. Beside it, a low stone house with rusted hinges and sagging shutters. A woman stood just outside it, gray-haired and bent with age, holding a bundle of dried lavender. When her eyes landed on Niev, the color drained from her face.

"Saints," the woman whispered, hand clutching her chest. "Sera Nieva?"

Niev's entire body went rigid.

Caelan barely caught the way her breath hitched—just a fraction, just enough—and then she drew her hood tighter to hide her face and kept walking.

He didn't ask. Her silence told him everything.

She didn't want to be seen here. Not like this. Not yet.

As they passed a crumbling fountain in the middle of the square, Caelan looked around with growing unease. Driftwood wasn't his home. The southern edge of Thornmere felt wild and strange, heavy with wet roots and old superstitions, the kind of place that swallowed secrets and spat them back up in riddles.

But even stranger was how much the town itself seemed to *recognize* her.

Like it had been holding its breath all this time—waiting for the girl who left to come back and claim the place she'd left behind.

And Niev?

She looked like she wanted to vanish inside her own skin.

It made something raw twist in his chest.

He hadn't seen her this vulnerable before. Not when she'd been stitched into red silk and carnage. Not even when she'd turned the sea into a battlefield and torn through Darrow's ship like divine punishment. Not even when she'd been telling him naked truths the night before.

But now—surrounded by familiar alleys, by whispers and half-remembered names—she was folding in on herself.

Like she wasn't sure she had the right to take up space here.

And God, he *hated* it.

Hated that this place had the power to make her question who she'd become. That it could reduce her to this girl with her head held low in shame.

He moved closer.

Let their hands brush again. Not quite touching.

But near enough.

If she stumbled, he'd catch her.

If the ghosts of this town tried to pull her back down, he'd bury them in the dirt.

Because whatever Thornmere had once meant to her... it didn't own her anymore.

They reached the edge of the town and found the horses waiting—a gift from Laughlan, who was already busy haggling with dockhands and shouting at his quartermaster to stock enough citrus to keep the crew from dying of scurvy.

Caelan helped the children into the wagon. Talia stuck close to Niev like a shadow with a heartbeat.

When Niev finally turned back toward the town, her expression was unreadable.

He saw her stare at the gates.

Then past them.

To something only she could see.

He watched her jaw clench. Watched her shoulders lift.

And then she mounted her horse like she wasn't afraid anymore.

Like the girl who'd been stolen from her bed a decade ago had finally come home.

✳ ✳ ✳

They left Driftwood behind just as the morning broke gold across the sky.

The town's crooked edges shrank in the distance, swallowed by the sea air and tangled branches that crept in from the wilds. Thornmere was unlike any place Caelan had ever seen—lush and overgrown, riddled with moss-covered stones and trees that looked older than memory. The forest seemed to breathe around them, each gust of wind carrying the scent of damp earth, salt, and something old that lived in the bark and shadows.

Their small group moved slowly along the winding trail. The children sat in the wagon behind them, swaying with each bump in the dirt road.

Caelan didn't speak. He couldn't.

Not when Niev rode just ahead of him, her back straight, her hair pulled into a loose braid that hung between her shoulder blades. She was quiet, eyes scanning the trees, her jaw set. The ride had a heaviness to it—not from danger, but from everything that still needed to be said.

The closer they got, the more he could feel it pulsing off her in waves.

The weight of coming home.

And of not knowing if home would still want her.

He didn't blame her for being afraid. He knew what it was to be shaped by pain. To carry shame like a second skin. But watching her now—this woman who had clawed her way out of hell, who had turned grief into fire and silence into strength—he couldn't imagine a world where someone didn't want her back.

But that wasn't his choice to make. It was Guinevere's.

And the thought of facing a woman who had once loved Niev and been left behind in the storm of her disappearance... It made Caelan's grip on the reins tighten just a little.

"Do you think she'll be kind?" one of the younger children asked at one point, as Niev slowed her horse beside them.

She didn't answer right away.

"She used to be. The kindest woman I know," Niev said, softly. "But that was a long time ago."

They rode on in silence after that.

The road sloped upward slightly as they passed into the deeper part of the forest. Roots clawed at the path, thick and gnarled, and the canopy above turned the world green and gold. Caelan's eyes shifted to the wagon as one of the children poked her head out from under the canvas. It was Talia—braids tousled, curiosity sparking in her gaze.

She caught his eye, then rode up beside him on her pony, trying very hard to look like she hadn't been waiting for the right moment to speak.

"Are you going to marry her?" she asked plainly.

Caelan choked on air.

Niev didn't turn around, but he saw her shoulders jolt once. Her ears straining to hear his answer.

"I..." Caelan cleared his throat. "That's not really up to me, is it?"

Talia gave him a look. "But do you want to?"

"That's... a complicated question."

She narrowed her eyes. "Seems simple to me."

He could've said a dozen things. Could've told her he wasn't the marrying kind. That he'd never imagined a future with anyone. Not because he didn't want one, but because wanting felt dangerous. Because planning meant believing he'd survive long enough to see anything through.

He could've told her that he'd been born in chains and every time he let himself want something, it got torn away. That he was carved from fire and iron and all the wrong things—built for war and survival, not softness or vows or rings.

But he had told her he loved her.

He'd looked her in the eye and said the words like they were ripped from somewhere deep and buried. Because they were. Because she was *it* for him.

And that hadn't changed.

But all that came out was: "She deserves better than what I've got to offer."

Talia stared at him for a moment, her arms crossed and her brow furrowed like she was trying to puzzle him out.

Then she rolled her eyes.

"Maybe," Talia said smugly, her eyes narrowing. "But it's not like you'll ever find better than her."

He stared at her, speechless.

God. From the mouths of babes, as they said.

Talia grinned, clearly pleased with herself, and drew her head back into the wagon to join the others.

Caelan let out a long breath.

He didn't look at Niev.

But she glanced back at him over her shoulder, and the look in her eyes said she'd heard every word.

His heart squeezed.

He wasn't sure if it was from fear, or hope.

Or both.

31.
Niev

The road into Helvast territory wound through hills draped in moss and bramble, thorn-strands arching overhead like skeletal fingers. A low mist hugged the forest floor, coiling around hoofprints, and somewhere in the gloom a raven's lone cry echoed—harsh and accusatory.

Here, the earth smelled of loam and rain, untamed and indifferent to court intrigues or noble blood. This was the wilderness her father had cherished, and the one her mother had fled.

At the thought, a hot spike of anger shot through Niev. If only her mother had stayed, stood her ground in Arenthia... if she'd never abandoned Thornmere, perhaps the last ten years of loss might never have been.

She didn't realize she'd been holding her breath until the trees broke apart and the estate came into view—half-shrouded in mist and framed by the rising ridge behind it. The manor stood at the edge of a sloping meadow, three stories of pale stone and green-tiled roofs, its windows glowing faintly in the morning gloom. The gates—ironwood and etched with the Helvast sigil—were older now, but still proud. Still strong.

Niev's fingers tightened on the reins as they approached. She could feel the children behind her shift, whisper, their tired eyes taking in the looming house.

Beside her, Caelan said nothing.

She hadn't spoken since they passed the boundary stone. Her pulse had crawled up her throat and stayed there.

The horse beneath her slowed as they reached the outer courtyard. There were no guards here. No staff lining the walk. Just silence and the rustling of leaves nearby.

She didn't realize she was shaking until Caelan reached over, his fingers brushing hers.

The gates opened with a heavy creak, ironwood groaning against iron. The horses shifted beneath them, hooves clopping softly on the stone as the carriage rolled into the estate courtyard. Niev's pulse thrummed beneath her skin.

She stayed seated as the coach slowed, the creak of the brake and the snort of the horses barely audible over the roar in her ears. Her hood was still drawn low over her face, shadows hiding every feature.

The great double doors of the estate cracked open. A woman emerged—tall, robed in green velvet, her shoulders squared. Her silver hair was pulled tightly into a bun. Her steps were brisk, and hurried.

Guinevere Helvast.

Her grandmother.

She didn't look at the carriage. Not at first.

Her dark eyes locked straight onto Caelan, who was just stepping down to the stone courtyard.

"You there," Guinevere said sharply. "Get off my estate! If it's more seedlings from Leighton's orchard, tell him I'm not interested. If it's tinctures again, you can leave them with the steward."

Caelan blinked. "I—no, I'm—"

She raised a hand, silencing him. "God, you lot never stop. I don't care how rare your rosebuds are or what glowing things they do to my skin. If I wanted to smell like honeysuckle, I'd roll in it myself."

Caelan tried again, stepping forward. "I'm not selling anything. My name's Caelan Galbraith. I—"

"No, thank you." Her tone sharpened. "I don't know who you are but if this is about some favor from my late husband, I assure you, I have no patience—"

"Guinevere."

Niev's voice cut through the courtyard like a blade through silk. Soft but laced with exhaustion.

Guinevere froze. Her brows furrowed—but her head tilted, eyes narrowing beneath the weight of something remembered.

Slowly, Niev stepped down from the carriage. Her boots hit the stone. She pushed back her hood with both hands.

Guinevere's breath caught. She didn't move. Didn't blink. For the first time since they arrived, the formidable woman staggered. Her lips parted.

Her gloved hand reached, faltered, and then pressed tightly to her chest, her voice barely above a whisper, "Sera Nieva?"

"Hello, Grandmother," Niev said softly.

It was the smallest voice she'd used in years.

For a second, time seemed to stand still.

And then Guinevere descended the steps so fast Niev barely had time to brace herself before she was enveloped in a crushing embrace. Her knees buckled. Her arms wrapped around the older woman's frame, clinging to strength she hadn't realized she'd missed.

"You're alive," her grandmother gasped. "God above—you're alive—"

Niev's throat clenched painfully around each breath, and her hands trembled where they clung to the back of the woman's cloak. She smelled like rosemary, smoke, and something familiar Niev hadn't felt in a decade.

Safety.

When they finally pulled apart, Guinevere took her face in both hands and stared at her.

"You're taller," she whispered. "And your eyes—they are just like your father's."

Niev tried to smile. It wobbled.

Guinevere's lips trembled again, but she didn't cry. She was too much of a Helvast for that. Instead, she cleared her throat, squared her shoulders, and turned toward the wagon.

Her gaze, sharp and silvering with age but no less piercing, drifted from face to face. The children were quiet, watchful. Most too exhausted to put up their usual shields. A few clutched the sides of the wagon, unwilling to let go of their only familiar landmark.

Guinevere turned back to Niev, confusion etched across her features.

Niev didn't explain. Not fully. Not yet.

She simply said, "They're with me."

Three words.

But Guinevere heard everything buried inside them.

She held Niev's gaze for a long moment, and then nodded.

With the kind of brisk authority Niev had nearly forgotten—softened now by age and memory—her grandmother straightened her back and turned to the children.

"Well," she said, dusting her palms on her dress. "There's food inside and a lit hearth. I suspect that makes this the most welcoming place within ten leagues. Come now. You'll all catch your death standing around like wary rabbits."

The children didn't move at first.

But then the smallest one—dark curls and missing shoe—slid off the wagon and took a tentative step forward. Guinevere offered her hand, not with gentleness but with matter-of-fact expectation. And somehow, that worked.

One by one, the children followed. Past the gates. Toward the manor. Toward the scent of warm bread and lavender soap and safety.

Niev stood watching until they all disappeared inside, trailing behind the formidable woman who'd once tucked her in beneath a wool blanket and read her tales of moonlight beasts and flame-winged birds.

The house was still the same.

But she was not.

She pulled her cloak tighter around her shoulders.

And then she went to find her grandmother.

They sat alone in the drawing room, the afternoon sun bleeding through the garden windows. Niev stood for most of it, pacing in slow, rigid lines, her voice hushed and even. She told her grandmother everything. Not just about the children—though that came first. The raid on the auction. The tunnels. The horrors they'd seen. But then she told her about the years before. About what had happened to her parents. To Elias. To herself.

Silent tears tracked down Guinevere's weathered cheeks, her expression caught somewhere between heartbreak and fury. She didn't interrupt. Didn't press for details.

She just listened.

By the time Niev sat beside her, she felt rung out. Hollowed. But not alone.

Guinevere wiped at her cheeks with the back of her hand, then exhaled like she was trying to let go of ten years of grief in one breath.

"Why didn't you ever come *home*, Sera?" Her voice trembled on the last word, heavy with both accusation and longing.

Niev's throat closed up. She stared at the shifting shadows on the wall before finally speaking, each word scraping its way out. "I—I didn't think I'd be welcome back," she admitted, shoulders hunched. "After everything I've done, I didn't believe this place had room for me anymore."

Guinevere watched her granddaughter's hands knot into her lap. "You believe too many lies."

"I spent years repaying my debt to Saeris," Niev went on, voice shaking. "Trying so hard to forget my grief. I thought if I stayed away, eventually the memories would fade." She exhaled hard, eyes flooding. "And... if it hadn't been for those children—"

Her voice caught.

"—I don't know that I would've come back at all."

Guinevere crossed the room without another word, closing the distance in two quick strides. She pulled Niev into a fierce embrace so sudden it nearly knocked the breath out of her.

"Not a day went by that you weren't missed," Guinevere whispered against her hair. "You're not just welcome here, Sera...this is where you belong."

Niev stiffened and pulled back a fraction, eyes flicking away. "I'm not the granddaughter you knew ten years ago," she said, voice brittle. "There's nothing left of Sera anymore."

Guinevere's eyes softened, and she reached out to cup Niev's cheek. "Yesterday, I had no grandchildren left at all," she said simply. "Today, I have you...and that's more than I ever dared hope for."

Niev's defiance cracked. She exhaled, letting Guinevere draw her back into a gentler hug.

When they returned to the garden, the sun had dipped toward the west, casting the stone path in honey-gold. A table had been laid out beneath the awning. Wooden bowls, steaming bread, fresh butter, and a soup that smelled like roasted thyme and root vegetables. The children were eating like they hadn't seen a proper meal in years, which, for most of them, was true.

The sight knocked the breath from Niev's lungs.

She didn't realize she was staring until Guinevere's hand closed gently over her arm.

"I have room enough to house a village, Sera," she said quietly. "This house grew cold after your grandfather passed. I wouldn't mind the company."

Niev's throat clenched at the mention of her beloved grandfather, but she didn't dare ask how he had passed. Guinevere squeezed her arm once more before walking forward to refill a pitcher of cider and scold one of the boys for feeding the estate cat under the table.

Niev stood still beneath the archway for another moment, watching the way the children leaned into the warmth of it all. Into comfort. Into peace.

And maybe—just maybe—into something that might eventually feel like home.

※　※　※

The estate had grown quiet by the time Niev slipped out onto the garden path.

The children were tucked into clean beds, bellies full, the scent of lavender and wool hanging softly in the halls. Some had asked for water. Some had asked for stories. One had asked, shyly, if they would still be there in the morning.

Niev had smiled and told him he was in safe hands from now on.

Now, the dusk air curled cool around her shoulders, brushing through the ivy-laced trellises and flowerbeds like it remembered her. The garden had once been her sanctuary. Before her world fractured.

The cobbled path wound beneath her bare feet as she padded past the hedges, past the birdbath and the sundial, toward the small stone arch that overlooked the western fields.

She found Caelan sitting on the low wall, his silhouette carved in shadows and moonlight. One foot planted on the stone, the other hanging loosely over the edge. His jacket was gone, sleeves rolled to his elbows, and the pale burn on his shoulder peeked from the open collar of his shirt.

His head turned at the sound of her steps, and for a long moment, they simply looked at each other.

Eventually, he scooted over—wordlessly making room.

Niev climbed up beside him, the stone still warm from the fading sun.

He didn't speak. Just passed her a half-empty flask.

She took a sip, grimaced, and handed it back.

"Burns like sin," she coughed.

"Better than tea," he said, shrugging.

"Blasphemy!" she replied in mock horror. "Nothing's better than tea."

Calean laughed and she smiled back, letting her shoulder rest against his. Feeling the steady weight of him beside her, grounding and quiet.

They listened to the wind for a while. To the rustle of trees, the creak of the weather vane, the distant sound of horses settling in the stables.

"Your grandmother's a force," Caelan said quietly.

Niev huffed a small laugh. "She always has been. The matriarch of Thornmere's most stubborn family."

"She loves you."

"I wasn't sure she would. Not after everything." She hesitated, and continued quietly. "Not after who I became."

"You mean a survivor who's saved over a dozen children?" he said, turning to look at her, eyes narrowing, "Ah yes, how *shameful*."

She snorted, elbowing him in the ribs. Her eyes fixed on a beetle crawling across the stone near her foot.

Then, she went on softly, "She used to read to me out here, you know. On summer nights. I'd fall asleep in the grass, and she'd carry me back to bed."

Caelan's hand shifted. His fingers brushed lightly against hers.

"Would it be selfish to say I envy you?" he admitted.

She looked at him with sorrow in her eyes, and laced their fingers together.

"I look at the warm home Guinevere's built, and I just—"

She squeezed his hand, her thumb brushing along the scarred skin of his knuckles, grounding him.

"You just wish you'd had something like it," she finished softly.

He gave a tight nod, eyes fixed somewhere beyond the garden. The last rays of dusk still clung to the sky, streaking the clouds in shades of lavender and dying gold. The warmth of the estate hummed behind them — voices murmuring low in the kitchen, the faint clink of plates, the soft scrape of wood as the staff moved through their end-of-day routines.

But out here, beneath the tangled branches of the garden's oldest tree, it felt like a different world.

"I don't envy people for their comfort," Caelan said finally, voice low. "I just... wonder who I would've been, if I'd been loved like that. Fiercely. Like you were. Even for a little while."

Niev didn't answer immediately. She leaned into him, shoulder to shoulder, letting the weight of their shared silence settle between them.

"You would've been more trusting maybe," she said at last. "Not weaker. Just... not so careful with your heart."

Caelan let out a quiet breath. Almost a laugh. "Careful? I kissed you in front of two dozen people after you turned into a sea monster and decapitated a man."

"Fair enough," her lips curved, a soft blush creeping up her neck.

He turned to look at her then. She could see him staring at the arch of her brow, the dark waves of hair pinned behind one ear, the way her eyes held his.

"But you're right about trust," he said, voice low, "I didn't think I was still capable of it."

She searched his face, every line softened by the dying light, and found herself whispering, "What changed your mind?" Her own question sounded foreign—terrifyingly hopeful.

Caelan reached for her hand, fingers brushing hers as though afraid they might wake from a dream. "You," he whispered, his hazel eyes burning bright in the moonlight. "I survived every single day after I escaped those slave camps by trusting no one. It was how I stayed alive— never expecting anyone to watch my back. But then I found you." He drew a slow circle on her palm, tracing lines she'd thought dead. "And every lie I ever told myself about never needing anyone just fell away."

Her breath caught, warmth flooding her cheeks. He spoke with a raw honesty she'd never seen before. He leaned closer, and she could count the faint scars on his jaw in the half-light. "I would cross any battlefield, plunge into any storm, if it meant standing with you. And I know that— this," he paused, voice thick, "—this love for you might be the thing that finally destroys me. But I'd choose it anyway."

Niev felt the ground shift beneath her feet as her heart threatened to burst from her chest. It felt like regret, relief, and terror all at once. *This love for you might be the thing that finally destroys me.*

Couldn't he see that this was exactly what she *didn't* want? She didn't want to be the cause of any more destruction. Didn't want anyone else she cared about to die. Niev's head swam with images of her parents' corpses, their blood painting the marble floor. Tears blurred her vision but she blinked them back fiercely. "We should probably get going," she said, stumbling back a step as she stiffened. Before he could see the fierce panic in her eyes, she turned and went back down the stone path.

The chill of night settled around her shoulders, but she kept moving until her chest burned with the effort of breathing. Then, halfway to the gate, she paused—heart pounding so loudly she barely heard his footsteps behind her. She turned, shoulders squared against the night, voice low but certain. "Just so you know," she said, each word a vow, "I would never let anything happen to you."

"Niev—"

She turned away once more, cloak billowing like a dark promise, and slipped into the shadows of the estate grounds. Behind her, Caelan watched, hand still outstretched, his lips parting in a silent plea, and then he followed her back into the quiet corridors of the Helvast estate.

The scent of rosemary and cedar met them at the door to the study.

Guinevere stood near the fireplace, a letter in one hand, her posture straight as a sword. But when she turned and saw them enter, her face softened. The lines around her eyes were deeper than Niev remembered, but her gaze was still sharp, still warm. Still home.

"You're leaving already," she said. Not a question. Not quite a statement either.

Niev nodded slowly, stepping forward. "There are still children who need to find their families."

Guinevere said nothing for a moment. Just studied her like she was trying to memorize her face.

"Thornmere is your home, Sera. Whether you want it to be or not." Her voice was firm, but not unkind. "You have a place here. Always. So does your brother."

A lump rose in Niev's throat. "Thank you."

"Then promise me you'll come back. Don't let me spend another decade wondering about you."

"I promise."

Guinevere crossed the distance between them, cupping Niev's face gently, as if afraid she might vanish if held too tightly. "You look so much like your father," she said again, voice thick with memory. "But most importantly, you still have his heart."

"I'm not sure he'd say the same," Niev tried to joke, but it landed brittle and frayed.

Her grandmother just kissed her brow. "You'll figure it out. You always do."

They hugged again—tightly, desperately. Niev buried her face in the crook of her grandmother's neck, breathing in the scent of hearth-smoke and crushed lavender. A part of her didn't want to let go.

But duty tugged at her spine like a tether.

When she stepped back, Guinevere looked to Caelan.

He stood straight, hands loosely at his sides, waiting—always waiting. Ready to follow her wherever she went.

Guinevere's gaze sharpened.

Then, to Niev's absolute horror, the old woman stepped forward and patted his cheeks like he was a boy come courting.

"You take good care of her," Guinevere said, eyes narrowing. "She may be stubborn as a mule, but she needs someone strong by her side."

Niev looked away mortified. "Grandmother—"

But Caelan only smiled.

"I won't leave her side," he said simply.

And Niev blushed so furiously she thought her face would catch fire.

They stepped outside into the rising sun, the air cool but filled with the promise of the day. The horses were already saddled near the front gates, tethered and waiting.

Caelan swung into the saddle first.

Niev was halfway into the stirrup when the door burst open behind them.

A blur of motion collided with her leg.

"Talia?"

The little girl clung to her fiercely, arms wrapping around her waist with enough force to almost knock her off balance.

"You didn't say goodbye," she whispered, muffled against Niev's side.

"I thought you were asleep," Niev said softly, crouching to meet her eyes.

Talia sniffed. Her eyes were red. "Promise you'll come back?"

"I swear it."

"As soon as you can?"

Niev smiled. "As soon as I can."

Talia stepped back reluctantly, then darted forward again and hugged her once more. "Tell the others hi for me. Especially the loud one."

Niev laughed. "You'll need to be more specific."

"The one with too many knives."

"Ah. Teagan."

Talia nodded solemnly and stepped back. "Be safe, Lady Niev."

Niev froze at the title.

But then she nodded. "You too, Talia."

As she mounted her horse, Caelan leaned over just slightly in his saddle, voice low and teasing.

"Lady Niev?"

"Shut your mouth."

He only grinned.

The gates of the estate creaked open ahead of them.

And with one last look back at the manor— the waving figure of her grandmother on the steps, the flicker of firelight in the windows—

Niev kicked her horse forward and rode into the morning.

32.
Niev

The gangplank creaked beneath her boots as she made her way up to the Sersha Mara, the scent of the sea rushing in to meet her—salt and tar, old wood and brine. Behind her, Caelan walked in steady rhythm, his silent presence, despite his earlier words, a welcome comfort she was finding harder to resist.

She was almost to the top when someone called her name.

"Miss Helvast!"

Niev turned, eyebrows lifting as she spotted the older wagon driver from the estate jogging toward them, red-faced and breathless.

He paused, hand bracing his side as he caught up. "Your grandmother sent these," he wheezed. "Said... you might need some help feeding that crew of yours."

He gestured behind him, and Niev blinked.

Three more wagons were rumbling down the dock behind him. Each one stacked high with crates and satchels tied in thick burlap and linen cloth. The scent hit her before she could even step down to investigate— roasted meats, fresh breads, baked pies, wheels of soft and hard cheeses, bundles of herbs, and a mountain of carrot cake that had been wrapped in wax paper like precious cargo.

"What in God's name..." she murmured.

The old man chuckled. "She said she's been cooking for ghosts long enough. Figured it was time to feed the living again."

Laughter bellowed from the ship.

Thorne stood at the helm, arms crossed over his chest and one brow cocked. "By the breath of the sea," he called down, grinning wide. "Is that a bloody dowry, or are we just exceptionally well-fed pirates now?"

The crew cheered behind him as the first crate was hefted aboard. Within seconds, they began pouring toward the goods like wolves scenting blood. Some began hauling the food into the galley. Others cracked open crates right there on the deck, already elbow-deep in fresh bread and lemon-roasted fowl.

"I'll say this," Caelan stepped closer beside her, chuckling. "Your grandmother doesn't do things halfway."

"She never has," Niev said softly, unable to stop the smile tugging at the corner of her mouth. He didn't make any mention of their earlier conversation, and for that she was thankful.

"I swear to you," Teagan declared from the shadows behind them. "If she wasn't your grandmother, I'd propose on the spot."

Niev turned, and there he was, already cradling a thick slice of carrot cake between both hands like it was holy. Crumbs dotted his shirt, and a streak of frosting painted the corner of his mouth.

Ayda stood beside him, arms crossed, lips twitching.

"Did you even wait for a knife?" Niev asked.

"He didn't," Ayda confirmed.

"No time," Teagan said through a mouthful of cake. "You didn't tell me she was a bloody kitchen sorceress."

"Ah, yes," Niev shook her head, laughing. "How did I forget to mention such *crucial* information in our current circumstances?"

Ayda stepped forward, her eyes softer now. She touched Niev's arm. "So? How did it go?"

Niev looked between them, and her smile turned quieter. "Better than I could have hoped."

Ayda didn't hesitate. She pulled her into a warm, wordless hug. No congratulations. No platitudes. Just silent understanding between two women who had both lost and found too much to explain.

When she pulled back, Ayda looked toward the crates, toward the crew laughing and eating and tearing into loaves like children who hadn't seen home in months.

Teagan, already halfway through a second slice, pointed with his fork. "I'm just saying—if you ever fall out with her again, don't expect me to take your side."

"You're going to give yourself a stomachache," Niev muttered, exasperated.

"And it'll have been worth every bite," he replied smugly, smacking his lips.

She rolled her eyes, but her chest was full. Warm in a way that had nothing to do with the sun cresting over the water, or the feast spread across the deck.

She watched them for a while—her friends, her found family—laughing and devouring what looked like an entire harvest's worth of food. Ayda was picking grapes off a vine straight from one of the crates, and Teagan had already disappeared below deck, presumably to "secure" the carrot cake from further pirate assaults.

Caelan hadn't moved from her side.

He stood quietly, one hand resting lightly on the rail beside her, his gaze sweeping over the deck of the Sersha and its now thoroughly spoiled crew. Every so often, his eyes drifted back to her.

She didn't look at him—didn't need to. She could feel it. That steady hum of awareness. That heat, low and simmering, that always curled around her ribs when he was near.

"You know," he said quietly, "I think they love her."

"My grandmother?"

He nodded. "Laughlan's going to write her sonnets."

Niev laughed under her breath. "God help us all."

He turned toward her slightly. "You alright?"

She nodded. "I think so."

And for once, she meant it.

Ayda approached again with a flask in hand and tossed it to Caelan, who caught it one-handed.

"She says it's rosemary brandy," Ayda explained. "Something her husband used to swear by after long rides."

"Is that code for 'it'll light your insides on fire'?" Caelan asked, uncorking it.

Ayda shrugged. "I wouldn't know. I don't drink things that smell like the underside of a herbalist's foot."

Niev grinned and accepted the flask when Caelan offered it to her. She sniffed it, then took a cautious sip, and immediately coughed.

"God Almighty," she wheezed. "I think that just erased my childhood trauma."

Ayda barked a laugh, doubling over, and even Caelan cracked a wide grin.

But beneath the laughter and sunlight and scent of roasted garlic wafting up from the galley, Niev felt the shift in the wind. Not just weather—though the breeze was stronger now, stirring the edges of the sails—but something deeper.

The calm before the storm.

She glanced toward the bow, where the ocean stretched endlessly into morning haze, golden and unbothered. But the weight in her chest hadn't disappeared. Not entirely.

She thought of Elias. Of Arenthia. Of the shadows still stretching beneath the surface of their world.

The food was a gift. Her grandmother's table, a blessing.

But peace... peace would take more than roasted lamb and carrot cake.

She drew in a breath, felt Caelan watching her again.

"What?" she asked, brow raised.

He shook his head. "Nothing."

But his voice was low, almost reverent.

She narrowed her eyes. "You're staring."

"Hard not to."

She rolled her eyes, the movement lazy and unconvincing. "*You* are an absolute menace."

Caelan took a long sip from the flask, his gaze never straying from hers. When he finally lowered it, there was the hint of a smirk tugging at the edge of his mouth.

"Menace?" he said, voice deep, rough, and far too pleased, "Darling, I'm a walking hazard. But I don't see you running away, which only leads me to believe you don't mind a little danger."

She huffed, but the sound lacked bite. "Oh, is that what you're going for?"

He stepped in just slightly, enough for her to feel the heat radiating from him, enough for her breath to stutter. His smile deepened.

"Depends," he murmured. "Is it working?"

Niev narrowed her eyes at him. "No," she said dryly, knowing fully well that her answer sounded like the blatant lie it was.

He stepped closer—closer than he needed to. The scent of the brandy lingered on his breath, curling with the warmth of his skin.

The wind caught the loose ends of Niev's hair, dragging them across her cheek. He reached up and brushed one back, deliberately slow, fingers grazing her jaw like he'd done it a hundred times before.

"And yet..." he murmured, his breath brushing the shell of her ear, "here you are."

Her pulse spiked.

It was infuriating. The way he could disarm her without trying. The way her body leaned into his without permission, like it remembered something her mind was trying desperately to forget.

She wasn't supposed to let anyone close. Wasn't supposed to feel this safe with a man whose touch could unravel her in *seconds*.

But stars help her, he knew exactly how to press.

Her breath caught. And when she looked up at him—his eyes were darker now. Full of desire.

And absolutely, devastatingly focused on her.

She opened her mouth. Closed it again. Her thoughts scrambled, too quick and too loud all at once.

He grinned—slow and wicked—and leaned in just a little more, as if he could hear the war raging inside her.

"Have I rendered you speechless, Tigress?" he teased. "Now, that's a first."

She narrowed her eyes at him, but the heat blooming across her cheeks betrayed her. "Don't get cocky."

He raised a brow. "I think it's a bit too late for that."

Her mouth opened again—this time with something scathing locked and loaded—but the words never made it out.

Because all at once, she was painfully aware of how close he was. Of how easy it would be to grab him by the collar and finish what they hadn't dared to start in the galley two nights ago.

Her gaze flicked to his lips. Once. Just once.

But it was enough for him to see. Enough for him to step back with a smug, knowing look that made her want to punch him. Or kiss him. Maybe both.

And the worst part?

He knew it.

The air itself bent around them, thick with salt, heat, and unspoken things that buzzed under her skin. She could've stepped away. Could've shut it down with a well-placed glare or one of her blade-sharp retorts.

But her body hadn't moved. And neither had his.

Just that single heartbeat of silence—his question hanging, her answer unsaid.

Her lips parted. "You—"

But then—

"Oi!"

A loud crash of footsteps up the stairs broke the moment like a slap of cold water.

Teagan appeared, chewing something that looked suspiciously like a third helping of cake, crumbs clinging to the corner of his mouth. He looked between them, paused, then grinned slow and wide.

"Am I interrupting?"

Caelan didn't move. Just took another slow sip of brandy.

Niev, however, exhaled through her nose and stepped back half a pace, shoulders lifting in a show of indifference she did not feel.

Damn him.

Damn him and his disgustingly handsome face.

"As usual Blackwood," Caelan muttered. "Your timing is abysmal."

"Sorry to ruin the smoldering tension," he said, waving a lazy hand between them, "but Ayda wants to talk to you."

Caelan exchanged a glance with Niev. The teasing burned off quickly.

"Lead the way," she said, already brushing past him.

They climbed the steps toward the captain's cabin, tucked snugly near the helm, overlooking the decks below. The wood creaked under their boots, worn smooth by years of salt and storm. The lantern above the door cast a golden ring across the weather-beaten planks, and the smell of sea brine and tar hung thick in the air.

Laughlan's cabin wasn't grand, but it commanded respect—map-lined walls, a massive desk cluttered with navigational tools and half-finished letters, and a flask never too far out of reach. The back windows overlooked the endless sprawl of ocean, moonlight slicking over the waves like spilled oil.

Laughlan was already inside, lounging in a chair with one boot propped up on the edge of the desk. A bottle of something probably illegal rested at his elbow.

"Well," he drawled, lifting an eyebrow as the others filed in. "If it isn't my favorite little chaos coven."

Niev shot him a deadpan look as she closed the door. "You're hilarious."

"Always." He winked, then tipped the bottle back for a long swig.

Caelan crossed his arms and leaned against the bulkhead, eyes narrowing on Ayda.

"What is it?"

Ayda didn't look up right away. Her fingers traced the edge of the parchment as if organizing her thoughts. "While you were gone," she said slowly, "I went through the ledgers again."

"Looking for more names?" Niev asked, brows furrowing.

"Patterns, mostly. And... something jumped out."

Ayda flipped a few pages, then held up the book, tapping a specific line of script with the tip of her finger. The handwriting was sharp. Precise. Next to the line where Niev's and Elias's names were recorded, a signature.

"Don Arin Alvania."

Laughlan blinked. "Who?"

"Exactly," Ayda said. "I've never heard of him either. But his name's all over this thing. And I can't find anything useful in the public registries or black market logs. He's not a noble I've heard of. Not a buyer. Not a trafficker with a known crew or sigil."

Caelan pushed off the wall and stepped closer. Niev could see that the name meant nothing to him either.

Ayda turned the page. "His name comes up again. Here—" she tapped another entry, "and here. It's always tied to high-level transactions. Children, yes. But also arcane weaponry. Restricted magical substances. Bribery records involving coastal port officials. He's connected to too much to be a middleman."

Teagan's brow furrowed. "So he's not just selling children. He's running the show."

"Maybe," Ayda nodded grimly. "Or at least he's one of the people who is."

Niev stared down at the name. The handwriting was crisp, elegant, and utterly unfamiliar. Her stomach turned.

"I have no idea who that is," she murmured. "He's not from my grandmother's court. Not from my father's lands. That name doesn't belong anywhere in my memory."

Ayda flipped to another marked page and tapped a black ink sigil—a jagged circle with three slanted lines through the center. Faded, but unmistakable.

Laughlan straightened, all traces of nonchalance vanishing. "I've seen that."

Niev looked up sharply. "Where?"

"Once or twice. On crates that went missing. On logs that led to dead ends. Once on a wreck that washed up near Mossgrove—crew gutted, nothing left but ash and bone. That mark was carved into the mast."

Teagan let out a low sigh. "And here I was hoping Darrow was the top of the food chain."

"He wasn't," Ayda said. "He was just the gatekeeper."

Silence fell.

Niev stared at the name.

Don Arin Alvania.

It meant nothing.

Not a single thread tugged in the back of her memory. No courtly introduction. No whispered political rumors. No signature overheard in her grandmother's council chambers. Not even a passing mention.

But somehow, *that* name was scribbled beneath the darkest day of her life. The day her family died. The day her entire world ended.

And that—that made *no sense*.

Her hands curled around the edge of the desk, knuckles whitening. "Why?" she whispered.

The others all turned to look at her.

"Why would someone I've never heard of order the death of my family?" Her voice was quiet but sharp-edged. "Why would a stranger send soldiers into the most guarded stronghold in Arenthia, kill the heir to the throne, slaughter her husband, and then sell their children off like livestock?"

The questions poured from her, breathless and bitter.

"What did he gain? There were no alliances to sever. No vendettas. Nothing."

Ayda placed a tentative hand over Niev's, grounding. But her skin felt hot, like the confusion and grief inside her were threatening to spark.

"And how did he get access?" Niev murmured. "How does a man I've never met reach *inside* the heart of the fortress and walk away unscathed?"

Caelan's voice came low, quiet, steady. "Unless someone on the inside helped him."

Niev turned to him slowly.

It was the kind of thought she hadn't let herself consider. Not for years. Not since the memories stopped coming back in jagged shards and started living inside her like ghosts.

"It's the only way this makes sense," Caelan said with what looked like an apologetic expression.

The room was still.

Ayda's brows had drawn tight, Teagan's jaw was tense, and even Laughlan had stopped fidgeting. The silence between them was louder than anything else.

"I don't know who he is," Niev rasped again. "But he knew *exactly* where to find us. He knew who to kill. Who to take. And he made sure I vanished."

Caelan's voice cut through the silence, low and grave. "We need to start considering the possibility that someone on the inside betrayed your family," he said, his eyes locked on Niev. "And if they did—we need to figure out what they gained from it."

A beat passed.

And then Niev looked back down at the ledger, at the name written so calmly beneath the destruction of everything she'd ever loved.

It stared back at her in careful, deliberate ink. As if it weren't holding the weight of a massacre. As if it didn't carry the echo of her mother's last scream or the iron tang of her father's blood on the palace floors.

A stranger's name.

A stranger who had reached into her life like a hand through smoke and torn it apart.

She traced the letters once. Slowly. As if committing them to memory could somehow grant her power over them.

"You made a mistake," she whispered to the cursed name etched on the ledger. "You should've killed me when you had a chance."

For the first time in a long, long while, Niev felt something solid click into place.

Purpose.

She looked at the four of them—Caelan, Teagan, Ayda, Laughlan—and her voice didn't tremble when she spoke.

"Whoever this *fucker* is—he has no idea the kind of hell he's brought upon himself."

Then she turned and walked out of the cabin, wind lifting the edge of her coat, salt in her hair, her steps quiet and lethal as a promise.

She wasn't the girl who had been sold.

She wasn't the assassin who had been forged.

She was the reckoning they never saw coming.

And she was done waiting in the dark.

33.
Niev

Sleep came slowly, and when it did, it arrived in pieces.

The kind that splintered around her like broken glass—each shard a memory. A scent. A voice.

Her mother's gentle humming as she brushed Niev's hair by candlelight. Her father's arms lifting her and Elias together as they raced down the golden halls of the palace, shouting with laughter. Her brother's face—identical to hers, a mirror image save for his blue eyes—grinning as they pressed palms together, swearing they'd never leave the other behind.

But then, like always, the light dimmed.

The corridors darkened.

The laughter dissolved into screams.

And her brother's face—so clear a moment before—morphed into something else.

Eyes. White-silver and ancient. Blinking open where they didn't belong.

Voices—too many, too close—whispered in a language she didn't understand, curling under her skin like frostbite. Her limbs refused to move. Her mouth opened to scream, but no sound came. Just water. Salt-thick and choking.

Niev jolted awake, her heart pounding against her ribs. The shadows in the corners of the hold looked too long. Too sharp. Sweat clung to her back despite the cool night air. Her fingers trembled as she slid from the hammock, careful not to wake the others.

The floorboards were cool beneath her bare feet as she climbed the steps to the upper deck.

Above, the sky was painted with a thousand stars, pale and cold and infinite. The moon floated low and waning, spilling silver across the sea. The air was brined and clean, the wind soft but steady. For a moment, she just stood there, her fingers curling around the edge of the railing, letting the salt air sting her lungs.

But the sense of being watched lingered.

And those haunting whispers—still echoed faintly in her ears.

I'm losing my damn mind, she thought.

But then came the voices—soft as tides, layered like waves, ancient and strange and full of something that made the hairs on the back of her neck rise. They sang, though not in any tongue she knew. The melody was not quite beautiful—too eerie for that—but it was mesmerizing. A music made of ocean and grief.

She leaned forward, eyes fixed on the water.

There were shapes moving beneath the surface. Sleek and pale, flickering just beneath the moonlight.

And underneath their song—*words*.

Whispers threaded through the music like reeds through a current.

"You listen well, Daughter of Shadows…"

Her breath hitched. She scanned the deck, but there was no one. Just the ship creaking softly, the ocean breathing around her.

The voice continued, coiling tighter.

"You wear the skin of the serpent and walk like a predator. But do you know what you are?"

Her magic stirred before her thoughts did—like something waking at the edge of her blood. The wind shifted. The water seemed to glow.

"Your blood remembers. Even if your mind does not."

She braced herself against the railing as a flicker of movement rose from the depths.

Sirens.

Half-shapes, graceful and terrible, swam just beneath the surface—eyes glowing faintly, their hair dark ribbons trailing in the tide. They watched her. Waiting.

The next whisper slid through the water like a blade:

"The currents are deeper than you know. And the silver-crowned liar still barters in bones."

The words turned her blood to ice.

"What silver-crowned liar?" she whispered aloud, her voice barely more than breath.

But the waves had already begun to still.

The shapes beneath the surface faded. The music dissolved.

Only one final whisper clung to the wind:

"The true master waits in the shadow of your birthright. The tide has only just begun to turn."

Niev stood motionless as silence reclaimed the sea.

Her hands rested on the railing, but her fingertips glowed faintly—silver and dark, like moonlight skimming the surface of a blade. Her magic hummed low and restless, tasting the air like it could sense what she could not yet see.

She was no longer dreaming.

And something had just awakened in the darkness—and within her—that refused to sleep again.

34.
Caelan

The streets of Breyvia greeted them like an old memory.

They'd made port mere hours earlier, the sails of the *Sersha Mara* folding like tired wings as they slipped into the familiar bay. After a brief council on deck, they'd agreed to split up — Niev and Caelan would escort Finnian home, while Ayda, Teagan, and a few of Laughlan's crew took the rest of the children to their families scattered across the southern quarter. There'd been no ceremony, no grand strategy, just a quiet understanding that some reunions deserved to happen without a crowd.

And so they'd gone.

Now, the homes around them stood tall and close, like a family pressed shoulder-to-shoulder in an embrace. Their red clay roofs sloped with the patience of age, weather-worn but sturdy. Iron signs swayed gently above doorways, and herbs and wildflowers spilled from cracked window boxes like they'd always belonged. The scent of forge smoke drifted lazily through the air — familiar and grounding — laced with sea salt, fresh bread, and something that might've been rot.

Children ran barefoot down cobbled lanes, laughter echoing off stone.

And for the first time in a long while, Caelan felt the breath in his chest loosen.

Niev didn't speak much as they passed the cobbled square, where market stalls had begun to pack up for the evening. Her hood was drawn low, obscuring the sharper edges of her face. Finnian shuffled between them, head bowed, wrapped in a wool cloak several sizes too large.

He hadn't spoken since they'd left the ship either.

Niev didn't push. Calean knew she never did when it mattered most. She just watched him with a quiet, unwavering steadiness, like a flame waiting for wind.

Eventually, they stopped in front of a modest two-story house nestled between a weaver's shop and an abandoned storefront. The windows were shuttered, the stone stoop worn smooth from years of use.

Caelan followed Niev up the steps, his boots heavy against the stone.

She knocked once sharply.

For a moment, there was nothing. Just the muffled echo of footsteps behind the door, then the scrape of a latch, and the creak of old hinges.

The door creaked open, and the man who emerged looked like he'd been forged in fire. Broad-chested and thick-armed, with soot embedded deep into the lines of his fingers and beard dusted in ash. The light caught the worn edge of a blacksmith's apron still tied around his waist.

Ewan Beylore's eyes scanned them without recognition at first. But when they landed on Niev, they froze.

"...Tigress," he rasped, his voice rough with heat and wariness.

Caelan felt it then—that familiar shift in the air that always followed her. Fear and reverence, braided together like smoke and steel. But she didn't flinch beneath it.

Instead, Niev reached into the folds of her cloak and drew out a leather pouch. She stepped forward and held it out, her voice calm but edged like a whetted blade.

"You gave me this to avenge your son," she said.

The man's brow furrowed as he took the pouch, his fingers grazing hers. He looked down at it, then back up, confusion cracking across his face. "I—I don't understand."

"We do not avenge the living, old man," she said softly, her voice almost too quiet to carry.

She stepped aside.

And Finnian stepped forward.

The boy hesitated just one breath. And then slowly, he reached up, grasped the edge of his hood, and pulled it back.

The world stilled.

Caelan watched the color drain from Ewan's face. His lips parted, and for one breathless moment, the man didn't move. Didn't blink. He looked like a man who'd stumbled into a dream and wasn't sure if it would shatter.

"Finn...?" His voice cracked.

The boy's eyes glistened. He nodded.

"Aye, Da. It's me."

Ewan dropped to his knees like his legs had simply given out beneath him. "My boy," he choked. "My dear, sweet boy—" His arms were around him in an instant, fierce and shaking, like he'd never let go again. "I thought I'd never hear your voice again."

The boy clung to him, silent tears streaming down his cheeks.

Caelan looked away without meaning to.

The air felt too thick. Too full of something raw and holy.

Eventually, Ewan rose, still holding Finnian like he might vanish again if he let go. He turned back to Niev—eyes wide and bloodshot, voice hoarse with emotion.

"I don't know what kind of creature you are, lass. I don't know what god you whispered to. But you brought him back."

"I didn't do it alone," Niev said, quietly. "But I want you to know I would've happily died trying."

He stared at her for a long moment. Then, slowly, he knelt.

Not as a smith. Not even as a father.

But as a man who had nothing to give but his name.

"My forge, my blade, my blood—whatever you ask. It's yours. If you ever call, me and my household shall come running."

Caelan glanced at her, half-expecting her to wave the offer off.

But she didn't.

She just looked at him, silent and still.

And nodded.

And even though Caelan wouldn't dare voice the thought to her out loud, in that moment, his Tigress looked *regal*.

Finnian's small voice cut through the silence. "Can I stay home now?"

Ewan pulled him tighter. "Aye, lad. You're home."

As they walked back down the steps, Niev didn't speak. But Caelan caught the way her hand brushed her collarbone. Like a knot had come loose inside her.

She didn't look back.

But he did.

And the image burned into his mind—of a father and son reunited, standing framed in the doorway. A fire lit behind them. A world stitched back together, just slightly.

"You okay?" he asked her quietly as they turned toward the square.

Niev didn't answer right away.

But when she slid her hand into his, she didn't let go.

And that was answer enough.

✳ ✳ ✳

By the time Caelan and Niev stepped into the alley behind The Wild Boar, where a rusted door was tucked beneath an arch of weeping stone, the others were already waiting.

Ayda leaned against the wall, arms crossed, her expression a taut mask of calm that barely concealed her worry. Teagan stood beside her, jaw clenched tight, tension coiled through his frame like a pulled bowstring. Myria flicked her cigarette into the gutter as they approached, her gaze sharp and unreadable. Laughlan, stars help them, actually looked amused — one boot up against the wall, the very picture of reckless delight.

"Ready to face the boss?" he drawled as they came into view.

"Hardly," Niev muttered, but her stride never faltered.

Caelan said nothing.

The moment his boot touched the threshold, something in his gut twisted.

They descended into the Red Dragon's Lair together, boots echoing down the winding stone steps, the scent of sweat, smoke, and old metal thick in the air. The door at the bottom was already ajar, voices drifting through — laughter, bargaining, the distant clink of coin and cutlery.

But the moment Niev stepped into the room, everything stopped.

The laughter died.

Chairs scraped backward.

A card table toppled as someone leapt to their feet, and the click of loaded weapons being set aside echoed like bones in a tomb.

Criminals scattered.

No one asked questions. No one stayed to gawk. One by one, they vanished — out back doors, into corridors, through trapdoors — until the only footsteps that remained were heavy and purposeful.

Saeris Morraine entered from the far chamber, firelight catching on the rings stacked up her fingers and the glinting edge of the short blade she always wore at her side.

She spotted Niev in an instant, closing the distance between them in two quick strides.

And smacked the Tigress right across the face.

The force of the slap echoed through the chamber like a thunderclap. Niev's head snapped to the side, her cheek blooming red, a trickle of blood biting the corner of her lip. She didn't move. Didn't raise a hand. She simply stood there — back straight, chin high, eyes locked forward.

"You arrogant, insufferable *child*," Saeris hissed.

Caelan moved before he could stop himself — fists clenching, boots sliding forward — but Teagan stepped hard in front of him, one hand gripping his shoulder.

"Don't," Teagan muttered under his breath. "Just... don't."

"Do you have *any idea* what I've had to clean up after you?" Saeris went on, circling Niev now like a storm looking for where to strike. "You burned down a noble estate. You commandeered a pirate ship. You paraded a dozen slave children across half of Eldhaven, dragged their little faces through every goddamned port."

Her eyes blazed.

"You gave the underground something *unforgettable*, Niev. Something uncontainable. I've had to burn names. Shift coin. Threaten allies. You've cost me thousands — *thousands* — in damage control, trying to keep your name out of the picture, not to mention the people breathing down my neck for answers."

Still, Niev didn't flinch.

But that only seemed to enrage Saeris more.

"You *vanished*," she spat. "Without a word. Without a plan. For *weeks.* You think I trained you for this? You think you get to wear the Tigress's mask and then piss on everything we built?"

Caelan's fingers ached from how tight he'd balled his fists.

She was shaking.

The Tigress, proud and deadly and impossible to rattle — was shaking. Not from fear, but from restraint.

Yet Saeris wasn't finished.

Her wrath coiled tighter, like a whip drawing back for another strike.

"You had the entire capital whispering your name again," she hissed, pacing now, her voice sharper with each syllable. "Not in fear — in *hope.* You think that's a good thing? You think it's *safe* for the Tigress to become a myth instead of a monster? You've drawn too much light, girl. And in our world, light is fatal. Have I taught you nothing?" she spat, throwing her arms wide.

"Traffickers. Enforcers. Even nobles are watching now. Waiting. You didn't just light a fire — you *declared war.* And do you have any idea what war costs in our business?"

Niev didn't respond. Her cheek still burned red from the slap, a faint line of blood tracing the curve of her jaw. But she held the line. Shoulders locked. Eyes unreadable.

Caelan's jaw ached.

He could barely hear over the sound of his own blood pounding in his ears. He had imagined this meeting with the woman who raised Niev — who carved her from iron and defiance. He had imagined a battlefield, verbal and brutal.

But this?

This was a reckoning.

And Niev was *bleeding* for it.

Still, she didn't step back.

Didn't offer any excuse or remorse.

Saeris ranted on.

"You commandeered *Laughlan Thorne's* goddamned ship without so much as a contract. Do you even understand how much I had to pay the people at the port to keep their mouths shut? They made me *haggle. Me.*"

From the corner of his eye, Caelan caught Laughlan smirking, clearly enjoying himself. Teagan muttered something under his breath like *you're not helping,* and Ayda rolled her eyes to the ceiling.

But Caelan wasn't focused on them.

He was watching Niev. Watching the way her fingers curled slightly at her sides. The way her jaw locked, eyes flashing with something darker than anger.

She was waiting.

Letting Saeris finish.

And when at last the storm broke — when the Red Dragon slowed, breath ragged, fury cooling to simmering disbelief — Niev lifted her chin and leveled her gaze.

Then, with perfect clarity, she asked, "Did you know he was alive?"

The older woman stared at her, eyes narrowing in confusion. "What the hell are you talking about?"

Niev took a single step forward. Her voice was barely more than a breath, but it cut through the quiet like a blade.

"Elias. Did you know he was alive?"

The silence that followed was absolute.

Saeris went still.

Her expression flickered — not confusion, not annoyance — but something Caelan couldn't name. A split-second of something raw.

She stared at Niev, as if seeing her for the first time. Her mouth opened. Closed again.

"Elias is alive?" she asked — hoarse now, the rage gone from her voice, stripped down to disbelief.

Niev didn't blink.

"He's in Zarenth," she said. "In the slave camps. And I'm going to get him out."

The silence shattered.

Saeris's face paled, as a breath left her lips like a curse dragging through her throat. "Fuck."

Caelan barely registered Saeris's reaction after that. The way she stepped back, bracing herself against the wall as if the floor had shifted beneath her. The way Teagan muttered *well, shit* under his breath while Ayda stared at the floor like the pieces were only just falling into place.

Because his world had narrowed down to one single, searing truth.

Niev was going to Zarenth.

Of course, she was going to break her brother out of the slave camps.

And he was going with her.

The thought hit him like a hammer to the chest. Because he hadn't stepped foot on that cursed red dirt since the day he clawed his way out. Since the day he swore never to return.

The whiplash of that vow, and the ease with which he was now willing to break it, knocked the breath clean from his lungs.

He would go back.

For her.

For Niev, who had dragged him back from the edge of everything more times than he could count. For the girl who sang to broken children in the dark. For the woman who, after all the blood on her hands, still clung to the thread of who she used to be.

And he loved her for it.

❋ ❋ ❋

They'd all left the Red Dragon's Lair behind in a slow drift of boots and silence.

Saeris hadn't said anything. Just stared Niev down with fire in her eyes and reluctant acceptance in her clenched jaw, as if she knew—had always known—that nothing could stop the Tigress once she'd set her sights on something.

Still, the parting had felt like a rupture. A quiet tearing.

Ayda, Teagan, Myria, and Laughlan all peeled off down the alley toward the docks, back to their own homes, wordless but watchful. Caelan lingered, eyes heavy on hers, until she gave him a tired nod and insisted she needed a few hours alone. He didn't press. He didn't try to follow.

He just watched her go.

So now she stood at her door, hand resting on the handle, staring at the scarred wood like it belonged to someone else.

The lock clicked open. She stepped inside.

Her apartment welcomed her with a familiarity that felt suddenly alien—like walking into a play she hadn't rehearsed. Everything was where she'd left it. The boots by the wall. The half-burned candle on the table. A rumpled blanket curled at the corner of the couch. Nothing had changed.

And yet everything had.

She closed the door behind her with a soft thud and leaned her back against it. Her eyes roved the space as her chest tightened, the stillness clawing at her skin like smoke with no fire.

Niev moved slowly, shedding her cloak like a second skin and draping it over the back of a chair. Her boots came next, then the outer layers of her clothes, until she was left in just her shift, standing in the center of a life that no longer fit.

This was the first moment in weeks she'd been alone.

No children to protect. No disguises to wear. No missions to plan. No leads to chase. No blood to clean off her boots.

Only silence.

And the unbearable weight of what she now knew.

Her brother was alive.

Somewhere, in the darkest pits of Eldhaven's biggest slave camp.

Niev moved to the middle of the room and stopped, her gaze fixed on nothing in particular. Her legs gave out and she sank all the way to her knees, hands braced on the floor as if the earth itself might give way beneath her.

She should be relieved.

She should be overjoyed.

She should be hopeful.

But none of those were things she knew how to feel anymore.

Her brother had been alive this whole time. Ten years. Ten years of believing his body had burned alongside their parents'. Ten years of surviving with a hollow where her twin should've been.

She'd buried him in her heart. And now he was alive.

Had he suffered?

Of course he had. No one ended up in a ledger sold to Zarenth without suffering.

Had he called out for her?

Had he hated her for not coming?

She bent forward slowly, arms trembling as they caught her weight. Her fingers clawed at the wood floor, nails scratching softly. Her mind wouldn't stop—images of his face as a boy, the way he used to grin crookedly at her from across the training yard, the sound of his laughter in the garden when their mother chased them, the time he gave her his scarf even though he was the one shivering.

He would've protected her.

She hadn't protected him.

And now she didn't know who he was. If he even remembered her. If he'd become something else entirely. If she'd find him—finally—and he'd be nothing like the brother she remembered. Or worse... if she found him dead, and had to mourn his loss all over again.

Tears blurred her vision, fell unbidden.

And for the first time in years—maybe since she stood before the burning gates of her childhood home—Niev broke.

Truly broke.

No shields. No teeth bared. No blade to hide behind.

Just a girl. On the floor. In a city that had taken and taken and taken from her.

"God," she whispered, the word catching in her throat like a splinter. "Please."

Her voice cracked, but she kept going, fingers curling into her palms until her knuckles burned.

It wasn't a prayer she remembered. Just the echo of ones she used to whisper beside her mother's bed. Back when she still thought someone might be listening.

"I know I've... I know I've sinned. I've killed. I've stolen. I've lied more times than I can count. I stopped asking for forgiveness a long time ago because I stopped believing I deserved it."

The tears came faster now, hot and unrelenting, streaking down her cheeks and catching on her lips as she gasped for breath.

"But please," she begged, her voice breaking, "please, don't let it be too late. Not for him. Don't let him be gone. Don't let me find a grave. Please, if there's anything good left in the world... if I've ever done anything that mattered... don't let him die in that place."

She pressed both hands to her face, curling into herself on the cold wooden floor.

"Give me the strength to bring him home," she whispered. "*Please...* I don't care what it costs."

There was no answer, save for a light breeze coming in through her window.

Only the quiet hum of the city beyond her window, and the slow, steady thrum of her heartbeat breaking beneath her ribs.

But still, she stayed there—on her knees, broken open and bleeding into the silence—until the tears slowed and her breathing steadied.

Until there was nothing left inside her but the fragile shell of a sister who had lost too much and refused to lose again.

She would save him.

Even if it broke her.

Even if it killed her.

Because Elias had deserved better than the world gave him.

And this time, she would not look away.

35.
Caelan

He'd been pacing for over an hour.

The cobblestones beneath his boots had long since memorized his pattern—up the alley, past the old spice merchant's stall, around the water barrel, and back again. Every turn brought him within sight of the same crooked window above Niev's apartment. Dark. Still. Silent.

He should've followed her.

He should've gone after her the second the light left her eyes and her shoulders curled inward like the weight of the past had finally become unbearable. But he hadn't. Because she'd asked for space. And he was trying—God, he was trying—to respect that.

But space felt a lot like silence.

And silence had teeth.

It gnawed at his gut, at the sharp, helpless ache in his ribs that warned him something inside her was unraveling. That she'd locked herself away, not to rest—but to fall apart where no one could see.

She always did that. Drew blood for strangers. Moved mountains for the innocent. But when it came to herself, she shut every door, barred every window, and sat alone in the dark until the damage settled into her bones like it belonged there.

He knew it deep in his bones, because he'd spent years doing the same. But he couldn't let that happen again.

And still—he stood there, frozen between impulse and fear, caught in the fraying threads of what he knew about her, and what he didn't know how to give.

Because the truth was, he didn't know what she needed.

Only that she'd never ask for it.

And if he waited for her to say the words, he'd be waiting until the world turned cold.

And then there was Zarenth. The word alone made his blood run cold.

He didn't let himself think about it often. About the chains. The stone mines. The way the sky there always seemed bruised, like it resented the things forced to crawl beneath it. He'd clawed his way out of that place once. Barely. And now, for her, he was preparing to walk back in.

Willingly.

The thought almost paralyzed him.

He blew out a slow, tight breath and turned down a quieter lane—now was not the time to dwell on that. The hour was late enough that even the rats had begun to retreat, the fog curling low between the stalls like smoke from some smoldering thing beneath the stone.

"Didn't think you were the type to sulk in alleys."

The voice made him jolt.

Myria Holloway emerged from the shadows with her usual quiet grace, a satchel slung across her shoulder, her expression unreadable beneath the hood of her slate-grey cloak.

Caelan straightened. "I thought you'd gone home."

She quirked a brow. "I did. But I came back to pick up a few things."

His gaze flicked toward the satchel.

Something about the way she carried it—too flat, too purposeful—suggested the "things" she was picking up weren't quills and ink.

He didn't ask. It wasn't his business.

Myria stopped a few feet from him and took in his face. She studied him like she was reading him line by line.

"You're worried about her."

Again, not a question.

He didn't bother lying. "She said she needed space."

Myria snorted, a sound that didn't quite qualify as a laugh. "The Tigress says a lot of things she doesn't mean when she's bleeding."

Caelan's gaze snapped to her face.

But she didn't flinch. Didn't soften.

"Look," she said, taking a step closer, "I've known her longer than most. I've watched her throw herself into fires for strangers without blinking. But when it comes to herself? When it comes to pain she can't fix with a dagger or a threat? She disappears."

Caelan exhaled harshly. "She asked me to let her go."

"And maybe you should've," Myria said calmly. "If she were anyone else."

She paused, then tilted her head, like she was weighing her words more carefully now.

"But based on the way you've been pacing, she's not. And if you wait for her to come back, for her to admit she's hurting—you'll be waiting forever. So if you care about her? If you really, truly want her in your life? Don't wait."

Her voice lowered.

"Trust your gut, Galbraith."

And then, as quickly as she'd appeared, she was gone—vanishing into the night with no more sound than the whisper of her cloak.

Caelan stood there for a beat longer, staring at the space she'd left behind.

Then he moved.

Across the square.

Up the stairs.

To her door.

He paused only long enough to press a hand against the wood, listening—hoping.

Nothing.

And then he knocked.

Once.

Twice.

Please open the door, he thought.

He didn't know what he was going to say. He didn't know what he'd find. But one thing had finally become clear. He'd rather face every demon in Zarenth a thousand times over than walk away from her again.

And so, he knocked again, softer this time—knuckles brushing wood like a question he wasn't sure he wanted answered. Still nothing.

A cold unease threaded down his spine.

He knew this apartment. Knew the way it usually hummed with tension, with life. Even in its stillness, it bore her presence—sharp-edged and restless, like it might rise up and bite you if you weren't careful. But now—

Now it was too quiet.

His jaw clenched. He glanced down the street below, as if expecting a witness, then let out a slow breath.

"She's going to kill me," he muttered, and pressed his palm flat against the lock.

The metal shivered beneath his hand, vibrating at a pitch only he could feel. His Materia powers hummed in his blood—matter giving way beneath intention, molecules loosening, sliding apart. With a quiet *click*, the bolt unlatched, and the door creaked open an inch.

He hesitated.

One last chance to turn around.

To give her the space she'd asked for.

But the memory of her face in the Red Dragon's Lair stopped him cold—the hollow in her eyes, the tension in her jaw, the blood dripping from her cracked lip.

He pushed the door open and stepped inside.

Darkness met him like a shroud. The air was thick with it—warm and stale, as if it hadn't moved for hours. Moonlight spilled in through the narrow window slats, casting slashes of silver across the floorboards. Shadows pooled in the corners like secrets left out too long.

"Niev?" he called softly, not wanting to startle her.

No answer.

He crept forward, his boots silent against the wood. The place was still familiar—organized chaos. Her satchel tossed over a chair. A half-empty mug on the table. Her weapons lined with precision along the wall.

Everything in its place, and yet... it felt abandoned. Like the pulse that usually ran through her home had vanished.

And then Caelan saw her.

She lay motionless on the floor, bathed in the slant of moonlight that spilled through the narrow window.

For a terrifying breath, his heart stopped.

Her limbs were bare, her shift rumpled—shoulders exposed to the cold air, legs curled beneath her like a collapsed marionette. Her coat and weapons were discarded at the door, and every line of her body looked... soft. Vulnerable in a way she never let herself be. Not even with him.

His first instinct was panic.

"Niev," he whispered, stepping toward her, already bracing for the worst.

But then he spotted the slow rise and fall of her chest.

She was breathing.

Asleep.

Just... asleep.

Relief struck him like a wave, crashing through his chest and robbing him of air. He pressed a hand over his sternum as if to hold the cracked pieces together, but it was too late. The sight of her like this—bare, undone, alone on the cold floor—it broke something open in him.

She must've collapsed here the moment she got home.

Carefully, he dropped to one knee beside her. Moonlight silvered the curve of her cheekbone, her collarbone, the dip of her waist beneath the threadbare shift. She looked so young like this. So unbearably human.

His throat tightened.

Slowly, reverently, he slipped an arm beneath her knees and another around her back, lifting her with a gentleness that bordered on worship. Her head lolled slightly, curls brushing his jaw. And just as he stood with her cradled in his arms, her fingers curled—grasping blindly—and caught in the front of his shirt.

His breath hitched.

She held on.

Like some part of her recognized the shape of him even in her sleep.

He carried her to the bed.

It was neatly made—of course it was—but he tugged the blanket back with one hand and eased her down onto the mattress. Her fingers slipped from his shirt as he pulled away, and a quiet, distressed sound escaped her lips.

"Caelan," she murmured, barely audible.

He froze.

Her brow furrowed in sleep, her lips parted just enough to whisper again. "Stay..."

His name from her lips wrecked him. And that word—*stay*—gutted him.

He wasn't sure his heart would ever beat the same way again.

He brushed a hand along the side of her face, voice low and hoarse. "I'm here, love."

Still holding his breath, he stepped back just long enough to shed his boots. Then his shirt, careful not to make a sound. The belt followed, until he was down to nothing but his breeches and the thundering weight of everything he felt for her.

He climbed in behind her, slipping beneath the blanket like he belonged there. Like this wasn't the most dangerous thing he'd ever done.

As soon as he lay down, she shifted.

Without waking, she turned toward him and curled into his chest—seeking his warmth.

His arms folded around her.

One beneath her shoulders, the other across her waist.

And there, in the hush of her apartment, with the moonlight trailing soft and silver over the sheets, Caelan Galbraith fell asleep with the princess of Arenthia wrapped up in his arms.

36.
Niev

The first thing Niev registered was the smell.

Not the usual sharp tang of bergamot and leather that lingered in her apartment, but something warmer—comforting. Smoky herbs and melted butter. The faintest hint of black tea.

The second thing was the way the sheets felt beneath her hands.

Warm. Rumpled. And not just from her own weight.

She sat up slowly, still wrapped in the thin cotton shift from the night before. Her body ached, bone-deep and weary in ways that had nothing to do with battle. Her eyes scanned the room instinctively, and her heart stuttered.

Caelan's boots were by the door.

Neatly placed. As if he'd meant to stay.

She stared at them for a long moment, mind still too fogged to reconcile what that meant. Part of her wondered if she'd imagined it—that memory of strong arms lifting her from the floor, of a quiet voice murmuring her name into her hair. But then she glanced at the sheets again, at the space beside her still faintly warmed.

He'd been there.

He'd stayed.

Niev exhaled, slow and shaking, and pushed the blanket off. Her legs felt like stone, but she moved anyway, pulling on a robe and tying it tightly around her waist. The wooden floor was cool against her feet as she padded silently through the living room, following the scent of something that—if she didn't know better—smelled suspiciously like breakfast.

When she reached the kitchen, she stopped short.

Caelan stood at the stove, shirtless, hair a mess, working a kettle over the flame like it was second nature. A plate of eggs, bacon, and warm bread sat on the counter, already waiting for her. Two mugs sat beside it, one already steaming.

He glanced over his shoulder as she appeared, and his mouth tugged into that stupid, soft smile of his. The one that made it too hard to breathe.

"Tea's just about done," he said casually, as if this were something he did every morning. "Milk, two sugars. The way you like it."

She blinked at him.

Her throat went dry, and all she could manage was, "How...how did you get in?"

He had the decency to look guilty, rubbing the back of his neck with one hand. "You didn't answer," he muttered. "So I, uh... broke the lock."

Her brows lifted, looking back at her front door in panic. "You broke it?"

He didn't even try to hide the grin this time. He wiggled his fingers, the tell-tale sign of his Materia abilities. "Gently."

She huffed, the tension draining from her shoulders. "Of course you did."

Silence stretched between them, thick as the tea leaves in the pot, until she found her voice. "Thank you."

He didn't answer.

Instead, he crossed the space between them and pulled her into his arms.

His chest was warm, solid muscle pressing into her. His arms tightened around her back, his skin hot where it touched her through the thin fabric of her robe. He didn't say anything. Just held her.

At first, she tensed—uncertain, her body still braced from everything that had come before. But his heartbeat was steady against hers. His hands didn't roam, didn't ask for anything. They just held her there, anchored her.

He smelled of sleep and warmth, and faintly of bergamot—the scent she always seemed to carry, now clinging to him too.

Her fingers curled into the bare skin of his back, and her breath loosened. She sagged into him, letting her body press against his until she could feel the slow rise and fall of his chest. Safe. Steady.

They stayed like that for a long time.

When he finally pulled back, his hand moved up to cradle the side of her face, thumb sweeping gently across her cheek, eyes searching hers.

"We're going to get Elias out," he said, voice hoarse with the weight of it. "Whoever did this—whoever's still out there pulling strings—we'll make them pay tenfold."

Her breath caught. Her vision blurred again at the edges, but she held it back. Just barely.

Caelan dipped his head, brushing his lips softly to her temple.

"But first," he murmured, "you're going to eat."

She let out a breath of a laugh, wiping beneath her eyes. "I still can't believe you cooked."

He scoffed, reaching for the mug of tea. "How do you think a single man survives in this godforsaken country if he can't even cook his own damn breakfast?"

She shrugged sheepishly, the smallest smile tugging at her lips. "Fair enough."

He set the mug in front of her and nodded at the plate. "Try it. Might be the best damn thing you've ever tasted."

She raised a brow—but took a bite.

Her eyes widened almost immediately. "Okay...this is unfairly good."

Caelan flashed his wicked grin again and shrugged as if to say, *what else did you expect?*

Niev took another bite, then another, chewing slower this time, savoring each bite. She swallowed, licked a crumb from her lower lip, and looked up at him with a narrowed, considering gaze. She sipped her tea slowly.

"You know... If the food's this good," she said, voice low and smooth, "I might actually be forced to keep you around."

Caelan stilled.

He reached out, took the cup of tea from her hand, and set it aside with slow, deliberate care. Then he stepped closer, between her legs, bracing his arms lightly on either side of her, caging the Tigress in where she sat on the stool.

The look in his eyes darkened.

"Is that so?" he asked, almost a purr.

She shrugged, all affected indifference, but her fingers tightened around the hem of her robe. "Might not have a choice. I'd be doing the realm a disservice, letting a great cook like you wander loose and unattended."

His smile was slow and deliberate, his hands slowly sliding to her hips beneath the robe. She could feel every inch of him pressed close—the heat of his breath, as he leaned in closer to her ear, his voice a low rasp that sent shivers racing down her spine.

"We definitely can't have me loose," he murmured. "Or leave me unattended..."

With you—he didn't need to add, but she felt the weight of it between every syllable. The truth that pulsed beneath the teasing tone. The way his fingers tightened slightly at her waist.

She gasped, the sound soft but sharp, as the heat of his palms continued to graze her thighs, slipping beneath the hem of her robe with maddening slowness. His breath was warm against her jaw, rough stubble scraping gently against her skin as he trailed his lips from her cheek toward her neck.

"Caelan..." Her voice was barely more than a breath, but it made him pause—just long enough to let the tension coil tighter between them.

His lips hovered above hers for a beat. Then, with the faintest smile tugging at his mouth, he dipped lower.

The first kiss landed just beneath her ear. Soft. Intimate. Her breath hitched.

"I'd make you tea in the mornings," he whispered against her skin.

Another kiss, lower this time—just beneath her jaw. Slow and reverent.

"I'd bring you breakfast in bed."

A third followed, pressed lightly against the hollow of her throat. Her hands tightened at his shoulders, breath catching in her chest.

"I'd rub your shoulders when you're tired..."

His mouth moved lower, trailing a line of heat down to her collarbone as she gasped.

"Warm your feet when they're cold..."

Each kiss was a promise, a vow, a thread pulling tighter around her ribs.

"I'd learn every curve of your body, every inch of your skin—"

She let out a quiet, breathless laugh, trembling as his lips got closer to hers.

Mother of stars.

He was *everywhere*.

His hands braced on either side of her hips, his torso flush against her front, the warmth of him seeping into every place her robe failed to shield. The scent of him—amber and mint and salt—wrapped around her like a second skin. Her back pressed to the counter, nowhere left to run, and yet she had never felt more still.

It was maddening, the way he didn't touch her lips, the way he held her there with the gravity of restraint.

He was undoing her with nothing more than a look. A whisper. The weight of him between her knees, his thumb brushing the skin just above her pulse, like he could feel it hammering beneath her skin.

And he didn't pull back. Not as he watched her like she was sacred, like she was *his*.

"You are an absolute menace," she whispered, voice thick.

Caelan leaned in even closer, lips brushing the shell of her ear.

"You keep saying that," he murmured. "And yet you're still here."

She turned her head just enough to meet his gaze, her eyes searching his. Then, quietly—trembling at her own vulnerability—she leaned in, her mouth barely a breath from his, and Niev could feel his heartbeat under her palms—racing, like hers, like thunder.

Then Caelan was crushing his lips to hers, hard and desperate, like a starving man desperate for water. Her hands flew to his shoulders, digging into muscle, while his arms locked around her waist, pulling her tight against the heat of his chest. Every pulse in his neck thundered beneath her palm, every frantic inhale she drew pressed between them like shared oxygen. His tongue swept urgently for hers, claiming and mapping her mouth in a single, overwhelming claim.

His body pressed more urgently into hers, as his hand came down to cup the back of her thigh—until a sudden thunderous crack tore through the moment.

BANG. BANG. BANG.

A *violent, explosive* knock rattled the door so hard the hinges *shuddered* in their frame.

"NIEV! You better be alive in there! Open the goddamn door!"

In a split second, the moment shattered.

Niev *jumped* so hard she smacked her elbow against the counter with a loud *crack*. The mug she'd just set down wobbled—then tipped—scalding tea *sloshed* down her front and splattered across Caelan's bare chest.

"SHIT!" they both shouted in unison.

She stumbled back, clutching her elbow, soaked and livid.

"Fucking Teagan!" she snarled, swiping uselessly at the tea dripping down her thighs.

Caelan hissed under his breath, grabbing a towel from the hook by the hearth and rubbing at the spill on his stomach.

Niev made for the door like a storm, but he caught her by the wrist.

"Where the *hell* do you think you're going?" he said, breathing hard, *still* obviously trying to calm the pounding of blood in his veins. "Are you seriously going to open the door—*in that?*"

She blinked. "In *what?*"

And then she looked down.

Her shift, already thin to begin with, was now clinging in all the wrong places. The tea had soaked through the entire front, turning it practically sheer. Her thighs, the curve of her hips, the swell of her breasts were *all visible* through the drenched fabric.

Caelan's gaze flicked down for only a split second before jerking away again like it burned him. He clenched his jaw. "Niev..."

Her eyebrows *shot up.* "I will open my own damn door however the hell I please—"

Caelan leveled her with a look that could've cut through steel. His eyes were dark, stormy, and *so close* to feral she felt the air tighten between them again.

He stalked toward her, closing the gap in two long strides. "For once," he growled, voice low and strained, *"could you do what you're told* and just—*just go change!"*

She blinked, startled by the edge in his voice.

His hands dragged through his hair again, the strands sticking up wildly. "Please," he added, quieter now but no less heated. "I am one wrong breath away from throwing that door open and beating the living shit out of Teagan. I do *not* have the strength to deal with your sheer nightgown and *his* big mouth at the same time."

Niev blinked once. Twice.

"Fine," she said, biting her lip to hold back a full laugh.

She batted her eyelashes mockingly at him and turned without another word, striding—*swaying*—back toward her room, casting a look over her shoulder that was all *triumph* as she disappeared through the door.

But not before she threw one last look at Caelan as he stood in the middle of her kitchen, shirtless, flushed, and still *aching*, visibly trying not to explode with the frustration of being *this close* to her and having the door almost kicked down by a screaming idiot.

Another round of knocks followed.

"NIEV! HELLO? I swear, if you're dead, I'll break this door to collect your corpse!"

Caelan muttered something very dark under his breath and stomped toward the front door, murder pulsing in every step.

37.
Caelan

The knock hadn't finished echoing before Caelan yanked the door open, jaw tight, barely refraining from snapping it clean off its hinges.

Teagan stood on the other side, hand still raised to knock again—his grin obnoxiously wide. Behind him were Ayda, Myria, and Laughlan, all blinking in surprise like they hadn't expected the door to be answered by *him*.

"Well, well," Teagan said, stepping back with exaggerated mockery, "*this* is new."

Caelan gave him a flat look. "She's getting dressed."

Laughlan let out a low whistle. "Is she now?"

Ayda arched a brow but had the decency not to smirk—*much*.

"Just out of curiosity," she drawled, eyes cutting back to Caelan with merciless precision, "do you make a *habit* of opening doors half-naked in women's homes, or is this a new development?"

Caelan, who had just started putting on his shirt, froze with one hand still at his collar. He looked up, deadpan. "Only when I'm interrupted at a *spectacularly* bad time."

"Ohhh," Teagan said, leaning forward, eyes gleaming. "So we really *did* interrupt something."

"Saints above," Caelan muttered under his breath.

Myria said nothing, but her eyes swept him once—shirtless, barefoot, hair still mussed from sleep, and the grin she wore made it perfectly clear she was filing this moment away for later torment.

"You going to let us in, or do you plan to interrogate us on the porch?" Teagan asked, already moving past him.

"I didn't *plan* to have you here—at all," Caelan muttered, stepping aside and gesturing with a dramatic wave of his hand. "But by all means, make yourselves at home."

They spilled into the living room like they owned it. Teagan dropped into one of the armchairs, stretching out like a king, while Laughlan flopped dramatically onto the edge of the couch, swinging a booted foot.

"In all fairness, we were here to check on *her*," Teagan said cheerfully, brushing past him without waiting. "None of us suspected you'd be here."

What a blatant lie.

Ayda moved more gracefully, settling in with her usual quiet poise. Myria took a seat beside her, but not before giving Caelan another once-over and a wink that made him rub the back of his neck.

"My question is—" she said, already smirking with feigned ignorance, "did you *arrive* at her house half-naked... or did you just *happen* to lose your shirt after crossing her threshold?"

"Ah," Laughlan sighed dramatically, leaning back in his chair with a hand to his chest. "The only regret I have in this miserable pirate life of mine," he declared, raising his flask, "is that I never got the chance to cross that woman's threshold."

There was a loud intake of breath from Teagan as everyone went silent.

"You'd need a map, a compass, and a miracle for your dick to *find* the threshold," Niev said sweetly, not even blinking as she walked into the room—fitted in a black tunic and belted trousers, hair loose and thrown over one shoulder, damp at the ends. Her eyes scanned the group, then flicked once to Caelan, and winked.

She looked pointedly back at Laughlan and went on, "and even then, my dear Thorne, I'm not sure the poor thing would survive the journey."

Teagan choked on his drink so hard it sprayed across the floor. Laughlan sat there, stunned, eyes wide as if he'd just been backhanded by the stars themselves.

And Caelan—

Caelan nearly *bent double*.

Laughter exploded out of him, loud and helpless, and only grew worse when Niev shot him a smug, unrepentant look over her lashes.

"Oh, saints above," Ayda whispered, eyes wide, somewhere between horrified and delighted. "You've finally done it. You broke them."

Laughlan blinked once. Twice. Then grinned slow and wolfish, tipping his flask toward her. "Marry me."

"Keep dreaming, darling," she said, sitting back smugly on her favorite armchair.

"Honestly Niev, I leave for a few hours, and suddenly *everyone* wants to be your bedmate." He grinned at Caelan. "First his cabin, now your apartment. You're getting more of *this man* in the last few weeks than you've had men in the last ten years."

Niev didn't answer, just took a sip of her tea, and smiled *into* the cup. Slowly. Like the tigress she was.

Laughlan caught it. "Stars above," he muttered to Myria, "she's *corrupting* him."

Myria grinned. "Or he's corrupting *her*."

Ayda, who had been half-successfully avoiding the commentary, finally groaned and threw her hands up. "Can *someone* please focus before Teagan starts asking for a reenactment?"

Teagan was already opening his mouth when Niev cut in, voice like honey and venom, "Finish that sentence and I'll test if a spoon can pierce cartilage."

He closed his mouth.

Wise man.

The laughter slowly died down. The reason they were all here now pressing at the edges of the silence.

Caelan could see the quiet tension in Niev's posture—the sunlight flickered across her face, throwing shadows beneath her cheekbones, gilding the anger already rising behind her eyes.

She knows why they're here, he thought.

Ayda broke the silence first.

"We're going with you."

Niev narrowed her eyes. "No."

"You're not going to Zarenth alone. Not a chance in the fucking underrealms." Teagan said, his annoyance clearly etched on his face.

"I didn't ask any of you to come," she snapped, but the anger was hollow.

"No," Laughlan said calmly, "you didn't. But we're not asking for permission."

"There's no way you can pull this off alone," Myria, still perched calmly beside the arm of the couch, crossed one leg over the other and tilted her head. "We're going."

"We're *all* going," Caelan said.

Her head snapped up to him so fast he thought it might break. ""The hell *you* are," she said, fire licking at every word.

"You can't stop me."

"Watch me," she threatened, shooting him a glare so fierce it would've made a lesser man tremble.

He took a step forward, meeting her toe-to-toe. "You don't get to play martyr with my life. I *know* that place, Niev. I know how it breathes. I know where it bleeds. You want to get in and out alive? You need someone who knows every twisted inch of it."

She shook her head, furious. "I am not *risking* you!" her voice cracked, just barely, "Elias is my brother, and I will bloody well get him out on my own!"

He slammed his hand on the table, the loud smack making her flinch. "I am not letting you get *killed* because you're too fucking stubborn to ask for help!"

The room held its breath.

"Let me do this," she whispered. "Please."

"You think I'm letting you go in alone?" he went on, voice low and rough. "After everything we've been through together—do you really think I'd let you face that hell by yourself?"

She looked away. It was the only sign of surrender she gave.

Caelan exhaled—tight, controlled.

They were going. All of them.

"Good. Now that this is settled," Myria said, standing at last. "You're going to want to see these."

She reached down and pulled out a satchel Caelan hadn't even noticed before. Unbuckled it, unrolling a thick set of vellum papers across the kitchen table.

The others crowded around as she smoothed the edges. Caelan stepped closer, his breath catching in his throat the moment the markings came into view.

He knew them.

He knew them *too* well.

Zarenth.

Specifically—*Camp Virell.*

Black ink etched with brutal precision. Rows of holding cells, barracks, auction pits, supply tunnels. Guard towers like ticks along the perimeter. Underground corridors crisscrossed beneath the living quarters, narrow chokeholds barely wide enough to squeeze through. A single high tower—the Overseer's post—stood like a skeletal fist in the center of the whole cursed thing.

"How the hell did you get ahold of these?" Caelan said quietly, tracing a finger along the outer boundary wall.

Myria shrugged. "Not legally, I'll tell you that."

"They're good," Caelan said. "Better than I expected. But they don't show everything."

"Like what?" Teagan asked, already bent over the left half of the diagram.

"The hidden channels beneath the auction pits. The rotways. They used them to move bodies. No official record of them exists—just stories passed between prisoners."

Ayda paled. "Do you know where they are?"

Caelan's jaw clenched. "Some. Not all. I was a child. But I remember the smell. I remember the feel of the walls when we were moved between cells in the dark."

Niev reached out, her fingers brushing his where they hovered above the map. "Show us what you do remember."

Caelan stared at her hand for a breath. Then at the blueprints.

The parchment felt like it weighed a thousand pounds. His throat burned.

He didn't want to do this.

Not because he didn't care—*God above*, he did. But going back, even in memory, was like wrenching open a locked door that he'd spent a decade reinforcing. It felt like slicing open his ribs and dragging his past into the light.

And yet—

He nodded. Slowly. Like every muscle in his neck resisted.

"The west wing," he said, his voice rough. "These cells here... they were overflow. When the regular holding pens got too full."

Teagan's jaw clenched. Ayda leaned in, reading every word on his face.

"They were less guarded," Caelan continued, pointing, "but worse. The guards didn't patrol as often. Nobody cared what happened in there."

He didn't say what happened in there.

Didn't need to.

"The foundation cracked once. Flooded the lowest units. They collapsed a whole tunnel trying to fix it. Eventually, they sealed it off and built a new one behind it." His fingertip hovered, then tapped. "Here. That collapsed tunnel might still be there."

Laughlan exhaled, raking a hand through his hair. "So that's our way in."

"Maybe," Caelan said. "If the damage didn't get worse. If the new tunnel didn't cave, too."

"Assume it didn't," Ayda said gently. "Where would it lead?"

Caelan stared at the blueprint, muscles locked. His finger traced slowly over the line of the eastern wall.

"If we breach the main gate and get through the east perimeter, we can cut through the yard to the barracks," he murmured. "Then down the old spiral staircase to the catacombs. If the tunnel's still there, we'd come out just below the lower housing blocks."

"And from there?" Niev asked.

He didn't answer right away.

His eyes met hers.

There was so much in her face—hope and fear and fury and *love*—and none of it dulled the terror slicing through his veins like ice water.

"Then we find Elias," he said.

38.
Niev

The maps were sprawled across the table—cut open, dissected, every hollow corridor and dark corner labeled with charcoal strokes.

The final strategy spoken aloud and debated until Niev's voice went hoarse.

And still, her thoughts would not rest.

The others had slowly filtered out, one by one. Myria had slipped away with a kiss to her cheek and a reminder to check her shop for something she'd been stitching. Laughlan had left grumbling about needing to whip his crew back into shape. Teagan was dragged back to his errands with a warning from Saeris about not making any more impulsive, heartfelt decisions. And Ayda... Ayda had simply pressed Niev's hand with a knowing look and disappeared, giving her the thing she both dreaded and needed most—

Time alone with Caelan.

The moment the door had shut behind them, Niev had begun to pace.

She hated how quiet the apartment felt. As if the silence would swallow them whole.

Caelan sat on her couch, hunched over the blueprints where he hadn't moved in hours. The charcoal in his fingers had blackened his knuckles. He didn't seem to notice, still drawing lines, symbols, annotations. Notes only he could make. Because only he had lived it.

Only he had survived the *horrific* slave camps of Zarenth.

She slowed her pacing and sat beside him on the couch, knees drawn up slightly. For a moment, she said nothing. Just watched his hand glide across the parchment, steady as always. She marveled at that calm — the iron strength it took to face the worst place in the world and not flinch.

His fingers stilled, hovering above the map.

"What is it?" he asked gently, eyes not yet lifting.

She hesitated.

"I don't want to ask," she said reluctantly. "Not unless you want to answer."

He finally looked at her then. Dark eyes, weary but waiting.

"Ask."

Her throat tightened, almost too scared to utter the words out loud.

"How did you get out?" she whispered.

The question hung between them like a knife, suspended and glinting in the low light.

For a long moment, Caelan didn't breathe. Then, slowly, he set the charcoal down. Leaned back, and let out a sharp and bitter breath.

"It took... years," he said, voice like sandpaper. "You don't plan an escape from Zarenth. You survive long enough to find the crack. And then you bleed through it."

He stared ahead, not at her, not at anything in the room. His eyes had gone distant.

"They put me in the iron pits when I was seven. It was where they sent the stronger ones if they disobeyed. Where the air was thick with soot and the walls were lined with barbed ore. You'd cough until your throat bled. And then you'd keep coughing."

Her heart clawed against her ribs, but she didn't speak.

"Most children died by fifteen," he said. "I got lucky. I learned how to be small when they needed me small, strong when they needed me strong. Learned who to bribe, who to avoid, who to blame."

His jaw clenched.

"But that only gets you so far. The guards were bastards, but the other slaves... some of them had given up on being human a long time ago. You had to sleep with one eye open, eat with your back to the wall, and never—*never*—show weakness."

He rubbed at the back of his neck. The memory must've felt like it was still there, still clinging.

"There was a boy," he said quietly. "He was maybe twelve. He'd been caught stealing moldy bread from one of the outer kitchens. They wanted to make an example out of him. But my father intervened. So, they took him instead. Tied him to the center post in the pit. No food. No water. No one was allowed to speak to him."

Niev's throat ached. She knew where this was going.

"They left him there for six days," Caelan whispered. "And when he finally stopped breathing, they laughed. *Laughed.*"

He closed his eyes for a long moment.

"The next morning my mother collapsed in the fields. The guards said she was faking. They kicked her. Over and over. I begged, and begged. But they wouldn't listen..." He stopped, breath hitching.

A silence like ash settled between them.

"She died three days later."

His eyes were distant now. Fixed somewhere in a memory far too vivid.

"After that, I didn't care if I lived or died. I started stealing scraps. Tools. Pieces of wire and stone. I watched the guards like a shadow, memorized the way they moved, the schedules, the weak links. Marked when the outer gates opened for shipments. It took me two years. Two years of crawling through sewage pipes, stealing tools, hiding shivs in the soles of my shoes. Waiting for the right shift. The right storm."

He looked at her now. Fully. Raw and open.

"Eventually, I found a gap in the eastern fence. Just wide enough for a severely underfed child to squeeze through. But it meant crossing the slag yard—open ground, no cover. I waited for the fog. One night, I made my run."

He rubbed a hand over his face. A tremor ran down his spine.

"I killed three guards before I even made it to the outer fence. Had to slit a fourth's throat with a broken shard of glass. The blood soaked through everything."

Niev didn't flinch. She couldn't. Her hands were frozen in her lap.

"They caught me halfway across. I was shot twice. One arrow in the thigh, one in the ribs. I climbed the cliffside half-conscious and barely breathing, and I don't even remember how I got to the coast. Just that I woke up three days later on the floor of a fishing boat. An old man had pulled me out of the surf. Never got his name."

The silence after that was deafening.

Niev sat there, shattered by the story. Not just by the horror, but by the sheer *will* it must have taken to survive it. To walk away from it. To still have enough left of himself to love someone else after it.

When she looked up at him, silent tears tracked down his face. He wiped them roughly with the back of his hand.

Niev couldn't take it.

She reached for him. Cradled his face between her palms like he might vanish if she didn't hold on. Her thumbs brushed away the tears, and her own vision blurred as she leaned closer, forehead touching his.

"You got out," she whispered. "You went through hell, but you got out. You're safe."

His eyes fluttered shut.

"And now you want to go back," she said, voice cracking.

He tensed, but she didn't let go.

"Don't," she whispered fiercely. "Please—don't. I've never asked anything of you, not like this. But I'm asking now. Don't go back there. You *survived*. You *escaped*. Don't throw yourself back into that hell because of me."

"Niev—"

"No, you need to listen!" she said, her voice rising, desperate for him to understand. "If you truly care for me, you will stay here. You will stay safe. Please, Caelan... I am *begging* you."

Her fingers trembled as they slid down to rest against the center of his chest, where his heart beat—steady and strong, louder than it had any right to be.

But Caelan wasn't done.

He exhaled slowly, shaking his head. "You still don't get it."

Her eyes flicked up to his.

"I won't lie to you. The fear I feel—about going back to Zarenth, about facing what's there—it's real. It's choking," he looked at her desperately. "But it is *nothing* compared to the fear I feel when I think about letting you walk into that place without me."

She opened her mouth, but he stepped in, closer, his hands cupping her face now, thumbs brushing her cheeks.

"I would *rather* go back to that nightmare a thousand times over than spend one second not knowing if you'll make it out of there. I'd rather bleed to death than wonder if I could've done something to stop it."

Her throat closed. Her vision blurred. "You don't have to do this to prove anything—"

"I'm not trying to prove anything!" he said, fiercely. "I've already made my choice."

She stared at him, willing his composure to break, waiting to see any crack in his armor. But there was none, his decision was made. There truly wasn't anything she could do to stop him from coming with her. Niev's heart broke as the realization dawned on her. As she finally understood the lengths this man was willing to go for her.

This beautiful, *infuriating* man.

She pressed her forehead to his, and his breath hitched. The air between them turned fragile, too full of words neither of them had dared to say.

Her hands gripped his shirt like it was the only thing keeping her tethered to the ground. Her heart pounded wildly, too fast, too loud.

And then, before she could talk herself out of it—before she could let the fear take over—she finally said the three words her heart had been singing for *weeks*.

"I love you."

Caelan went deathly still.

Her voice was hoarse, but she didn't flinch. "I love you, Caelan Galbraith. With every broken part of me. With every scar I carry and every shard of whatever heart I have left. *I love you.*"

His chest heaved once. His hands shook—actually shook—where they cupped her face, fingers trembling like he couldn't quite believe he was touching her.

"Say it again," he rasped.

She reached up, traced the curve of his jaw with soft, trembling fingers, and whispered, "I love you."

One second they were apart, and the next they were two worlds colliding.

Caelan crushed his mouth to hers.

It wasn't gentle. It wasn't careful. It was fire and wind and the collapse of all restraint.

His lips claimed hers like he'd been dying for this—for her—and no longer had it in him to wait. His arm locked around her waist, the other tangled into her hair, pulling her closer, anchoring her against him like the world was ending and she was the only thing worth saving.

Niev gasped, and he swallowed the sound like a lifeline. Her fingers clawed at his shoulders, then curled around his neck, desperate to drag him closer even when there was no space left between them.

His body pressed her into the couch cushions, his knee slipping between hers. She arched into him, and he groaned into her mouth—low, guttural, the sound of a man losing control after holding it in far too long.

He tasted like tea and sorrow and something she hadn't dared name until now.

Love.

When he finally pulled back, it was only because they needed air, and even then, he didn't go far. Their foreheads touched. Their breaths mingled.

And his voice was a broken thing when he said, "Then there's nothing in this goddamn world that could keep me from walking into hell with you."

Her eyes burned. Her heart cracked open wider.

And this time, she didn't try to stop him.

She just pulled him in again, and kissed him like she never wanted to stop.

39.
Niev

The sky was still ink-stained when Niev arrived at the docks the next morning.

A soft wind skimmed across the harbor, tugging at her coat and sweeping salt through her hair. The mist curling over the cobblestones hadn't yet burned off.

They'd chosen to forgo Port Veyne, since it was too exposed, too heavily watched. If word of their voyage leaked, they'd lose the only advantage they had—secrecy.

Instead, they opted to board the ship from Hollow Harbor—a near-forgotten stretch of wharf, south-east of Greyhaven—launching at dawn like ghosts slipping between the cracks of the waking world.

The *Sersha Mara* waited in the fog like something half-awake, her black sails furled and her lanterns dim. A few crewmembers moved along the deck, quiet and efficient, prepping lines and securing cargo without a word. They knew what this mission was. They knew who it was for.

Niev stood at the edge of the wharf, the wood damp beneath her boots, and tried to breathe.

But her lungs felt too full. With nerves. With dread. With hope.

It was a strange thing—to be afraid and steady at the same time. Her thoughts clashed beneath the surface, loud and merciless, a battlefield of noise behind the still mask she wore. Every breath she drew seemed to birth a new emotion, crashing against the next like waves against stone.

Fear coiled through her chest like wire. Zarenth waited on the other side of the sea, and it loomed in her mind like some great, devouring thing. She didn't know what they'd find when they got there. If Elias would be waiting. If there would even be anything left of him to find.

But under the fear, there was something steadier. Something she hadn't felt in years. Purpose. It ran like iron through her bones—unfamiliar, anchoring. She wasn't just surviving anymore. Wasn't running, reacting, adapting like a cornered thing. She had direction now. A mission she would see through, even if it burned her down to nothing.

And threaded through it all, soft as breath—gratitude. Strange, unwelcome, but impossible to ignore. Her brother might be alive. And Caelan had come with her. Despite the weight of what it meant. Despite what it might cost. Despite the place they were headed to. He had chosen her. Again. And again.

And so had her friends.

For the first time in as long as she could remember, the Tigress of Solhaven didn't feel alone. Not anymore.

She glanced down the dock just in time to see him step aboard, flanked by Teagan and Ayda. Teagan was already making some off-handed joke, one that had Ayda smirking and Caelan shaking his head. They looked like family. Her family.

"Myria," Niev called out as the seamstress emerged beside her with a cloak wrapped around her shoulders, and a satchel slung over one arm. Her expression was unreadable as she stared up at the *Sersha*, the mist curling at her boots.

"You really don't have to come," Niev said softly, her voice barely above the hush of waves slapping wood. "You've already done more than enough"

Myria didn't respond right away. She simply looked at her. As if peeling back all the layers until only her soul remained.

Then, with a fond smile, she said, "You know I usually avoid tagging along on your missions because they're just that. Missions. Jobs. Coin in, blood out." She turned to face her fully. "But this isn't a job. This is your heart. And I'm not letting you face it alone, sister."

A knot caught in Niev's throat as Myria reached out and squeezed her arm before turning and heading up the gangplank. Thorne's crew greeted her with casual nods, as if she's been sailing with them for years.

Niev exhaled, long and slow, her breath curling in the mist like smoke.

Behind her, the fog parted as soft steps shifted in the air.

"I was wondering when you'd step out of the shadows," she said, not needing to look.

Saeris stood half-wrapped in shadow, the deep crimson of her coat flaring like blood against the pale light. Her arms were crossed, back straight, the wind tangling through her raven-dark hair. That piercing, storm-born gaze was trained on Niev with a weight that was impossible to ignore—one part challenge, one part caution, all parts unspoken grief.

She looked exactly the same as she always did—impenetrable, deliberate, unflinching.

Niev's throat tightened.

This woman. This relentless, unforgiving woman. She had forced her to stand when everything else begged her to crawl. Had turned bone into steel, and heartbreak into armor. Had taken a shattered girl and carved something fearsome from the wreckage.

"I know you don't approve," Niev said quietly, "but I'm going."

"I know," Saeris said.

"And I know you think this is foolish. That I'm throwing away everything I've built."

"I do."

Silence.

The wind rolled over the docks. Somewhere far out, a gull called once—sharp and lonely.

"But before I go," Niev continued, "I need you to know something."

In case I don't make it back, she didn't have to add.

Saeris raised a brow but said nothing.

So Niev stepped closer.

"When my parents died, I lost everything I knew. When I was dragged into that brothel, I lost everything I believed in." Her voice faltered, just for a breath. "But the day you pulled me out, you saved my life. And you've been saving it every day since. With every lesson, every scar, every brutal word you used to make me strong."

Something flickered in Saeris's eyes.

"I know I haven't always made it easy," Niev continued, the words thick in her throat. "But I want you to know that if my parents raised me until they died... you raised the part of me that clawed her way back."

She moved forward, and before the older woman could pull away, Niev wrapped her in a fierce hug.

For a long, aching heartbeat, Saeris stood frozen in place.

But then—slowly, so slowly—her arms lifted and encircled Niev's shoulders, holding her like something rare. They stood like that in the fog, the salt-laced wind threading around them, two ghosts made flesh in the hush before dawn.

When they finally pulled apart, Saeris's face was tight, unreadable. But her voice was rougher when she spoke.

"I spent ten years trying to beat that heart out of you," she muttered. "Figured it would make you stronger. Less reckless."

Niev snorted, trying to hide her watery smile.

"I failed," Saeris said, shaking her head. "But now I see it. That heart of yours... it's the strongest damn thing you have. So whatever happens... Whatever you find in Zarenth—don't lose it."

Niev's expression softened at the woman's words. "I won't," she promised.

Saeris cleared her throat, and stepped back. "Now get on that damn ship before I change my mind and chain you to this damn harbor."

The Tigress huffed a laugh, her eyes shining, as she turned away from the Red Dragon.

The planks creaked beneath her boots once more as she crossed back to the gangway. The deck of the *Sersha Mara* waited for her, mist-wreathed and silver-lit in the rising dawn. Her crew—her friends—watched her ascend, saying nothing.

The sky blushed soft with morning behind them.

And for the first time in ten long, blood-stained years, Niev stepped into her future.

And she wasn't afraid.

40.
Caelan

They'd been at sea for most of the day, the steady churn of waves beneath the *Sersha Mara,* the groan of her timbers, and the rhythmic slap of wind in her sails quickly becoming familiar to him. The water stretched in every direction, endless and indifferent. The kind of silence that could lull a man into forgetting they were sailing toward hell.

Caelan didn't forget.

He stood at the starboard rail, boots braced, arms crossed against the salt-laced wind. His eyes scanned the horizon—pointless, really. Zarenth wouldn't appear like a ghost on the sea. It waited far beyond the veil of water and dread. Still, his gaze lingered, the old tension alive in his shoulders, a low thrum in his spine.

Behind him, the crew murmured in bursts of laughter and familiar curses. Niev was among them—her voice a low hum in the background, the curve of her smile catching sunlight as she handed Teagan a canteen and said something that made him nearly spit water out his nose.

She looked... happy.

Or if not happy, then close to it.

There was ease in her posture, a glint in her eye he hadn't seen in weeks. Her laugh was unguarded. Her face softer than it had been since they boarded. She stood shoulder to shoulder with Laughlan, Myria, Teagan, and Ayda—joking about something crude he didn't quite catch—and God help him, Caelan felt his chest ache at the sight.

Not with jealousy, though that was always there, simmering beneath the surface whenever *Captain Thorne* got too close or too smug or too damn charming. No, this was something deeper. The kind of ache born from watching someone you love remember what it felt like to live without the weight of the world pressing down on them.

He hadn't even realized he was smiling until the wind shifted and pulled her laugh to him again.

He turned his gaze back out to sea.

They were sailing toward a graveyard.

There was no telling what they'd find. If Elias was even still alive. If they were too late. The questions pressed in on him like fists. They always did when the horizon was empty and the stakes were too high to say aloud.

Let him be alive, Caelan thought. *Let us find him. Let this end with more than just bloodshed.*

He didn't ask for a miracle. Just a fighting chance.

A flash of movement caught his eye.

Niev had peeled off from the group and was making her way up toward the quarterdeck, her hair tousled by the wind, face flushed from the sun. She looked radiant and untouchable and entirely too tempting.

Caelan pushed off the rail and crossed the deck, falling into step beside her like it was the most natural thing in the world.

She raised a brow at him, amused. "You've got that look again."

"What look?"

"The one that means trouble."

He gave her a crooked grin. "That's not true. Sometimes it just means fun."

"Which is just another word for trouble," she smiled, narrowing her eyes at him.

"Mm. You say that like you didn't enjoy it."

Niev snorted, but her cheeks darkened a shade, which he took as a victory. She tried to keep walking, but he caught her wrist gently, slowing her pace.

His voice dropped as he leaned just slightly toward her ear, lowering it to something meant only for her. "You know, I've been thinking... there has to be at least one private corner of this godforsaken ship where we can finish what we started."

She blinked, a breath hitching.

"Oh?" she managed, glancing sidelong at him, trying to keep her face neutral. Failing spectacularly.

He let his fingers graze hers, teasing and slow. "Somewhere quiet. Far away from Thorne's annoying voice and Teagan's incessant wheezing."

"You're forgetting Ayda's glare."

"Ayda's glare can't reach the cargo hold," he said with a grin. "I checked."

"You did not."

He leaned closer, his voice nearly a purr. "Darling, I'd comb this entire ship if it meant finding a place to kiss you without someone interrupting."

A shiver rolled down her spine. He saw it. Felt the electricity bloom between them.

But before she could respond—before he could drag her below deck and make good on every word—Teagan's voice echoed across the deck behind them.

"Oi! Galbraith! Stop whispering sweet nothings and get your brooding ass back here. We need you for whatever stupid plan Thorne's cooking up now!"

Caelan sighed, head slumping on Niev's shoulder. "I'm going to strangle him."

She just laughed, her eyes glinting with mischief.

"I guess the cargo hold will have to wait," she said, brushing past him, hips swaying just enough to drive him mad.

Caelan muttered a curse under his breath as he made his way back down the deck toward the gathering by the helm.

Laughlan stood at the center of it all, one boot propped against the railing, a map stretched across a crate beside him, held down by a knife plunged through the corner. His coat was half undone, sleeves rolled, and he was grinning like a man about to gamble away his last coin, and somehow convinced he'd win.

Ayda, Teagan, and Myria were already there, circling the crate like vultures over a war table. Niev had drifted toward them too, her face shifting back into the cool, analytical mask of command. Caelan stepped up beside her and caught the quiet flick of her hand—her fingers brushing his as if to say *behave.*

He didn't return the gesture. But leaned in just a little closer, close enough for her shoulder to graze his, and make it very clear that he had *no intention* of behaving around her.

"Alright," Laughlan said, drawing their attention with a clap of his hands. "We've got about two days left before we hit Thaelon waters. But the sea never makes it easy, does it?"

"Let me guess," Teagan said, arms crossed. "Our road to hell just got a scenic detour through sea monsters and certain doom."

"Well, yes—but also—" Laughlan tapped the map. "—a stretch of cursed waters we call the Needle's Teeth. Sharp reefs. Strong current. And if that wasn't enough, we're close to naval patrol routes for Thaelon's eastern fleet. Meaning if we're spotted, we'll be lucky to sink before they set us on fire."

Ayda leaned forward, frowning. "Isn't there a way around the Teeth?"

"There is," Laughlan said. "But it's slower. And slower means risking more exposure. Plus, we'd be docking closer to the southern shores—less populated, but more heavily watched." He gestured to a cluster of shaded terrain near the northern edge of the map. "Our best bet is to slip through the Teeth, hug the coast near Morrow Bay, and dock at a half-forgotten cove south of the ruined stronghold here. No towns, no traffic. Just an old harbor mostly swallowed by rock and moss."

Niev's eyes narrowed. "And we can get inland from there?"

"It's a trek," Laughlan admitted. "But there's an old smugglers' pass that cuts through the ridge. I've used it once before—years ago. It'll take us right into the outskirts of Zarenth."

Caelan exhaled slowly. "So we're sailing through a kraken's nesting ground, dodging patrols, and then hiking through a cursed ridge with a bunch of stolen maps and hope."

Laughlan grinned. "Exactly."

"This is getting worse by the minute," Caelan muttered.

"Don't worry, Galbraith," Laughlan said. "I plan on getting us there in one piece. Mostly."

"*Mostly*?" Teagan echoed.

But Niev cut in, voice calm and focused. "And if we are spotted?"

Laughlan sobered. "Then we don't outrun them—we disappear. Between the cliffs, there are false inlets and hollow caves. We'll take her in and drop anchor where no one can see her. If they come close, we pull sails and shut lanterns. We'll wait it out. But I'll need everyone ready."

He looked pointedly at each of them.

"Anything goes wrong, we vanish. No heroics. No flair. We do this quietly."

Ayda nodded. "Then we should start bracing ourselves for the worst."

"Agreed," Myria added. "No offense, Captain, but 'false inlets' sounds like something you made up drunk."

Laughlan clutched his heart. "Myria, love, the only thing I've ever fabricated drunk was a love song for a duke's wife. And I stand by every line."

Niev sighed. "Let's focus."

Caelan leaned in, scanning the maps again, eyes locking on the jagged inked lines surrounding the Needle's Teeth. "If the current's as bad as you say, we'll need to time it perfectly. Hit the pass on the turn of tide, when the pull shifts. Otherwise we're dragging the *Sersha* across rocks."

"I'll chart it to the minute," Laughlan said. "I've done worse."

"That's exactly what I'm afraid of," Caelan muttered, dragging a hand across his face.

He looked up, across the deck where the crew was already moving— checking sails, coiling rope, sharpening blades. Everyone understood what they were walking into now. There were no illusions left.

They were sailing straight into hell.

He looked at Niev, who stood still as stone beside him, studying the waters beyond with that same stormy stare. Her hand rested over the hilt of her blade. Her jaw was set. He knew she wasn't afraid of the sea, or the Teeth, or the soldiers waiting beyond.

She was afraid of not reaching her brother in time.

Caelan swallowed the knot in his throat and turned back to the map.

* * *

The skies darkened faster than they should have.

What began as a ripple on the horizon bloomed into a black-bellied leviathan of a storm—bloated clouds cracking like whips overhead, the wind howling through the rigging like a warning too late to heed. The *Sersha* pitched beneath his boots, the wood groaning with the strain as waves began to slap the hull like fists. Salt burned in the back of his throat. He moved instinctively, shouting orders alongside Laughlan, hauling rope, securing what he could.

Below deck, Ayda had tied the barrels together. Teagan had reinforced the storage with double knots. Myria had battened every hatch and lashed herself to the nearest column, just in case. Everyone was doing what they could.

But it wasn't enough.

The storm was coming too fast. Too hard.

Thunder cracked so loud it seemed to split the heavens, and then the sea lifted—rose like something alive and furious.

Caelan stumbled back two steps, blinking rain from his eyes, as the creature erupted from the deep, its bulk silhouetted by lightning, slick and glistening and impossible.

Tentacles the width of ship masts slithered from the deep, curling over the bow and snapping two of the forward harpoons like matchsticks.

"KRAKEN!" someone screamed.

The word carried only a second before it was drowned out by another thunderclap and a spray of water that doused the deck in freezing salt.

"Lass!" Laughlan roared from the helm. "Portside! MOVE!"

The *Sersha* lurched, and Caelan slammed his shoulder into the storage hatch, yanked it open, and tore a small metal gauntlet from his belt. His fingers trembled—slick with rain and seawater—but they knew the feel of it, knew the grooves.

He shoved one of his cylindrical creations into the socket of his gauntlet and twisted until it clicked.

The air around his hand shimmered and crackled.

The ship tilted violently as a tentacle slammed into the aft rail, splintering the wood, sending Teagan skidding across the deck. Caelan dove, catching the stabilizer lever mid-fall, wedging himself between two cargo crates to find balance. With a guttural yell, he released the charge.

A whip of solidified vapor and lightning shot across the deck, lashing one of the kraken's limbs as it curled toward the mast. The beast recoiled, letting out a furious screech that vibrated straight through Caelan's chest.

But it didn't back off.

It writhed and curled, readying for its next attack.

"Show me what you've got, you piece of shit!" Caelan snarled, already charging up another strike.

Above, Laughlan wrestled with the wheel like it had grown teeth. Rain lashed across his face, his coat torn and plastered to his back. "You've got two minutes, Galbraith! Or I'm jumping in myself and strangling the bastard with my bare hands!"

"You'd be kraken bait in thirty seconds!"

"I'd die *spectacularly*!"

The kraken struck again.

This time, it took the mast with it.

Caelan watched—helpless—as timber exploded, sails shredded, rigging whipped across the sky. Debris rained down. He barely ducked in time.

The ship screamed.

Wood groaned. Nails tore loose.

"We're going to break apart—" Ayda's voice rang out from somewhere near the stern, panic threading through every word.

No. Not yet.

Caelan stumbled to the second stabilizer and shoved his gauntlet into the socket again, pouring the last of his charge into the core.

Lightning forked across the sky, and another wave slammed into the starboard side, tilting the ship so violently he felt the deck tilt beneath his boots.

A snarl—not human—ripped through the chaos.

Caelan whipped his head around.

Niev was already halfway across the deck, soaked through, a dark blur of rage and muscle as her body shifted mid-run. Bones cracked, skin darkened, fur erupted. In the span of a breath, the woman was gone, and the Tigress unfurled in her place.

She launched at the kraken's nearest limb, claws flashing like silvered scythes. She sank her teeth into thick, wet hide and ripped. Blood, dark and briny, sprayed across the deck—but the kraken didn't even flinch.

Another tentacle rose. And Caelan saw the Tigress look at the deep waters and hesitate.

Laughlan caught the look too. "Don't you *fucking* think about it!" he bellowed from the helm, catching her movement toward the edge of the ship. "You leap into those waters and you *will* die, beast or not! These seas are crawling with more of them. You shift into that serpent and they'll tear you apart before you even get a strike in."

Niev snarled at the captain.

Her paws scraped deep gouges into the soaked deck as she turned from the railing. Fury radiated off her in waves. Caelan saw the wild indecision flash in those glowing, golden eyes.

And then she shifted again.

Back to her human form. Tall. Wild-haired. Blood-slicked. Her mouth bared in a silent scream as she lifted both hands and called the shadows.

Her newly found powers came instantly.

From the corners of the storm, from the cracks in the deck, from the space between lightning and breath—they poured around her like ink, thick and writhing. Power shimmered up her arms in smoky tendrils, her fingers glowing faintly at the tips. The wind howled louder, as if answering her call.

Caelan stared, stunned, a heartbeat too long.

She raised her hands, and the shadows obeyed.

They surged forward like living chains, wrapping around the kraken's nearest limbs. The beast screeched—its eyes flaring—tentacles jerking violently as they were yanked back by invisible force.

"Hold it!" Caelan shouted, stumbling upright again, voice hoarse. "Just keep it still!"

Niev didn't look at him.

Didn't speak as she tried to keep all her focus on the writhing beast infront of her.

The wind screamed. The sea crashed.

And in that maelstrom of violence and darkness, Caelan sprinted across the deck, his gauntlet sparking with fresh energy.

One shot left.

He dodged a broken sail beam, leapt over the cracked railing, and skidded to the edge of the deck—where the kraken's limb still writhed, pinned by shadow and rage.

He aimed the gauntlet.

Focused.

And fired.

The charge exploded like a bolt from the heavens—searing into the exposed, glowing cluster near the base of the kraken's massive eye. The blast landed with a sound like stone shattering underwater—deep, brutal, final.

The kraken screamed.

Every limb recoiled. The beast thrashed violently, knocking barrels and men across the deck as it withdrew. The sea hissed and frothed as it slipped beneath the surface, leaving behind a swirl of blood and churned water.

The silence that followed was worse than the noise.

Because the sea itself was changing.

The wind dropped suddenly. The thunder paused.

And then a wall of water—*a wall*—rose on the horizon, tall as a cathedral, roaring toward them with the rage of a dying beast.

"Oh saints," Caelan whispered.

He turned and locked eyes with Niev who was already running.

"Grab something!" Laughlan bellowed. "Now—NOW—"

Caelan vaulted across the deck, reaching for her—he got her arm just as the wave hit.

And the world *disappeared.*

Sound shattered into silence.

Light vanished into the dark.

Water swallowed everything.

Caelan was airborne for a heartbeat—*weightless*—before the ocean swallowed him whole.

The cold was instant. Brutal. A punch to the ribs.

He tumbled, spinning, couldn't tell up from down—salt in his nose, his mouth, his eyes. His limbs thrashed but there was no surface—only cold and pressure and *depth*.

No.

NO.

He kicked harder. Reached.

Saw a flicker of fabric—black. Dark hair.

He reached for her again.

Then something *slammed* into him from below.

Pain exploded through his side.

And the world went black.

41.
Niev

Darkness pressed in from all sides, the ocean relentless and crushing, like a fist clamped around her chest, broken only by shards of moonlight filtering through the distant surface.

She was sinking.

Her limbs moved sluggishly, useless in the water, her body heavier than stone. Her lungs burned, throat locked in a scream that never made it past her lips. Her instincts begged her to shift, to release some form that would save her—but she could barely remember what her body was made of, let alone command it to become something else.

Caelan—

Her heart stuttered. Her thoughts thinned.

And then—like a thread of silk brushing against her skin—something stirred.

The water trembled, and a slippery, melodic sound found her in the dark.

Daughter of Shadow...

Her limbs went still.

You breathe our tide. You dream our name. Yet you do not know the depths of what you are.

The ocean shivered around her. Faint lights—bioluminescent and beautiful—began to pulse in the distance like a constellation mirrored in ink. Niev was losing consciousness.

You are not meant to drown, little shadow. There is still much ado.

Her body trembled. She didn't know if the voice was real, or just a fragment of death playing tricks on her mind. But the current had changed. Something was pulling her now—upward.

The slave burns for you, the sirens whispered. *He will burn the world for you.*

The image of Caelan rose unbidden—his eyes locking on hers in that final moment, just before the sea devoured them both.

But he cannot protect you from what awaits.

The voice grew deeper. Colder.

A silver-crowned liar barters in bones. Bloodlines buried in ash. Power forgotten by your kind.

They wait. They wake. Remember who you are, shadoweaver.

Her fingers twitched. She reached blindly for something, anything.

Rise, Sera Nieva.

With the last scrap of strength, she summoned the shadows.

The water folded around her in a cocoon of darkness, a velvet current pulling her up instead of under. Her limbs began to move—jerky, slow—but moving. The pressure lightened and the light grew, as the sea turned her over, and spat her out.

She broke the surface with a choked cry, salt water burning her lungs as she coughed, gasped, sputtered. Her vision blurred, her limbs too numb to paddle. The world rolled and reeled and then—

Sand.

Her body collided with the shallows, dragged forward by the tide and thrown onto rough, wet shore. She coughed violently, spitting salt and foam, hands clawing into gritty sand. Her hair was soaked and tangled, her body trembling with cold and exhaustion.

She could hear voices, and feet pounding through the sand.

And then—

"*Niev!*"

She tried to lift her head. Her throat burned but no words came out.

Caelan was there in an instant, dropping to his knees beside her like the sky had cracked open and dumped the sun into his chest. His hands were on her face, her arms, her back—*real*, warm, shaking. He looked like hell—bruised, bleeding, soaked—but he was there.

Alive.

She let out a half-choked sob and he hauled her into his arms with a strength that didn't seem possible. His forehead pressed to hers. She clung to him, fingers fisting into the fabric of his torn shirt like she needed proof he wouldn't vanish again.

"I've got you," he murmured, voice raw. "I've got you."

Teagan waded through the surf and knelt beside them. "Come on," he said gruffly, slipping an arm beneath her shoulders. "Let's get you up."

Together, they guided her toward a jagged rock further up the beach. She collapsed against it, shivering, her breath still uneven. Her gaze lifted, finally catching sight of the ruined silhouette of the *Sersha Mara* in the distance—listing to one side, sails torn, hull cracked. Smoke and steam rose from parts of the deck. It was alive, but barely.

"We've lost two men," Laughlan reported grimly as he trudged up from the shore, dragging a length of rope. "Half the rigging's shot. It'll take ages to patch her up."

All his banter and swagger had vanished, leaving only a tired man with too many losses in his eyes.

But he was already shouting orders, rallying the crew to drag supplies off the wreck, sort what could be salvaged, and start a fire. The survivors moved with grim purpose, too cold and shaken to argue.

Niev sat back, her body aching, mind still spiraling. The sirens' whispers echoed in the hollow of her ribs, like ghost-touched warnings burned into her marrow.

Myria crouched beside her, draping a blanket over her shoulders, as Ayda took a seat on the jagged rock next to her.. Both women looked like they'd seen death and spit in its face.

"You're safe now," Ayda said softly.

❅　❅　❅

The fire crackled softly, tucked between a ring of stones and the broken timbers of the wrecked Sersha Mara. Flames danced in the salt-heavy air, casting long, flickering shadows across the stretch of shore where survivors gathered to dry off and regroup.

Niev sat near the edge of the firelight, wrapped in a thick wool blanket, sand clinging to her damp skin and the taste of salt still bitter on her tongue. Her hair was drying in heavy waves, tangled with bits of seaweed and blood. Her body ached—muscles screaming, lungs raw, magic frayed to the edge of breaking.

Ayda and Myria sat quietly nearby. The others were busy tending to the injured, patching sails, salvaging what they could from the beach and the half-capsized hull.

Niev hadn't spoken much since they dragged her from the surf.

But now, sitting here in the aftermath, the silence pressed too tightly against her chest. It buzzed in her ears. Stirred the thoughts she'd tried to bury since the kraken rose from the deep.

She looked down at her hands. At the thin dark tendrils of magic that had curled from her fingers like smoke when she'd reached for the creature, at the way the sea had seemed to pull her out on its own.

"Ayda," she said softly, still watching her fingers. "Have you ever heard of a shadoweaver?"

Both women stilled.

Ayda tilted her head. "What do you mean?"

"I mean—" Niev swallowed. "My mother was a threadreader. She could see multiple branching futures simultaneously. Her mother, Adrianna... is a mindweaver. That's what our bloodline is. Cold magic. Visions. Mindrot. Not..." She trailed off. Her voice came rougher. "Not *whatever I am.*"

Ayda frowned. "I've read about affinities shifting over generations. It's rare, but it happens."

"But shadows?" Niev pressed. "I've never read of a single Nivola in the last thousand years wielding shadow. And the water—" She shook her head. "It's like it responds around me. Like it's sentient."

Myria leaned forward slightly, her expression thoughtful now.

"You've felt that before?" she asked.

Niev nodded once. "When I shifted beneath the surface during Darrow's attack. When the kraken came. And when I was drowning..." Her voice thinned. "I heard the sirens calling me."

Ayda's expression changed at that—something cautious flashing in her eyes.

"They *speak* to me," Niev went on, her voice low. "Not with words. Not always. But they *call* me. They've been whispering since the powers first came. And they—" Her throat tightened. "They called me *Daughter of Shadow*."

Niev was met with silence. Even the fire seemed to still for a moment.

Ayda's brows drew together slowly, something old and wary in her face. "You're sure that's what they said?"

"I'm sure," Niev said. "It's not the first time."

Myria looked at Ayda, then back at Niev. "Have you ever heard that name before?"

Ayda didn't answer right away. She stared into the flames for a moment, as though digging through memory. Then she spoke, slow and deliberate.

"Before she met my father, my mother was a Librarium archivist," she said, "And when I was a child, she would tell me of the stories she read there, myths, really. One of those myths spoke about a witch born outside the laws of her house. The first of her kind. They called her the Daughter Who Was Promised. Said she'd carry the darkness in her veins and wield the shadows like silk. That she'd rise when Arenthia was on the edge of ruin." Ayda's gaze met Niev's.

Niev's mouth went dry.

"No," she said quietly, shaking her head. "No, I'm not—this isn't—"

"Niev—"

"I'm *not* part of some prophecy," she snapped, sharper than she meant to. "I just want to know what's *happening* to me. I want to understand why this is happening *now*, after twenty-four years of *nothing*. Why I can feel things I've never felt before. Why the shadows *move* when I reach for them. Why the *sea* listens." Her breath hitched.

Neither woman spoke. They just stared at Niev until her shoulders slumped.

"I just want to save my brother," she whispered.

Ayda's voice softened. "I know."

"But what about after that?" Myria asked gently.

Niev looked down at her hands again. At the remnants of a magic she didn't understand, tangled in a future she never asked for.

"I don't know," she whispered.

They were silent for a long time, and then Ayda murmured, "Maybe you were never meant to be what Adrianna wanted. Maybe your power doesn't come from Arenthia at all."

Niev blinked at her.

"Maybe it comes from somewhere deeper," Ayda finished. "Somewhere older."

The words chilled her more than the cold in her bones ever could.

Her grip tightened on the blanket.

She didn't want a destiny. She wanted her brother. She wanted them all to make it out of this alive.

Myria's fingers gave hers a soft squeeze.

"We'll figure it out," she said gently.

Ayda leaned back beside her, shoulder to shoulder now. "Together."

Niev nodded slowly.

42.
Caelan

The wind carved sharp lines across Caelan's face as he made his way down the cliffside path, sea spray dampening his cloak. The sun hung low, but the adrenaline hadn't faded. Not since the water spat Niev out like the ocean had suddenly grown a conscience. Not since he saw *him* standing at the shore, eyes fixed, hands clenched in focus.

He found Teagan at the edge of the bluff, staring out at the waves with weariness. The waves below rolled in quiet procession now, nothing like the chaos earlier.

Caelan stopped a few paces behind him. His boots skidded slightly on the slick stone. "Tell me the truth, Teagan."

Teagan didn't turn. "About what?"

Caelan's jaw tightened. "Don't play dumb. I saw you today. And before, when Niev was on Darrow's sinking ship."

Teagan shrugged, the movement slight. "I have no idea what you're talking about."

"Do not *insult* me." Caelan's voice was sharp now. "You stood there like the sea was answering you. Like it *knew* you."

Still, Teagan didn't face him. "You're seeing what you want to see, Galbraith."

Caelan stepped forward, closing the distance between them. "No. I'm seeing what you *didn't* want anyone to see. You controlled the water, Teagan. You turned it inside out to spit Niev back onto the shore."

There was a long pause. Then Teagan sighed, almost like he'd been dreading this moment. "What else would you have had me do? I couldn't stand back and watch her die."

"So you're a water elemental," Caelan said slowly. "Why hide it?"

At last, Teagan turned, slowly, as if dragged by the weight of the moment. His dark eyes were clouded with something deeper than guilt— fear.

"You were never meant to see any of this."

"That's not an answer."Caelan stepped in, voice low, dangerous. "You waited until the last possible second to act. Why? Why hide it? Why let her nearly die before you showed your hand?"

Teagan flinched, just barely. He looked past Caelan, eyes on the horizon. "Because once you reveal something like this, you can't take it back."

"You think people wouldn't understand?" Caelan folded his arms. "There are plenty of elementals all around Eldhaven."

"I think they'd expect me to use a power I have no business using." His voice dropped. "Control is fragile. Especially with something as alive and wild as the water. One mistake, one surge of fear or rage, and I could drown half a village."

Caelan stared at him. "So you hide? Pretend to be normal while carrying a power that could *change everything*?"

"Yes," Teagan said, more forcefully now.

Caelan was quiet for a beat. The wind howled in the silence between them.

"And Niev?" he asked finally. "Did she have the right to know? She's your best friend Teagan, and she almost died. You could have saved her sooner."

A muscle in Teagan's jaw twitched. "If I had, she'd ask how. And I'd lie. And that would be worse."

"That's bullshit," Caelan snapped. "You wanted to stay invisible. You didn't save her for *her* sake. You did it because you couldn't stand the guilt of doing nothing."

Teagan turned away again, silent.

Caelan let out a slow, bitter breath. "You're afraid of who you are. I get it. But secrets don't stay buried forever. You may have saved her life, but if she finds out from someone else—"

"She won't."

"Don't be so sure."

Teagan closed his eyes, shoulders heavy. "Be quiet, Caelan. You don't understand the things you're bringing up."

"Then explain it to me!" Caelan's brow furrowed. "What happened, Teagan?"

The wind howled past as Caelan watched the war of emotions crossing the other man's face.

"My father was a water elemental," Teagan finally said, voice brittle. "He thought pain was the best teacher. Said the sea only obeys those who master fear. So he—he'd take me under. Hold me down. Again and again. Said if I panicked, I'd never be worthy of the gift."

Caelan felt his stomach tighten. "He *drowned* you? On purpose?"

Teagan looked away. "He called it training."

There was a terrible pause. A seagull cried overhead. The sea roared below.

"I was six. Seven. Younger, maybe. I don't even remember how early it started."

Caelan's breath caught. He didn't move.

"He'd hold me under. Let the sea fill my nose, my mouth, until my chest burned. Until I stopped thrashing. Said that was the moment control began—when panic died."

Teagan's jaw worked like he was forcing the words out of stone.

"Sometimes he let me up. Sometimes he didn't. Just watched me claw at the water, watched me *drown*, again and again. Said this was the only way to master it."

"God, Teagan..."

"I learned to stop fighting. That was the first lesson. Learned to go still. Learned to let the sea in." His eyes glistened now, but no tears fell. "But then one day—something shifted. I got so tired, so damn tired of the constant panic I'd feel in his presence. I became *furious*. And the water—"

He swallowed hard.

"It listened. Just once. He was dragging me under again, and I broke. The current snapped like a whip. I didn't even know I was doing it. One second he was above me, yelling. The next—"

Teagan exhaled shakily.

"The current twisted around him like a snake. Dragged him under. Smashed him against the rocks. I came up for air, and he didn't. But the worst part?"

His voice dropped to a whisper.

"I found him. Caught in a tangle of kelp on the reef, face half-bloodied, half-drowned—but alive. Gasping. His arm was broken. He couldn't swim."

Caelan stared at his friend, unable to form words, as Teagan's eyes glistened, but he didn't blink.

"He begged. For the first time in my life, he *begged*. Said he was sorry. Said I was strong now. Said he was proud. Said all the things I needed to hear."

Caelan swallowed hard. "And?"

"I stood still and looked him straight in the eye as the water filled his mouth. Watched the panic set in as he drowned in front of me, and the ocean claimed him."

Caelan's chest ached for that little boy.

"I went back to shore. Told everyone he fell off the boat. Said the sea took him. They believed me."

Teagan looked back at the water, his voice ragged.

"After that, I never touched my power again. I locked it away. Because water had caused me more pain than joy. And I couldn't stand the feel of it. What if I let it out and it never stopped? What if it turned me into *him*?"

The tide crashed below them, relentless and unbothered, as both men stood silent.

"You're not your father, Teagan," Caelan finally said.

Teagan gave a hollow laugh, bitter as sea-brine. "You didn't see me that day. I didn't cry. I didn't scream. I didn't feel anything. Just... stillness. Like the ocean had carved me out and filled me with something cold and quiet."

He pressed his fingers into his temples, as if trying to scrub the memory from inside his skull. "I was ten, Caelan. Ten, and already hollow. And when I stepped onto the shore, I swore I'd never let the water touch me that way again. Not like that. Not through *me*."

Caelan's voice softened. "And you've kept that vow."

Teagan turned, frustration flickering in his eyes. "And what good has it done? I almost let Niev *die* because I was too afraid to touch what I am. She trusted me. And I stood there, paralyzed, because I was haunted by a man who's been dead for over fifteen years."

Caelan took a breath. "But when it counted—you saved her. And you didn't lose control."

"She'll hate me if she finds out," Teagan whispered. "Not because I have this power. But because I didn't trust her enough to tell her who I really am."

"She won't hate you," Caelan said. "But she might hurt. And you'll have to face that. You'll have to let her. But that's part of love, Teagan. You don't get to protect people only on *your* terms. God knows Niev is learning that lesson as well."

Teagan's expression cracked at the edges. For a second, he looked impossibly young. Just a boy who had never been taught to be gentle with himself.

"I'm scared, Caelan."

"We all are, most of the time," Caelan stepped closer, voice steady. "But you're not alone. And the next time you feel that power rising—you don't have to cage it. You just have to *choose* to do good with it."

They stood in silence, the wind softer now, the tide murmuring below them like a lullaby.

Teagan turned back toward the horizon. "I'll tell her," he said after a while. "Not tonight. But soon."

Caelan nodded. "Good."

"I loved him," Teagan said quietly. "Even when he was hurting me. Isn't that sick?"

"No. That's human," Caelan placed a hand on his shoulder. "But your father was a monster for what he did to you. And he deserved the death he got."

Teagan didn't reply. But he didn't shake the hand off either.

They stood there until the last light bled out of the sky. Two figures on the edge of the world, trying to make peace with the tides inside them.

43.
Caelan

Caelan leaned against the port rail of the *Sersha Mara*, one hand gripping the wood, the other hanging limp at his side, fingers still trembling with spent energy. The sky had cleared just enough to reveal a pale strip of dawn, like a wound slowly scabbing over. The salt-streaked air scraped across his skin, and though the sea was calm now, a storm of another kind still churned behind his ribs.

The *Sersha* groaned as it shifted with the tide. Her hull—patched hastily with both wood and will—creaked with every swell. They shouldn't have been able to make her seaworthy so soon. A crew that size, a wreck that devastating—it should've taken days.

But Caelan had bent the rules again.

His materia powers were never meant to be used at this scale for this long. Reshaping planks. Sealing fractures. Reforging bolts and locks with trembling hands and tunnel-vision focus. He hadn't stopped, hadn't rested, hadn't even *breathed* properly until Laughlan declared them seaworthy again.

And now he could feel the cost of it like a lead weight behind his eyes.

His reserves were drained.

If something waited for them in Zarenth—if they were walking into the kind of trap his worst instincts whispered about—he wouldn't be at full strength. He hated the thought. Hated the vulnerability of it.

But more than that, he hated the look that had been on Niev's face as she broke out of the water.

He turned slightly, eyes scanning the deck until he spotted her standing at the bow, half-shadowed beneath the curve of the sail. The wind pulled at her coat, dark hair lifting like smoke, her eyes locked on the horizon. She hadn't spoken much since the island. Since the kraken. Since *whatever happened* beneath the waves had dragged her halfway to death.

She'd emerged from the water alive, but haunted. She was always quiet when she was hurting. Always sharp when she wanted people to back off.

And right now, Caelan wanted nothing more than to pull her in, wrap himself around her, and *keep* her from whatever the hell was eating at her spine.

But she wouldn't let him.

Not yet.

He dragged a hand through his hair and let out a slow breath, forcing his muscles to unclench. Rest. He needed to rest. There would be no backup in Zarenth. No rescue party. No allies on the inside. Just a mission carved in bone and desperation, and the woman who would walk into the darkness for a brother she hadn't seen in ten years.

And he'd go with her. Even if it killed him.

But first... he needed to get stronger.

So he turned from the rail, walked slowly across the deck, and settled into the shaded corner beside the helm. Not far from Niev—never far—but not close enough to spook her walls back up.

She didn't turn to look at him, but he knew she felt him there. She always did.

And for now, that was enough.

❋ ❋ ❋

Night fell on the crew of the *Sersha Mara*, as they sailed the newly repaired ship, stars so close they looked painted on.

Caelan sat at the bow, elbows braced on his knees, the ocean still as glass around them. A windless quiet pressed against the sails, interrupted only by the occasional groan of the ship's hull and the hushed rush of water parting beneath them.

He heard the Tigress before he saw her. Her footfalls were always light, but his body had become too attuned to hers. She sank down beside him without a word, blanket around her shoulders, legs folding beneath her, gaze tipped upward to the sky.

For a few moments, they sat in silence.

And then he said, quietly, "Don't shut me out, Niev."

She didn't look at him right away. Just tilted her head back farther, eyes closed, breathing in the salt and night like she needed it to keep from unraveling. "I'm not."

He waited patiently until eventually, she opened her eyes again. "I'm just not ready to talk about it. Not yet."

Caelan nodded, swallowing the ache of disappointment. Not because she owed him anything—but because he didn't know how to help if he didn't understand. Still, he leaned his shoulder lightly into hers.

"When I woke up on that beach without you," he said quietly, "I thought I was going to lose my mind."

She turned to look at him then, brows pinched.

He stared out at the sea. "I called for you. Until my voice broke. I searched that shoreline like a madman. Teagan and Ayda had to hold me back from jumping back in. I couldn't... I couldn't breathe knowing you were out there and I wasn't with you."

Niev's throat bobbed. She reached for his hand, fingers threading through his.

"I should've come to you after," he said. "But I threw myself into fixing the damn ship instead. Like a coward. Like if I worked hard enough, I could distract myself from how terrified I was of losing you."

She squeezed his hand. "You're not a coward, Caelan. And I don't blame you. I get it, you know? I'm scared too."

He looked at her then. Her eyes full of nothing but fondness.

"I love you," he whispered.

Her breath caught. Her eyes glistened, but she smiled, and there was something vulnerable and beautiful in it.

He shifted slightly. "Can I ask you something?"

"Anything."

"If things were different—if we weren't who we are, if none of this had happened. If your family lived. If mine did. If we met in some world that was kinder... what would you want your life to look like?"

She blinked. Looked at him with startled, earnest eyes. And then she laughed, softly. "You're going to laugh."

"I swear I won't," he said, now even more curious to find out.

She looked away, the night breeze playing with the ends of her hair. "I used to dream of owning this little cottage in Thornmere. Near the riverbend. Have my own garden and a fence. I'd read all day. Raise too many children. I'd bask in their laughter and keep their drawings on the wall. I think... I mostly just wanted to get out of Arenthia."

Caelan stared at her.

"You?" he breathed, eyes wide with mock disbelief. "The Tigress of Solhaven wanted to be a barefoot kitchen wench with jam-stained toddlers clinging to her legs?"

"Hey! You're the one who asked!"

She gave him a withering look, but there was no real heat behind it.

"Besides" she muttered. "I didn't say it made sense. I just... always dreamed of a life that was safe. You forget I was raised in a castle among royalty," she said mockingly. "I wasn't exactly born a ruthless killer."

He chuckled, low and warm. "You baking scones while a herd of children tears through the garden might be the best thing I've ever pictured."

She snorted, nudging his shoulder with hers, but her lips curved upward. "You're impossible."

"And you're terrifying. But apparently full of domestic fantasies." He leaned over, taking her hand into his and kissed her knuckles, his voice quieter now. "You surprise me every damn day."

She didn't answer right away. Just exhaled, slow and soft, before resting her head on his shoulder.

And for a moment, neither of them said anything. Just sat there beneath the stars—two warriors chasing a dream neither believed they deserved.

Then, quietly, Caelan tilted his head down toward her.

"But... just to be sure," he murmured, mischief threading through his voice, "how many children are we talking about here?"

She groaned and buried her face in his shoulder.

"*Caelan.*"

"I mean, I need to prepare—mentally. Emotionally. Strategically. Are we looking at a small unit or a full battalion?"

She slapped his chest without lifting her head. "You'll be lucky if I give you one."

He grinned. "One's a start. Although if it has your scowl and my charm, the world may not survive any more."

"You are *so* full of yourself."

Caelan leaned in, his lips brushing her ear as he said—voice low and shameless—"I think in this case... *you* actually need to be full of *me*."

Niev lifted her head, eyes wide, jaw dropped low enough to wipe the floor. "*Oh my God!*"

He just arched a brow, smug as sin. "What?"

Her mouth opened. Closed. Her face flushed all the way to her ears as she buried it in her hands. "I cannot believe you just said that," she hissed.

"You walked right into it."

"I walked into nothing," she hissed. "That was a *trap*."

He tilted his head, trying not to laugh. "A well-*laid* one."

She shot him a look that could've melted steel. "Stop. Talking."

But her voice cracked around a laugh, and when she peeked at him between her fingers, her eyes were still wide, still flustered, still way too into him for her own good.

"You're the worst," she said.

Caelan draped an arm around her shoulders like he'd done it a thousand times before. "And yet, here you are. Curled up against me, thoroughly scandalized, and only thinking about one... single... thing."

She elbowed him hard.

He grunted—but his grin didn't budge. If anything, it widened.

"You can act as scandalized and bashful as you want," he murmured, his voice dropping as he turned his head, nose brushing her temple. "But we both know how this ends."

Her laugh faded, and she turned just enough to look up at him, brows drawing together. "What do you mean?"

Caelan didn't hesitate.

"I'm going to marry you, Niev Helvast."

He saw the second his words registered, her breath hitched and her eyes searched his face like he might be joking—but his gaze didn't waver. There was no teasing in it now. Only quiet, devastating certainty.

"Not tomorrow. Not next week. But one day," he said, the words curling around her like armor and flame. "You're going to be my wife."

She stared at him, struck silent. Caelan could almost hear her heartbeat hammering in her chest as he leaned closer, lips brushing the edge of her cheek.

"And until then," he whispered, "I'll just keep making it impossible for you to imagine choosing anyone else."

Niev blinked again—caught entirely off guard. A slow, stunned smile crept onto her face. She opened her mouth—

Probably to tell him he'd *completely lost his mind*.

But before she could say a word, a voice called from the deck.

"Oi, lovers! Dinner's getting cold!"

Niev's blush erupted down her neck. She stood so fast the blanket slipped off her shoulder, her eyes avoiding his entirely.

"I'm starving," she announced, already walking toward the main deck.

Caelan sat there a beat longer, still half-dazed, still smiling like a man who'd been hit with a revelation. Then he got up and followed her into the firelight—his heart absolutely wrecked in the best way.

The warmth of the crew's fire spilled golden across the deck, flickering against the worn planks and casting lazy shadows against the sailcloth. Plates clinked. Laughter rolled low and steady like the tide. The Sersha Mara was a patchwork of scars, but tonight, she floated like a sanctuary on still waters.

Caelan followed Niev to the circle, his grin not quite wiped clean, though he tried to school it. She was already seated beside Ayda, who raised an eyebrow at her flushed cheeks but, blessedly, said nothing. Teagan, however, was less merciful.

"Took you long enough," he said with a shit-eating grin, holding out a tin plate. "We were beginning to think you two had started dessert early."

Niev accepted the plate with the poise of someone barely holding herself together. "Careful, Blackwood," she said sweetly. "You've got one good kneecap left. I could change that."

Teagan only chuckled and scooted back exaggeratedly, raising his hands in surrender.

Caelan took a seat beside her, bumping her knee as he crouched. She didn't look at him—still not recovered, clearly—but when her hand slipped over his, her thumb tracing the ridge of one of his knuckles, his chest went tight.

He would have walked into Zarenth blindfolded and unarmed for that touch alone.

"Alright, alright," Laughlan said, lifting a flask. "Before we all lose our appetites from watching Galbraith moon over my lady, a toast."

Caelan, who usually let the captain's jabs slide right off him, looked up slowly with a razor-sharp grin. "Funny. I was just about to toast to the captain's last remaining brain cell. God knows it's worked overtime ever since he imagined he had a shot with her."

The entire circle *howled*.

Laughlan threw his head back and laughed so hard he choked on his own drink, while Teagan damn near fell off the bench.

"Oh, saints," Myria cackled, wiping her eyes.

Niev was biting the inside of her cheek so hard to keep from laughing that her eyes were watering.

Ayda just shook her head, lips twitching. "It's a miracle this ship hasn't sunk under the weight of your egos."

Laughlan, still laughing, raised his flask higher. "To bad decisions, unexpected miracles, and the beautiful bastard who stole the heart of a Tigress."

Caelan bumped his cup against Laughlan's with a smirk. "To better taste."

Niev, finally unable to hold it in, snorted into her drink.

Ayda rolled her eyes, but raised her tin cup. "To surviving krakens, storms, and each other."

Caelan saw Niev look around the circle—at Laughlan, still trying to act like he didn't care half as much as he did; at Teagan, whose smirk masked how tightly he gripped his blade these days; at Ayda, who never missed a detail; at Myria, who might've been the closest thing she had to a sister, and finally at him.

"To family," she said quietly, lifting his own cup.

They all raised their cups, and the clinking of tin echoed across the quiet sea.

The meal was simple—salt pork, root mash, flatbread warmed over the fire—but it tasted like decadent after all the shit they'd just gone through.

As the night stretched and the fire burned low, laughter mellowed into quiet conversation. The stars above spun on, unbothered by the weight of what lay ahead.

And eventually, Niev leaned into Caelan, her lips a breath away from his ear.

"You should go rest."

He smiled faintly. "I'll stay up a little longer."

She rose from the bench, brushing her hands on her trousers as the firelight danced across her face. She turned to Caelan, eyes dark and unreadable in the glow, and then she held out her hand.

Come with me.

Caelan blinked once. His pulse ticked faster. The others were still laughing around them, trading stories and half-finished jabs but the world narrowed to her hand, her soft but certain gaze, and the promise that lived somewhere in between.

He reached out and took her hand, calloused fingers lacing with hers, and stood.

Around them, the crew noticed. Of course they did.

"Oi! Where do you think you're going?" Teagan crowed.

"'I don't want to catch any funny business on my ship!" Laughlan shouted, raising his flask.

"I think our company's gotten too boring for them, lads," Myria howled drunkenly.

Ayda just rolled her eyes and sipped her drink, though a faint smile tugged at her lips.

Caelan didn't even spare them a glare. His focus was solely on the woman at his side.

Niev squeezed his hand slightly, lips twitching into something between fondness and smug victory.

Together, they walked toward the stern, toward the steps leading below deck—past the laughter, past the clinking mugs, past the knowing looks—until all that remained was the hush of the sails and the distant lull of the sea.

❋ ❋ ❋

The door to their small quarters shut behind them with a soft click, sealing out the sound of laughter and wind.

Inside, it was warm—dimly lit by a single lantern swinging gently with the motion of the sea. The air was tinged with salt, cedar, and the faint, lingering sweetness of the soap Niev had started using again since their stop in Thornmere. The scent hit him low and deep, tightening something in his chest.

She still hadn't let go of his hand.

Caelan stood there a moment, watching as she slipped off her boots and undid the buckle of her belt. Her movements were slow—not sensual, not deliberate—just tired. Bone-deep tired. But he also saw the way her shoulders had loosened since they walked in. The faint weight that left her brow, the silence that wasn't heavy between them.

It was... calm.

He stripped down to his breeches and undershirt, tossing his coat over the trunk in the corner. She was already under the blanket when he turned again, wearing nothing but her loose shirt and undergarments. The Tigress curled on her side, watching him with a soft kind of alertness. Her hair tumbled across the pillow, half-twisted from sea spray and wind, her eyes darker than usual in the flickering light.

"Are you going to stand there all night?" she asked.

Her voice was a rasp of amusement, faint and warm. It undid him.

Caelan slid into the bed beside her, careful not to crowd her, but the second he was close enough, she reached for him—hands fisting in the front of his shirt, dragging him until his body pressed flush to hers. Their mouths met with aching hunger, slow at first, but deepening with every breath. Her fingers slid into his hair. His hands skimmed the curve of her waist, the dip of her spine, the silk of her skin beneath the blanket.

She made a soft sound against his lips—something between a sigh and a moan—and he drank it in like salvation.

"*Stars save me,*" he murmured against her mouth, voice rough.

Caelan kissed her like she was already his.

And maybe she was.

When he pulled back, barely an inch, his voice was rough against her lips. "You have no idea what you do to me."

She exhaled, a breath that trembled just a little. "Then tell me."

His fingers skimmed along her hip, possessive yet gentle, like he was reminding himself she was real.

"You've crawled under my skin and made yourself home, Tigress," he whispered.

Her lashes fluttered. He could feel the heat of her blush even in the dark.

"You're mine," he murmured, kissing her again—softer this time, reverent. "Every stubborn, reckless, breathtaking inch of you is mine."

"You're—" Her voice broke on the word as he kissed the hollow of her neck. She tried again. "You're not playing fair."

"No," he said, curling his fingers into her hair and tugging her mouth back to his. "I'm not."

Niev's breath hitched, her fingers tightening in his shirt. "You keep doing that, and we won't get any sleep tonight."

He kissed the corner of her mouth, then lower, to the edge of her jaw. "Sleep's overrated."

Her lips curved into a smile, teasing but breathless. Her fingers skimmed down his chest, trailing slowly under the soft linen of his shirt, and Caelan hissed between his teeth.

He pressed her back harder into the pillows, their breaths tangling. "Tell me to stop."

She didn't.

Instead, she pulled him closer, her bare legs wrapping around him.

His breath caught. Fire surged through every vein like a tidal wave—demanding, ravenous.

And still... he held himself with all the self control he could muster.

Because he'd promised her.

Caelan braced himself with one hand beside her head, the other curling tightly at her hip, like he could anchor himself there—on the edge of surrender.

"Niev—" His voice cracked, raw and strangled. "If we don't stop now..."

She opened her eyes—dark, dazed, utterly wrecked by him—and something in his chest shattered.

"I won't be able to," he whispered.

She blinked, slow and heavy, but didn't pull away. "Then don't."

His whole body screamed to listen. To take her. To give them both what they wanted.

But he didn't move.

Instead, he dropped his forehead to hers and squeezed his eyes shut, fighting to breathe, to remember who she was. What she'd told him.

Her body was temptation incarnate.

But her soul?

Her soul was sacred.

"I made you a promise," he rasped, trembling. "I'm not breaking it. Not even for this. Not even for you."

Niev stared up at him, lips parted, throat working as she tried to speak. She didn't.

Caelan kissed her once—deep and slow—like it broke him to stop. Like she was already his in every way that mattered but one.

Niev shifted as she slid her arms around his shoulders and held him close—pulling his arm around her waist and pressing her back into his chest. He went easily, wrapping himself around her, letting the steady rhythm of her breathing begin to slow his own.

For a while, they said nothing.

Then—

"I meant it, you know," he murmured, lips brushing her hair. "Back on the deck."

She didn't answer right away. Just twined her fingers with his where his hand rested against her stomach.

"I know," she whispered.

Caelan pressed a kiss behind her ear, gentle and lingering. "You surprise me every day. You love like a weapon—but when you dream, you dream like a princess."

She let out a breath, more shiver than laugh. "Don't make fun."

"I'm not," he said, pulling her closer. "I think it's the most dangerous thing about you."

She was quiet again.

"Caelan?"

"Hmm?"

"I love you."

He buried his nose in her hair and held her tighter. "I love you too, darling."

And in the quiet that followed, with her heartbeat steady under his palm and the creak of the ship beneath them, Caelan Galbraith closed his eyes and prayed that dawn would wait.

That time might stop here—for just a little longer.

Before they reached the dark coast of Zarenth.

Before war, or grief, or the universe came to collect.

✳　✳　✳

She fell asleep before he did.

Her breath evened out first—long, steady exhales against his arm. Then her grip on his fingers loosened, her muscles softened, and he felt the weight of her begin to truly settle against him, as if her body had finally accepted—for this moment, at least—that she was safe.

Caelan didn't move. He didn't dare.

He just stared at the low ceiling, tracing the seams in the wood, letting the quiet rise around him.

Sleep should've come easy. He was exhausted—more spent than he'd let on after draining nearly all his powers just to hold the Sersha together. But his mind wouldn't still. Not with the sound of her voice still echoing inside him. Not with the heat of her body pressed so perfectly against his, her thigh tangled between his, the scent of her hair still filling every breath he took.

Not with the memory of how close he'd come to losing her. Again.

He glanced down.

The blanket had slipped low on her shoulder, baring the line of her collarbone, the bruise blooming just beneath it from the wave's impact. There was another mark near her hip—faint, but real. And her ribs... he'd seen the way she winced when she twisted earlier. The kraken had nearly gutted them all. But Niev had held it off like a goddamned force of nature.

And then there were the shadows.

He still didn't know what it was she'd summoned on that deck. That terrifying, impossible power. Those clawing streaks of black magic that had come out of her like something ancient.

His chest ached. With pride. With fear. With the weight of not knowing what would come next.

He shifted slightly, brushing a hand up her arm to tuck the blanket over her again. Her skin was warm. Too warm. He would've worried about fever if he didn't know better. But no—this was something else. The kind of heat that came from power left untapped. From energy pooling in the blood, hungry for release.

She stirred faintly at the touch, murmuring something in her sleep.

His heart clenched.

He brought his lips to her temple and whispered, "I've got you."

She didn't wake. But her body shifted again, nestling closer, as if even in her dreams she was searching for him.

Caelan stayed like that—watching her, listening to the sea lap softly against the hull, feeling every breath she took—until finally, the tide of sleep claimed him too.

❋ ❋ ❋

Hours later, he woke to her voice.

"Caelan."

He blinked against the darkness, heart kicking. Her hand was on his chest, fingers curled lightly.

"I'm here," he whispered, voice gravel-thick.

She looked up at him through strands of mussed hair, eyes still glazed with sleep. "Bad dream," she said simply.

He didn't ask. Didn't need to.

"Come here," he murmured, pulling her up against him. Her limbs folded around him easily, like she'd been made for it. Her cheek pressed to his shoulder, her breathing shaky.

He held her until it smoothed again.

Until she stopped trembling.

Until she slept once more—her hand still clinging to his shirt like an anchor.

And Caelan?

Caelan stared into the dark, one hand stroking her back, and promised himself something he knew might get him killed:

If they made it out of Zarenth alive,

He would build her that cottage in Thornmere.

Fence and garden and children and all.

Even if he had to tear the world down to do it.

44.
Niev

The boat rocked gently beneath her as the first sliver of light bled over the horizon.

Morrow Bay wasn't much more than a memory carved into the southern edge of Thaelon—an abandoned cove strangled by stone, sandy moss, and time. It had once been a harbor, she could tell by the half-rotted pylons jutting from the surf like broken teeth, and the remnants of a crumbled dock clinging to the jagged shoreline.

They had chosen this place precisely for its obscurity. A forgotten cove, far from the main trade routes and miles beneath the watchful eyes of Zarenth's garrisons. It was the only place they could land unnoticed, and even that was a risk.

The *Sersha* groaned as it dropped anchor in the shallow inlet, the hull brushing rock and sand. The crew moved in practiced silence—more solemn now, every man and woman suddenly aware of where they were. Of what lay ahead.

Zarenth was no longer a story on the horizon. It was here. It was real. And the air had changed.

Niev stepped onto the dock first, her boots landing with a soft crunch of sea-slick grit and broken shell.

Niev stood at the edge of the Sersha's deck, her coat fluttering in the wind, eyes fixed on the pale, cracked hills that stretched inland like bones buried in sand. The desert loomed just beyond, sun-scorched and endless, its dunes already beginning to shimmer with heat. There were no lush forests here. No cool shade. Just rock, grit, and the slow-baking breath of a land that had long forgotten mercy.

Behind her, the others disembarked slowly—quiet, watchful. Even Teagan didn't crack a joke. Ayda's eyes were hard and sharp, her weapons already strapped tight. Myria pulled her scarf higher. Laughlan barked a few soft orders to what was left of his crew and tied the ship down tight.

And Caelan...

He said nothing.

But his eyes hadn't left her once.

Niev breathed in slowly, the memory of his body pressed against her still vivid in her mind. She let the scent of sand, salt, and stone fill her lungs. The stoneridges beyond the cove loomed like giant beasts, and beyond them... the dunes that would carry them to the gates of hell.

The trek ahead would not be easy. There were no roads this way— only forgotten hunting trails and smuggler's cuts winding north through shadow-thick palm trees and ridge passes. But it would keep them unseen. Off the charts. Exactly as they needed.

She turned to the others as they gathered their gear and slung weapons over their backs. The Sersha wouldn't come with them. It would wait in the bay, hidden, until their return.

If they returned.

Niev's fingers tightened around the strap of her pack. "Everyone ready?"

A chorus of tense nods answered her.

Myria slid a small throwing knife into her belt. "No time like the present."

Ayda adjusted the hilt on her shoulder. "This path is cursed. I can feel it."

Laughlan spat into the dirt. "Good. Maybe it'll curse the bastards that built Zarenth too."

Teagan checked the sun through the thinning fog. "We'll reach the tower before nightfall. If we move fast."

Caelan came up beside her, silent as always, and brushed his fingers once—lightly—against hers. She didn't reach for him. But she didn't move away, either.

She looked forward.

To the place where her brother was still waiting.

The land around them was thick with old magic—she could feel it—the blood and grief that lingered in the earth like a bruise.

But she was not the girl who'd once cowered in a brothel's cell.

Niev turned toward the ramp. Her boots hit the sand with barely a sound, as the sun began to rise fully,

She was the Tigress of Solhaven.

And she had come home to raise hell.

❄ ❄ ❄

After what felt like hours of trekking, Niev had to finally admit that the desert did *not* welcome them.

From jagged cliffs and hollowed canyons, from the pale sun that climbed higher and harsher with every hour, to the heat-slicked air that shimmered like a mirage above the cracked earth. Thaelon's landscape was not golden like the coastlines of Breyvia. It was rust. Burnt red and ash-brown.

Niev adjusted the scarf around her mouth, already coated in dust, sweat clinging to the back of her neck. The heat was a weight—pressing on her shoulders, sinking into her bones. The terrain stretched out endlessly, broken only by brittle brush, thorned shrubs, and the occasional skeletal ruin of old waystations long abandoned.

Behind her, the others walked in silence.

Ayda kept to the rear, her hood pulled low to shield from the sun. Myria walked with effortless grace despite the heat, her pace steady and precise. Teagan was less graceful, grumbling under his breath every few minutes as his boots caught on loose gravel or dry roots.

Caelan stayed close beside her, always just a step or two behind. His shirt was soaked through, his daggers wrapped to avoid sun-glare, but his eyes remained sharp and focused.

They moved at a careful pace. Fast enough to keep momentum, slow enough to conserve strength.

Hours went by with no shade or reprieve from the excruciating heat.

They passed what might've once been a caravan post—crumbled stone walls and a rusted sign post marking a crossroads now long forgotten. Niev paused, placing a hand against the wall, feeling its heat pulse against her palm. She could almost hear voices from long ago—travelers, merchants, smugglers—now swallowed by the sand.

"Water break," Caelan called quietly, voice rasping.

They all paused in the shadow of the half-collapsed arch. Packs were lowered. Scarves loosened. Niev dropped to one knee, letting the warmth bleed from her limbs into the stone beneath her.

"Remind me," Teagan croaked from where he slumped beside a rock, "why we didn't just blast our way into Zarenth with a warship and a cannon?"

"Because we'd all be dead by now," Myria said, pouring a thin stream of water over her pulse point. "Also, you'd still complain."

"I'm not complaining. I'm critically analyzing our choices while sweating out what's left of my soul."

Ayda chuckled softly.

Niev took a sip from her canteen, then handed it to Caelan without a word. He took it, their fingers brushing. She didn't miss the way his gaze lingered on her face—always searching for signs of strain. He didn't ask if she was okay. He already knew the answer.

But when the others had turned away, his hand slipped to the small of her back, grounding her.

"We'll get there soon enough," he murmured, just for her.

She nodded once. Then pushed herself back to her feet.

The journey continued—over rock bluffs and narrow ravines, skirting old cliff paths that crumbled if you so much as looked at them wrong. Once, they spotted vultures circling in the far distance—slow, deliberate spirals.

❋ ❋ ❋

By midday, the heat had become unbearable.

Her boots sank into dry, fractured clay with every step, and her lungs felt like they were breathing sand. The ridge ahead shimmered under the relentless sun, and the path snaked around it in a way that set her teeth on edge.

So Niev gave in to the call under her skin—the one that hummed every time the wind shifted.

Without a word, she stopped, closed her eyes, and let the change take her.

Bones shifted. Skin dissolved into feathers. And the world dropped away beneath her feet.

A moment later, a hawk soared where a woman had stood.

She cut through the sky like a blade, letting the wind cradle her wings. The air was thinner up here, but cooler. Cleaner. Below, her companions shrank to silhouettes trailing through the red dust. Even from the sky, Caelan's stride was unmistakable—shoulders tense, gaze forward.

She flew higher, wheeling over the ridge, scouting the path ahead. The land stretched outward like a wound—scarred and sunbaked, with little sign of life. But she spotted the ruins of a watchtower in the distance, its crumbled base hidden behind a bluff of jagged stone.

A good place to rest. Or get ambushed.

She banked and circled once more, then dove.

The wind shrieked past her feathers as she arrowed back toward the earth. Her wings folded just before she reached the ridge, and she landed in a silent burst of dust—shifting back mid-step.

"Clear," she announced as the others reached her, panting. "But there's an old tower ahead. Looks deserted, but... we should go wide."

Teagan narrowed his eyes. "That's the third time you've done that today."

"What?"

"Shifted into a hawk and left the rest of us to fry like salted meat."

"You want me to scout ahead or not?"

He waved a hand. "Oh, I'm not complaining. Just... making sure we're all aware that the rest of us are slowly being cooked alive while her feathered majesty here gets all the breeze."

Niev rolled her eyes and shifted again—this time into a small, sleek fox. The wind ruffled her rust-colored fur as she darted past him, kicking a small puff of dust into his face.

Teagan coughed. "Rude."

"Now she's just mocking you," Ayda said dryly, brushing sand off her scarf.

"I could squash her tiny fox body with my boot!" Teagan declared, glaring after her as she darted up a ridge.

"She'd bite your ankle and vanish before your foot even hit the earth," Myria chimed, deadpan.

"She wouldn't dare," Teagan huffed.

No sooner had the words left his mouth than the little fox whipped around in a blur of russet fur. She darted straight at him, fast as lightning, and sank her tiny teeth into the back of his calf—not hard enough to hurt, but enough to make her point.

"OW—bloody hell!" Teagan yelped, spinning as Niev danced just out of reach, tail flicking with smug satisfaction.

The others burst out laughing.

"I think she just dared," Ayda said, biting back a grin.

Teagan was already chasing after the fox, boots kicking up sand as he ran. "I'm gonna turn you into a bloody throw rug, you little menace!"

Niev squeaked and zipped ahead, easily keeping out of reach, clearly thrilled with herself.

Caelan chuckled low in his throat, arms crossed as he watched the scene unfold. "You'd think he'd know better than to test her by now."

Ayda snorted. "He never learns. You should've seen him last week when he tried to steal her sweetbread."

"I'd be careful if I were you," Myria added, grinning at Caelan. "You might be next."

Caelan's smile turned wicked as he looked back at the seamstress. "The Tigress is welcome to leave teeth marks on me whenever she wishes."

That earned a mock scandalized gasp from Ayda and a sharp laugh from Myria.

"She's going to hear that, you know," Myria warned, nodding toward the fox still perched smugly on the ridge.

"Good," Caelan said, eyes narrowing affectionately. "Maybe it'll inspire her."

And sure enough, the fox's ears twitched. Niev's sharp little eyes flicked to the three of them as she circled back, and without a single sound, she stood, turned in an elegant spin, and shifted back before they noticed.

She stepped out behind them, arms crossed, voice dry as dust. "You planning on showing me a chart of all the places you want me to bite next, or should I just improvise?"

The conversation died instantly.

Caelan froze mid-smirk, eyes locking on her like a man caught with his hand halfway down the biscuit jar. Myria made a choked noise somewhere between a snort and a wheeze, and Ayda barked a laugh so loud it drew Teagan's attention back.

Caelan, for once, looked like he might be rethinking his life choices.

Niev strolled past them casually, the picture of feline grace, and flicked a hand toward him. "Though if you wanted me to mark you like territory, you could've just asked."

Teagan, panting as he stumbled back into the group after his failed fox-chase, wheezed out, "What in the hells did I just walk into?"

"Nothing you're invited to," Niev said sweetly, and tossed a smirk over her shoulder at Caelan—who was now rubbing the back of his neck, half-laughing, half-mortified, but his gaze was full of nothing but heat as it trailed her.

Myria leaned toward Ayda and muttered, "We're going to need more wine if those two keep talking like this."

Teagan sighed, long and dramatic. "I miss when she used to just stab people."

"Well, lucky for you," Niev said, grinning as she passed them. "I can multitask."

❋ ❋ ❋

The sun was a molten coin, sinking slow and heavy into the desert's throat by the time they crested the last ridge.

The watchtower rose from the sand like the jagged vertebra of a long-dead beast — crumbling, skeletal, and stubbornly defiant against the decay of centuries. Half-swallowed by dunes, its stones were worn smooth by wind and sun, its top broken like a snapped neck. But still it stood, silent and waiting, the last sentinel on the road to hell.

They stopped at its base in silence.

They wouldn't march into Zarenth weary and frayed at the edges, muscles aching, vision dulled. Even fools didn't court death on an empty stomach and half a night's sleep.

And they weren't fools.

So they would rest.

And gather.

And at dawn... They'd infiltrate the camps.

Niev climbed the fractured spiral stair alone, each footfall echoing softly against stone, her fingers grazing the pitted wall as if the ruin might whisper back its secrets. At the top, the desert opened wide around her — endless, blistering gold now cooling into amber and rust beneath the dying light. The wind carried the scent of dust and salt and something older, something like memory.

Zarenth lay ahead, tucked between scorched ridges and cracked hills, its silhouette a bruise on the horizon. The sun caught on the spires of its outer wall, and for one terrible second, it looked like the city was on fire.

Caelan stepped up beside her, silent as a shadow, his gaze fixed on that same distant outline.

He didn't say a word. But his silence spoke louder than any scream.

The tension rolled off him in waves — quiet, coiled, barely leashed. She watched him from the corner of her eye, watched how his jaw ticked, how his knuckles had gone white where his hands gripped the stone ledge. He looked like a man standing on the edge of a grave he'd crawled out of — and now had to crawl back into.

Her throat tightened.

And yet, she didn't reach for him. Didn't speak. Instinct told her not to.

Instead, she simply stood beside him, let her shoulder brush his, and stared down the beast with him.

The wind curled around them, dry and restless. Far below, the others were setting camp — Myria laying out bedrolls, Teagan muttering as he struggled to light a fire with flint and grit, Ayda unpacking what little food they had left.

But here, on the tower, the world narrowed to the man beside her.

She could feel it — the thunder in his chest, the pull of every muscle trying to stay calm, the crack in his breath every time it hitched.

But she could do nothing other than pray she hadn't made an enormous mistake letting him step back into this godforsaken land.

As night fell, they settled beneath the hollow ribs of the tower, curled against cold stone and tattered bedrolls, the stars wheeling silently overhead.

Teagan took the first watch, climbing the worn stairs with his crossbow slung over his back and a flask tucked into his belt. He winked at her as he passed, and she gave him a tired smirk in return.

Niev lay beside Caelan, her body still humming from the ghost of his tension on the ledge earlier. The others drifted off one by one. Even Myria, who usually took an hour to fidget and mutter about comfort, fell quickly into sleep. Ayda's breathing had evened out ages ago. The fire dimmed to embers.

Niev stared at the cracked stone above her and tried to keep her mind still. Tried not to think about the city waiting for them. But eventually, exhaustion won and darkness claimed her.

She was floating again — no, not floating. Suspended. Held in a current she could not control. Shadows curled around her limbs, warm and heavy, like silk soaked in ink.

The sirens' voices coiled through the dark.

"The blood remembers, even if the world does not..."

"Daughter of Shadow... you are the last of your name."

"The silver-crowned liar waits in the dark, and she fears what you will become.""

The words echoed through her, like wind down the spine, and teeth on skin. Niev opened her mouth to scream.

And woke with a violent gasp.

Her heart was pounding. Her body was slick with sweat despite the night chill. She sat bolt upright, the nightmare still clawing at her lungs. It took a few seconds before she realized she was alone on the bedroll.

Her blood turned to ice.

"Caelan?"

No answer.

She got to her feet in an instant, boots half-laced, cloak forgotten. Her eyes scanned the shadows, but all she saw were the shapes of the others, still asleep. A thread of panic wound itself through her chest.

She crossed to the base of the tower and looked up, barely spotting the flicker of Teagan's silhouette near the top.

"Teag," she hissed.

He turned his head over his shoulder. "You good?"

"Is Caelan up there?"

He blinked. Frowned. "No. I thought he was with you."

Her stomach dropped.

"I haven't seen him come past," he added, quieter now. "He's not in the camp?"

She shook her head. "No."

They both knew Caelan — knew what Zarenth meant to him.

Panic edged into her bones.

"Check the ridge," Teagan said quickly, his voice sharpening. "I'll keep watch from above."

She turned without a word and descended quickly, boots silent against the sand-smoothed stone. Her heart pounded, faster than she could reason with, and her breath started to come too sharp. Not him. Not now.

She searched the camp's perimeter first. Then beyond it. The night was thick with wind and silence.

Eventually, a flicker of movement caught her eye, low and hunched, barely visible behind the collapsed arch.

There.

She found him crouched at the base of the tower, wedged between two fractured beams of stone, hidden like a wounded animal. His knees were pulled to his chest, arms clamped over his head, fingers tangled tight in his hair. His breathing was erratic—shallow, fast, desperate—and his whole body trembled like it might tear itself apart from the inside.

"Caelan," she breathed, dropping to her knees before him.

He flinched violently, eyes flying open—but he didn't see her.

Not at first.

There was terror in his gaze. Real, bone-deep terror. A man not on a desert floor, but in the belly of some buried cell. Somewhere far, far away.

"I can't—" he gasped. "I can't—breathe—"

His voice was hoarse, broken, barely human. He clawed at his chest as if trying to rip the air into his lungs.

Niev reached for his hands, voice shaking. "Hey, hey—look at me. Caelan. It's me. It's Niev. You're safe."

He tried to look at her. But his pupils were blown wide, his shoulders locked, and panic was still crashing over him like waves that wouldn't stop.

She took his hand and pressed it against her heart.

"I need you to match me, alright? Just breathe with me—just one breath. Slowly, in...and out."

He opened his mouth. Nothing came out. His body curled tighter.

A muffled sob tore from his throat.

Niev's chest cracked wide open.

She wrapped both arms around him from behind, tucking her chin over his shoulder, holding him like she could shield him from everything that ever hurt.

"Please," she whispered, her own voice starting to break. "Come back to me."

He trembled harder. One breath. Two. He tried again. Failed. Tried again.

Niev didn't let go.

She rocked him, quietly and steadily, like the tide. Whispered the first words that came to her mind — nonsense, old lullabies, old prayers, anything to drown out the ghosts.

"You're alright. I've got you," she said, trying hard to keep her own panic at bay. "I've got you, my love."

A small shuffle drew her attention — Teagan, at the top of the ridge, halfway through climbing down.

Niev met his eyes.

And without a sound, she raised her hand and shook her head.

Not now. Not like this.

Teagan stopped. And she saw the second his expression cracked at seeing his friend like this. But he gave her one small nod. Then disappeared back up into the dark.

She turned back to Caelan. His fists had loosened slightly, and his breathing — ragged though it still was — had begun to even out.

"You're safe," she whispered again, her own throat burning now. "You got out. You're safe, my love."

His shoulders shook once more, a dry, heaving sob escaping from between clenched teeth. He pressed his forehead into her chest, clutching at her tunic like he was afraid she'd disappear.

"I'm sorry," he rasped.

She held him tighter. "Don't you dare be." she said, her tone final.

Her Caelan — her steady, selfless, brilliant man — reduced to wreckage by the scars Zarenth had carved into him.

She kissed his temple and closed her eyes, her heart aching with a pain too vast to name.

And somewhere deep inside her, a darker thing stirred.

Black, bottomless fury that threatened to consume her.

She would burn that place to the ground.

Not just for Elias or the stolen children.

But for this.

For what it had done to the man she loved.

And before this was over — the desert would remember the Tigress of Solhaven.

45.
Caelan

The sky was still dark when Caelan woke.

For a few blissful seconds, he didn't remember where he was. Just warmth. A soft weight curled into his chest. The steady cadence of another heartbeat pressed to his ribs.

Niev's legs tangled with his beneath the blanket. Her hand still clutched the fabric of his shirt — like she'd stayed up half the night afraid he might run away.

He swallowed hard and slowly, carefully, untangled himself from her.

He didn't deserve this.

Not after last night.

Not after the way he broke.

The stone floor beneath his boots was still cold with desert air as he rose. He didn't let himself look back. His limbs felt heavy, his joints stiff from a night spent curled up in terror.

He packed in silence.

Methodically. Sword, dagger, cloak. Tied his boots with shaking fingers. Checked the satchel twice though he already knew everything inside.

Behind him, he felt her stir. Heard the soft rustle of her moving, the brush of hair over her shoulders. But still — he didn't turn. He couldn't. Not yet.

Shame sat like a stone in his gut.

He had promised himself — *promised her* — he'd be strong. That whatever hell Zarenth dredged up from his past, he'd handle it. Keep it buried. That he'd stand beside her like the man she deserved.

Instead, she'd found him curled at the bottom of the tower, gasping like a sniveling boy locked in the dark.

He tightened the straps of his scabbard.

"Caelan," she said softly.

He didn't answer.

She came closer anyway. Step by step, until her presence wrapped around him like the desert wind — quiet but insistent.

"Caelan," she said again, firmer this time.

And then her hand landed on his wrist. "Look at me."

He hesitated. Then finally — painfully — he turned.

Her eyes met his without flinching. No pity. No judgment. Just that same unflinching, iron-willed gaze he'd fallen in love with.

"I love you," she said, plain and sure.

He blinked, throat thick. *Out of all the things she could've said—*

"I love you," she repeated. "And I am proud of you. Do you hear me?"

Caelan tried to look away, but she stepped closer, lifting her hands to frame his face.

"You are the strongest and bravest man I've ever known, Caelan Galbraith," she said, voice steady. "Not because you've never broken, but because every time you did—you put yourself back together. You survived what would've killed most men. You built a life your parents would be proud of. And last night doesn't make you weak. It makes you human. And I love you all the more for it."

He closed his eyes. Her thumbs brushed the edge of his jaw.

"You don't have to go in there to prove anything to me," she whispered.

"I know," he rasped. His voice was hoarse. "But I *am* going in there anyway. There's no way in hell I'm letting you walk into that shithole alone."

Her eyes searched his. And then, with a single quiet nod, she stepped back.

No argument. No fight.

And *God,* how he loved her for it.

His breath left him like a slow exhale, some of the weight in his chest easing.

"Thank you," he whispered.

She didn't answer. Just brushed her lips to his cheek and moved to pack.

A beat later, a quiet voice interrupted him.

"Hey," Teagan said, stepping up beside him, putting one arm on his shoulder. "You alright?"

Caelan looked at his friend. The man who's secret he kept, who'd seen him fight, seen him bleed, and probably knew without needing to be told exactly what last night had been.

"I will be," Caelan said.

Teagan nodded once, his jaw set, then clapped a hand on his shoulder. "Let's burn the bastards down."

The others were already up and ready—Ayda adjusting her satchel, Myria murmuring something under her breath as she surveyed the trail beyond the dunes.

The sun had yet to rise.

And the towers of Zarenth stood in the distance, like teeth against the sky.

Whatever waited inside, they would face it together.

❋ ❋ ❋

As they continued their trek, the walls of Zarenth rose from the sand like jagged scars—iron and stone twisted together in ways that made Caelan's stomach churn. Even from a distance, he could feel the wrongness of it. The way the air thickened. The silence that pressed in like a weight. He kept his breathing slow, steady, one hand wrapped tight around the grip of his gauntlet.

They moved under the cover of darkness.

The camps sprawled in a half-moon shape along the southern ridge, where forgotten mines and broken supply roads funneled into the larger fortress. These weren't the central barracks—those were deeper in, fortified like the vaults of kings. But this? This was where the overflow bled out. Where the desperate were warehoused like livestock. Easier to slip through.

If they were lucky.

Watchtowers loomed like skeletal fists, and lanterns swung on creaking chains, casting trembling light over the rusted gates.

Niev shifted just beyond the edge of the path—her hawk form vanishing into the stars without a sound.

He tried not to fidget. Tried not to look at the broken fences and imagine exactly what was waiting on the other side.

But a few moments later, he heard a rush of wings.

She landed beside them in the dust, already shifting back. Her body snapped and reshaped in a matter of heartbeats—feathers giving way to skin, eyes blazing as she pulled the black scarf back over her hair.

"Six guards," she whispered. "Two on the perimeter. Four inside. There's a gap in the north post—they rotate patrols every ten minutes. We'll go in through the south gate. Quieter. Fewer sight lines."

Caelan nodded once, adrenaline sharpening his focus. Teagan grunted approval. Ayda murmured a quiet blessing under her breath.

Niev padded ahead, her breath shallow. Her body glistened with sweat, skin half-shifting as if her instincts couldn't decide what form she needed to be in.

She raised a hand, and her shadows rippled.

But it wasn't like before. The darkness stuttered, then thickened— crawling along the wall and pooling beneath the archway like smoke turned solid. Caelan watched in awe as it spread, curling around them like a second skin, blotting out sound and movement from any nearby guards.

But it was unstable.

He could see her tremble. She didn't have enough training or control yet. Her jaw clenched as if she were holding back a scream. The magic flickered at the edges—untamed. Hungry.

"Niev," he whispered.

"I'm fine," she hissed back. "Just—move."

Wrapped in the unnatural stillness, they crept forward—silent as ghosts—until the hulking form of the first guard emerged through the dark.

Niev struck first.

A whisper of motion, a glint of steel, and he dropped like a felled tree—his body caught before it could hit the ground. Teagan dispatched the second with brutal efficiency, muffling the sound of his collapse beneath the shifting sand.

As they reached the gate, Caelan stepped forward, heart pounding as he pressed his palm against the rusted lockplate.

His hand hummed, his blood stirring with familiar power.

Focus.

He could feel the structure of the lock—its flaws, its stress points, the way time had thinned the iron from within.

He exhaled.

Then twisted, and the bolt gave with a soft, clean click.

The gate opened to reveal the biggest slave camp in all of Eldhaven.

Rows of low shacks and steel-barred cells. Faint torchlight flickering across the gravel. The scent of rot, blood, and desperation thick in the air.

"*God Almighty,*" Myria whispered in horror.

Niev sucked in a breath and took the lead again, slipping into the shadows, her movements as fluid as smoke.

Her shadows bending the light, distorting their outlines. Caelan had never seen anything like it. Her magic flickered and rippled as she moved ahead, her hand brushing the air now and then to reinforce the veil. Unstable. Fractured. But enough to hide them from sight.

They crossed the threshold into the camp, and the world changed.

Even after all these years, even braced for it, Caelan wasn't prepared for the smell.

Burned metal. Rot. Sweat. Human waste. The stench of suffering layered into the very bones of the place choked him.

The outer yard was wide and packed dirt, sloped slightly so the runoff from rain and blood didn't linger long. Iron stakes lined the perimeter, some still strung with chains. Above them, the towers loomed— watchposts of scorched black wood and splintered beams, where soldiers leaned lazily against spears, bored and oblivious under the illusion of control.

They ducked into the shadow of a long, crumbling wall. Caelan pressed his back to the cool stone, his eyes scanning the grounds.

There were five long cell blocks—low, narrow buildings constructed from mismatched slabs of rock and steel, like someone had stitched them together in a hurry. Their roofs sagged under sand and rust. Doors reinforced with thick bolts. No windows. Just narrow slits.

Air holes.

Or maybe just reminders that the people inside weren't dead. Not yet.

To the east, he spotted the smokehouse—where they processed their "unfit" for labor. His stomach rolled. Beyond it, a blackened pit of scorched earth where the cremations took place.

Everything was smaller than he remembered.

Or maybe he'd just gotten bigger.

Maybe he'd grown into the space once built to contain him.

But the dread in his chest—the helplessness—it felt exactly the same.

He could hear it now. The coughing. The chains. A distant cry, cut short.

Ayda stepped up behind him, her breath barely a whisper. "How many guards inside the cells?"

"Too many to fight outright," he murmured back. "But if we keep low, we can cut between the blocks during the changeover."

Niev raised her hand in a silent signal to wait.

Then she flicked two fingers forward.

They slipped along the side of the first block, keeping low. The torchlight above flickered—briefly dimming—and Caelan realized she was manipulating the shadows as they passed, blurring their movement in the periphery of the guards' vision.

The four of them paused behind the next corner. From here, they could see more.

There was a courtyard at the camp's heart—gravel and dust, marked by the outline of shackles driven into the ground. A single bucket of water sat in the center. Half-spilled. One of the guards kicked a chained man in the ribs before wandering off.

Caelan's jaw tensed.

Teagan, crouched beside him, muttered a curse. "This place..."

"I know," Caelan rasped.

Because he did. Every stone. Every chain. Every scream.

He knew this place in his bones.

They had to keep moving. Niev shifted her stance and looked back at him, her eyes sharp even in the dark. They paused behind a crumbling stone wall near the center of the camp. Caelan crouched low, glancing toward the nearest bunkhouse.

"We don't know where he is," Teagan murmured. "And we can't check every building without being seen."

"There's the central records room," Caelan said, pointing to a domed building across the compound. "If he's here, he's in one of the ledgers."

It was too far. Too exposed.

And the veil was breaking.

Caelan could feel it.

The shadows around them, once smooth and fluid like ink in water, had started to fray at the edges. Wisps peeled away with each step, curling like smoke in the dry canyon air. The magic that had hidden them so well now flickered—faint pulses of darkness trembling with each of Niev's labored breaths.

He looked back.

Her jaw was clenched, a fine sheen of sweat on her brow. Her eyes were narrowed in concentration, fingers twitching subtly as she tried to hold the spell together.

But it was unraveling.

They didn't have much time.

They crept low between two storage shacks, the ground beneath their boots cracked and dust-dry, the scent of sunburnt metal and scorched stone pressing in on all sides. The watchtowers loomed overhead—rusting spires with flickering torches and lazy silhouettes pacing behind the crossbars.

If anyone glanced down now, the shadows wouldn't hide them.

Not for long.

"There," Ayda whispered, pointing toward a squat, circular building across the open yard. Iron-banded stone. Reinforced slats on the narrow windows. The central records room.

Two guards flanked the door.

Clad in sand-colored armor, they stood too rigid, too alert—professionals, not the half-asleep louts stationed elsewhere in the camp. Both carried long blades and compact crossbows strapped across their backs. Their eyes scanned the courtyard with the mechanical rhythm of men used to violence.

And the overseer would be inside.

Caelan swore under his breath.

They were exposed here—out in the open, barely twenty yards from the guards. Any sudden movement, any flicker of shadow, and they'd be seen. Worse, they'd trigger the alarm bells mounted to the watchtowers.

Niev's magic pulsed again, a ripple that faltered and then snapped back into place.

He saw her stagger slightly and moved to catch her, steadying her elbow.

"I'm fine," she muttered, but her voice was frayed. Raw.

"No, you're not. We need to move. Now."

He turned to the others, eyes sharp. "We can't rush them from here. We'll be seen."

"Distraction?" Teagan whispered.

"Too risky."

Ayda leaned in. "What about above? If you and Niev climb the side wall to the rafters, you could drop behind them."

"I'd have to shift," Niev said hoarsely. "And I don't think I can keep the shadows up and shift at the same time."

"Then don't," Caelan said. "Drop the veil. Just for a second. We'll strike fast."

Niev met his eyes, and nodded once.

He turned back to the group. "On my signal."

Together, he and Niev slipped toward the outer wall of the records building. The stone was old and pockmarked, offering just enough hold. Caelan scaled first—quick and silent—his dagger scraping once against the wall before catching the lip of the roof.

He glanced down.

Niev crouched, eyes glowing faintly in the low light. She let out a breath, and the shadows disappeared.

They were visible now.

But only for a moment.

Caelan hauled her up. She climbed with sharp, agile movements, catlike in her precision.

From the roof, they could see both guards clearly.

Timing had to be perfect.

He counted the rhythm of their patrol.

One step forward. Two steps back. Turn. Pause.

Now.

Caelan dropped.

He landed in a crouch behind the first guard and slammed the pommel of his dagger into the man's temple. A crack of metal on bone. The man crumpled silently.

Niev was faster.

She shifted midair—half-woman, half-shadowed beast—and landed atop the second guard. Her claws sank into his shoulder as she dragged him back, muffling his cry with a hand over his mouth before slamming his head into the stone.

Silence.

Both guards down. No sound. No witnesses.

Caelan dragged the bodies to the side of the door, hiding them behind a stack of crates.

Niev shifted back, panting hard, her hands shaking slightly. "I don't have much left," she murmured.

"You've done enough," he said, brushing a hand down her spine. "We're in."

He stepped to the door, pressing his palm to the iron latch. His powers sparked.

Stone shifted beneath his hand with a deep, quiet grind.

The door creaked as it swung open into dim torchlight and the stench of dust, sweat, and ink.

Caelan moved first, his power crackling faintly, scanning the room. It was tighter than he expected—rows of shelves packed with ledgers, all bound in weathered leather. A narrow desk sat wedged near the back, cluttered with parchment, quills, and a cold cup of something that had once been tea.

And behind it, the overseer stood.

A gaunt man in a desert-worn uniform, a thin scar running from brow to cheek. He was mid-turn when he saw them—eyes going wide, mouth opening to shout—

But Niev was already there.

She moved like a flash of silvered death, her dagger pressing into the tender spot just beneath his jaw.

"Make a sound," she whispered, "and I'll paint these shelves with your blood."

The man froze.

Caelan shut the door behind them, locking it with a quick flick of his wrist—metal groaning quietly back into place. His heart was pounding. The air in the room was heavy with heat and tension that made his skin itch.

Niev had donned the calm mask of Solhaven's infamous assassin, and seemed wholly unaffected.

"What can you tell me about a slave by the name Elias Helvast?" she said, voice low and even.

The overseer's brows pinched. "What?"

"Elias Helvast. He was sold to this shithole ten years ago. Where is he?" she said urgently, choking the man with her dagger.

"I—there's no one here by that name," he stammered. "We don't—names aren't—we use designations."

Disgust twisted Niev's face. "You number them?"

The dagger pressed harder into his throat. A bead of blood welled.

"I don't know who that is, I swear!" He whimpered. "L-Ledger's over there. Wall on the right. Adult males, eighteen and over. Brown spine. Top shelf."

Caelan was already moving.

He yanked the ledger down, the old leather cracking in his hands as he flipped it open. The pages were dense, scrawled with column after column of dates, brands, assignments. Hundreds of numbers, names reduced to ink and order.

His fingers skimmed the rows. His eyes darted left and right, his breath catching.

There.

Slave #626.

Nivola, Elias. Age: 24. Assigned to Camp Virell, Quarry 4. Section 3-C.

He stared at it. Elias was alive. He was still here.

His lungs shuddered on a breath he hadn't realized he was holding—something caught between relief and disbelief. A sound burst from his chest. Not quite a laugh. Not quite a sob.

He looked up at Niev, his heart crashing into his ribs. "He's here," he said hoarsely. "Niev. He's alive."

Her gaze snapped to him. Then softened.

And that smile—small, fierce, unspoken—lit something inside him.

Niev turned back to the overseer, who trembled under her blade.

"Thank you for your cooperation," she said, almost sweetly.

Then slit his throat.

The man gurgled, slumped forward, and the ledgers the man had splayed over his desk soaked up the spill of red like it had been waiting for it.

Caelan didn't flinch.

Neither did she.

They moved quickly, efficiently, memorizing Elias's cell number, and slipping back into the shadows.

46.
Niev

The air outside the overseer's office hit Niev like a wall—stale heat tinged with smoke, the scent of sand, sweat, and something sharp underneath. Alarms hadn't sounded yet, but something was off.

The shadows she cast had all but flickered out, stretched too thin to cover the distance. Her breathing was shallow now, fingers twitching faintly as they darted along the outer corridor—her shadow magic burning out like a dying ember.

"We need to find the others," she muttered. "Now."

Caelan nodded once and tucked the bloodstained dagger tighter beneath his coat. They moved quickly through the narrow alley between stone bunkhouses, boots silent against cracked earth, ducking past barred windows and trailing plumes of dust.

And then they heard raised voices.

Too many for it to be normal.

They rounded the far corner of the building, and stopped cold.

Across the wide, open yard near the central courtyard, Teagan and Ayda stood flanked by two armed guards. A third loomed behind them. Steel glinted in the lantern light. A crowd was forming—half-curious, half-hostile.

Niev's gut dropped.

One of the guards barked something in Thaelonic.

Ayda's hand hovered near her belt.

Teagan, ever the charming bastard, was smiling. That lazy, too-easy grin that said he had everything under control even when he *clearly* did not.

"Gentlemen," he was saying, arms raised slightly, "I assure you, we're merely here for inventory—"

The guard shoved the butt of his spear into Teagan's chest.

"Or not," he staggered back but kept his tone light. "You know what? That's fine too."

Caelan swore under his breath.

They were outnumbered. Too many guards, too open a space. No shadows to hide in. And Niev's magic was spent.

She tensed beside him, eyes locked on Teagan.

"Don't," Caelan said in a hushed tone. "Not yet."

But it was too late.

One of the guards yanked Ayda's satchel off her shoulder. She shouted, twisting to grab it—magic already crackling in her hands.

The guard raised his blade—

"Shit," Caelan hissed. "Go."

Niev launched forward in a blur of motion. Sheer speed and fury, blade drawn and silent as death. Caelan surged after her, the sword in his hand already filling with the charge he's imbued it with.

Teagan ducked as Niev slammed into the first guard, driving her dagger up beneath his chin with a wet crack.

Ayda spun, a burst of fire exploding from the vial she's just thrown, searing across the shoulder of the second.

Caelan reached the third, swiping his sword with a crack that crumpled the man's spear and sent him sprawling across the ground with a wheeze of air and blood.

Screams erupted from the watching crowd. Slaves ducked away. More guards shouted from the edges of the camp.

"All hell is breaking loose," Teagan said, hauling himself upright.

"You think?" Ayda shot back, panting.

Niev turned to Caelan, her hair wild, blood smeared along her sleeve.

"Did you find him?" Ayda demanded.

Caelan yanked the ledger page from his coat and slammed it into Ayda's palm. "Quarry Four. Section 3-C."

"Take Niev and go!" he shouted. "Now!"

"I'm not leaving you—" Niev started to argue.

"I'm not asking," he said firmly.

Niev stared into his eyes as her entire form rippled with light and shadow—bones stretching, limbs snapping into shape as the tigress exploded from her body in a shimmer of silver and shadow. Her growl shattered the air like a warning bell.

And then she launched.

Fur and fang tore through the distance between them, and before the guards could blink, she was on the first one—jaws clamping down around his throat with a sickening crunch. Blood sprayed. Screams erupted. The other two guards backed up instinctively, trying to regroup—

He ran to her—brushed a hand over her soaked fur and crouched beside her massive form.

"You need to go," he said, low but firm. "Take Ayda. Find your brother. You don't have enough left to cover all of us, and Teagan and I can handle the rest."

She growled in protest.

"I'll be fine," he said again, meeting the glint of her wild, golden eyes. "You've done enough. Let me hold the line."

For a moment, the Tigress didn't move.

Then her body twisted—ribbons of shadow unspooling around her bones as she shifted back to human, blood-streaked and breathless, her bare skin glowing with sweat and exertion.

"You better not fucking die, Caelan Galbraith," she panted.

Caelan flashed his wicked grin. "Not on your watch."

"Ayda!" she called, grabbing a sword from one of the fallen guards. "Let's go find my brother!"

They disappeared into the alley beyond the courtyard.

Just as Caelan turned, sword humming with energy, as more guards swarmed in like vultures to a battlefield.

❋   ❋   ❋

The halls of the prison reeked of blood, piss, and death.

Niev's boots slapped against the stone, every breath a rasp in her lungs as she and Ayda tore through the narrow halls, eyes straining in the dim light. Her muscles screamed, magic fraying at the edges of her skin, and still she pushed on.

They turned a corner.

Rows upon rows of cages stretched out in front of them.

Shackles. Bedding made of rags and dirt.

Men stared out at them with hollow eyes, not even bothering to rise—like they didn't believe what they were seeing.

Niev didn't hesitate.

She slammed her palm into the first rusted lock. Her power, raw and crackling, surged. The metal burst open with a groan, the door swinging inward.

Stunned faces looked up from the straw-lined floor.

"Go," she rasped. "Get the *hell* out of here."

She moved to the next cell.

Crushed the lock.

And the next.

And the next.

Ayda caught up behind her, eyes wide. "Niev, there's no ti—"

"I'm not *leaving* them here," she hissed. "Not if I can help it."

Every shackle she broke, every cage she opened—it sent something deeper unraveling in her chest. These weren't strangers. Not really. They were boys who could've been Elias. Men who could've been Caelan. Ghosts of everything she'd lost and everything she still had to save.

By the time she reached the cell at the far end—larger than the others, packed with a dozen gaunt, silent men—her hands were shaking.

She stepped closer, peering through the bars. Her breath caught.

"Elias?"

Her question was met with nothing but silence.

She scanned the men—one after another, faces hollowed by starvation and silence. Nothing. Until—

One of them stirred.

In the corner, half-shadowed, slumped against the wall like a discarded rag.

Slowly, he lifted his head.

Niev's chest caved inward.

He looked nothing like the boy she remembered. No longer the grinning fourteen-year-old who raced her through palace gardens. This was a man now—battered, sunburnt, bruised. His hair was jagged, as though it had been hacked off with a dull knife. A scruffy beard clung to his jaw, and his blue eyes were sunken, dark... but familiar.

So goddamned familiar.

"Eli?" she said again, softer this time.

His eyes found hers. And after what felt like forever, she finally saw the flicker of recognition in them.

"...Sera?" he rasped, voice broken and unsure, like he didn't dare believe it.

Her hands clutched the bars, heart cracking open as his name escaped again, this time a sob. "Brother—"

And then Ayda was at her side, already at work on the lock with trembling hands, her fingers flickering sharp and fast.

The door groaned open, and Niev was inside the moment it did, dropping to her knees beside him. Her hands hovered over his face, his shoulders, afraid to touch too hard, afraid he might vanish like a dream.

"You're real," he whispered, eyes wide. "You're—how?"

She shook her head, tears slipping free. "Doesn't matter. I'm here now."

But Elias's expression shifted—twisting in sudden fear.

"No," he said, his voice a harsh, broken whisper. "No, no—what are you doing here? Did they catch you too?" He gripped her arm with shaking fingers, wild-eyed. "Sera, you can't be here. You don't know what they'll do to you—what they've done to us—"

"Hey." She caught his face gently, grounding him. "Listen to me."

She pressed her forehead to his, eyes burning.

"I'm not a prisoner, Eli," she whispered. "I'm here to get you out."

He stilled.

She could feel the trembling in his bones, the disbelief warring in his blood.

His chest heaved, breath shallow. "They'll kill you. They'll kill all of you. You've lost your mind—there's no getting out. Not from here."

"Watch me," she said, voice low and lethal.

Niev turned from her brother, the fire in her chest burning hotter than it ever had.

She looked at the other prisoners—men crammed into cells like cattle, eyes hollow, limbs gaunt, their chains rusted into their skin. They stared back at her in stunned silence.

"Get out," she said, voice hard as iron as she flung her hands toward the open cell door. "Run for your lives."

None of them moved.

So she took a step forward and raised her voice, letting it ring through the corridor like the crack of a whip.

"These walls won't be standing by sundown. If you want to live, GET MOVING!"

That did it.

The first man staggered forward—then another. Chains clanked to the ground as they surged out in waves, bruised bodies scraping against the walls in their rush. Some limped. Others crawled. A few had to carry those too weak to stand. But they moved. They ran.

Behind her, Ayda stood frozen.

"Niev..." she said quietly, eyes wide as the realization dawned on her. "What the hell did you do?"

Niev didn't answer.

She needed her friends in the dark until the last minute.

She needed them safe.

Because the promise she'd made to herself—to her brother, to every child dragged screaming into these walls—was no longer something she could contain.

This place would fall.

She would make sure of it.

"Later," she rasped, not looking into her friend's eyes. "Help me with him."

Together, they pulled Elias up between them. He could barely stand, but he clung to them with the last scraps of strength he had left.

The corridors were chaos. Guards shouted, tripped, and were overrun by stampeding prisoners. Smoke had begun to curl along the ceilings—someone must've set fire to something. The alarms were screaming now, shrill and wild, but no order remained. Only fury. Only escape.

As they rounded the southern corridor, Niev caught sight of a familiar figure—Teagan, shirt torn and bloodied, a cut slashing across his brow, swinging his sword like a goddamned berserker.

Next to him, Caelan moved like a force of nature. His sword blazed with raw energy, turning steel to smoke and stone to dust. She didn't know what kind of magic he'd imbued that weapon with, but whatever it was, it was effective. A guard lunged, and Caelan shattered the man's weapon with a flick of his hand, then slammed his fist into the man's ribs. The guard crumpled.

"Caelan!" Niev shouted.

His head snapped up.

And when he saw her—saw Elias draped between her and Ayda—relief cracked across his face, fierce and aching. But it vanished just as quickly as another wave of guards charged forward.

"Move!" Teagan bellowed. "We've got the east path open!"

Niev gritted her teeth as she adjusted her grip on her brother, slinging his weight tighter against her side. His breath was shallow, rasping like torn cloth against his ribs, but he held on—barely.

They ran as the world around them descended into chaos.

Flames licked up the sides of the barracks. Smoke choked the narrow corridors, thick and acrid, clinging to her lungs like a curse. Ash snowed from the ceilings. The ringing of alarm bells had morphed into something animal—screams, steel, the sound of bones breaking.

Prisoners flooded the compound like a tidal wave of fury. Some scrambled for the exits, desperate for the sun and sand beyond these cursed walls. But others—others turned. Snapped. Became something else entirely.

She saw one man seize a guard by the collar and rip him off his feet with nothing but brute, feral strength. Another straddled a fallen soldier, pounding his fists into the man's face until it caved beneath his hands. Fury had given the slaves inhumane strength.

A prisoner, near what she assumed was the kitchen, emerged with a cleaver, eyes wild, blood splattered across his chest. He hurled it like a throwing knife—blade spinning end over end—and it sank into a guard's neck with a wet, meaty thunk. The man didn't even pause. Just picked up another and kept going.

To her left, a woman staggered into the hallway, covered in soot, barefoot and limping—but her eyes were alight with madness. She let out a shriek, half laugh, half sob, and tackled a guard twice her size.

Years of cruelty were being repaid in seconds.

Smoke blurred the edges of her vision. Sparks popped in the rafters above. Flames chewed through the floorboards behind them. Every breath she took tasted like metal and ash.

The walls of Campy Virell—the place that had stolen her brother, broken her lover, destroyed hundreds of lives—were cracking.

"Don't stop," she whispered to Elias, more to herself than him, as she dragged him around a collapsed beam. "Don't you dare stop."

Ahead, Caelan cut through two guards like water parting around a blade—his sword burning white-hot, his face a storm of resolve. Teagan was beside him, bloodied and grinning like a devil, his twin swords dripping, eyes blazing with battle fire.

Ayda threw one of Elias's arms over her shoulders to adjust him, helping Niev carry his weight, breath ragged but focused.

They plunged through the last corridor as a thunderous crash echoed behind them—stone caving, the last guard tower engulfed in fire.

And as they neared the blasted gate—smoke curling behind them, screams echoing from cells, and the entire camp unraveling at the seams—Niev looked to Caelan.

His eyes met hers across the madness.

And all five of them ran towards the gate.

The desert wind hit her like a wall the moment they crossed the outer gate—hot, dry, and too bright after the gloom of the camp. Smoke clawed its way into the sky behind them, billowing like a funeral pyre for every soul still trapped behind those stone walls.

Elias's weight dragged between her and Ayda, every step heavier than the last. He was barely conscious now, mumbling words that didn't make sense, his feet tripping over the ground.

"Almost there," Niev whispered, tightening her grip around his waist. "Just a little further."

They'd done it. God above, they'd actually done it. Her brother was in her arms. Alive.

And yet—her chest ached.

Because it wasn't enough.

The screams still echoed behind them.

And something in her—something deep, cold, certain—knew it wasn't finished.

They reached the base of the dunes where Myria waited for them. Teagan and Caelan surged forward to meet them, taking Elias's weight off her shoulders. The moment Caelan touched her, her body almost gave out.

"Got him," Caelan said, pulling Elias against his side. His eyes scanned her face, frantic. "Niev? Are you alright?"

She nodded.

A blatant lie.

Her heart was pounding. Her hands were slick with blood—some of it hers, most of it not. And her shadows, her power... they pulsed beneath her skin, alive with fury.

"Go," she said. "Take him. Get him away from here."

Caelan's eyes narrowed. "What are you talking about?"

She didn't answer.

Instead, she grabbed the front of his shirt, fisted it in her trembling hands, and pulled him into her. Her mouth crashed into his—fierce, desperate, tasting of blood and dust. It wasn't gentle. It was a desperate goodbye.

When she pulled back, her breath hitched.

"I love you," she whispered fiercely, forehead pressed to his. "I love you more than life, Caelan. You deserve everything good in this world. Be safe, my love."

He looked stricken, like something inside him was unraveling. He tried to grab on to her but she was already turning away.

She faced Teagan next, and pressed a hand to his chest, just over his heart. "Keep them safe, brother."

Teagan's eyes went wide. "Niev—no. No, don't you dare—"

"Don't let him follow me," she whispered, and spun back before he could stop her.

"Niev!" Ayda shouted behind her.

But she was already moving.

The desert roared in her ears. Her lungs burned. Her legs screamed. But she didn't slow.

The sound of Caelan shouting her name cut through the wind.

She didn't look back.

Couldn't.

Because if she did, she'd stop. She'd cave. And this—this—was something only she could do.

She reached the gate again as the fires blazed higher, and slipped through the smoke like a blade through silk.

47.
Caelan

"**N**IEV!"

His voice cracked like thunder across the open desert—but she was already gone.

One second, she was at his side—bloodied and burning and alive—and the next, she was running straight back toward the screaming gates of Zarenth like she hadn't just fought her way out of hell.

Caelan lurched forward, the dead weight of Elias dragging from his shoulder like a shackle. Every muscle in his body screamed to let go—to run after her, to dive back into the fire—but Elias's limp arm and sagging frame held him back.

Teagan stepped directly in front of Caelan. Blocking him.

"Move," he snapped, fury breaking loose in his voice. "I can still reach her—I can still *get to her!*"

"No," Teagan said, his voice low and full of sorrow, palms planted on Caelan's chest like a shield.

"*Take him!*" Caelan roared, half-turning, shoving at Elias's weight with trembling arms. "*Take him and let me go!*"

But Teagan didn't move. His face was streaked with blood and soot, and his eyes burned with fury. "She made her choice."

"*Fuck* her choice!" Caelan snarled. "She's gonna get herself killed!"

"Caelan—" Ayda started.

"She's your friend—and you just let her—*let her go?*" Caelan's voice broke at the end, sharp with disbelief, chest heaving. "She's going to die in there!"

"You think I don't know that?" Teagan snapped back. "You think I don't want to go after her too?!"

Ayda stepped in front of him now, placing both hands on his shoulders, holding him like a tether. "We have to *trust her,* Caelan."

"I *do!*" he shouted, tearing free from her hands. "That's the damn problem! I trust her with everything—*everything.* Except her own life! And now she's in there alone, and you're all just standing here like it's fine—"

"It's not fine!" Teagan barked.

Silence cut through the rising wind.

Caelan stared at him—furious, breathless, devastated.

Teagan's eyes softened, but only barely. "You think you're the only one who loves her? I've had her back for ten years, Cael. You don't survive someone like Niev unless you learn when to run beside her... and when to *let her go.*"

Caelan staggered back a step like he'd been struck. His jaw clenched hard enough to ache. His heart pounded so loud it drowned out everything else.

He shook his head, his voice barely more than a whisper. "I should've stopped her..."

Myria spoke then, quiet and steady. "You couldn't."

He turned sharply to her. "*You knew?*"

She didn't flinch and didn't deny it either.

"You knew she was going back in, and you didn't say a goddamned word?!"

Myria's gaze didn't waver. "She made me swear."

Caelan's voice rose, ragged and breaking. "You let her walk into that hell alone!"

"She gave me a job," Myria said, quietly but firmly. "A contingency. If she didn't make it out, I was to finish what she started. Burn Zarenth to the ground. That was the plan all along."

Silence cracked across the desert.

Caelan stared at her like she'd slapped him. "After everything I told her... She still decided to throw herself away... and all of it *behind my back*..."

"She didn't want you to carry that," Myria said, her voice softer now. "She trusted you with Elias. She trusted *me* to be the knife in the dark if she couldn't be."

"And you just—agreed?" he shrieked.

"No, Caelan." she said, her voice rising, her temper finally getting the better of her. "I didn't just *agree*! I fought with her for HOURS! But she would do it with or without me. There was nothing I could do to dissuade her."

He looked like he couldn't breathe. Like the weight of that secret was crushing the last air from his chest.

Myria exhaled shakily. "You think it was easy? Watching her run back in? You think I don't hate every second of this? But this is bigger than all of us. And Niev knows this."

"Fuck you, Myria Holloway" Caelan threw back, his voice soaked in venom as he forcefully shoved a half conscious Elias into her arms—ready to run back after the woman he loves.

"Caelan." Ayda's voice cut through the haze like a blade—sharp, urgent, laced with something raw beneath. "Look!" she pointed back to the gates.

He turned.

And everything else fell away.

From the heart of Camp Virell's crumbling fortress, fire and smoke surged like a living thing—pushed outward by something far more terrible than a blaze. The air pulsed with heat and magic, the desert wind itself recoiling.

The earth trembled.

And stone exploded outward as a colossal shadow tore through what remained of the fortress gates—wings unfurling like banners of war. The sun, barely rising, caught the ridges of scale and fang and claw, as a massive dragon rose up within the walls of the prison.

This creature was all fury and glory and ancient might—a massive mountain of sleek obsidian and silver-veined scales, wings like stormfronts, talons like carved obsidian. And the beast's eyes—

Stars above.

He knew those eyes.

Molten amber, ringed in dark shadow. Unmistakable. Unyielding.

Niev Helvast.

Caelan staggered back a step as a wall crumbled beneath the crush of her tail. She spun, wings snapping wide, and swept a line of guards into the air like leaves—before bringing one clawed limb down and flattening a watchtower with a sound like thunder cracking open the sky.

"*Stars almighty,*" Teagan whispered beside him, as he fell to his knees in reverence.

Caelan couldn't look away.

The dragon reared, jaws opening with a sound like the world was being ripped apart, and *unleashed* a breath of pure shadow flame that caught the western wall, melted it to slag, and sent stone and screams hurtling skyward—exposing the massacre happening within.

Guards ran. Screamed. Fired arrows that bounced uselessly off her hide. One leapt with a spear, and was caught midair between her teeth and *thrown* across the yard like a rag doll.

Another tried to flee.

She crushed him beneath one paw, wings flaring as her tail lashed across the yard again—splintering scaffolding, igniting stores of fuel, sending bodies and debris spinning into fire-lit sky.

The prison that had broken Caelan's family, that had stolen Elias, that had turned countless children into nameless numbers—was being *torn apart* by the very girl it failed to entrap.

She hadn't just come to free her brother.

She'd come to *end it.*

To turn pain into power.

To bring the slave camp down.

Caelan dropped to his knees. His hands clenched in the sand.

And for the first time since he was a boy, held captive within those walls, he felt something he never thought he'd feel.

Deliverance.

48.
Caelan

The sky had gone dark with smoke and ash—thick, suffocating, stirred by the hot breath of what had once been Zarenth.

Caelan stood frozen on the ridge, Elias half-sagged against his side, the others flanked around him in stunned silence. No one spoke. No one moved.

Because the fortress in front of them no longer existed.

Its walls—once towering and immovable—lay in ruins, blackened and buckled like the bones of some ancient beast. The guard towers had collapsed inward. The barracks had been flattened. And the gates—the same gates they had crawled through, bleeding and desperate—had been torn apart like parchment.

And standing at the heart of it all, a force carved from nightmare and salvation—

The dragon.

Her scales were a shimmer of shadow and moonlight, each movement rippling like silk. She towered above the wreckage, her wings vast as stormclouds, her tail a whip of destruction. With a roar that split the earth, she slammed it into a crumbling wall, and stone rained down like gravel.

Guards fled in every direction—what few remained. But they didn't get far.

Niev hunted them one by one.

She moved with precision, with fury. She bit and tore and flung them like broken dolls, the ground cracking beneath her rage. Again, and again, for what felt like hours. Until nothing could be heard but the whisper of the wind and the scuttling steps of the freed slaves running away.

"She...she destroyed the entire fortress," Ayda whispered behind him, her voice thin, awed.

Elias, who has been quiet until now, gazed towards his sister. "Beware the endless wrath of a provoked Helvast."

His words sounded like prophecy, but Caelan just nodded slowly, unable to find his voice.

Eventually, the dragon stilled and the wind shifted as smoke twisted around her frame. Ash billowed in great clouds, swallowing the wreckage.

The massive form shimmered, warped—

And the mountain of muscle and wing vanished into the ash, until there was nothing but dust and ruin and silence.

Caelan's heart seized. He started forward—but the smoke was too thick. The air too heavy. The heat still unbearable from the scorched earth. He covered his mouth, eyes stinging.

He held his breath for what felt like ages. Waiting. Praying.

His eyes roamed the shadowed abyss in front of him until finally, a lone figure emerged from the rubble.

Barefoot. Covered in soot. Bloodied and bruised.

She walked slowly through the swirling ashes like some terrible wraith reborn from flame.

The smoke parted around her. The ground gave way beneath her steps.

And Caelan released a breath of relief as Niev limped towards him.

Caelan didn't feel his feet move—only knew that he was running.

Ash whipped through the air like snow in a storm, coating his skin, stinging his eyes, choking his breath. But it didn't matter. He pushed forward, boots skidding through the scorched dirt, slipping on blackened stone.

She moved like a ghost. No—like a wraith returned from the underworld. Her feet were raw, bleeding. Her hair hung in tangled ropes down her back, half-singed, half-soaked. The shirt she wore clung to her frame in shreds, torn at the seams, soaked with blood and soot. Her skin was a canvas of ash and sweat, and her eyes—

Her eyes burned like twin coals in the dark.

He reached her just as her steps faltered, and without thinking—he caught her.

She collapsed into his arms with a broken breath, her body trembling, heat still rising from her skin.

"I've got you," he whispered hoarsely, voice shredded with relief.

She clung to him, her arms wrapping around his neck, her fingers digging into his back like she didn't trust the world beneath her to hold.

"*You insane, insufferable woman,*" he breathed, echoing the words she'd said to him back in Port Orynth.

She didn't speak but he could feel her smile against his shoulder.

The ruins groaned behind them as the last tower crumbled in on itself, a final monument to a fallen empire of chains and cruelty. Smoke curled lazily around them, rising like incense to the heavens.

He pulled back just enough to look at her face—at the dried blood on her cheek, the cracked lips, the wild flicker still in her eyes.

"You just destroyed the biggest slave camp in all of Eldhaven," he said, wonder thick in his voice.

"I told you," she rasped, her words more breath than sound. "I'd burn it all for you."

He crushed his mouth to hers in a hard and desperate kiss. Like the battlefield still lived in their bones and she was the only safe thing left in the world.

Caelan groaned into her mouth, one hand sliding into her matted hair, the other anchoring at her waist as he kissed her back like he needed her to breathe. Her lips were chapped, her skin gritty with ash, and none of it mattered. All that mattered was the feel of her—*real*, solid, *alive*—in his arms again.

She bit his lower lip, and he growled, dragging her closer, deepening the kiss until they both forgot the ruined world around them.

Until they were just a tangle of breath and lips and salt and need.

When they finally broke apart, gasping, foreheads pressed together, the taste of smoke still lingered between them.

"*You are an absolute marvel,*" he breathed in awe. "But I will murder you with my own hands if you ever scare me like that again.."

She smiled through cracked lips. "Don't make promises you can't keep."

Behind them, the others were beginning to draw close—Teagan limping, face pale with disbelief; Ayda cradling Elias, eyes wide and wet; Myria moving like she'd just seen her sister conquer the world.

But in this moment, all Caelan could see was her.

He cupped her face in both hands, brushing a smear of soot from her cheek with his thumb.

From behind them, someone whistled low.

"Not to interrupt this whole post-apocalyptic love scene," Teagan called, voice ragged but teasing, "but I think you *technically* just declared war on half the empire."

Niev didn't even look at him.

Still pressed to Caelan's chest, her voice came low and rough, but every word laced with steel.

"Good."

She pulled back just enough to turn her head, locking eyes with her brother across the ash-swept ruin.

"The empire could use a little landscaping, don't you think?" she said with that feral, wicked grin.

Caelan stared at her for a heartbeat—then huffed a breathless, disbelieving laugh.

Teagan whistled low under his breath. "Saints save us."

49.
Niev

The Sersha Mara rocked gently beneath her boots, its battered frame groaning as it pushed away from the blood-soaked coast. The sea had never sounded so good.

The sails strained against the wind, and the horizon stretched wide and open before them, the smoke of Zarenth still a faint shadow behind.

Laughlan stood at the helm, his coat tattered, one arm wrapped lazily around the wheel. His voice cut through the hum of waves.

"Well then, Tigress," he said with a grin, "where to?"

Niev stood beside him, barefoot, her skin still streaked in ash. The desert wind tugged at her torn shirt, now half tucked into a belt someone had given her, and her hair had been messily tied back to keep the soot from her eyes. She looked behind her. To Elias.

Her brother sat on the railing, swaddled in a blanket and sunlight, one arm resting on his knee. He looked exhausted, but there was a slight color in his face again. And his eyes weren't quite so hollow.

She met his gaze.

He gave her a tired, crooked smile.

She turned back to Laughlan and said, simply, "Home."

The captain tipped an imaginary hat. "To Thornmere then."

The sails caught, and the Sersha turned, cutting a sharp line through the water.

❋ ❋ ❋

By midday, the sun was warm again. The wind steady. Niev's crew moved about the deck in slow, deliberate rhythm. It wasn't the frenetic energy of a chase, or the desperation of war—it was the steady lull of after.

Everyone was bruised. Bandaged. Bone-tired.

But they were breathing.

Alive.

And for that, she was eternally grateful.

Below deck, buckets of seawater and old soap were passed around, and one by one, the crew sloughed off the battle. Niev had washed the worst of the blood and grit from her body, standing beneath the pouring rain-barrel, letting it run through her hair and over the marks Zarenth had left behind.

Now, she leaned against the railing, letting the salt wind do the rest.

Behind her, she heard the sound of low conversation—voices soft, casual.

She turned just enough to catch Caelan lowering himself beside Elias, who now wore a clean shirt two sizes too big and looked like he still didn't quite believe this wasn't all a fever dream.

"It's good to see you, brother," Caelan said, voice low and warm as he wrapped one arm around Eli's shoulder. "Though, if we're being honest... you're in *dire* need of a haircut."

Elias snorted. "Talk to the man who tried to trim it with a hunting knife."

Niev winced.

"It's not that bad," came a soft voice.

Niev glanced over just in time to see Ayda step closer, the tips of her fingers brushing the edge of Elias's sleeve as she tucked her hair behind her ear.

"I mean," Ayda added quickly, a little pink in the cheeks, "not the part where it looks like it was cut with a knife. But I can... help with that. If you'd like."

Elias looked up at her, surprised, and then, slowly, nodded.

Niev blinked.

Oh.

Ayda turned to her, almost shy. "I can take him below. There's salve for his bruises, and I'll clean him up." she gestured towards his hair and beard.

Niev raised a brow, the corners of her mouth twitching. "Elias," she said lightly, "This is Ayda Ravenscroft. Elarian witch. Healer. Miracle worker. Occasionally saves idiot men from themselves."

Ayda made a sound of protest. Elias gave an imperceptible grin.

"You're in good hands," she continued softly.

They disappeared down the stairwell, Ayda already scolding him gently for trying to limp his way down without asking for help.

"You don't miss a damn thing," came a voice beside her.

Thorne leaned against the railing with a flask in hand, watching the distant plumes of ash still curling into the sky behind them.

"That was a hell of a storm," he said, gesturing vaguely toward where Zarenth had once stood. "Though I gotta say... the smoke cloud I saw from the Sersha didn't look like a six-person escape."

Niev lifted her chin, the wind brushing hair across her cheek. She didn't smile.

She *smirked*.

"You know me, Captain," she said, cheekily. "Always overachieving."

Laughlan let out a low, appreciative whistle. "Remind me never to piss you off."

"I feel like that lesson's well established by now."

He took a long swig and handed the flask to her.

She drank greedily.

❋ ❋ ❋

The sky stretched endless and deep above them, stars scattered like salt across black velvet. The ship rocked gently beneath them, sails furled, her hull creaking with the steady rhythm of a vessel finally at rest.

Niev sat beside her brother at the helm, arms folded loosely over her knees, her shoulder brushing his. They'd barely spoken.

Elias leaned against the wooden rail, face half-lit by moonlight. Clean-shaven now, his features had started to emerge again—still hollowed by hunger, still painted with bruises in various stages of healing—but there was something familiar in the angle of his jaw, in the quiet intensity of his stare.

It was like looking at a ghost of the boy he'd once been.

His skin was marked. Faint scars along his collarbone. Red welts on his wrists from years in shackles. She'd seen them all when she'd helped him clean up. She hadn't said a word about them then.

She still didn't.

Her eyes just traced the curve of his temple, the tangle of dark hair that fell over his brow, and the steady way he watched the sea.

He was alive.

Here.

And yet, every breath still felt borrowed.

"Can't sleep?" came Caelan's voice, low and familiar, as he approached with a folded cot in his arms.

Niev noticed Elias stiffening subtly, but she knew now it was more out of instinct than fear.

"Didn't think you'd want to sleep below," Caelan added, holding the cot up like a peace offering. "Too many walls down there. Too quiet. Thought maybe the deck and stars would be... easier."

Elias looked up, surprised. He nodded once. "Yeah. Thanks."

Niev watched the moment pass between them.

Something unspoken. Something forged long before she'd found them both again. There was a language in the silence—the kind built from shared ghosts and the weight of survival. Elias looked at Caelan like he understood him in a way no one else ever could.

And Caelan—he just gave her brother a small nod, respectful. Steady.

"I'll let you two talk," he said, setting the cot gently beside the helm. His hand brushed Niev's shoulder as he passed, the touch brief but grounding. "You know where to find me."

When she turned to look at him, he was already halfway down the deck.

But the glance he threw her over his shoulder—full of warmth and promise—made her heart stutter.

Beside her, Elias chuckled softly.

Niev looked at him, startled.

He was grinning faintly, eyes still rimmed with exhaustion but clearer than they'd been earlier. "Of all the people in Eldhaven," he said, "you fell in love with a slave from Zarenth."

She rolled her eyes, smiling despite herself. "And he fell in love with a murderous bitch. So, I'd say I got the better bargain"

"Good for you then," Elias said with a dry laugh.

Niev bumped her shoulder gently against his. "He's the best man I've ever known."

Elias didn't answer right away. He just stared out at the water for a while, letting the silence wrap around them again.

"I'm happy for you, Sera." he finally said. "Or is it Niev now?"

Her throat caught, she didn't know how to answer him. The distance between them felt endless, so she just gave a curt smile.

Niev sat quietly with her brother, until they both fell asleep under the stars. Elias's head nestled in his twin sister's lap.

❈ ❈ ❈

Their voyage passed like a blur, the sea wind not stinging like it used to.

And after the smoke and ash and fire-choked screams—the salt air felt almost gentle. Niev stood at the prow of the Sersha, hands braced on the rail. The skies above Thornmere were grey, the coastline wreathed in mist, and yet the land looked... softer. Greener.

She hadn't spoken much since they set sail from Thaelon. There hadn't been much to say. Her voice had burned out with the last of the fire. Her body hadn't stopped aching since she collapsed in Caelan's arms that night, half-naked and scorched and shaking.

And even now, standing under open skies again, free and whole—she didn't feel it.

Freedom.

Not really.

Not while she could still taste ash on her tongue. Not while her dreams were filled with the scent of burning stone and the distant sobs of dying men.

Not while there were still names she didn't know.

Still monsters walking free.

Niev barely registered the moment Driftwood came into view, its moss-covered docks wreathed in fog. The ship gave a soft lurch as they got closer to Thornmere's port, where it all began. Where she had first let herself hope again.

The others were stirring behind her. Teagan was helping Laughlan shout orders to the crew. Ayda sat quietly near the stairs to the lower deck, her head bent, her hand resting gently on Elias's shoulder as she murmured something to him softly. He hadn't spoken much during the journey. But after what she'd seen, she didn't expect him to.

Her fingers curled tighter around the railing, knuckles bone-white. The salt wind tangled through her hair, tugging strands free to dance around her face, but she didn't move.

Her scars itched beneath her tunic. Her body ached in places she'd stopped counting. Her magic was dormant again—quiet, coiled like some sleeping beast just under her skin. Waiting.

Everything about her was waiting.

She was so lost in thought she didn't feel Caelan come up behind her until his arms slid around her waist, slow and sure, and a breath exhaled against the side of her neck.

He buried his nose in her hair, one hand resting flat against her stomach, the other curling possessively beneath her ribs.

"You didn't come back to me last night," he murmured.

"I—" Her throat tightened. "I stayed on the deck with Eli."

"*I missed you,*" he whispered against her skin, pressing a kiss to her temple.

His scent filled her nose—smoke, leather, salt—and she leaned back into him, just enough to feel the warmth of his chest at her spine.

The sounds of the ship blurred around them. Somewhere below, a bell tolled faintly as the ship docked fully into port.

"I don't know what to do now," Niev said quietly, fingers still braced on the railing. "Zarenth's biggest camp is gone. Elias is safe. And I'm still..."

"I know," he whispered.

She tilted her head, just slightly, as his lips trailed down to her throat. The kiss he placed there was slower—more lingering.

And then he did it again.

And again.

A soft, lazy rhythm, like he could kiss the pressure right out of her.

One hand splayed over her stomach. The other slipped beneath the hem of her shirt, calloused thumb finding the bare skin of her waist.

He brushed upward, slow and deliberate.

A featherlight caress.

Niev shivered.

Her breath stuttered, and she knew he felt it—her body trying so hard not to melt into the touch. Not to give in. But she couldn't stop the small noise that escaped her throat.

"You're distracting me," she whispered, eyes fluttering shut.

"Mmhmm," he hummed against her skin, his lips grazing just beneath her ear. "And doing a damn good job by the sound of it."

Her fingers tangled in the front of his shirt. She blinked at him, dazed.

"Cael," she rasped. "We're on the *deck.*"

He didn't move. Just continued pressing soft kisses to the hollow of her throat.

"*The entire crew* is gonna see," she added, cheeks flushed red beneath the layers of soot. "The ship's literally docking—people can see us *from shore.*"

He still didn't move.

Instead, his gaze flicked briefly toward the gathered crew—Teagan grinning like the smug bastard he was, Myria looking politely elsewhere, Laughlan not even pretending not to stare—and then returned to her, eyes gleaming with zero remorse.

"Let them look," Caelan said, voice low and wicked against her ear. "It's about time this *unruly crew* sees who you belong to."

She inhaled sharply.

And he kissed her.

Slow, but no less possessive. His lips moved over hers like a promise, like a *claim*—one hand fisting in her shirt, the other splayed possessively against the small of her back. The heat of him was everywhere.

When he finally pulled away, her knees nearly gave out.

She blinked up at him, dazed. "You're insane."

"Only about you."

Her mouth parted—but whatever reply she might've given was lost to the chorus of catcalls from the rail.

Teagan's voice rang out, as smug and obnoxious as ever. "Stars above, *get a room!*"

"Gladly!" Caelan shot back without missing a beat, eyes still locked on her.

Niev choked.

Laughlan let out a bark of laughter. "I'm just impressed she can still walk after the shit she pulled the last few days."

"Not for long," Caelan murmured, wickedly soft.

Niev smacked him on the chest, scandalized, and utterly unable to stop the shiteating grin slipping up her face.

50.
Caelan

By the time the ship touched the dock in Driftwood, Caelan could barely believe they were still breathing.

The Sersha groaned softly as her hull kissed the worn wood, salt-stained and scorched but intact—just like the crew who spilled off her in cautious, exhausted relief. The sun had barely crested the sky, casting a golden haze across Thornmere's shores, but for the first time in days, Caelan could hear birdsong again.

He followed the others down the ramp, boots thudding against the dock, each step heavier than the last. Every muscle in his body ached, and all he could think about was getting to Helvast Manor—stripping off the grime off him beneath scalding water, and collapsing into a bed that didn't smell like sand and sweat.

Elias stepped off behind him, still a shadow of himself, still thin and quiet, but walking.

Caelan watched him for a moment—watched the way his shoulders hunched just slightly at every noise, how his eyes darted to every movement, how he kept his arms tucked in close like he didn't quite believe he was allowed to take up space yet.

He knew that posture.

He'd worn it himself.

And God, did he hate that Elias knew what it meant now too.

The scars would never fade.

But at least they were out.

At least they'd *survived*.

Caelan's gaze drifted to Niev, who stood at the edge of the dock with her head tilted toward the sea, her hair tangled with wind, her eyes far away.

She hadn't spoken much since Zarenth burned.

Not about what she'd done.

Not about what it cost.

He didn't push. But he felt her restlessness like a second heartbeat beside his own.

They mounted the horses that had been waiting for them, a small cluster of mounts and a carriage sent ahead by Guinevere's staff. Niev rode in front, and Caelan behind her, his arms loosely wrapped around her waist, her warmth a constant reassurance as the forest thinned and the dirt path curled toward Helvast Manor.

The others followed in the carriage—Teagan, Ayda, Myria, and Elias—though Teagan had griped the whole time about being stuffed between everyone "like a very attractive sardine."

But the moment the gates appeared, carved and familiar and ivy-clad, Niev tensed in anticipation against him.

The horse cantered up the gravel path, hooves crunching rhythmically until the looming figure of the house rose behind the trees—grand and sun-dappled, exactly as they'd left it. The carriage rumbled behind them, wheels kicking dust into the morning light.

As soon as the horse stopped, Niev was already off—swinging down with practiced ease and hurrying to the carriage.

But as she tried to help her brother down—

"Stop fussing," Elias muttered, though his voice lacked any real bite as he batted her hand away.

"You're still as stubborn as ever," she shot back.

He rolled his eyes and stumbled into her shoulder, letting her catch him before he straightened. "And you're still as bossy."

"Thank you," she countered, taking it as the compliment it was *not*, and for a second they were just siblings again—bickering, breathing, *alive.*

Caelan smiled as he dismounted, watching them like a man trying to memorize sunlight.

The manor doors opened before they reached them. The housekeeper—Marna, if Caelan remembered right—gasped aloud and bolted back inside with a "*Madam Helvast!*" that echoed down the hall.

They didn't wait long.

Guinevere appeared a heartbeat later, robes trailing, white hair pinned in soft coils. Her eyes locked on Niev instantly, and Niev ran to her, arms wrapping tight around the older woman's frame.

"I have a surprise for you," Niev whispered, her voice thick.

And then Guinevere looked past her, and saw Elias.

One second the grand matriarch was standing in front of Caelan, the next she was falling to her knees in the gravel and gathering her grandson in her arms like she'd never let go again.

"My boy," she sobbed, pressing kisses to his hair, his cheek, his shoulder. "My sweet sweet boy."

Caelan didn't dare interrupt, even though he could see Elias fighting for breath as his grandmother crushed him.

Niev's eyes filled, her knuckles white at her sides as she fought the tears rising.

He moved to her silently and took her hand in his.

She squeezed back.

A door slammed upstairs.

"*Talia!*" Guinevere bellowed, voice still shaking with tears. "Talia, they're here!"

Scuffling followed.

Then a blur of chestnut curls and flying feet as the girl tore down the stairs and launched herself like a cannonball into Niev's ribs.

"*You're back!*" she screamed. "I *knew* you'd come back!"

Niev stumbled a step, laughing through the tears as she caught the girl mid-air. "You nearly broke my spine, you menace."

Everyone laughed—wet and exhausted and still a little stunned that the world hadn't ended.

Guinevere finally pulled herself to her feet, dabbing at her cheeks and snapping into command like she hadn't just crumbled in front of them.

"Get the cook!" she barked at a nearby servant. "Tell her I want a feast—no, *two!* My grandchildren have returned and we will *celebrate.*"

Talia tugged at Niev's sleeve. "The other kids are upstairs. They're with the tutor. I snuck out when I heard the carriage."

Niev narrowed her eyes and flicked her forehead. "You little traitor."

Talia giggled and ran off before she could be scolded again.

The old Helvast estate was quiet by the time they reached the upper floor.

Caelan leaned against the carved balustrade of the upper hall, watching as Niev quietly slipped her arm through Elias's and murmured something close to his ear.

He couldn't hear her words, but her smile said enough—hopeful, bright, and fragile in a way he rarely saw from her. She led her brother slowly down the corridor, past the open windows where sun spilled over the polished wood floors. Caelan followed at a distance, silent, shadowed by the knowledge of what this moment meant to her.

She thinks she's bringing him home.

He heard her voice drift faintly back through the still air.

"Remember when we used to race down this hallway? And you always cheated—pushed me into the wall?"

Elias didn't reply.

She chuckled softly. "You cracked your chin on the corner that one time. Mama nearly skinned you alive."

Still nothing. Elias gave her a tired half-smile—just a flicker—and even that seemed like it was too much effort for him.

Niev faltered. Her voice quieted.

By the time they reached Elias's old bedroom, Caelan had slowed to a respectful distance, lingering just far enough to keep watch. He saw her push the door open, fingers still wrapped gently around her brother's wrist. The air in that room felt different. Like it was frozen in time.

Elias blinked at the threshold. His face was unreadable. A thousand years too old for the twenty-four years he carried.

She stepped in with him, pointing to the window, the shelves, the spot where he used to pile his toy swords. Every word out of her mouth carried something raw, trembling on the edge of joy.

Caelan stayed at the door, silent. He watched as Elias's eyes flicked around the room, pausing on an old wooden shelf, a pale stain on the windowsill where sun once hit a favorite plant, a childhood sword tucked in the corner—wooden, worn, barely clinging to its handle.

He said nothing.

And then finally, after a long silence:

"...Thanks," Elias muttered. His voice was flat. Not cold. Just dulled. Numb.

Niev smiled, faint and hopeful. "Of course. I thought maybe it might feel familiar."

Elias just nodded. He sat down heavily on the edge of the bed and didn't look at her again.

Her smile wilted. She cleared her throat, voice softening further. "I'll let you rest."

She turned, her shoulders too stiff, her eyes locked on the hall ahead.

Caelan's heart ached as he watched her walk away. She'd burned down an empire for him. Torn the sky apart. And he couldn't even lift a smile for her.

He didn't blame Elias. He just wanted to take the hollow in Niev's chest and carry it for her.

He'd lived that hollow silence. Joy took time when all you'd known was survival.

Caelan waited a beat before following her down the hall, toward her room at the far end. She stepped inside, fingers fumbling with the door behind her—only to nearly jump when she realized he was slipping in after her.

Her eyebrows shot up, scandalized.

"What are you *doing?*" she hissed, peeking out into the hallway before slamming the door shut behind him. "You can't just—*Caelan,* this is my *grandmother's house!* Do you want her to *skin me alive* for having a boy in here?!"

He blinked at her.

Once.

Twice.

"...Did you just call me a *boy?*"

"That's not the point!" she whisper-yelled, waving her arms. "This is *Thornmere,* not Breyvia! Strange men don't just *waltz* into a single woman's room without a chaperone—*especially* not under her grandmother's roof!"

"Niev," Caelan stared at her like she'd grown an extra head. "You literally set a prison on fire *as a dragon* three days ago."

She crossed her arms. "That's entirely unrelated."

"You dragged me into your bed, in your own apartment. Not to mention, in the cabin of that bloody ship," he murmured, voice dropping low, heat curling around every word. "And now you're acting scandalized?"

"Lower your goddamn voice!" She swallowed. "And I didn't *drag* you—"

He took a slow step forward. "You've got a body count in the dozens, a glare that terrifies grown men, and *this* is the moment you decide to uphold traditional modesty?"

Her chin lifted. "It's about *respect,* Galbraith."

Caelan's mouth curved. He stepped closer.

"So let me get this straight..." he said slowly, dipping his head, letting his breath brush across her cheek. "You're worried about what people think I'll do to you?"

Her throat bobbed. "That's not what I—"

He crowded her gently, fingers brushing along her waist. "Tell me," he murmured, sliding one hand to the small of her back, "what *exactly* do you think I'll do, Tigress?"

She opened her mouth but no sound came out. Caelan bent, caught the back of her thigh, and lifted, just enough to guide her backward onto the bed. She landed with a breathless huff, blinking up at him, her hair spilling across the blanket like a siren's lure.

"*You really can't be in here,*" she said, breath shaky.

"And yet..." Caelan smirked, lowering himself slowly, one knee pressing into the mattress as he hovered halfway over her, "...you closed the door anyway."

She glared up at him, cheeks flushing. "I *hate* you."

He dipped his head, kissed the corner of her mouth. "Liar."

Her lips parted, but she didn't answer. Because Niev's hands fisted in his shirt as she pulled him down, her mouth finding his with that same fevered ache. The world around them faded beneath the gravity of their bodies.

Caelan kissed her deeper, slower now. His hand slipped beneath the soft fabric of her shirt, fingertips grazing across the curve of her hip. She gasped against his mouth, her nails digging into his back, and he felt himself unraveling again.

She was heat, hunger, and wilderness beneath him.

But something shifted. Barely perceptible at first.

Her mouth slowed. Her breath hitched but not from desire.

Her fingers curled tighter, but no longer in want.

Caelan froze, pulling back just enough to see her face in the silver wash of moonlight bleeding through the open tent flap. Her eyes weren't on him. They were somewhere else entirely. Far away.

"Hey." His voice was low, the word soft against the shell of her ear. "Talk to me."

She blinked and turned toward him, eyes wide. Like a deer caught in lantern light.

He eased off her gently, slipping out from between her legs and settling beside her on the narrow cot, one arm beneath his head. He didn't say anything again. Just reached over and took her hand.

For a moment, she stayed quiet.

Then she let out a long breath and turned her head toward him on the pillow. Her lips were still swollen from their kiss. Her hair tangled and he longed to run his fingers through it. But it was her eyes that made his heart pull tight. They were full of storm.

"I thought..." she started, then shook her head, frustrated. "I thought saving Elias would mean I'd *have* him again. My brother. Like it would all... reset or something. That after everything, he'd look at me and I'd *know* him again."

Caelan didn't interrupt.

She swallowed hard. "I get it. I do. He's been to hell and back. He doesn't owe me anything. But it's just..." Her voice cracked slightly. "It's awkward. Every word. Every silence. He feels like a stranger, and I *hate* that."

Caelan turned to face her fully, brushing a curl off her cheek. His chest ached at the admission, at the guilt lining her voice. "It's okay," he said softly.

Niev didn't reply, but her fingers closed tighter around his.

He inhaled slowly, thinking. "When I got out of Zarenth, I didn't know how to talk to anyone. Everything felt... wrong. Too loud. Too *clean*. I didn't trust anyone's kindness because I didn't remember what kindness felt like."

She blinked at him.

He gave her a faint, tired smile. "I forgot how to be a person. I didn't know how to let people in again without it feeling like a violation."

The wind shifted outside, carrying the scent of moss and early rain.

"I'm not saying it's the same," Caelan added. "But if he's anything like I was... he's still waiting to wake up and find himself back in a cell. Still learning how to breathe air that doesn't reek of blood."

Her throat bobbed.

"It's not that he doesn't want to reach for you," he murmured. "It's probably that he doesn't know how to...yet."

Silence settled between them. She stared at the ceiling for a while. Then rolled onto her side and curled against him again, resting her cheek against his chest. Her breath was softer now. Less jagged.

"I just miss him," she whispered.

He held her tighter. "I know."

Caelan brushed his thumb over her cheek, about to say something— maybe something soft, maybe something stupid—

When the door *slammed* open.

They both jolted upright like they'd been caught committing a crime.

Standing in the doorway, framed by the dim hallway light and a thundercloud of suspicion, was Guinevere Helvast. Arms crossed. Back straight. Eyes narrowed in the precise way that said she'd already seen everything, measured it, and was prepared to pass sentence.

Caelan froze, his hands still hovering around Niev's waist. Niev scrambled back, cheeks flaming, hair a tangled mess as she ducked her head and cleared her throat.

Guinevere's eyes didn't leave him.

"I don't know how things are done where *you're* from, Mr. Galbraith," she began slowly, her voice icy and imperious as a queen, "but in Thornmere—*in my house*—men do not linger in an *unmarried woman's room*, alone, *at night*, on her *bed.*"

Caelan opened his mouth. Closed it again.

Niev bit her lip to stifle a laugh, the sound escaping in a muffled cough as she hunched her shoulders and looked everywhere but at her grandmother.

"I was just—uh—I mean, we were just—" Caelan cleared his throat. "I was making sure she was okay."

Guinevere's eyes sharpened.

"Is that what they call it these days?" she said, lifting one skeptical silver brow.

Caelan went bright red. "Nothing happened."

Niev snorted.

He looked at her, his eyes full of lethal betrayal. "*Nothing happened.*"

"Mm-hmm." Guinevere didn't blink. She simply walked to the door, grabbed the handle with perfect, deliberate grace, and opened it wider. "You have a perfectly clean and acceptable room across the hall, should you require rest." Her voice dropped just enough to be sharp. "*Alone.*"

Caelan hesitated. Looked at Niev, who buried her face in the crook of her shoulder, shaking with silent laughter. And that sealed his fate.

He sighed and stood. "Of course. I—thank you. For the room. I'll just…"

He gestured vaguely.

Guinevere gestured back—directly toward the hall.

He walked past her with as much dignity as he could muster, though he could feel her eyes on the back of his neck like twin daggers.

And just before the door shut behind him, he heard Guinevere murmur, "At least he has the decency to look ashamed."

Then the door clicked closed.

And Caelan was left in the hallway, barefoot, flushed, and absolutely certain of two things.

One: Guinevere Helvast terrified him more than any battlefield.

Two: He was hopelessly, completely, and irrevocably in love with her granddaughter.

51.
Niev

Niev took a moment just outside the dining room, pressing her palm lightly against the smooth wood of the door. Steam still clung to her skin from the long, glorious shower she'd just taken. Her hair—finally returned to its natural glossy brown—fell in a damp curtain down her back, and her face was flushed from the heat of the fire. She breathed in, feeling the slight ache of over-scrubbed muscles. Despite the comforting warmth of being clean again, there was an odd tension in her belly, a twisting mix of relief and nerves.

She smoothed a hand down the front of her dress and pushed the door open. Laughter and chatter spilled out, warm as the candlelight that lit the long table. A dozen faces turned toward her—children and staff dotted along the left side, her loyal crew interspersed on the right, and at the head of the table sat Elias, right beside Guinevere.

Ayda sat on his other side, leaning in to murmur something that made her brother's eyes flicker with shy appreciation. Caelan caught Niev's gaze from his seat a few chairs down and gave her a crooked smile that set her pulse thrumming.

"Ah, there she is," Guinevere said, bright with affection. She gestured to the empty seat between herself and Caelan. "Come, Sera. Dinner's nearly begun, and Talia might actually burst if you make her wait any longer."

Niev didn't bristle at the sound of her real name. Everyone else had taken to calling her "Niev," but Guinevere clung stubbornly to that piece of her old life. It jarred her at first. But now, it was just one more reminder that she belonged here, no matter what she called herself.

A smattering of giggles erupted from the children, and Talia herself attempted a remarkably indignant scowl. Niev slipped into her seat, exchanging a quick glance with Elias—he looked paler than usual, though that could be the lamplight. Or perhaps it was the sheer exhaustion lining his face.

"How are you feeling?" she asked him softly, leaning forward.

He gave a tight nod, the barest hint of a smile ghosting across his lips. "I'm...here," he said. His voice was low, but at least it wasn't absent. Niev caught the way he swallowed, like the myriad sights and smells—the bustling staff, the endless candleglow—were too big, too bright for him.

He's still getting used to it, she reminded herself.

A sudden clatter of serving dishes near the hallway made the door slam shut with a sharp crack. Elias flinched—a slight jerk of his shoulders and a flick of panic in his eyes. Even Ayda's reassuring hand on his arm made him tense briefly.

Niev's heart squeezed in her chest. Gently, she placed a piece of bread on his plate, trying not to hover but wanting him to know he was safe here. She caught Ayda's eye, and the witch gave her a small nod, as if to say she'd noticed too.

"Elias dear," Guinevere said, softening her voice. "It might help to remember that once upon a time, *you* were the terror slamming doors around this house. Don't think I've forgotten your habit of riding the banister down the grand staircase either."

Niev groaned. "Grandmother..."

But her grandmother pressed on, lifting her chin in that regal way she had. "He and Sera were nightmares together, practically unstoppable." She turned to Caelan, who looked far too intrigued. "I recall a certain summer when they decided to test Elias's new slingshot on my prized rosebushes—said they needed to *improve their aim*."

A ripple of laughter circled the table. Teagan, perched between a pair of housemaids, snorted. "When she came to *us*, Niev's aim was less than impressive. So I'm guessing your rosebushes survived."

"Oh, they survived all right. Her aim was abysmal," Guinevere pointed out wryly.

"That didn't stop her from causing havoc," Elias said, a faint hint of a grin breaking through. "In fact, she missed the rosebushes entirely and ended up clocking our grandfather. Left a welt on his forehead the size of a silver coin."

Niev groaned and dropped her face into her hands. "That was *one* time," she muttered, voice muffled by her palms, while the table erupted in fresh laughter.

"Besides, It's not like your aim was any better," she looked pointedly at her brother. "You almost took the neighbor's eye out."

Elias shrugged innocently.

Teagan shook his head, eyes dancing with amusement. "Remind me never to stand too close when you two start a shooting contest."

A chorus of chuckles swept around the table, and Niev turned bright red. Caelan, of course, leaned closer to her, a gleam in his eye, clearly delighted with each embarrassing new detail. Her chest warmed at the sight.

"Don't encourage her," she muttered under her breath, earning an unrepentant look from her grandmother.

Guinevere spread her hands as if she'd only just begun. "There was also that time they scaled the orchard fence at night. Came back covered head to toe in mud and insisted it was all in the name of discovery.' To this day, I don't know what they were testing—only that they left footprints all over the library while trying to hide."

Niev closed her eyes, cheeks burning. "Please, can we not—"

"And let's not forget," Guinevere continued loudly, "the time they decided the old clock tower was haunted and attempted an *exorcism*, which involved—"

"Oh no," Niev mumbled, burying her face in her palms. Caelan, of course, looked utterly delighted by her humiliation, resting his chin on his hand and leaning in to hear more.

"I remember that," Elias said, his voice carrying a little more strength now. He sat straighter, though his posture still hinted at caution. One of the younger children, perched beside Talia, reached for his sleeve in curiosity, and Elias instinctively pulled back, uncertain. Then, noticing the child's confused blink, he forced a tentative smile and let the little one tug him closer.

Niev watched the tension ripple through him, noticed the tremor in his shoulders as he fought not to recoil from friendly contact. A pang cut through her chest. But at the same time, seeing him try—however small the step—felt like a spark of hope.

Guinevere beamed, delighted to see him engaging, even if only for a moment. "Yes, you were quite convinced spirits needed coaxing out with a broom and an old fishing net. And you managed to drop both on my poor groundskeeper."

A soft, collective laugh followed. Elias's lips twitched, and then, finally, a faint, genuine smile. It was like sunrise breaking over his face, subdued but real.

Niev exhaled a breath she hadn't realized she'd been holding. She reached for her glass, ignoring the burning in her cheeks as Caelan angled closer with a smirk. "So, you've always been an absolute menace. I see that hasn't changed."

"You're one to talk," Niev sniffed, though her tone was warm.

The rest of dinner passed in a patchwork of gentle teasing and stories—some about Elias, some about Niev, some from the crew's latest escapades. Servants flitted around with trays of roast vegetables, steaming potatoes, fresh bread, and honey-sweet pastries. Every so often, Elias would stiffen at a sudden movement or pull back when someone tried to top off his drink without warning. But each time, someone—Ayda, Guinevere, or Niev—calmly eased him back into the moment.

By the time the plates were cleared, he looked exhausted but...lighter, somehow. There was still strain around his eyes, but that fleeting smile lingered, and Niev clung to it like a promise of better days.

When Guinevere finally called for dessert, Elias ran a hand over his face, taking in the swirl of conversation and lamplight with an odd reverence. As if even the simple act of sharing a meal felt startlingly unreal.

And when he glanced at Niev with that small, tentative smile again, her heart soared.

✳ ✳ ✳

As dinner stretched into late evening, the chatter around the long table mellowed; a few of the younger children began nodding off in their chairs. Guinevere stood, smoothing her skirts and fixing the assembled little ones with a firm, grandmotherly look.

"All right, my darlings, that's enough excitement for one day. Off to bed with you now."

A chorus of groans rose from the children and for a moment they tried bargaining for just a bit more time. But under Guinevere's practiced glare, they grudgingly gathered their things, grumbling halfhearted goodnights. The staff ushered them gently out, and once the younger ones had disappeared through the double doors, the mood in the dining room shifted. The warmth of candlelight remained, but the buzz of childish laughter faded into something a little more adult, a little more weighted with the complexities of the world.

Niev caught Elias's eye—he still looked tense, but at least he hadn't flinched in a while. A near-silence settled, broken only by the clink of silverware being gathered from the table.

She exhaled slowly, re-centering her thoughts. "Grandmother," she started, though her gaze flickered between Guinevere and Caelan, "I've been thinking. Now that Eli is out of Zarenth...we can finally hunt down the person who did this to us—" She paused, voice trembling with renewed fervor.

Elias lowered his gaze, expression guarded.

Niev forged on, pushing the words out in a rush. "We can start in Breyvia—someone there must know which slaver rings were operating back then. Then we can use those Librarium robes Myria sewed for me ages ago to get into Arenthia's archives. The Librarium keeps records of almost everything that happens in the empire. And Elias"—she leaned toward him, her pulse quickening—"you could stay here in Thornmere for a bit while you recover. Dig through local intel, check old Helvast contacts. The Helvast name still carries weight. Between that and the librarians' notes, we can figure out *who* this Don person really is, *why* he wanted us dead—"

"Sera," Elias said softly, trying to slip a word in.

She didn't hear him, too focused on the momentum of her plan. "And once we figure it out, we can hunt them down. And make them *pay*—"

"Sera," Elias said again, a bit louder, his brow creasing.

But she kept going, unstoppable in her fervor. "At this point, we've fought worse. Hell, we brought down the biggest slave camp in Zarenth, why not—"

His voice snapped through the room like thunder. "Sera!"

She froze. The force behind the single word brought every head around the table up. Guinevere's hand stalled in midair where she'd been reaching for her teacup. Myria and Teagan exchanged wary glances.

Elias exhaled, jaw set. "I won't be a part of this."

It took a moment for his meaning to register in Niev's mind. She blinked at him, certain she'd misheard. "What... what do you mean?" Her tone wavered, swinging between confusion and a rising edge. "You don't want to find out who did this? Who got our parents killed and destroyed our lives?"

Elias shook his head, eyes flicking away, but not before Niev caught the flash of conflict in them. "No."

It felt like the room was suddenly airless, the hush so absolute that Teagan coughed just to slice through the tension. Niev's chest tightened. "So you're content to sit here, doing nothing—?"

"Niev," Caelan tried gently, "Let's maybe think about—"

"I want to move on," Elias said tersely, but his gaze never left Niev's. "There's no point in dredging all of it back up."

"No point..." she echoed, her voice scaling higher in disbelief. "That's our family, our childhood—! We were *sold* like cattle. Does that not matter to you?"

"Of course it matters!" Elias said, suddenly sharper. His shoulders hitched, and he forced them back down. "But that's all in the past. We can't change it. We can't bring them back."

Niev inhaled. "So you're willing to just *accept* it? Accept that someone got us imprisoned, got them killed, and you don't even want to know who or why? You don't want payback?"

Elias pressed his lips together. She saw the pulse beating at his temple, his left hand clenched so tightly his knuckles were white. "It's *over*," he said, voice barely above a hiss. "I survived long enough to see you again, and I'm done chasing ghosts."

"Nothing's *over*!" Niev snapped, words trembling with frustration. "That person is still out there. You'd let them walk free? Let them do it to someone else?"

In the corner of her vision, Myria opened her mouth, no doubt intending to calm them down, but the siblings' voices were escalating too quickly.

"Sera," Elias growled, "I said *no*. Stop pushing—"

She slammed a hand on the table, rattling the empty plates. "So you're just going to *sit* there and accept your fate like a *coward*?"

He shot to his feet, face twisted with an anger she'd never seen before. His blue eyes suddenly turned bright gold as *something snapped*.

It wasn't a sound, not one the others could hear—but Niev felt it. Like pressure exploding inward. A force slamming into her skull.

She gasped as if struck. Her hands flew to her temples, body lurching back in her chair as her breath hitched.

Then she *screamed*.

The room erupted into chaos, but all she knew was the feeling of *Elias inside her head*. Not just a whisper or a touch—*inside*. His consciousness crashed into hers like a tidal wave, claws dragging through her thoughts, her emotions. Her own senses short-circuited—flashes of wolves snarling, hawks diving, a serpent coiled in burning sand. And behind it all—*him*, Elias, furious and frantic and *not himself*.

She'd always known Elias was a spiritcaster who could send his consciousness into nearby animals, seeing, hearing, and feeling through them. He could do it to her when she was in her animal form. They'd done it before as children, to train, or heighten his own senses willingly. But never, *never* had he been able to force himself into her mind, especially not in her human form.

How much power had he kept pent up those last ten years?

Niev choked on a breath, eyes wide with panic as she collapsed to the floor, limbs twitching. She felt like her mind was being *peeled open*.

"Elias, *stop!*" Myria's voice cut through, panicked.

"What are you—what the hell are you doing?!" Teagan shouted, stumbling toward him.

But Elias didn't hear them.

He stood rigid, face twisted in fury, *eyes glowing* with golden sigils that pulsed like brands across his irises. The power that had slept for ten years now flooded out of him—wild, furious, unchecked.

"You think you're so righteous?" he spat down at her, his voice ragged and distant. "You think slaughtering your way through the empire makes you better than me? You don't know what I've lived through. What I've had to *survive*. You're just some bloodthirsty *bitch* who spat on everything our parents taught us!" he snarled. "Look at you—You think they'd be proud of that?"

Niev writhed, tears streaming, mouth open in a silent scream. Her lungs locked as the invasion overwhelmed her.

But her brother could not be reasoned with.

Until Caelan moved, *slamming* his hand down on the table with a crack like thunder.

"*Elias, STOP!*"

The sound jolted through the room like a whipcrack of command, the energy breaking like shattered glass.

Elias staggered backward as if struck. The golden light in his eyes flickered—then extinguished. His breath came in short, panicked gasps, and he blinked like he was waking from a nightmare.

Niev curled on the floor, coughing violently, her face soaked with tears and sweat. Her hands clutched her skull like it might split open.

Elias looked down at her and went deathly still.

"Oh, God," he whispered, horror dawning in his expression. "Sera..."

She raised her head slowly. Her eyes were red-rimmed and gleaming, her face pale, but *expression* held nothing but pure and unyielding betrayal.

"This..." Her voice shook, jagged and raw. "This 'bloodthirsty bitch' is the reason you're breathing free air."

The silence was deafening.

"I tore down Zarenth the second I thought you were still alive," she rasped. "But you—" her voice cracked, trembling with rage and heartbreak, "you knew I wasn't dead when they dragged me away. You *watched* them take me. What did you do to get me back?"

Her eyes locked with his like steel. "*Nothing.*"

Elias's face crumpled. "Sera—I didn't—I wasn't—"

"You just accepted your fate like the spineless coward you are."

Guinevere stood, her voice sharp with fury. "That's enough! Both of you!"

But Niev was already pushing herself off the floor, swaying unsteadily as Caelan moved to steady her. She didn't let him.

She took one last look at her brother, her voice a whisper laced with venom and sorrow.

"You got your freedom, Elias. Try not to waste it like you did mine."

"Niev—" came Caelan's quiet plea, but she was already on her feet, whirling away. Her eyes burned, her hands shook, and the blood in her ears roared so loudly she barely registered the frantic hush of voices around the table.

She wrenched open the dining room door—then slammed it behind her with enough force to echo through the house.

Niev took the stairs two at a time, her vision tunneling with each stomp of her boots. Rage churned in her veins, but it wasn't just fury anymore—it was *shame*, *violation*, and the crackling aftershock of power forced into her mind like an open wound. Her heartbeat throbbed at her temples, too loud, too fast. At the top of the landing, she yanked open her bedroom door and slammed it shut with a sound like thunder, dust cascading from the rafters.

The walls felt like they were closing in. The candlelit room, once serene, now pressed down on her like a trap. She couldn't stop pacing, couldn't breathe without tasting the remnants of Elias in her mind—his fury, his chaos, the echoes of beasts clawing against her thoughts.

She pressed her palms to her skull and *screamed*.

How could he *do that* to her?

After everything—after she burned down half of Zarenth to find him, after she bled for him, killed for him—he had the gall to hurl her pain back at her and then *invade her mind* as if she were nothing.

She spun, her body taut with wrath, and struck the wall with her fist. A sickening crunch of knuckle against plaster echoed as white dust and blood flew. Her skin split. She welcomed the pain—*real* pain. Hers.

She cradled her injured hand against her chest, breath ragged. The fury in her began to wane, cooled not by reason, but exhaustion. Her mind felt scraped raw, nerves frayed from Elias's psychic touch. He hadn't meant to do it—*had he?*—but that didn't matter. He *had*. And he hadn't even stopped until Caelan's voice snapped him out of it.

A soft knock sounded at the door. She stiffened instantly.

"I'm not in the mood for a lecture," she muttered, not bothering to mask the bitterness in her voice.

The door opened anyway, revealing her grandmother's silver-white hair and concerned eyes. Guinevere shut the door behind her gently, crossing to the bed. She didn't speak immediately, just sat down beside her granddaughter and regarded Niev with a weary sort of compassion.

"You're bleeding," Guinevere said softly, reaching for Niev's injured hand. Niev snatched it away, still too raw to accept help.

"I'm fine," Niev snapped, though her voice wavered at the edges.

"You're *not*," Guinevere said gently.

The words dropped like stones in the quiet room.

"I couldn't breathe," she said after a long moment, her voice hoarse. "I could feel him inside my head. I—I couldn't push him out."

"I know," Guinevere said. Her voice trembled just slightly. "We all saw it."

Shame rippled through Niev like acid. "I don't think he even realized. Not until Caelan shouted. God. If he hadn't—" She broke off, her breath catching. "What if I hadn't gotten him out?"

"You would have," Guinevere said with quiet certainty. "But Caelan was right to intervene. And your brother..." She sighed. "He lost control of something he's been denying for far too long. That doesn't excuse it. But it should give you enough perspective to understand."

Niev sank down onto the edge of the bed like her legs had given out. Her fist throbbed in time with her heart.

"How can I ever trust him again?" she whispered.

A sigh left Guinevere's lips as she folded her hands in her lap. "When your father died," she asked, her voice low. "It destroyed me. I couldn't bear the grief. I refused to accept what had happened and cursed the God who allowed it. I raged for *years*—convinced that if I stayed angry enough, I'd never really have to face the fact that my Feodor and his children had died."

She paused, her expression twisting with a distant sorrow. "I travelled all the way to Arenthia to confront Adrianna. I screamed at her. Blamed her. Accused her of letting you all die under her watch."

Niev blinked, momentarily startled out of her own misery. She'd never heard that story before—never realized how deep and vicious her grandmother's grief had been.

Guinevere's gaze flicked down to the blood on Niev's knuckles. "But at the end of the day, no amount of rage could bring back my son. Couldn't bring back the two of you." Her voice went quiet. "I understand your anger, Sera. It's kept you alive all these years. And that woman who saved you in Breyvia, she taught you how to wield your fury like a blade."

Niev swallowed, her throat tight.

"But Elias was put in a place designed to break him every single day," Guinevere said gently. "He survived by shutting out the world, by learning not to fight. Because if he fought, they would have crushed him. That was *his* reality."

Niev closed her eyes. She could still picture her brother's haunted face, the near-flinches at sudden noises, the anger that finally burst out when she accused him of being a coward.

"It's going to take time for the two of you to see eye to eye," Guinevere said, resting a hand lightly on Niev's shoulder. "You're both scarred from your experiences. But you're the only family you have left. I'm not saying you're wrong for raging at the injustice of it all. Nor is he wrong for wanting peace at any cost. You're just two people who coped in opposite ways, and now you have to find common ground again. Or at least...learn to accept each other's differences."

A shaky breath shuddered out of Niev. The sting in her hand was a dull throb now, matched by the ache in her chest. She swiped her uninjured hand across her eyes to banish the traitorous tears. "He said they would be *ashamed* of me," she said, voice cracking.

Guinevere's grip tightened, not in reproach, but in reassurance. "He's hurting, child. You both are. But if your parents could see you now, they'd feel nothing but pride in how fiercely you've fought to stay alive."

"I just wanted him to *fight* for once," Niev murmured. "To stop hiding."

"And he did," Guinevere replied. "In the worst possible way. But he did."

Niev let out a choked laugh, short and bitter. "That's one way to put it."

Silence stretched between them, broken only by the murmurs of late-night staff in distant corridors. Slowly, Guinevere eased Niev's injured hand toward her lap, examining the damage. Niev let her, too drained to resist.

"You'll need bandages for this," her grandmother murmured, rising to retrieve a small medical kit from the bedside table.

Niev pressed her free hand over her face, exhaling shakily. Everything in her felt raw—guilt twisting around anger, heartbreak tangling with the memory of her brother's bitter voice. But Guinevere's steady presence kept her grounded, a reminder she was not alone, no matter how divided she and Elias felt.

After a moment, Niev dropped her hand and looked up. The old woman dabbed gingerly at the split knuckles, her breath soft with concentration. Niev allowed it, grateful for something tangible to focus on.

Her grandmother's words echoed in her head.

"I'm sorry," she whispered, not entirely sure for what—slamming doors, lashing out, letting vengeance consume her. Possibly for all of it.

Guinevere simply patted Niev's arm once the bandage was tied in place. "You have a right to your anger, dear. Just make sure it doesn't consume you."

And with that, she pressed a gentle kiss to her granddaughter's hair, then stood. Niev watched her go, chest heavy. She didn't have answers tonight—maybe she wouldn't for a long while—but at least she knew she wasn't alone in the ache that raged behind her eyes.

As the door clicked softly shut, Niev lay back on the bed. The quiet felt uneasy, but Guinevere's words kindled something small and cautious in her, a reminder that she and Elias were different but they had each other, and that would have to be enough to start again.

52.
Caelan

Caelan stood in the flickering glow of the dining-room lanterns, his hands braced hard on the back of a chair. The echoes of what had just happened—the door slamming, Niev's choking gasps, Elias's voice like venom made flesh, still reverberated through the floorboards and the marrow of his bones.

Guinevere had gone after Niev. Caelan had wanted to do the same, but part of him hadn't trusted himself not to drag Elias out into the street by the collar.

Across from him, Elias stood frozen. His chest rose and fell in uneven bursts, sweat beading at his brow. The gold sigils in his eyes had faded but Caelan could still feel the residue of power lingering in the air. Like smoke after a lightning strike. Like a storm that hadn't finished breaking.

Ayda lingered near his shoulder, arms folded tightly across her chest. Teagan and Myria had drawn back toward the sideboard, casting wary glances at Elias as if unsure whether he might lash out again—*whether he could control it if he did.*

Caelan's own pulse hadn't settled. He'd seen plenty of arguments. He'd watched Niev threaten people with knives and fire. But he'd never seen her *afraid* until tonight.

She hadn't run from his words.

She'd run from what he *did to her mind.*

Caelan stepped forward slowly, measured, as if approaching a wounded animal.

"Look," he said quietly, every syllable deliberate, "I know that didn't go how you wanted. But before you judge her too quickly, there's something you need to understand."

Elias didn't look at him. His fists were still clenched at his sides, nails dug into his palms. Caelan could see a faint tremor in his shoulders.

Caelan continued gently, "You have no idea how single-minded she's been about getting you out of Zarenth. Ever since she learned you were alive, she hasn't been able to sleep, or even breathe properly, everything she did revolved around rescuing you. It...it tore her up, thinking she'd missed those ten years with you. Thinking maybe if she'd known sooner, she could've saved you sooner. It crushed her."

A flicker of something—guilt, pain—crossed Elias's face. He exhaled shakily, but still said nothing.

Caelan lowered himself into the chair across from Elias. "She is furious," he agreed, voice careful. "But that fury isn't about causing pain for its own sake. Niev's rage is... protective. She hates injustice with a passion. She'll throw herself in front of whatever monster she sees threatening the people she cares about. And yeah, sometimes that means she runs hot. She can be brutal. She's learned how to survive by hitting first, hitting hardest—but it's never without purpose."

A bitter laugh escaped Elias. "And in the process, she's turning into the kind of monster she claims to hate." His voice wavered between anger and a hollow sort of resignation. "I'm not saying it's the same as what our captors did, but I saw what she did in Zarenth and—"

"Yes, and you *invaded* her mind," Caelan continued, voice harder now. "She was *screaming*, Elias. You didn't hear her because you were too wrapped up in your own pain, but *we did*."

Elias flinched, just slightly, but it was the first break in his armor.

"You say she's turned into a monster," Caelan went on, "but she didn't just burn that camp down. She freed the slaves first. And carried you out of it, remember?"

Myria stepped forward, her posture calm but her gaze direct. "Elias, the Niev you're seeing now is the product of ten years of heartbreak, survival, and guilt. She didn't become this overnight. You don't have to agree with everything she does. But don't dismiss her just because she learned to survive differently than you."

Elias's shoulders stiffened. Shame flickered over his face, or maybe it was regret—Caelan couldn't be sure. But his words had been spat in anger, and they both knew it.

"Look mate," Teagan folded his arms across his chest. "I've known that woman for a decade. I've seen her break bones and burn bridges, she's the scariest person I've ever met, and I mean that in the best possible way," he said with a rueful grin.

Caelan let out a small, humorless laugh. "Trust me, you don't want her on your bad side. But if she's got your back? Hell, that's the safest place in the world to be."

Elias exhaled, pressing a trembling hand to his forehead. "I just…" He paused for a long moment, and the hush weighed heavy in the room. "I want to forget everything that happened. I don't…have it in me to keep digging into the past. I'm so tired."

Myria spoke up gently, stepping forward. "Nobody's saying you have to do anything you're not ready for. We all understand you've been through hell. Your sister knows it too, she does. But Niev's been burning for answers for a decade. That rage is her way of staying alive. She's not trying to hurt you. She's trying to make things right. However she defines that."

Ayda nodded. "She's been telling herself for ten years that if she only fought hard enough, if she just *pushed* harder, she could find you. She wouldn't rest until she did. And now that you're here, she wants to keep pushing—this time for whoever took your parents from you both." Her voice went softer. "It's her way of coping. It's not necessarily right or wrong. Just… different."

Elias kept his head down, knuckles still pressed against his brow. Caelan could practically feel the swirl of conflict roiling under those carefully controlled features. It was the same chaos he'd grappled with in the beginning, the urge to bury everything in a shallow grave, to lie still and breathe free air without stirring up more bloodshed, but also the gnawing knowledge that wrongs had never been righted.

"I don't know if I can be part of that," Elias whispered finally. He looked up, gaze shifting from Ayda to Teagan to Myria, and finally settling on Caelan. "I really don't."

Caelan considered him for a moment, weighing the next words carefully. "That's okay," he said quietly. "Nobody here wants to force you into a war you can't fight. We've all seen enough battle. But if Niev charges forward, are you going to condemn her for it? Or stand back and let her chase ghosts alone?"

"I...I don't know," Elias said, voice raw. "I don't want her running off on a crusade that destroys her, and I don't want to be dragged in either. I don't have a better answer for you than that. Not yet."

Teagan pinched the bridge of his nose. "Look, I'm not the best with delicate talk," he said bluntly. "But I've seen Niev do some crazy things for the sake of others. She's a savage in a fight, yeah. But if the world was all kindness and light, she wouldn't feel the need to bare her teeth. The fact that you're alive right now, free, is partly because she's *that* kind of woman."

The words hung in the air, Caelan could see each one settling on Elias's shoulders like a weight he couldn't quite shrug off. He nodded, just once, a small concession.

Ayda gave Elias's arm a gentle squeeze, though he seemed too lost in his own turmoil to flinch at her touch. "It's not just about revenge, you know," she said softly, "It's about answers. She's convinced that Don Arin Alvania—" she hesitated, glancing around as if she might be treading on sensitive ground, "—the man who sold you both to those slavers might be the key to understanding what really happened to your family. She wants to know *why* a complete stranger tore your lives apart."

As the words left her lips, Caelan noticed Elias go perfectly, horribly still. His spine went rigid, his head snapping up.

"Wait," he whispered, tone laced with alarm. "What—what did you say?"

Ayda blinked, caught off guard by the abrupt change in his demeanor. "I said... she wants answers," she repeated slowly.

"No!" Elias said impatiently. "The name—what is the name you just said?"

"Don Arin Alvania." Ayda replied slowly, looking at the others in confusion.

Then, seeing the fear sparking in Elias's eyes, her voice wavered. "It was the name signed off in that ledger Niev found—" She stopped herself, drawing back as Elias jerked away from her grip. The motion made the lantern light bob, shadows dancing erratically across the walls.

His sudden shift was palpable, a tension that made even Teagan stand up straighter, and Myria step forward as though preparing to intervene. Caelan's heart picked up speed.

"Show me," Elias demanded, voice threaded with near-panic. It was the tone of someone who'd seen a ghost. "Show me the name."

Ayda's mouth opened, but no sound came out for a moment. She cast an uncertain look at Caelan, who gave a minute nod. Then, swallowing hard, she backed away from Elias. "All right," she said, voice unsteady. "I—I have the ledger upstairs, in my room. Just... let me go get it."

She turned to leave, but Elias shadowed her immediately, following so close that Caelan could see the nerves tighten in Ayda's shoulders. She glanced back over her shoulder, clearly unsettled by Elias's urgent proximity. Teagan and Myria exchanged looks that said, *What in the world is going on?* before trailing after them.

Ayda led them up the winding stairway, her steps hurried as though trying to outrun Elias's intensity. He kept on her heels, eyes fever-bright, jaw set in a tense line that made Caelan's pulse thrum with unease. When they reached her small guest chamber, Ayda slipped inside first and hurried to rummage through her belongings. Moments later, she emerged clutching the battered ledger.

"I'm—trying to find the page," she stammered, flipping through yellowed sheets filled with transaction records and coded references. Her hands shook, and Elias's presence loomed so close that she nearly fumbled the book. "Just...give me a second," she whispered.

But Elias was already leaning in, his eyes fixed on those pages like a starving man catching scent of food. Caelan watched from the threshold, Teagan and Myria hovering behind him, a collective dread coiling in the pit of his stomach.

He could almost hear Elias's heartbeat in the hush. The man was trembling with contained urgency, his breath coming in quick bursts. No one else spoke. Teagan had gone tense and watchful, ready to step in if Elias lost control.

Finally, Ayda found the line she sought. She turned the ledger so Elias could see the neat columns of data, her finger tracing down until it landed on the name:

Don Arin Alvania.

"There," she whispered.

Elias's gaze locked on the words as though they'd jump off the page at him. His reaction was immediate and severe. His eyes went wild with recognition, color draining from his face. The ledger threatened to slip from his grasp as he all but snatched it from Ayda's hands, scanning every inch of the surrounding text with desperate intensity.

"Dear God Almighty," he breathed, voice wavering on an edge that terrified Caelan more than any anger.

53.
Niev

Niev sat on the edge of her bed, staring at the bandage now wrapped around her split knuckles. Her grandmother had left only a few moments ago, but Guinevere's words still lingered in the hush of the room: You have a right to your anger, just don't let it consume you.

She exhaled a long, trembling breath. She could still feel the echo of Elias's accusations, the white-hot fury that had blazed between them. The guilt gnawed at her—guilt for calling him a coward, for dismissing his pain. He was her twin, the only other living piece of the family they'd lost, and she'd lashed out with the same venom they both abhorred.

I have to fix this, she told herself, heart pounding.

Rising to her feet, Niev flexed her sore hand and winced at the flare of pain. She'd lived with broken bones and deeper wounds before, but the ache in her chest felt worse than any physical injury. Her temper had cost her that quiet, uncertain bond she'd begun to rebuild with Elias.

She opened her bedroom door cautiously, stepping into the hallway. Everything seemed oddly still, as though the entire household held its breath. Her eyes flicked to the staircase, half expecting to see Elias pacing at the bottom, but no. It was empty. Taking a fortifying breath, she headed toward his chambers to search for him.

But before she even reached them, she spotted Myria, Teagan, and Caelan bunched together outside a doorway a few paces down. Ayda's room. All three looked tense, standing too close, as if they were watching something unfold inside and weren't sure how to intervene.

Niev's steps slowed. Her pulse hitched in alarm.

"What's going on?" she demanded, keeping her voice low but urgent.

Caelan turned toward her, relief and confusion battling in his eyes. He shook his head slightly, jaw tight. "We're...not entirely sure."

Teagan shoved a hand through his hair. "Ayda mentioned Arin Alvania and your brother just...lost it. Asked to see that ledger you'd brought back from Breyvia."

Niev's pulse stuttered. Arin Alvania. The name had haunted her since she found it linked to her family's tragedy, the name she'd been intent on tracking down. "Why would he—?" She swallowed hard, pushing past them before the thought could fully form. "Let me see."

She stepped inside Ayda's room, where the air felt charged and unnaturally still. The small space was dimly lit by a single lantern on the side table, its light throwing shadows across the bed and walls. Her gaze landed on Elias instantly as he stood by Ayda's side, shoulders taut, face stark white. In his hands, he clutched the battered ledger that had ignited her search for answers.

He wasn't moving. Niev's stomach twisted as she approached. The pages of the book lay open, words swimming in the warm lamplight, but Elias's eyes were locked on a single line. Ayda hovered near him, fear evident in the way her hands fidgeted against her skirts.

Niev cleared her throat softly. "Eli?"

Slowly, as if dragged from a trance, he turned his head. Their eyes met, and the look on his face—some mix of dread and realization—made her chest constrict. He knows something, she thought, heart hammering.

"Eli," she repeated, gentler this time. She glanced at Ayda, who gave a small, helpless shake of her head. "What happened?"

Niev was so focused on her brother's white-knuckled grip on the ledger, she hardly noticed the others fall silent behind her. She could feel their collective tension, the press of fearful anticipation. Her heart hammered as she waited for her brother to explain whatever had him so shaken. Just moments ago, she'd been ready to apologize—now she stood on the precipice of another battle, one that crackled in the narrow space between them.

Elias finally tore his gaze from the page. He sucked in a ragged breath, as if surfacing from dark waters. "She...she killed her own daughter," he whispered, voice trembling with grief and rage. "She sold her grandchildren...." He swallowed hard, and a pained sound caught in his throat.

Niev's pulse thundered. She'd heard him, but the words were so surreal, so monstrous, that her mind refused to process them. "Elias," she began, stepping closer. "What the hell are you talking about?"

He barely seemed to hear her. "She—murdered her," he repeated brokenly, his eyes darting across the ledger. "In her own bed—Under her own roof... She let their blood seep into the tiles of her palace—" He clenched his jaw, as if the words were acid on his tongue. "I can't—I can't believe I didn't see it."

"Elias?" Niev's throat constricted. She placed a tentative hand on his forearm, feeling the way he shook with contained fury. "You're scaring me."

He yanked his arm free, but not violently, just driven by a desperate need to speak. "Arin Alvania—" he spat, voice cracking, "is Adrianna Nivola."

The air rushed out of Niev's lungs as if she'd been punched. Adrianna Nivola. Her maternal grandmother. The woman whose grief had been heard all around Eldhaven. Who had wept with Guinevere at their parents' funeral, who was rumored to have vanished into her tower in Arenthia for days on end after losing her 'precious daughter', Niev's mother Elowyn.

All her life Niev had believed Adrianna was merely distant, cold, perhaps disapproving of them. But this?

"You're lying," Niev said, shaking her head. Rage and disbelief sparked in equal measure, making her voice shake. "How do you know? We've asked about Arin Alvania all over the continent, and nobody's heard that name—"

"Because he doesn't exist," Elias snarled, jabbing a finger at the ledger. "Arin doesn't exist. It's Adrianna. I saw her sign documents as Arin

Alvania when we were little, before—before everything went to shit." His eyes shone with a frantic urgency, like he was trapped in a nightmare he couldn't escape. "I asked her about it once, and she just said it was something the Matron of Arenthia had to do sometimes, to hide her identity, protect the family name. I was a kid. I believed her. Like an idiot!"

A thick silence descended, broken only by Elias's ragged breaths. Niev's mind whirled, her thoughts careening from memory to memory—childhood visits to Arenthia, glimpses of Adrianna frowning at their father, at Guinevere, at Niev herself. She'd always felt unwelcome there, a stain on Adrianna's pure bloodline.

And then it clicked—

"The silver-crowned liar still who barters in bones," she whispered.

Elias looked at her in bewilderment. "What?"

But Niev didn't answer. Her anger flared as she remembered the sirens' words, then froze into something colder, more precise than any rage she'd ever felt. She remembered Adrianna's sharp jabs, her condemnation of the 'mixed blood' in Niev's veins, the side glances at Elias's budding witch powers that were, by Arenthian law, worthless in a male heir.

Niev wet her lips, speaking slowly. "It makes sense," she said, and her voice sounded strangely flat to her own ears. She glanced at Elias, who watched her with an almost fearful expression. Was this how she looked when the lethal calm took over?

"She never wanted us," Niev went on, soft but steady. "Elias... you inherited witch powers, but you're a man. You can't ascend Arenthia's throne or hold a formal seat in the Council. And me?" She gave a small, hollow laugh. "I'm a half-breed with no real magical gifts. Adrianna made her feelings clear when she said our mother sullied the bloodline by marrying a Helvast."

Elias's eyes flickered with pain, the ledger trembling in his grip. "So...she needed a fresh heir, one untainted by scandal. Couldn't risk the people finding out her legitimate grandchildren were, in her eyes, a disgrace."

"Exactly." Niev closed her hand over Elias's wrist. This time, he didn't shake her off. "So she wiped us off the board. Sold us away, orchestrated our parents' murders, and played the grieving matriarch to keep her hands clean. And then Aunt Milah would be the undisputed heir, and her daughter Lydia after her."

Behind them, Ayda sucked in a sharp breath. Teagan muttered something too low for Niev to catch. Myria's expression was grim, her fists clenched at her sides. Caelan stood in the doorway, jaw set, eyes bright with fury.

Elias raised his head, meeting her gaze. Anger and heartbreak warred in his eyes. "What do we do?"

Niev inhaled slowly, struggling to leash the maelstrom in her chest. For a moment, she let herself look at him—truly look—seeing not just the fury etched in his features but the deep, soul-crushing hurt that matched her own.

She reached out, resting a trembling hand on his shoulder. "You don't have to do a damn thing, brother," she said, voice hushed but steadfast. "You've been through enough for a lifetime. You've earned your rest. And I never should've said the things I said earlier."

He studied her in silence, the muscles in his jaw working. Then, with a sharp exhale, he shook his head. "No." His voice was raw, underlined with trembling resolve. "I'm done letting other people fight my battles. She murdered our parents, sold off her own grandchildren, and still sits on her cushy throne without a shred of guilt. I'll kill that bitch with my bare hands if I have to."

Ayda lifted her chin, stepping into the narrow space between them, one hand half-raised in alarm. "Hold on...you're talking about overthrowing the most powerful Matron in Eldhaven, in the most impenetrable fortress of Arenthia. This is—"

"Suicide," Teagan stated, matter-of-factly.

Caelan, who had been silent at the threshold, let out a dark, rueful chuckle. He angled a glance at Niev, a look so charged with wicked confidence it sent a pulse of heat through her core. "We've got a fucking dragon," he said simply, one corner of his mouth pulling into a dangerous smile. "I'd say the odds are pretty even."

A hush followed, charged with electricity. The steady tick of an old clock in the hall seemed to pound a countdown to war. Niev locked eyes with her brother, then with each of the friends who'd become her family, as a cold, vicious certainty settled over her like a steel cloak.

"Adrianna's first mistake," she said, voice dropping to a lethal calm, "was not killing us when she had the chance."

Acknowledgements

First and foremost, I want to thank my mentor, Jonathon Kendall, whose guidance, knowledge, and belief in me lit the spark that made this book possible. Without your faith in my skills, I would never have had the courage to write these pages.

To Yasmine Maher, thank you for patiently enduring my endless questions, for your wisdom, and for inspiring me through your own novels. You helped me bring this story to life in more ways than you know.

I'm deeply grateful to the incredible team who helped format and design this book. Your talent turned a dream into something tangible and beautiful, and I will forever treasure what you've created.

To my boss and friend, Sean Garner, thank you for giving me not only a job I truly love but also the trust and freedom to pursue this dream alongside it.

A huge thank-you to my best friend, Merna Fahmi, and my brother, Stephane, for walking with me through every brainstorm, every late-night idea, and every corner of this world I built. This book would not exist without your patience and support.

To my cousin Jolie, your fangirling, feedback, and enthusiasm gave me confidence when I needed it most. I'm so thankful for your excitement and love for this story.

To my family, and especially my dad, thank you for cheering me on, even though fantasy isn't your genre. Your pride and encouragement meant the world to me.

To my husband, Mina, you are my backbone, my partner, and the love of my life. For eleven years, you've stood beside me, and I am the woman I am today because of your unwavering support and love.

To Alina, my sweet daughter...I dedicate this entire book to you, because no words can ever express how much joy, courage, and love you have given me. You are my sun and I thank God every day for giving me the honor to be your mom.

And to your little sibling, my sweet second baby, who, as I write this, is still just a tiny hedgehog kicking in my belly, know that you are already the final piece of the puzzle that completes our family. Your dad, Alina, and I cannot wait to meet you, and we love you to the moon and back.

And finally, to you, the reader, thank you for picking up my very first novel. Your time, your curiosity, and your willingness to step into this world mean more to me than I can ever say. I'm endlessly grateful you're here. And I hope you're as excited as I am to dive into the rest of Caelan and Niev's story in the upcoming sequel.

About the Author

Nathalie Edward is a Swiss-Egyptian copywriter, marketing manager, foodie, and self-proclaimed bookworm. A lifelong lover of stories, she has finally stepped from the world of reading into the world of writing with her debut novel *Vows of Vengeance*.

She lives in Egypt with her husband and daughter, where she balances full-time marketing work with the beautiful chaos of family life. When she's not at her desk, Nathalie can usually be found curled up with a book, experimenting in the kitchen with new recipes, or chasing after her energetic toddler.

www.ingramcontent.com/pod-product-compliance
Lightning Source LLC
Chambersburg PA
CBHW030847030726
47495CB00005B/1409